MW01042501

SLEEPWATER STATIC

INTERNATIONAL BESTSELLING AUTHOR
KATHRIN HUTSON

Books by Kathrin Hutson

Gyenona's Children (Dark Fantasy)
Daughter of the Drackan
Mother of the Drackan

The Unclaimed (NA Dark Fantasy)
Sanctuary of Dehlyn
Secret of Dehlyn
Sacrament of Dehlyn

Blue Helix (LGBTQ Dystopian Sci-Fi)
Sleepwater Beat
Sleepwater Static

Copyright © 2020 Kathrin Hutson

Cover Design by OliviaProDesign

https://www.vecteezy.com Free Vector Art by Vecteezy

ISBN: 978-1-7331613-4-3 (Exquisite Darkness Press)

 Exquisite
Darkness
Press

A Note from the Author

When I wrote *Sleepwater Beat*, the first book in the Blue Helix series, I truly thought the story was finished—self-contained, wrapped up neatly in a dark, gritty, somewhat oppressive bow that still left room for hope. That book was a big leap of courage and self-awareness for me. I poured more of myself into Leo Tieffler than I'd ever pushed into one of my own characters before. And honestly, I was terrified that people wouldn't understand the messages I was trying to portray about society; about the way this country and the world are headed; about the lights needing to be shed on so many marginalized groups (LGBTQ+, drug addicts, children of neglect and abuse, the homeless, the destitute, the underprivileged and underappreciated); and yes, about myself.

Then *Sleepwater Beat* became an International Bestseller in 2019 and an Award-Winning Science Fiction Finalist in the 2019 International Book Awards, and that terror subsided. People were getting it. Readers understood what I was aiming for, and I received nothing but appreciation and thought-provoking insight from those who'd read that book. Apparently, it was a timely release for Sleepwater's story, which I'd finished writing *before* my daughter was born in

October of 2016 and *before* the 2016 Presidential Elections in November. And then the world I'd created for myself—Sleepwater's world in this Dystopian America—became less fiction and more of a twisted, preemptive reflection of reality.

Then I knew the story wasn't really over. Readers wanted more. These characters wanted more. *I* wanted more, and I couldn't stop with Leo. There was so much still left to be said and illuminated and discovered—for myself, yes, but more importantly, I wrote *Sleepwater Static* with this country and those who have been struggling painfully through it for the last four years, as I have, specifically in mind.

It goes without saying that everything an author writes is—or perhaps *should* be—completely intentional. But I feel compelled to make the statement anyway.

The setting in Hollywood and Charleston, South Carolina was intentional. I moved to Charleston shortly after I met my husband in 2012, and we lived there for three years. We were married in Edisto on Brick House Plantation, which just so happens to be my husband's ancestral land (and yes, an actual working plantation back in the day). After spending the first twenty-two years of my life in and around Denver, Colorado, I really wasn't prepared for the culture shock of moving to the South and the Low Country, of discovering that the deep-seeded roots of racism and inequality were still so prevalent anywhere in America but especially the place my husband—a man so aggressively and unapologetically accepting and supportive of all marginalized people—called home. My eyes were opened during our three years in Charleston, and part of *Sleepwater Static's* intention was to help others open their eyes, to bring to light racial injustices and the intricacies of transracial relationships and families while also comparing these to and contrasting them with the fictional "minority group" Sleepwater, who becomes even more marginalized and targeted by hate and violence than any other marginalized community in this Dystopian world. The aim wasn't to highlight black versus white but instead love versus hate, acceptance and alliance versus bigotry and closed-mindedness, working with race as an avenue to highlight those glaring differences.

Bernadette's romantic relationship with Darrell, a white woman disowning her racist family to love and build her life with a black man, was intentional. I'm also a white woman, and while I married a white man from the South, I know love, and I know pain, and I know what it is to stand up for what's right and for the people for whom I care so deeply, even if it means cutting out the sources of toxicity. Even if it means cutting off some of my own roots. I don't know what it's like to have a biracial daughter or to live in this world as a transracial family. But as a queer person, a woman, an ex-heroin addict, I know what it is to be marginalized, misunderstood, feared a little, and I understand what it means to do whatever I have to do to protect my family through love, acceptance, security, and stability on all fronts—physically, emotionally, mentally. Our biracial niece, my daughter's cousin, is a gorgeous, smart, hilarious little girl, and I know what it is to be a mother and to want the best for my own child, no matter the sacrifices.

Writing a main character as a white woman in her seventies through the present timeline of the story was intentional. There is so much knowledge, perspective, understanding to be gained from our elders, and as a society in this country, I think we've forgotten that. We have slipped away from the necessary practice of caring for and about the elders in our lives, not on a physical level of medical elderly care but on an emotional and spiritual level. A *human* level. Bernadette is a woman in her seventies with so many demons in her closet, and in bringing her new Sleepwater family into her past, there is so much to be learned about who she is and what Sleepwater never took the initiative to discover. She had a life. She experienced pain, betrayal, love, growth, youth, motherhood, sexuality, danger, and everything in between. And she is no less badass because of her age but perhaps in spite of it. And as I try to do in everything I write, Bernadette is one more stereotype I've flipped on its head—an elderly person who is *not* a burden, who still fights in more ways than one, who is both strong and haunted and still has so much to give despite everything that could have torn her down. And how often do we see motherhood and sexuality combined? How often do we see *ageing* and sexuality combined? If you want surprises, here's a seventy-one-year-old woman who can love and fight and endure *and* bring sexuality and pleasure right to the forefront because *that is her beat*. It may make some people squirm, sure. It doesn't have to. And I hope that, within all the juxtaposing work I've sewn through this book, it doesn't even hit the top three most squirm-worthy topics.

There is so much more to touch on in *Sleepwater Beat*

than I ever anticipated—emotional abuse, gaslighting, mental illness, open relationships, sexual orientation and the exploration of it, familial relationships and especially those between mother and daughter. My daughter is only three as I write this, but since the day she was born (and her birth was the blueprint for the birth of Brad and Mirela's first child in this book, only my child was born on the couch at home and not the floor of a cabin-safehouse), I have been painfully aware of the eventuality of losing her—not as poignantly as Bernadette loses her own daughter and hopefully without any of the fear and betrayal. But I know I'll lose her as my "little girl", who sings the whole house awake every morning and who needs a kiss and a hug every time I leave the room. And I understand the importance of holding that kind of sacred close to my heart before it's gone.

In retrospect, I suppose, I've written *Sleepwater Static* in the same way I wrote *Sleepwater Beat*—for myself, as a reflection of myself, as a glimpse into the future at both what I want and what I hope will never come to pass. But I also wrote it for everyone else who picks up this book and is brave enough to explore its pages, who wants to see the world from a different perspective, who may in fact discover a new perspective without ever having seen it coming. I wrote it for you, and if any part of this story makes you feel something more by having read it, then I've done my job.

Thank you for taking the dive into the darkness with me. I'll see you on the other side in the light.

—Kathrin Hutson (March, 2020)

For those who stand with love
against the tides of oppression and uncertainty.

We will always be stronger together,
louder in grace,
unstoppable in hope.

The world is changing. We *are* the storm.

Acknowledgments

There are more people to thank for their invaluable advice, support, and insight throughout the entire process of bringing this book to life than in any of my other novels to date. I think that means I'm doing something right.

First, I want to give a special thanks to my publicist Mickey Mikkelson of Creative Edge Publicity. He took a chance on me just because he liked what he saw, and I couldn't be more grateful for all the hard work he's put into getting this book out into the world. Mickey, here's to a dream working relationship that's turned into an irreplaceable friendship.

To my highly skilled and incredibly proficient editor Christie Stratos with Proof Positive. I can't say enough what a joy and a relief it is to work with an editor who knows her stuff *and* understands exactly what I'm doing with my fiction. Working with you eliminates the nail-biting aspect of waiting for edits.

To all my beta readers, advanced readers, and self-professed fans who read this book before publication, especially: V.S. Holmes (my soul twin), for their dedication to the craft we share and their constant availability to talk me down out of a head-spin; Jason Lavelle, for their unwavering enthusiasm and late-night delves into darkness with me; Brandon Palmer, for his hours-long discussions, opinions that made me teary, and all the work he pours into crafting my audiobooks as a professional and a long-time friend; and Salt & Sage Books, for their outstanding accommodations in matching every book with the best-suited sensitivity reader to make each work shine (especially mine).

And as always, I must and forever will thank my husband Henry, who puts up with my one-track writer's brain and makes it possible for this to be my sole focus. We made it, babe.

1

THERE WERE VERY few days now when *something* didn't hurt. Bernadette sighed as she shifted the commercial-sized van into park, knowing her knees would give her hell the minute she stepped out. She let herself sit there just a few seconds longer.

"*This* is your safehouse?" In the middle row of passenger seats in the back, Cameron almost pressed his face against the window.

"It's not officially registered or anything, if that's what you're asking." Bernadette glanced up at the rearview mirror and smirked at him. He didn't see her.

Randall nodded in the passenger seat beside her. "Looks good to me."

"As long as there's a bed big enough for this baby, I'll be happy." Mirela let out a long sigh and rubbed her hand in circles over her swollen belly.

Beside her in the first row of seats, her husband feigned insult. "I hope you'll let me share it with you."

"If it's big enough." Mirela turned to give him a slow, exhausted smile. "Spooning's a little out of the question at this point, don't you think?"

Brad chuckled and rubbed her belly with her.

"Oh, for fuck's sake." Cameron rolled his eyes but didn't turn away from the window. "Get a room."

"That's literally what we're talking about," Mirela told him.

"Ya think?"

"All right." Randall slapped his long, lanky thighs and opened the front passenger-side door. "Let's check it out." He didn't wait for anyone else's agreement before slipping out of the van and closing the door behind him.

Brad slid open the van's single back door and helped his pregnant wife out first. She groaned a little, having to duck through the doorway, and steadied herself on the side of the van when her feet landed in the dirt driveway studded with browning crabgrass. Cameron puffed out a sigh and followed after them.

Bernadette stayed in the driver's seat, watching Don and Tony in the third row all the way in the back. The twins were still struggling with the massive wall between them, she knew. Six months on the road after they'd broken Tony, Kaylee, Leo, and John out of that fucked-up lab, and Tony still hadn't said more than a few words a day, if that. Whatever else Vanguard Industries had done to the poor guy couldn't be summed up in any amount of words anyway, but they all got the gist of it.

Some people were just damn unlucky. Some people were snatched up from their homes or their jobs, carted off to the middle of nowhere, poked and prodded beyond imagining, and forced to endure a kind of torture she could never fathom. Tony was one of those people. He was one of even fewer who'd had his beat stripped from him while the rest of the world lauded the excellence of scientific advancement. It was all bullshit, and every person here knew it. Tony more than any of them.

Like an amputee who hardly remembered how he'd lost his limb, the guy was still working through the scars left by that severed part of him. Bernadette wished she knew how to comfort him—both of them. Don was just as clueless as to how to be with his twin when the entire dynamic between them had changed. But there wasn't any way to fix something like this.

The others might have known, maybe. But the others had either turned against the small tribe this faction of Sleepwater had made for themselves, or they'd run from the pain of losing one of their own. Who was to say if any of the scattered others would come looking for them again? Bernadette wasn't a pessimist by any means, but she didn't screw around with wishful thinking, either.

The driver-side door opened, startling her out of her thoughts. A quick glance in the rearview mirror showed her only an empty seat. She hadn't even noticed the twins getting out of the van.

Randall stood there beside the open door, smirking at her, his thick, black-framed glasses slipping down over the bridge of his aquiline nose. "I don't think we can get inside without you."

She smiled up at him. "Oh, I'm sure you could. Nobody locks their doors down here anyway. Can't remember if I did or not." She left the keys in the ignition and pushed herself out of the driver's seat. When Randall extended a hand to help her out, obviously expecting her to take it, she snorted and waved him off. "Put that hand away. I'm not senile, and I'm definitely not handicapped."

Randall chuckled as she managed to get both of her brown loafers onto the ground. "Not yet."

Bernadette ignored him, fighting back most of a grimace at the sharp pain in her knees but refusing to comment on them or bend to try rubbing out the pain. That never worked, anyway. Randall shut the door behind her.

"I thought anyone over sixty-five was a senior citizen," Cameron said, his arms folded as he watched Bernadette and Randall step away from the van. The others made their way slowly toward the cabin at the end of the dirt drive. "You're *way* over that, aren't you?"

Bernadette raised an eyebrow at him and pointed. "Watch it."

"Yeah, I'm watching." To anyone else, Cameron's impassive expression looked a lot like apathy and condescension. She knew him well enough to recognize the tiny flicker at the corner of his mouth that served as his small smile. "Gotta make sure you don't fall and break a hip."

"Oh, Lord." Bernadette shook her head and headed toward the cabin. When she passed Cameron, she lashed out to slap his arm with the back of her hand. "And if I did that, you'd still just be watching me, wouldn't you?"

"Maybe."

She chuckled and fished around in the pocket of her denim dress. "Did you try the door?" she called to Brad and Mirela.

"It's definitely locked." Brad slipped his arm around his wife's waist and whispered something in her ear.

Mirela just shook her head with that small, tired smile. She removed one hand from her hip to wipe at the sweat on her forehead. "Is everyone else this hot, or is it just me?"

Bernadette reached the front porch with its semi-rotted wooden steps and the rocker missing one of its armrests. A sharp, painful longing twisted her gut. Karl would've made fixing that chair his first job when they got here. But Karl was gone, wasn't he? And no one but Leo had gotten a chance to say goodbye.

Swallowing, she shot Mirela a sympathetic smile and nodded. "That's just the South in August, honey. We'll turn the fans on first thing." The key in her hand stuck in the doorknob for a few seconds, and she had to jiggle it a little before it finally turned. "Assuming there's still power running through the place."

Mirela sighed. "Oh, boy."

"Hey, we'll figure it out." Brad rubbed her back. "If we have to get a generator, I'll pick one up, no problem. Not gonna let you cook in the heat, okay?"

"I'm already cookin'." His wife closed her eyes and took a deep breath. "And the timer on this kid's gonna go off at any minute."

The door jammed on the warped boards of the cabin floor, and when Bernadette grunted against it, Randall reached over her shoulder and gave it a little shove. The door creaked, and then it opened. Bernadette immediately stepped back and turned her head away, covering her mouth and nose. Her eyes fell on the twins, both of whom flared their nostrils and leaned away from the door. At least with something like this, they were their old, synced selves again. They'd be fine.

"*Oh*, no." Mirela heaved and waddled off the porch, followed quickly by Brad.

"Are you gonna puke?" he called after her. "Can I get you anything?"

"Not smothering me would be nice…" The sound of dry heaving came from the bushes on the side of the cabin.

Cameron folded his arms again and stepped inside. "Okay, what died?"

Bernadette cleared her throat, made an effort to breathe only through her nose, and waved a hand toward the dust-covered furniture in the cabin's main room. "Just check everywhere," she said. "Or follow the smell. You'll find it."

Without a word, Cameron went to the light switch on the wall first and flipped it up. The yellow, dusty bulb in the ceiling fixture flickered then came on. "Guess there's power." Then he stepped down the single step into the living room and went looking for the source of the stench.

Randall met Bernadette's gaze and shook his head. "Nothing phases him, huh?"

"Well, almost nothing." She fanned the air in front of her nose. "It's been a while since I've smelled death like this."

The man leaned against the outer wall just beside the door and folded his arms. "How long's it been since you were here?"

Bernadette ran a finger over the windowsill between the door and the rocking chair, swiping up a thick layer of dust and a few streaks of mostly dry mold. "A long time. With everything that's happening now, though, it feels right to come back."

He studied her with slightly squinted eyes, the corners of his mouth lifting in a smile that was half admiration and half intense curiosity. "We're not here just for the safehouse, are we?"

Wiping her dirtied finger on the side of her dress, Bernadette swallowed and glanced up at him. "Well aren't you Mr. Observant."

Randall chuckled.

2

"I'M STANDING RIGHT here. Not outside." She put her hands on her hips and smiled at Darrell.

He turned from the window of the cabin with wide eyes and laughed when he saw her raised eyebrow. "I know where you're standin', girl." Slowly, he stepped across the small living room decorated with a historically eclectic mix of nineteenth-century muskets, buck antlers, her family's coat of arms, and the quintessentially Southern framed photographs of live oaks, palmettos, the Cooper River at sunset. "I always know where you're standin'."

Bernadette stepped toward him, holding his dark, shimmering gaze with her own. "So why are you staring out that window like you're looking for someone else?"

"It's who I *ain't* lookin' for." Darrell stepped toward her until they were only inches apart. His dark brows flickered together as he studied her and raised a hand to run his fingers through her light-brown hair.

She gently gripped his wrist; the sight of her pale fingers settled around the smooth, dark-amber skin of his forearm made her heart beat a little faster in her throat. It was impossible to be anywhere with him—right where she belonged—without some flutter of tension rising in her belly. Almost impossible. Bernadette reached up to cup his cheek, moving her thumb along the thick stubble following his jawline. "I told you he went down to Virginia."

"I know." Darrell licked his lips, staring at her. "And you can't blame me for wondering just how much your daddy tells you about where he's goin'. When he's comin' home."

Smiling, she gripped the back of his neck and pressed herself against him. "Good thing this isn't home for anyone, then. I *can* blame you for thinking about my daddy when I brought you *here*…"

His snort of laughter made her grin. "I always knew you was trouble, girl."

"For everyone else, maybe. Not for you." Bernadette wrapped both arms around his neck, against the cords of muscle stretching down to his broad, rounded shoulders. "Nobody knows we're here. Right now, though, I don't give a fuck what anyone else thinks." She pulled him down and pressed her lips against his. Darrell grunted, his hands slowly sliding down her ribcage and over her hips. Then he wrapped her in an embrace far gentler than most might have guessed for the size of him and the hardened strength of those soft-skinned arms. When she pulled away, Bernadette blinked up at him and narrowed her eyes. "Come on." She grabbed his hand from the swell of her hips and moved backward through the cabin, pulling him along with only a hint of pressure. But she wouldn't have had to pull him at all toward the bedroom; they both knew Darrell would follow her anywhere. And Bernadette, for all her restlessness, had only stayed this long because of him.

Darrell stepped up onto the slightly raised landing into the kitchen, his dark eyes burning as they moved straight back toward the largest bedroom that had been the cabin's only bedroom for the last fifty years. Now there were two. "Trouble, girl." He shook his head and bit his lip when she opened the bedroom door behind her. "Too much trouble."

"Then come make trouble with me."

"You plannin' on talkin' me up into a sweat? That it?" He shut the door softly behind him and stood there with a barely discernible smile on his slightly parted lips.

"Wasn't plannin' on it, no." Bernadette grinned. "But I will if you want me to."

His gaze flickered over her from head to toe, and he shook his head. "Naw. You and me? We gon' talk a different kinda talk. Ain't no words for that."

Bernadette kicked off her wedges and ran her hand down his tight t-shirt, his chest hard beneath the brown cotton broken by zigzags of bright orange and yellow. She lifted the bottom hem of it from beneath his brown slacks. "Then stop talking."

When she lifted the shirt just above his navel and the patch of dark, curly hair dipping below it, Darrell covered her hands with his own and stopped her. Smirking, she removed her hands, and he brought his lips just an inch from hers again. "Yes, ma'am."

Then he pulled the t-shirt over his head, tossed it on the floor, and stepped toward her until she had no other choice but to lie back on the bed that no one knew she shared with Darrell Wilkins from Columbia, least of all her daddy.

3

I CAN'T BELIEVE you took him there, Bernie. I shouldn't be surprised, but I didn't think you'd really do it. Part of me wishes I'd come with you, just so I could give this town the one-fingered salute right next to you. When your next letter rolls around, you better give me the skinny on everything. I mean it. Don't leave anything out.

Everything's pretty mellow for me over here. That sounds like nothing's happening, but I guess that's a straight-up lie. I met someone. It just happened. I wasn't looking for it. Went to this disco in Birmingham, and she just... found me, I guess. Maybe it was the booze got me to chill, but she's far out. Donna. I thought she was a dancer that first night, but it turns out she just knows them all. At least where we were.

We've been going around for almost two weeks. There's too much booze with her, Bernie, so I can't tell her about my words yet. Maybe when I come down off these vibes a little more, I'll bring it up. I think some of the other dudes she knows at the clubs are already in on it. Like, they know. Or they can do the same thing we can do. Maybe I'll ask. Maybe they'll ask me. Not sure I'm down to talk about it with anyone else. You're still the only one who knows.

Write me back about D. I want to hear everything. *I could tell you to be careful too, but we both know you'd just tell me to quit being such a drag. I'm trying.*

—Janet

P.S. Did you hear about that test-tube baby? It feels freaky and heavy at the same time. Like, what if those doctors end up making babies like us? Different. Who can do what we do. Or maybe the question is what if they figure out how to do something different to *people like us? Or maybe I'm just stoned.*

4

THE SINGLE OVERHEAD fan swung back and forth below the ceiling of the screened-in porch. The crickets and
cicadas droned in a never-ending buzz, pulsing, crying out
that they were here too. That they'd never left in the first
place. That Bernadette had.

She sipped on the bottle of poorly sweetened tea from
their stop at the gas station off Highway 17 before the longer,
much more hidden stretch down 165. The drive she'd made
countless times in the back seat of her parents' car, in her
own Oldsmobile when she'd gotten her license, in the passenger seat of Darrell's Monte Carlo after her dad had stolen
her keys from her purse and refused to give them back. So
many drives and adventures. So many nights spent on this
porch in the heat of so many South Carolina summers. This
time, though, Bernadette had come to this cabin looking to

escape a lot more than the everyday boredom with which life had plagued her when she was young.

Not to say that it hadn't been dangerous almost every time she'd waltzed up those warped wooden steps and heard the screen door slam shut behind her. Back then, she'd pretended she didn't give a damn about any of the consequences. In more ways than one, revisiting this place now came with very much the same warning—they had to keep it quiet, couldn't stay long, couldn't let anyone they didn't trust know where they were. The consequences, too, were just as real and maybe more severe. And Bernadette cared very much about what might happen if the wrong people found them.

The second door from the cabin onto the porch opened with a soft, sticky peeling away from the mostly insulated frame. Bernadette paused in the rocking chair and turned slightly to see Mirela stepping slowly through the doorway. She didn't look at the older woman until she'd closed the door behind her—a soft whisper and thump in the thick humidity. Rubbing a hand over her swollen belly, she used the other to brace her lower back and waddled barefoot onto the porch.

"Can't sleep either, huh?" Bernadette asked with a knowing smirk.

Mirela settled herself onto the wicker bench and the old, lopsided cushions they'd pulled out of the shed. A little groan escaped her. "All that work to get the sheets on that queen-sized bed, and Brad's the only one who gets to enjoy them."

Bernadette nodded in understanding. She'd told Randall more than a few times as they'd readied the cabin to be slept in—if nothing else that night—that she didn't need to take the second bedroom in the back. That she didn't sleep much these days anyway, and it would only be a waste of a good bed. But he'd insisted that the couch was better for him anyway. Cameron had passed out in the recliner, Tony and Don had each taken one of the twin beds in the corners of the living room, and there had been no one else to debate giving *the old lady* her own room. She wanted to think that the memories of sharing that back bedroom with her sister growing up had nothing to do with the fact that she'd only been able to lie in that bed for a few hours before having to get up and step outside.

"Men are idiots," she muttered into the top of her tea before taking another sip. Mirela snorted, as if she'd followed the older woman's thoughts with perfect clarity, and they shared a short-lived chuckle. "Maybe that's why they're all asleep in there without a care in the world."

That wasn't necessarily true, but she was willing to make the concession that a person's troubles could momentarily disappear in the darkest hours. If that person ever managed to get to sleep.

Mirela leaned her head back against the frame of the wicker bench. "I can't remember the last time I slept all the way through the night."

Bernadette chuckled, resumed her rocking, and sipped at the bottle that would never hold up to the standards of homemade Southern sweet tea. "That might be the only part of motherhood you'll be prepared for once that little one gets here."

The younger woman rolled her eyes and leaned back against the cushions, though her lips still curved in a fine line of amusement. "They must've skipped that part in all the birthing classes we didn't take."

With a hum, Bernadette gave her a dismissive wave. "Women have been having babies forever. Most of them without birthing classes or doctors, if we're looking at the entire history of women having babies. Definitely makes it easier if you're around someone else who's done it before, but it's not a requirement."

Mirela smoothed her long, thick curls of dark hair away from her face. It took more than one try before she managed to peel most of it from the sweat-slickened flush along her forehead, cheeks, and neck. The oversized t-shirt she'd picked up at a Goodwill in Mississippi the minute her own clothes stopped fitting now stretched incredibly tight over her pregnant body, distorting the printed image of an electric guitar on the front. It made Bernadette think of Kaylee and the girl's collection of overlarge shirts with heavy metal band names peeling from the cotton.

"Well." Mirela let out a heavy sigh. "I guess I'll be one of those women having babies without anyone else around who knows what they're doing."

The rocking chair paused mid-swing. For a few seconds, both women became intensely aware of Bernadette's frozen movement before the rumble and creak of the chair picked back up again. Bernadette stared at the dusty wooden slats of the porch, her heart pounding painfully in her chest above the hollow emptiness in her gut. She's spent two decades trying to ignore that emptiness, and she couldn't blame Mirela for having brought it back to her attention. Mirela couldn't have possibly known, because Bernadette had never said a thing about it to any of them. And she hadn't planned on it.

The drone of the warm-weather insects suddenly felt a lot less relaxing and a lot more stifling than she remembered.

"John's a nurse, right?" Mirela stared at the floor too now, still rubbing her belly. The tight, attempted cluelessness in her smile wasn't fooling Bernadette at all, and they both knew it.

All right. They could play the game. Bernadette had been doing it for most of her life anyway.

"That's what he said." Bernadette nodded and rocked. The bottle of tea sat forgotten in her lap, cradled by a hand that had become quite cold, now. "I don't think he spent much time in the maternity ward." When she looked up at Mirela with a wry smile, the younger woman burst into laughter, then quickly covered her mouth and glanced at the door into the cabin.

John had to have been six-foot-five at the very least, built like a football player. It had surprised them all at first to learn that he'd been a nurse in his old life, before abductions and experiments and Sleepwater. Before the only option left to any of them now was to run and just keep running.

"Have you heard anything from him?" Mirela's large brown eyes glistened in the faded yellow light of the fan's single dusty bulb.

Bernadette liked to think that glisten was hope—if not for word of the few who'd become like family to them in such a short amount of time, then at least for the immediate future. A new baby could always bring more hope, no matter the circumstances into which they were born. As long as the people in that child's life actually let themselves feel that hope again. Brad and Mirela were the kind of people who let more joy and love into their lives than most. Both of those things were so hard to come by these days.

She shook her head. "Last time I talked to John was when he shipped out to find Leo in Aberdeen."

"At her bar, right?" Mirela chuckled. "I never would've expected that from her. Good for her, though. If Leo found a way to slip under the radar after all this mess..." She shrugged and let the open-ended thought speak for itself.

They all knew why John had decided to head out on his own just a few days before they'd left Mirela's sister's house in San Antonio. That stop was only ever meant to be a temporary reprieve, just like every other stop between there and here over the last five months. But the giant of a man with a nurturer's softness wasn't quite like the rest of them. Not anymore. Sure, he had that inexplicable power in his words, could spin a beat and call himself one of them in that way. But his beat was changed. *He* was changed, just like Leo and Kaylee and Tony after Sleepwater had busted them out of that awful place. Now they were all scattered to the wind again.

Bernadette figured the guy just didn't want to be dragged around with a bunch of people reeling from Karl's death, walking on eggshells around Tony's stolen beat, and expecting Brad and Mirela's little bundle of joy all at the same time. She couldn't blame him. After all, Leo was the only other one who knew exactly what had been done to them in that hellish lab the rest of the world knew as Vanguard Industries. Then again, her beat had been affected just like John's. Not stolen, as Tony's was, but strengthened, somehow. John could connect with her that way.

The women were silent on the porch in the middle of the night. The bugs and the hollow rustle of palmetto fronds in the breeze and the rhythmic roll of Bernadette's rocking chair, back and forth, formed a different conversation.

Finally, Bernadette looked up at the younger woman and swallowed. Her thin smile felt tight and heavy, and that was only because she hadn't spoken the words she was about to say in a very long time. "I *do* know what it's like, actually."

Mirela took in a sharp breath, paused, then met her friend's gaze. "What do you mean?"

Glassy, light-blue eyes trailed down Mirela's jawline, her neck, over her chest, until Bernadette settled her gaze on the other woman's swollen belly. She didn't have to say anything at all.

"Really?" Mirela's dark eyebrows flickered together, as if she couldn't for the life of her imagine the woman barely in her seventies at one point in her life young and beautiful and filled with that same kind of hope.

Bernadette just raised her eyebrows and kept rocking. It was hard enough to admit to herself, in front of someone else, that she'd been in Mirela's position before. Apparently, it was still too hard to form the actual words. Of course, she hadn't been running from government agencies at eight and a half months pregnant in 1995, but the looks people had given her then were the same Mirela received now. The fear of bringing a child into this world—a child who was so different than everyone else and who didn't deserve to be hated for it—was very much the same too. So were the types of people who'd come after them for years, just for being who they were. The only difference now was that the catalyst for the world's hatred had changed. These days, Sleepwater and anyone else who could spin a beat like they could were the targets, and the electricity in the air was starting to feel like the Miami Riots all over again.

Shifting forward a little on the bench, Mirela blinked and pressed her hands against her belly. She looked at Bernadette now almost as if through new eyes, as if they'd just met and this shared secret between them was the first and only bond they had. "And the... having babies part?" She licked her lips.

Bernadette just kept rocking, though she did dip her head enough to hint at a nod. It could also have been taken as the motion of her body in the chair. "That too."

"I... had no idea."

"Most people don't. I'd like to keep it that way." The older woman lifted her head and stared through the screen lining the porch. The moon behind the cabin just barely lit up the silhouettes of palmettos a dozen yards away and the draping live oaks in the distance. "Honestly, that might be harder to do once everyone else figures out what I'm up to while we're here."

From the corner of her eye, she caught Mirela wrapping both arms around her rounded belly in that protective gesture so natural to expectant mothers. Thinking of it all now—being so close to the beginning and what had been a heartbreaking kind of end—burned in her chest with both grief and longing. It was almost as powerful as Bernadette's beat, when she used it. If it *had* been as powerful, maybe she never would have left.

Tears pricked the corners of her eyes, and she just couldn't keep it in any longer. "Her name's Olivia."

"Oh…" Mirela nodded slowly. "Is she here?"

The bottle of tea clinked down on the high, round table beside the rocking chair. Bernadette's hand, wrinkled now but still as strong as ever, fumbled for the pack of cigarettes and the lighter she hadn't yet touched since stepping onto the porch. "I hope so. Only a few ways to find out, and even then, they're just shots in the dark. But I have to try."

"It's been that long, huh?"

"Twenty years." Bernadette opened the pack without looking, slipped a cigarette into her mouth, and raised the lighter. Then she glanced at Mirela and stopped rocking. "Oh, I'm sorry. I'll step out for a few—"

"No. You stay right there." Mirela steadied herself at the edge of the bench and rolled herself laboriously to her feet with a little grunt. Then she sighed and tugged the bottom of the huge t-shirt until it dangled again just below her belly. "I think trying to sit up and be awake finally made me tired again."

With a knowing smile, Bernadette dared herself to meet the younger woman's gaze and nodded. "Good luck. It's amazing how functioning a person can be on just a few hours of sleep. Maybe not *fully* functioning…"

A chuckle escaped them both as Mirela shuffled across the wooden floor. She stopped beside the rocking chair, put a gentle hand on Bernadette's shoulder, and leaned down to kiss the fading scar over the older woman's eyebrow. A wave of honey, nutty herbs, and a stronger, sour smell wafted from that long, dark hair. Bernadette patted the hand on her shoulder and nodded again. This had to be what it felt like to live in a nursing home. Quick visits, short conversations that brushed the surface of meaning but never quite dug in, and everyone going back to their lives, leaving her with her memories and the sensation of frailty she'd always despised.

When Mirela's hand slipped from her shoulder, she felt like she could breathe again.

The younger woman grabbed the doorknob and paused. "We'll stay with you as long as you need to stay. You know that. If it's more than a couple days anyway, I'm pretty sure this kid'll be born in the South. Never thought I'd say that."

Bernadette snorted.

"But if that's what happens," Mirela added, "I do really want someone around who knows what they're doing."

Nodding slowly, Bernadette found she couldn't bring herself to look up at the woman who still had so much more to understand about the different ways a mother carried her child—the ways she couldn't *stop* carrying. "Well, you have her. And if you like, I think I still know a few midwives I could dig up out of their caves for you."

Mirela's soft chuckle spilled through her nose. "Anything's better than a hospital. Good night."

"'Night, sweetheart."

The door whispered open, the floorboards creaked, and then the thick wood clicked back into place. Bernadette stared at the dark shapes around the cabin that had watched over her entire childhood and all the recklessness that had followed it. She stuck the cigarette between her lips, lit it, and started rocking again.

The first cloud of smoke spilled from her mouth. "Fuck."

5

"HEY. DAD WANTS you to help in the kitchen."

Bernadette looked up from the letter she was writing and gave her sister a vapid stare. "Why?"

Candace leaned against the worn frame of the doorway into the cabin's second bedroom, folding her arms and crossing one glossy platform pump over the other. "Gosh, let me think about that… Oh, yeah. Because Mom said she needs help, and you're just sitting on your ass doing nothing."

"I'm busy." Bernadette slowly lowered her head to return to the letter propped in her lap on top of her crossed legs. "You go help."

Her sister scoffed. "*I* actually have work to do."

"You don't have a job."

"School *is* my job. Trust me. Once you start your first semester, you'll get it. Until then, I'm pretty sure me studying is more important than whatever you're scribbling right now."

Bernadette blinked at the letter and tapped her pen against the last sentence she'd written. She hadn't told anyone that she'd decided not to start her freshman year at the University of South Carolina in a few months with the full-ride academic scholarship they'd offered her. Her family thought she'd filled out all the paperwork and enrolled, because she had. But she wasn't going.

Candace's foot tapped slowly against the wooden floor.

Bernadette added another sentence to her letter. *'My sister's so far up my ass, I think she's forgotten that we're not actually the same person.'*

"Hey." Her sister snapped her fingers. "Are you deaf?"

"It's July."

"What?"

She scanned the letter again, not really able to focus on the words. With Little Miss Perfect standing there, tapping her foot and snapping her fingers and spouting a bunch of shit, it was amazing that Bernadette hadn't already chucked something at her. Maybe she should have. "How are you so busy with studying when it's the middle of the summer?"

A halting, stuttering vowel spilled from Candace's mouth. Bernadette knew that if she looked up again, she'd find her sister's wide eyes blinking furiously, mouth open in a mute gape so very much at odds with how smart she was supposed to be.

"You little—hey. Is that my *textbook*?"

Bernadette lifted a shoulder in a halfhearted shrug and pretended to write again.

"You've got to be kidding me. Do you have any idea how much new books cost?" Candace stormed into the room toward the double bed where Bernadette sat. Bernadette's mouth twitched into a smirk. "You can't just take whatever you want."

In a glaring act of defiant hypocrisy so inherent in older sisters—or at least in this one—Candace yanked the textbook out of Bernadette's lap. The letter went right along with it.

"Okay. Come on…" Bernadette rolled her eyes. "I didn't write on or in your book. Chill out."

"Look at this. You might as well have just slashed the cover with a knife." Candace stared at the textbook in one hand, holding away the offending letter with the other.

"You haven't seen *any* slasher films, have you?"

Her sister stared at her exactly the way Bernadette wanted—like she'd just been wildly insulted. "I don't know why you waste your time on that crap."

"I don't know why you waste your summer doing adult homework." Bernadette stuck out her hand and successfully hid the full-fledged grin fighting to break through. "You can have your book. Just give me back the paper."

Candace started to do just that, then apparently reconsidered and stepped away from the bed. "What are you even writing, anyway?"

Great. Now Bernadette had to keep acting like she didn't give a shit about the letter or the possibility of her sister reading anything in it. Except for maybe that last line. "Nothing."

Miss College Undergrad held the letter away from her younger sister—both of them definitely too old for this but neither quite able to resist. That was what coming down to Hollywood did to them. The obligatory family vacation every summer. The shitshow it inevitably turned into every year since Candace started high school. Six years of this bull. "Who's Janet?" Candace asked.

"Obviously not you." Bernadette stuck out her hand again with a little more force. "Seriously."

With raised eyebrows, Candace tossed the textbook onto the bed. The sharp edge of the corner struck Bernadette's bare ankle. She grimaced at the sting of it and jerked her foot out from beneath her to kick the heavy book off the bed. It slid over the light quilt with a flutter of pages and thumped onto the floor. But her sister wasn't paying any attention to her precious textbook now. Candace was in full spy mode, scanning everything her little sister had written and no doubt scheming up some master plan to use any or all of it against her.

Bernadette hunched over her crossed legs and watched her sister's reaction. If she tried to snatch the letter away now, Candace would know how much it meant to her—how many secrets were actually buried within a few not-so-subtle lines. She was just glad she hadn't gotten to writing the really juicy parts before the interruption.

Frowning, Candace finally looked up from the piece of paper and gave it a little shake. "What is this?"

"I thought they only let smart people into college."

"I guess you're the exception to the rule then, huh?" Candace stepped toward her and shot a quick glance through the open bedroom door before leaning over the bed. "Do Mom and Dad know this Janet person?"

Bernadette fought to keep from staring at the letter, so close and still just far enough out of her reach. There were very few times anymore when her sister took on that conspiratorial tone, where she made the choice to take her sister's side instead of their parents'. Right now, that put Bernadette in a precarious position. One wrong move, and her only sibling would turn on her in a heartbeat and say it was for her own good. Like any of them actually knew what was good for themselves, let alone her. So Bernadette could play her sister's game, at least for now. And then it would all blow over, and they could forget this ever happened.

She sighed. "No. They don't know her."

"So how do *you* know someone in Alabama?" Candace's voice was much lower than her regular speaking volume, but the venomous accusation didn't lose any of its insinuating sting.

"Through a friend, okay? We're just... pen pals, or whatever."

"Pen pals."

"Yeah." Bernadette widened her eyes and pumped as much sarcasm as she could into a slow nod. "That's when people write letters to each other—"

Candace scoffed. "I know what it *means*. You can't just... write stuff like this to someone you don't even know."

"I know her, okay? And it's really none of your business. So just drop it."

Then came the staring contest, which Bernadette always won because she could go a long time acting like she had nothing better to do. Her sister couldn't.

With another glance at the bedroom door—completely unnecessary with their parents in the kitchen on the other side of the cabin, their dad most likely outside checking the hog on the spit anyway—Candace straightened from leaning over the bed and cleared her throat. "Would Dad approve?"

Bernadette's heart felt like it had stopped completely, the cold emptiness of rage filling her belly in a fraction of a second that lasted forever. Then time and space came rushing back to her in an instant, and her hands clenched into fists. "Don't."

All euphemisms were nasty, but this one sat high up on her list. Maybe even at the top. Their mom had coined it years ago, when both of the Manney sisters were still in grade school. An apologetic *nicety* for their unapologetically racist father. *Your father just doesn't approve of those people.* That was their mom's line, her lie, as if using duller words made any of it less painfully disgusting. Then Richard Manney had started using it every chance he got. And now, as a grown woman who was supposed to be broadening her mind through higher education, Candace had tossed it out of her mouth like a bag of moldy Wonder Bread headed for the trash.

There was no shortage of concern in Candace's frown now and even more pity. Whether it was from having just said the words herself or from hoping she was wrong about her sister—honestly, it could have gone either way at this point—the oldest Manney sister's light-blue eyes brimmed with the first glisten of tears.

Good, Bernadette thought. If Candace was choosing to let that shit thinking into her own head, she deserved to be in this much pain, no matter what had caused it.

"Would he?" Candace asked again. Her voice quivered.

Bernadette's nostrils flared. "Give me my fucking letter."

"Bernadette!" Her sister ducked and glanced at the open door again, as if either of their parents would care about their grown daughters shouting at each other at the other end of the cabin. She thrust out her hand toward the living room, the paper fluttering in her grasp. "I swear, if you don't answer me, I'll take this into the kitchen right now and let you explain to *them* what you're really doing."

"It's a *letter*—"

"Answer my question."

"Yes!" It wasn't quite a scream, but it burst from Bernadette's mouth with just as much power. Yes, their dad would fucking approve of her writing a letter to a girl named Janet who lived in Vincent, Alabama. He'd even approve of Bernadette meeting her in person—hell, he'd invite the girl over for dinner. Because Janet was white, and that was really the only qualification that mattered to Richard Manney.

Candace's face paled a little, and she swallowed. Then, as if that one magic word that Bernadette should never have had to say was enough to flush out all the gunpowder in the air around them just waiting for a match, she sighed. "Okay. Well… you really shouldn't even be writing a letter like this and sending it to someone you hardly know. This is really personal stuff."

No shit. Bernadette glared at her sister and didn't say a word.

"If I were you, I'd stop whatever *this* is and just forget about it. Even if she's... what you say she is, you don't know what else she might be into. The kind of *people* she might hang out with. Do you even know what *part* of Alabama she lives in?"

Bernadette's chest flared with the white-hot, searing heat she'd never dared use on her own family. If they were this bigoted against the color of someone's skin, she could only imagine what they'd do to someone like her, someone who could make them feel what Bernadette made people feel just by a few well-placed words. There was no doubt in her mind that being Richard and Mary's daughter and Candace's little sister wouldn't mean shit if they'd known. But Bernadette was out of high school, this close to starting her own life on her own terms, and that in and of itself was enough of a reason not to hold back anymore.

Right now, she couldn't have stopped herself if her life depended on it.

"Dripping honey." She said the words the same way she would have told her sister to eat shit, but these held so much more weight. These words, just like those she'd been able to pick from thin air minutes after meeting a person, were just for Candace. Special. These words would tear her sister down.

Candace lurched a little where she stood, as if she'd been hit with sudden nausea and was about to vomit. But the little twitch hadn't come from her stomach, and they both knew it. She blinked quickly. "What?"

"Slow, dripping honey."

Her sister's lashes fluttered as her eyes rolled back in her head. "You…"

"So sweet."

A small moan came from Candace's throat, and she tipped her head back, arching her back.

"Golden in the sunlight when I unscrewed the lid of the honey jar and dipped my spoon into it."

Fast breathing. Glazed eyes. Candace's thighs pressed tightly together in a useless attempt to stop the onslaught of her sister's words. Her lips parted as she swayed, feet glued to the bedroom floor despite the rest of her body lighting up in response.

Bernadette just kept talking, the words burning in her chest, up her throat, out of her mouth. She'd known there was magic in them for the last seven years, and she'd known how to perfect them at this point into whatever she wanted. The only trick she hadn't figured out was how to quit while she was ahead, before the target of her words could finish what she'd started. But she couldn't stop herself now. The words had taken over, and even if she'd had a mind to leave her sister breathless and startled and wholly unsatisfied at the end of this, what she really wanted was complete humiliation. It wouldn't change anything, but it would make Bernadette feel a hell of a lot better.

"It was sticky on my fingers, running off the sides of the spoon in thin, sweet lines." She uncrossed her legs from beneath her and slid off the bed. "I had to taste it. The sweetness. Forget the butter. Forget the toast."

Candace writhed where she stood, her chest heaving in an ecstasy she couldn't stop and would never understand.

"So much honey. More than I ever imagined in one place, all for me."

By the time Bernadette had walked the few feet toward her sister, Candace was already touching herself. One hand fumbled clumsily at her own breast and the padded bra covering it. Her other wrist pressed tightly against her pelvis, trembling there as she still fought against the power of Bernadette's words, wanting to slide that hand between her own legs and unable to fathom how to do it when her body shuddered beneath an unseen caress. The letter fluttered in her hand, somehow still held between loosening fingers.

"So I lifted that first spoon of honey," Bernadette said. She stopped just beside her sister, who let out another breathless moan, and gave herself just a few seconds to take in the sight of it. This was what real control looked like, and it had nothing to do with their dad's hatred or their mom's euphemisms or how much Candace studied for classes she hadn't even started yet. She snatched the letter out of her sister's weak fingers, then leaned in closer to whisper in Candace's ear, "And I put the whole thing in my mouth."

The grand finale—she felt it in the fading heat within her chest just as much as her sister clearly felt it in the growing heat between her legs. Or wherever else. Candace nearly shrieked, her body spasming with the release of orgasm brought about by the power she'd had no idea existed in her little sister's words. Then she gasped and staggered forward toward the bed, stumbling over herself and falling halfway onto the mattress, quivering.

Bernadette took a deep breath and gazed at the open bedroom door. "Looks like you need a minute." She couldn't tell if the next sound from her sister's mouth was a sob or another gasp of lingering pleasure. Pressing her lips together, she walked out of the room, folding the letter and creasing it in half.

She reached the door from the living room onto the porch at the same time as her dad. He stood on the other side when she opened it, blinking at her in surprise. "Where are you going?" he asked.

"I'm taking a walk." His confused frown deepened, so she added, "I think there's something wrong with Candace."

The door to the second bedroom slammed shut with a bang.

Bernadette shrugged at her dad, grinned, then slipped past him onto the porch and hurried for the screen door. She couldn't get out of there fast enough. She couldn't get out of this town, the entire state, fast enough.

6

I HONESTLY CAN'T say it's any better in Alabama than it is in South Carolina. I wish I could, Bernie. Sometimes, though, I wonder if so much change is what's making the rest of the world lose their minds. Where we live, things move too slowly, you know? They've been moving slowly forever, like we're frozen in the same never-ending loop of living the same phony lives our parents and grandparents lived. Probably even their parents and grandparents too. But we're the only ones who can see what a drag it is to keep being stuck. That all this craziness has to change.

I don't really talk about this, but I tell you everything, so I know I can lay this down here. I say all this stuff about needing to stand up and speak. Raise our voices and make the Man pay attention, even if it means screaming. Donna's all about it now, actually. I guess she was when we met, and I was just diggin' her too much to notice. She takes me to these parties, right? But they're not really parties. Like, they are, and we have a bitchin' time, but there's always something deeper goin' down. Some kinda vibe everyone's keepin' on the down low. And I'm freaking out a little about what's gonna happen when the secrets get out, you know?

The "parties" are for people like us, Bernie. Wanting to change things so we don't hit the same problems as everyone else who's tried to do this before. About to scream that we're just people trying to do our thing. Donna says it's gonna happen soon. That big things are coming, and she says I'm just trippin' out about the whole thing. I don't know, though. Isn't it safer to be a little worried about things turning out wrong?

Like, that's what just happened in Miami a few months ago, right? All these people standing up and screaming to be heard, and they tore that city apart. Actual goddamn riots. I mean, I know why they're angry. Like, what if the same thing that happened to Arthur McDuffie happened to your man? Or to Donna ... Fuck. I'd be angry too, and I honestly don't want to know what you'd do. You'd stand against all of it, wouldn't you? Bernie, I don't know if I would.

That's the thing Donna keeps reminding me of over and over. That people like us with magic in their words don't have it nearly as bad. You can see the color of a person's skin, and that's one way to judge. You can see two lesbians holding hands or kissing, and that's another way to judge. But what about us? Nobody can see what we are. Not until they're right up in our faces and too close to turn away once those burning words start, you know?

She says we have to be inclusive. That anyone with "something special to say" should be welcomed with open arms. It's not like I'm a racist, and I obviously don't have a problem with lesbians (what kinda person would that make me if I did?), but I'm scared about what's gonna happen when this shit blows up. There's this guy here named Charles. Bernie, I'm not foolin' around, this cat was a legit member of the Black Panther Party. Lived in a pad and everything in Oakland. He's older. Thirty-something, I think. But his stories make me want to run as far as I can from this whole thing. It's some heavy shit.

Donna keeps talking about someday making a lesbian "chapter". Like, yeah, it's cool to stand up, and I'm chill about what I am and who I love. But isn't it just asking for more trouble if you take a bunch of women people already don't want to understand and then add on top of it people like us who are still hiding from the whole world? I swear, in my head, it feels like that idea of hers is gonna turn out to be like the McCarthy trials all over again (yeah, I've been doing some research. Plus my dad never stops talking about watching them on TV right before my parents got hitched).

I don't wanna get dragged into a war just by being who I am. We've already had too many wars. Even in our country. Oakland, San Francisco, Miami, Chicago, Boston, New York City. Hell, King and Kennedy shot down almost at the same fucking time. We were just kids, and we didn't know each other yet, but I know you remember.

It feels like that's about to happen again, and I can't sleep thinking Donna's gonna end up just like them. Or the people Charles keeps talking about who got picked off for no reason in California. Or Arthur McDuffie.

You're lucky, Bernie. Like, yeah, it sucks about your family. But you have D, and it's not like he's trying to convince you to do things you don't think you can do. He just wants to love you. He's not like us, sure, but he's not trying to turn you into a weapon, either. If I wasn't so into her, I would've stepped out a long time ago.

I think I love her.

I just hope it doesn't get us killed.

7

BERNADETTE WOKE WITH a jolt, which made her groan. Everything hurt. Again. This time, it came from the fact that she'd sat outside for so long the night before that she'd fallen asleep in the rocking chair on the porch. Her lower back was on fire, and when she straightened her knees, they flared up again with that breathtaking ache that was too deep for even her own strong fingers to reach.

Propping both feet out in front of her and gritting her teeth through the discomfort, she sighed. "I'm too old for this shit."

She grabbed her smokes, and as soon as she lit the first one, the side door from inside the cabin burst open with a quick puff of tepid, humid air. Bernadette almost put out her cigarette again but stopped when she saw Brad's face poking out through the door.

Mirela's husband—five-ten with a stocky build, fiery red hair cut short, and a beard to match—blinked at her with wide eyes. "How long have you been out here?"

Bernadette lifted her cigarette and dipped her head. "All night."

"Woah." Brad glanced back inside the cabin, then quickly stepped out onto the porch and shut the door behind him. "Can't sleep, huh?"

She let out a wry chuckle and blew out another breath of smoke. "Oh, I can. And apparently in a rocking chair."

When she bent her knees before attempting to stand, another flare of pain shot through them, and she just left them where they were, kicked out straight from the rocking chair. Brad just stood there in front of the door, his eyes on her but with a certain vacancy behind them. Smirking, Bernadette watched his cautious but urgent posture until it was time enough to put him out of his misery.

"Brad."

"Yeah."

"Why do I get the feeling you stepped out onto the porch for a reason?"

The man blinked quickly, huffed out a laugh completely devoid of amusement, and scratched his head. "Mirela's still in bed. She hasn't been sleeping well lately, so I figured I'd just leave her there until she's ready to get up. But she kept talking about wanting pickled okra last night. I don't... I don't even know what that is."

Bernadette chuckled. "You're in the perfect place for it."

"Oh, yeah?"

She dipped her head and shot him a pointed look to get on with it already.

Brad folded his arms, unfolded them halfway to stroke his nearly orange beard, then scratched his head and rubbed both palms down the legs of his jeans. "I should go get her *something* she actually wants, right? I mean, I get that cravings are cravings, and she's been trying to eat healthy as much as she can…"

"Little hard to do that on the road, huh?" Bernadette tried to rock again in the chair, gave up after another zing of pain radiated from her lower back, and took another drag.

He snorted. "Yeah. Just a little. It's not like we could've just stayed home and waited for this whole thing to blow over."

"Are you talking about Vanguard Industries," she asked with a raised eyebrow, "or the baby?"

Brad bounced a little on his toes and scratched his head again. "Both, I think. Maybe. I mean, one of them we can actually run away from"—he chopped both hands to one side, then the other—"and the other's completely unavoidable, and I think I'm having a hard time telling which is which right now. Am I crazy?"

Puffing out a cloud of smoke through her chuckle, Bernadette put out her quarter-smoked cigarette in the ashtray and finally mustered the willpower to push herself out of the chair. The furniture creaked and groaned, but fortunately—at least for now—the woman did not. Brad let out a huge sigh when she approached him and pressed her hands together. "Can I give you a piece of advice?"

"Is it about having a pregnant wife?" Brad cleared his throat. "'Cause I'm pretty sure I'm the only one here who has any experience with that."

"True. But I *am* a woman, in case you haven't noticed. I might be gettin' up there in years, but I have definitely seen my fair share of births."

The man blinked at her, and the corners of his mouth twitched up into a hesitant, confused smirk. "Seriously?"

"Enough to count them out on my hands, so yes. Seriously." She gave him a reassuring nod. "What your wife needs right now is support. A *strong* support, right? She's been doing her job and cookin' up this kid for the last nine months. It's almost your turn for the hard work now. Understand?"

"The hard work." A bark of a laugh escaped him, and he gestured toward the door into the cabin. "*She's* the one who has to actually... you know."

Brad spread his legs and mimed pushing with both hands. Bernadette wanted so badly to start cracking jokes at that, but it would just do the opposite of what the man needed. She honestly hadn't expected this man, Mirela's husband, to react like this to the impending birth of their first child. With a wife who cooked every meal from scratch, used tea and herbs instead of a few Advil, and opened her house to any number of people like them—whether coming to join Sleepwater for a while or just passing through on their way to somewhere else hopefully safe—Brad should have been a lot more prepared than this.

43

Then again, the days of sitting in silence and relative peace, enjoying the last bit of time they'd have alone for almost two decades, talking out plans for their child and picking out names and soaking in the energy of having created a life—all of it had been stripped from Brad and Mirela since the very beginning. Maybe Brad would have taken a nine-month pregnancy to settle into the role of birthing partner and father and pillar of strength for his soon-to-be family of three—if he'd had the chance to do so in his own home. But the couple had spent Mirela's entire pregnancy on the road with an old woman, a lanky and middle-aged hacker, a thirty-one-year-old brooder, and two twins of Italian descent who still hadn't figured out how to make things right between them after being separated by far more than just physical distance.

For the first time in over twenty years, Bernadette really appreciated the fact that, when it had been her time, things could have been so much worse.

"Bernadette?" Brad spread his arms and gave a pathetic shrug. "Seriously, any advice is better than none. I have no idea what I'm doing."

"So act like you do." She smiled, shot him a quick nod, and tried to step around him toward the door.

He stepped in front of her just a few inches, blocking her path not with a threat but with desperate, begging sincerity. "How the hell am I supposed to do that?"

Bernadette laid a gentle but firm hand on his shoulder and held his gaze. "The best way to show your wife that you know she can do it is by convincing her that *you* can handle it. I never thought I'd have to say this to you, but just know I say it out of love."

He swallowed. "Okay."

"Your balls didn't fall off when you made the kid. But you need to find them again before he's born." She patted his shoulder a few times, then slipped past his completely startled gaze and grabbed the doorknob.

"*He*?" Brad ignored her jab completely and shot her a goofy, baffled smile. "I'm gonna have a son?"

Bernadette rolled her eyes. Sure, maybe she'd opened her mouth a little too much just to get him to shut his.

"Just a feeling," she said. "Don't hold me to it."

She opened the door, paused, and nodded toward the opposite side of the cabin facing the road. "Keys are in the van. Go ahead and take it now before everyone else wakes up. They *are* still asleep, right?"

He cleared his throat again and swallowed. "Far as I know."

"You want local okra, if that's what she's craving. Best place for that close by is King's Market. About ten minutes down the main road."

"Yeah, okay. Thanks. I'll just…" He turned away from her, paused, then headed for the door leading off the screened-in porch.

"You need another reminder?"

He didn't turn around when he stepped outside and let the screen door shut quickly behind him. "Yeah, nut up. I got it."

Chuckling, Bernadette shook her head and stepped into the cabin again. Immediately, she wrinkled her nose and pulled the door shut. The other four guys sprawled out across all the furniture in the only room besides the kitchen and the bedrooms at either end. How was it that a room full of sleeping men managed to work up such an unconscionable stench?

Right on cue, Cameron let out an impressively loud fart in his sleep and rolled partially over in the recliner he'd stretched out and back to its full length. A rumbling snore rose from Randall's open mouth. The twins were silent enough—for now.

With a hard, heavy blink, Bernadette moved silently across the main room, stepped up into the kitchen, and pulled the sliding pocket door completely closed. When she glanced at the door to the master bedroom just off the kitchen, she paused.

Despite knowing Mirela was in there, hopefully sleeping deeply enough to give her a little more energy today, she could only think about Darrell and all the nights they'd spent together on the other side of that door. After that came the glaring, always painful knowledge of how many nights they *hadn't* spent together after she left. It shouldn't have hurt this much to think about it. Not after twenty years and everything she'd accomplished between then and now. But wanting to forget the past and all the things she could have done better didn't change the fact that her mistakes had piled up on top of her like broken trees after a hurricane. Didn't make any of this less painful.

Moving on autopilot, Bernadette shuffled toward the fridge beside the bedroom door and opened it. Puffing out a breath, she closed it again and checked the cabinets.

Of course they were all empty. Of course no one had used this place since Richard Manney passed away, followed six short months later by his wife Mary. Of course their youngest daughter hadn't come home for the funeral. Either of them. And Candace was too busy running her chain of *consignment boutiques* out of Mt. Pleasant, and Summerville, and Goose Creek, and whatever other town from which she could squeeze a few thousand more dollars to stuff into her reputation. Far too busy to come take care of the few acres of land and the cabin that had been in the Manney family for more generations than Bernadette really knew.

Maybe Bernadette was the only person left who found any meaning in this place anymore. Any value. Sure, a few distasteful memories stood out over the others. But weren't the good ones worth even more? Eleven years of running through the live oaks and napping under their thick, draping canopy; of driving ATVs down to the creek for a swim in saltwater as warm as a child's bath; of Mary's Southern cooking and Richard's steady patience as he taught his kids how to fish and set crab traps, chop wood and build fires, smoke a hog and skin a deer. All the things a man took to heart when he always wanted a son and got two daughters instead.

For eleven years, Bernadette had wished it were easier to be the son her father never had. Wished it were easier to make her daddy proud the way he wanted to be proud of something. But eleven years of an innocent, relatively decent childhood didn't erase another seven of struggling to understand her parents and then hating them when she finally did.

And all the wisdom in the world—the kind that came with age, heartache, shameful mistakes, overwhelming love, and the type of beauty that was quick to bloom and even quicker to be snatched away—couldn't convince Bernadette to forgive her father for what he'd done.

"That won't ever change." She pulled out a dust-covered chair from beneath the kitchen table and lowered herself into it. Apparently, sitting here in an empty kitchen was the only option she had until everyone else woke up. Not that she minded. Bernadette had spent plenty of time sitting alone at kitchen tables, namely her own. Without family. Without the two people who should have been sitting in two other chairs. They'd never had a chance to sit together at *this* table.

Still, it gave her a little bit of hope to think that both of them still lived within a few hours' drive of where she sat. There was always that hope—that despite her own wandering ways and her refusal to turn away from who and what she was, from what she could *do*, a small part of the world stayed still, right where it always had been. What she'd always resented about the South had somehow, now, become her last lifeline. Bernadette could clutch at it and not let go all she wanted, but a ladder leading out of a deep, dark pit was just so many pieces of wood nailed together if she never made the decision to climb.

Twenty years changed a lot, though. She'd hardly recognized Charleston when they drove through on their way here, and she wasn't so blind as to think that time would have done any less to those she'd left behind. No, it was bound to have changed them enough to practically make them strangers. Maybe Bernadette had become a stranger too.

She leaned forward and rested her elbow on the kitchen table before raising a hand to her forehead. "I'm really about to do this, aren't I?"

The squeak of the turning doorknob nearly startled her out of her chair, and then the bedroom door opened and a very pregnant—albeit refreshed-looking—Mirela stepped out into the kitchen. Rubbing her belly, the woman yawned, smacked her lips a few times, and glanced around. "Who were you talking to?"

Bernadette gave her a sympathetic smile and slid the chair out from beneath the head of the table with her foot. "Nobody but myself. Just a snapshot of old age, sweetheart."

Mirela stopped and shot her a playful frown. "You're the youngest old person I've ever met."

"Ha. I said old age, Mirela. Not death."

The expectant mother slowly sank into the offered chair and puffed out a long, slow breath. "I thought sleeping would make me feel *better*."

"Did it do the opposite for you, then?"

"No." Mirela stuck her elbow on the table and propped her chin in her open hand. "Pretty much the same, actually."

Bernadette pressed her lips together and nodded.

"I didn't know there was a door there." Mirela nodded at the pocket door closing them off from the man stink in the main room.

"Yep. My granddaddy put it there before he married grandmama. My dad's parents. It's a little outdated, but so is everything else in this place. So I guess it fits."

The other woman's low, tired chuckle made the kitchen feel a little brighter. "Did you spend a lot of time here?"

"Sure. When I was still a baby." Bernadette snorted. "For the record, the last time I came down here, I was nineteen. That falls into the baby category. Remember that nineteen years from now when you start thinking yours is all grown up."

She glanced down at Mirela's rounded belly and dipped her head toward the child they'd all be meeting any day now.

Mirela laughed. "Good advice. You know, if things got cleaned up a little, this wouldn't be a bad place to raise a family."

"It needs more than a *little*." Bernadette studied the cobwebs in the corners, then the layers of dust, dirt, and dead palmetto bugs scattered across the kitchen's linoleum floors. "We'd need a whole crew to make any of this look remotely like it used to. Nobody's been here for a long time."

A small frown flickered across Mirela's brow. "Then who's been paying the utility bill?"

Bernadette snorted. "Candace, probably. My sister."

"A *sister*. You have a family cabin going back at least three generations, a sister, and a—"

"We all have a past, honey. And sometimes, things are just better off if that's exactly where we leave them." Bernadette nodded slowly and pretended to study the warped kitchen walls again. The knots clenching tighter and tighter in her stomach made the constant ache in her joints feel like a dull, forgivable irritation. Honestly, she didn't know which sensation she preferred.

Mirela pressed her lips together and glanced at the table, swiping her hand slowly back and forth across the smooth wood stained decades ago and now boasting nicks in the edges and divots in the surface and a charred ring in the center from the year Mary Manney drank too much wine and set down the casserole dish without a potholder beneath it. Even all these years later, Bernadette still had a feverish urge to scrub that burn mark out of the table forever.

"I know." Mirela swallowed, glanced through the window on the other side of the kitchen above the sink, and sighed. "I bet this was an incredible place to grow up, though."

"Huh." Bernadette sucked on her lower lip and cocked her head. "It sure was somethin'. I'll tell you that much. Oh, Brad stepped out a while ago. Took the van to grab some food."

"Good." Mirela's neck made a graceful, shallow C between her chin and her chest when she looked down at her swollen belly and rubbed it again. "I hope he's quick about it. It's obviously impossible, but I feel like I could eat two foot-long subs and a whole bag of Sun Chips. Family size."

"I hope that's not a real craving right now. Because I definitely sent your husband to the wrong place if that's what you have your heart set on."

"Not my heart." Mirela tossed her long, dark hair over her shoulder and laughed. "Just my stomach. At this point, I'll eat anything."

"Good." Bernadette's smirk widened into a full-fledged grin. "Trust me. The way he was bouncing all over the place, he'll be back any minute."

"What?" Mirela let out an unsure puff of a laugh. "Is he okay?"

Bernadette wanted to tell the woman no. That any man on the verge of becoming a father was *not* okay. Instead, she just sat back in the creaking wooden chair, folded her arms, and shrugged. "He'll be fine."

8

DARRELL'S DARK EYES lingered at the corner of her mouth when Bernadette stretched her body to its fullest length along the bed. She let out a heavy sigh and coiled into herself again, rolling toward him until his lips followed the path of his gaze and settled not quite on her lips, not quite on her cheek. A soft hum of approval escaped him, and he drew his large, calloused hand—still so warm and gentle despite the rough proof that built on his skin, day after day, as he built his own life—down her bare thigh.

He could have trailed a finger, or his knuckles, or even his mouth across her skin if he hadn't already pressed his lips half on hers and half off. But that was what she loved about the man lying beside her on the bed in her family's cabin. Darrell didn't touch anything with hesitation or try to lure it out of hiding with an implied promise or whisper of intention. He touched her because she was already there, already his, curled up against his dark, bare chest damp with sweat on top of the quilt they hadn't bothered to turn down before pulling each other onto it. Darrell's hand moved over her skin like he was trying to touch all of her at once, as much as he could. Like there still wasn't enough.

When he squeezed her upper thigh, long fingers curving at the end of a broad palm, Bernadette let out an airy chuckle—part physical pleasure, part satisfaction in the fact that he always seemed to respond with something physical to her corresponding and unvoiced thoughts.

"What?" he murmured, his lips brushing against the corner of her mouth and sticking just for a moment to her skin.

She reached up to trace the line of stubble along his jaw, under his chin, almost down to his neck but not quite. "Just feels good."

"A thing feels good, and it makes you laugh." His rough hand went down her thigh again, paused at her knee, then moved back up and settled for one more squeeze just below her ass. "I ain't never gonna understand why it hits you like that, B. I tell you what. A thing feels good to me, laughin' is the last thing on my mind."

"Somebody's trying way too hard to be serious all the time."

"Naw." Darrell rolled toward her and pressed his lips to her neck, then pulled back just enough for her to feel a cool rush of air when he took a deep breath through his nose. "I think you're laughin' 'cause a thing feels good *and* you're still thinkin' about somethin' else at the same time."

"I'm not thinking about anything else." She took a sharp, shuddering breath when he drew his hand up her thigh again, this time along the inside. "Except maybe the next thing that'll feel good."

When he leaned away from her and met her gaze, the only proof of his surprise was a raised eyebrow over hooded lids heavy with pleasure. Then he barked out a deep laugh and rolled onto his back. "You—" Darrell laughed again and rubbed his mouth, then his chin, trying to hide the smile Bernadette wished he'd let out in the open a little more often.

"See? It's not so bad to laugh."

"Girl, I just gave you everything I got, and you're thinkin' about *the next thing*—" Snorting, he pushed himself up off the stacked pillow and rested a forearm on his bent knee to rub his head. Then he looked at her and grinned. "You're crazy."

"You like it." She shifted to lie on her side and propped her head up with a hand. "And I wasn't thinking about *that* kinda next thing."

"Oh, sure. You're already somewhere else, outta this bed, outta the middle of nowhere and somewhere nice and big and fancy. Ain't you?"

"Actually…" Bernadette sat up and pulled him toward her for another kiss. He laughed through his nose but kissed her back until she leaned away, pushing lightly against his bare chest and the small patch of black hair across his breastbone. "It's not *that* far away. Still in your car, I think."

"*My* car." Darrell's lips twitched on the edge of laughter again. "Your mind went all the way out to my car."

"Just for a second." Biting her lip, she trailed her gaze up over his shoulder and down his arm roped with muscle, and her fingers followed. Then she looked quickly back up at him and added, "That feels good too."

"You want this man lyin' bare-ass naked in your bed to get on up and fetch you that grass you forgot to take out his car." Another low, subdued laugh escaped him when Bernadette only grinned in response. "Lucky I can read your mind, girl."

"I'm lucky to have this man lyin' bare-ass naked in my bed. Everything else is just the cherry on top."

"Uh-huh." Licking his lips, Darrell stared her down as he climbed over her bare legs and slid off the bed. "Big fuckin' cherry. You gon' owe me one now."

She watched him pull on his brown slacks just a few shades lighter than his skin. "I'll pay you with a special kinda story. How 'bout that?"

"Oh, uh-uh." He shook his head, hiked his pants up the rest of the way, and buttoned them. "That's just you showin' off. I don't need more words from you."

"Then what do you want?"

"Lemme think 'bout that while I go fetch the next thing that feels good." He smacked her thigh and disappeared through the bedroom doorway into the kitchen. The pillow Bernadette chucked at him missed by an inch and thumped against the wall.

Laughing, she threw herself down onto her back again and stared at the ceiling fan swaying in slow, lazy circles above the bed. Six months, so far, and Darrell hadn't said a word one way or the other about the surprisingly impossible things she could do with that *special kind of story*. Six months, and he hadn't asked her how she could do it, how it worked, why she used it at certain times and not at others. He hadn't explicitly asked for her to use that ability on him,, nor had he tried to stop her when the words burned in her chest and his eyes glazed over after a few seconds of hearing the story meant just for him. When it came to the very real and unexplained magic in Bernadette's words, the secret formula for Darrell was anything having to do with fur.

Not that he had a special attachment to animal fur. Not that he'd be caught dead wearing it. The man didn't have any pets, wasn't especially drawn to animals in general. But that was his weakness. Different for everybody, and Bernadette had no idea why. The only thing that mattered, she supposed, was that at twenty years old, she could pick out the right story for anybody on the second try, if not the first.

She'd never used this power over Darrell to get anything from him. They'd been going together—in the bedroom and out of it—for over a month before she figured what the hell and gave it a shot. He'd surprised her that first time by tearing himself out of the brain-addled fog her words induced, combined with the way they'd quite obviously made him feel, to roll over on top of her and do with his body what she did with that special kind of story.

That was when she'd realized there was something different about Darrell. Something she wanted to keep with her for as long as she possibly could—that he saw her no differently after she'd exposed what she could do, that he still wanted her, that one way or another, what she had or what she lacked or where she came from didn't make a lick of difference. The only thing that mattered was that they'd found each other, as unlikely as it had always seemed.

Bernadette reached out for another long, languid stretch, grinning like a drunken idiot.

Outside in front of the cabin, tires crunched down the gravel drive. She hadn't heard the car door shut again, and Darrell wouldn't have left without saying something. They were here for the night.

The crunching gravel drew louder, followed by a thick, scattered spray of small rocks against the cabin's siding and the squeal of worn brakes. Bernadette froze. Then she did hear a car door open and slam shut, and it definitely wasn't Darrell's car.

"Just what the goddamn hell do you think you're doin', boy?"

"Shit." Bernadette scrambled off the bed and snatched her thin-strapped sundress off the floor. The fabric fluttered around her shaking hands as she tried to find the stupid hole to stick her head through.

"Mr. Manney." Darrell's voice was calm, collected, low.

"I asked you a question!"

"Bernadette brought me down here, sir."

"Like hell she did. You step back from that car right now."

Bernadette finally jerked the dress down over her hips and barreled through the kitchen. Her palm slammed up against the light switch for the front porch light, instantly lighting up the image of her dad pointing an accusatory finger at Darrell.

"What the—" Richard Manney whirled toward the porch and roared, "Bernadette!"

"Dad!" The front door creaked when she swung it open, same as the screen door, but that one slammed shut behind her as she leapt off the porch. "Dad, stop."

"This piece of shit said you *brought* him here." Her dad jerked his finger at Darrell again. "*Here*. So you tell me right now, Bernadette. Do you know this man?"

For a brief moment, time seemed to stop. The yellow porch light lit up Richard Manney's face so perfectly—rage, disgust, disbelief shadowed in the wrinkles around his blazing eyes; Darrell standing barefoot on the gravel drive, shirtless in the humid night air under the moon, his jaw clenched and his arms hanging loosely at his sides; the outline of another person sitting in the passenger seat of her dad's tan Buick, impossible to make out against the glare of the light on the windshield. There had always been a chance that they'd be found out, her and Darrell, but she never expected her dad to come barreling down the drive with an audience for the whole affair.

"I asked you a question."

She gave up trying to see the passenger in his car and met her father's gaze. "Yes. His name is Darrell, and I brought him here. On purpose."

"You…" Richard's face contorted in a mixture of betrayal and shame, followed by a crazed fury that made Bernadette quite sure he'd already decided to bring these emotions with him in the first place. "You're telling me you went behind my back and brought a fucking—"

"That's exactly what I'm saying," she shouted and stormed across the grass toward the drive and her father, who looked ridiculously surprised to see that she could still move and talk and think on her own. "And it's none of your business where I go or who I'm with. You *gave* me the keys! I should be asking *you* why you came all the way down here in the middle of the night. This is ridiculous."

Richard's mouth hung open beneath his wide stare, which moved from his daughter to the man he'd never met standing beside a car he'd never seen. Then he seemed to notice for the first time that Darrell stood barefoot on the gravel, wearing nothing but his trousers. Darrell, for all the tension of the moment, hadn't made a sound or moved an inch.

When Bernadette's dad turned back toward her, he looked her over and took in her mussed hair, her own bare feet, and if she hadn't been partially silhouetted by the porch light, he would have probably seen the flush on her cheeks that had already been there before he'd ruined her night. Richard blinked and muttered, "It's all true. I thought she was lying."

Bernadette's heart fluttered in her chest, and she shook her head. "What are you talking about?"

Her dad didn't answer. Richard Manney was never one to talk about his feelings, and more often than not, words failed him anyway. But this time, he took it too far. The man stormed in front of his car, and when his shadow blocked out the light from the front porch, Bernadette finally saw who was sitting in the passenger seat.

Her sister Candace looked away from their dad and met Bernadette's gaze with wide, glistening eyes. The terror in them—so unmistakable and so irreversibly condemning— told Bernadette everything she needed to know. She thought she was going to be sick.

"Dad!"

Richard Manney's fist slammed into Darrell's jaw and sent the young man staggering backward into the grass. But he didn't go down. And Bernadette's father didn't stop.

"No daughter of mine is gonna run around with a—"

"Dad, stop it!"

"—piece a shit from the—"

"You can't do this!"

Richard swung again, but this time, Darrell stepped swiftly aside, ducking the man's wild fist. "I should've brought my fucking gun!"

Bernadette's bare feet pounded across the gravel and into the ground again just before she shoved both hands into her dad's back. Richard stumbled forward with a shout of surprise and whirled to face her. The back of his hand smacked against her cheek with a deafening crack, and the world tilted around her. Then everything stopped.

Blinking away hot tears, Bernadette straightened and took in a quick, halting breath. He'd done it. The bastard had finally hit her, just like she always knew he would.

"Now, see…" Richard choked on his next breath. "That was an accident."

"No it wasn't," she muttered, glaring at him.

"Bernadette, you got in the way of a man handling his business—"

"That doesn't fucking matter. *None* of this is your business!"

The passenger door of Richard's car clicked open, and Candace's quiet, trembling voice filtered out. "Bernadette…"

"You stay put," Richard shouted, pointing at his oldest daughter and barely sparing her a glance. Candace stayed where she was, but the passenger door stayed open, too.

"Don't worry," Bernadette seethed. "I'll make this easy for you." She wished in that moment that the force of all the shame she felt burning behind her eyes could physically hurt him. Instead, her lower lip trembled, and she stormed away from her dad and toward Darrell's car.

"Sweetheart, please—"

"Don't even try. I'm done."

"Bernadette, you're making a mistake."

"And you're a goddamn coward."

Richard took a few steps after her and stopped when he saw Darrell slip behind the wheel of his own car. "I swear to God, if you get in that car—"

"Fuck you!" Bernadette paused beside her dad's car and slammed her hand against the open doorframe. Candace jumped in the passenger seat and recoiled when her little sister leaned forward. "Is this what you wanted?" Bernadette spat. Her sister blinked, her mouth opening and closing without any sound. "I *never* want to see you again."

Without waiting for a reply, Bernadette slammed her hand against the side of the car again. Candace let out a startled squeak, and the next thing Bernadette knew, she'd finally reached Darrell's car. She wanted to jerk the passenger door off its hinges, but she settled instead for slumping into the front seat and slamming it shut behind her. Through the windshield, she stared at the blurred image of her dad staggering toward her down the gravel drive. She wished her eyes hadn't filled with tears again, only because she wanted to see the baffled pain on her father's face as he watched her leave him for the last time. It made her feel a little better that he probably thought she could.

Darrell started the engine. "B, you sure you—"

"Just go." She choked on the last word, making it sound like a sigh and a repressed sob at the same time.

The Monte Carlo reversed just a little off the gravel drive so Darrell could turn it around toward the main road. Before he did, Bernadette caught the backlit shape of her father stumbling sideways against the trunk of his car, supporting himself with one hand while the other might or might not have clutched at his chest. It surprised her that she wasn't more worried about him in that moment—that she didn't feel anything at all. Because if Richard Manney were having a heart attack in front of his family's cabin, he had nothing to blame it on but his own hatred.

9

I'M PROUD OF you, Bernie. That part of me wishes that I'd been there to see it. Or maybe even to help. I think it means one thing to stand up to your own family and a totally differ- ent thing to not take shit from strangers. The other part of me just wants you to be careful. I know I've said it before, and maybe you've ignored it. Maybe it stuck. But I just have to say it, because I'm seeing things out here that make me just as proud and scared.

Something's coming, and it's unlike anything else mak- ing waves right now. Civil rights in a way that cuts through race and sexuality and economic whatever whatever. I'm honestly getting a little tired of hearing about it every single day. Donna's a machine when it comes to this stuff. She says pretty soon, no one's gonna care about the color of a per- son's skin or if they love a man or a woman or if they speak a different language or how much money they spend. She says the world's going to fall on its ass when everyone hears about people like us with our words and the things no one else can do. She says that'll be what's important, that it'll make everyone else see how useless it is to hate a person for something they can't help.

I don't think it's gonna happen the way she expects. She's so sure. All the people here in the clubs and the bars and under all the dark lights are gearing up for this one big reveal, like it's going to change the world in a good *way. Everybody tells me I need to loosen up. That I've just been programmed to be scared. That it's just the Man talking in my head. Seriously, though, I don't think coming out to the world right now is a good idea for any of us. People who hate what they don't know aren't gonna stop just because we step up and say, "Look what we can do with our words! Let's stop fighting!" They'll just end up looking away from the problem now because all their focus will be taken up by hating people like us even* more *than every other kind of person they can't understand.*

Donna thinks we'll be holding up a mirror to the world. Nobody's gonna see it that way, Bernie. If we try to hold up a mirror, all the world's gonna see is a bomb.

It feels like I'm the only one who can see it, but I see it like someone took a photo and hung it up on the wall. I see it coming. I feel it coming. I don't know how to step away from this without the whole thing falling apart. It's going to anyway, whether or not I'm a part of it. I think that's why I can't make up my mind.

I wanted to write more, but Donna and I haven't had

much time to sit down and breathe and take a few minutes to do nothing. I'm on a bus right now, actually, which is completely to blame for the awful handwriting. Definitely send me your new address when you write back. I don't mind mailing these out to a motel, but I definitely don't want our letters to get mixed up before you find another place.

Just be careful.

—Janet

P.S. You did the right thing. .

10

"YOU SURE THERE'S no AC in this place?" Cameron scowled at the walls of the kitchen and popped a cracker loaded with way too much pimiento cheese into his mouth. With the back of the same hand, he wiped at the sweat dripping down his forehead.

Bernadette glanced at Tony, who didn't give any reaction to all the comments about the heat. Until seven months ago, the kid's beat would've helped them all with the heat problem. It had through the worst days of a summer or two in Wyoming, which really couldn't compare with South Carolina in August. At least he didn't have any trouble putting away two slices of tomato pie.

"*Thank* you." Mirela slid the now-empty jar of pickled okra across the kitchen table and sat back in the chair with a sigh. "It's not just the pregnant lady with overheating issues."

"Aw…" Brad feigned insult again. "I thought that thank you was for me."

She laughed and leaned toward her husband in the chair beside her. Gently touching his cheek, Mirela crooned, "Oh, you get your own special thank you, buddy." Then she kissed him and sat back in her chair again.

"You taste like pickles."

"You shoulda tried one."

Bernadette laughed and fanned herself with a hand. Not even ten o'clock in the morning, and it was already sweltering and muggy outside. The cabin didn't feel much better. "Good thing we're so close to the ocean. And Russel Creek. Nothin' like taking a dip when you can't cool off."

"Oh, yeah. That's just what I need. Covered in sweat now just to go jump into *more* saltwater." Cameron grabbed a bottle of water from the table and chugged half of it.

"Down here, kid, you just gotta get used to never drying off in the summer." Bernadette slid the container of pimiento cheese toward herself and dipped her own cracker in. Her eyes rolled dangerously close to the back of her head when she put it all in her mouth, and she shook her head. "Never thought I'd be happy to say some things down here never change."

Leaning back against the kitchen counter beside the doorway into the living room, Don snorted. "Check it. Bernadette spins a beat on herself with chunky cheese dip."

Beside him, Tony lifted his hands and mimed a newspaper headline spreading across the air in front of him. Don blinked at his brother, let out a wry, airy chuckle, and nodded in approval.

"Hey, I'm allowed to enjoy myself however I want." Bernadette pointed at the twins, then reached for another cracker. "When you get to be my age, that's hard enough to do."

And that was only because, for so long, Bernadette had refused to believe that she deserved any of it. The thought made her pause, then she dug the cracker even deeper into the cheese.

"What about the swamp cooler?" Randall asked, sticking his empty plate and fork in the sink.

"If you wanna spend your time cleaning out at least a decade of mold and rotting leaves and whatever else wiggled its way into that thing, be my guest." Bernadette waved a hand toward the living room. "That'd make a big difference."

Randall shrugged and headed toward the front door off the kitchen. "I'll give it a shot."

"Wiggled in, huh?" Cameron squinted at Bernadette and tapped his fingers against the water bottle in his hand. "You mean like more dead squirrels?"

Mirela groaned in disgust. "Come on, Cameron. We're still eating."

"What? It's not like you can still smell it. Trust me, the one I found under the couch had probably been there for—"

"Dude." Brad gave the other guy a warning glance as his wife swallowed thickly and stared at the spread of food on the table. Her nostrils flared.

"Okay, okay." Cameron lifted his hands in surrender and drained the rest of his water in a few loud gulps. "Man, it's like growin' a baby turned you into glass or something."

Mirela glared at him. "Just my stomach. And my patience."

Tony mimed dropping something huge and heavy onto the floor with both hands, and Don made a long, drawn-out crashing sound.

Bernadette swallowed her last mouthful and waved toward the front door. "Cameron, go see what kinda help Randall needs with the swamp cooler, huh? You'll have better luck making friends with the squirrels right now."

"Yeah, even the dead ones." With a snort, Cameron left his empty water bottle on the counter and turned to follow Randall outside toward the swamp cooler.

Don let out another dry laugh, and beside him, Tony's smirk was a genuine grin, considering how little he'd shown any emotion in the last six months.

"Well." Bernadette slapped her thighs and pushed against them to stand. Her joints gave her so much hell, she figured everyone else in the kitchen was just being polite by not mentioning the groaning mechanisms of a body too old now for this kind of living. Too old for the kind of shit she'd pulled here in this very cabin. "If I don't keep moving, pretty soon, I won't be able to walk at all."

"Yeah, we'll clean up," Don said, turning to grab Cameron's half-cleared dishes. Tony nodded and headed toward the table.

"Thank you."

"Where are you going?" Mirela drained the last of her water and absently held out the bottle for Tony, who offered a mocking bow she didn't see. Brad bit back a laugh.

"For a real walk. Outside and everything." Bernadette winked at the other woman. Mirela's eyes widened. "Now I know it sounds like a load of crap, but when the breeze comes in off the water, it's a lot nicer outside than it is in here. And if those two get the swamp cooler up and running, we'll be steppin' back into relative comfort instead of a sauna."

Mirela squinted and rubbed her belly, obviously weighing the pros and cons of getting up onto her own swollen feet and walking for two.

Bernadette nodded at the t-shirt stretched tight over Mirela's bump. "A good walk helps bring on labor, too."

Brad slung his arm over the back of his wife's chair, as if that alone would cover up the terror behind his eyes at the word *labor*. "I don't think that's—"

"I'm coming with you," Mirela stated firmly and gripped Brad's knee to help support her up out of the chair.

"Wait, what—" He grimaced at her grip on his leg, then abruptly stood to help support his wife as she found her footing.

"We've got two choices, babe. Have this kid here, in a cabin with a bedroom and a door and electricity, or pop the little nugget out in the van on the side of the road. I guess that also depends on how long we're staying…"

Pressing her lips together, Bernadette dipped her head. "As long as it takes, sweetheart."

"Good." Mirela waddled across the kitchen toward the closest door out to the porch, waving off her husband's hands.

Shooting Bernadette a baffled stare, Brad froze, his mouth hanging open, until the woman nodded after his wife. That seemed to propel him into action. "Don't you think we should talk about—"

"Nope. I've made up my mind." The screen door screeched open and banged shut behind Mirela as she stepped barefoot off the porch and onto the grass. Her husband lurched after her, his unfinished sentence lodging in his throat with an awkward, urgent hum.

Sharing a silent glance with the twins, Bernadette just licked her lips and patted down her pockets for her pack of cigarettes and lighter. Tony shooed her with both hands for the door, and she chuckled. "Oh, by all means. Don't let me get in the way of your work."

She heard the twins snicker together behind her as she crossed the kitchen. The sound of them picking up after the group's early lunch cut off the minute the kitchen door clicked shut. Rotting boards groaned beneath her feet, and she paused for a brief moment with the screen door propped open just a few inches. It was such an odd feeling to be standing here again, in the middle of the day, poised to step calmly off this porch instead of leap from it to cross the gravel drive in desperation and burgeoning rage. But here she was, and this time, she made choice after choice for a good deal more people than just herself.

"But we don't know anyone here." Brad's voice cut through Bernadette's floating memories as he caught up with his wife. "We should at least find a list of midwives, babe. Or *someone* who knows what to do when it's time to—"

"Well, that's what Bernadette's for." Mirela gestured toward the woman standing at the edge of the porch. "Right?"

"Bernadette?"

They both stared at her with such completely opposing expressions of hope and cluelessness that it almost made her laugh. "Like I said, I'll make some calls."

"So like... now?" Brad stroked his bright-red beard, glanced nervously at his wife, then folded his arms. "Or do we wait until the minute she's in labor, or—"

"It's just a walk, Brad." Mirela waited for him to meet her gaze before she raised an eyebrow. His open mouth worked silently, and she turned away from him again to take off across the open grass toward the live oaks beyond the cabin.

Bernadette finally let herself off the porch, making sure to gently release the door before it could slam again. A pregnant and slightly annoyed Mirela wasn't breaking any speed-walking records, but the woman set a pace that made Bernadette grateful for the opportunity to push herself. Driving across the country in a van with six other wanted criminals was one thing. Hoofing it across the flattened peninsula surrounded by saltwater marsh and the ocean breeze was something else. She wished, for a moment, that it could have been as rejuvenating as it sounded.

When she reached Brad, he leaned toward her and muttered, "Will this *actually* make her go into labor?"

She shrugged. "It'll be her time when it's her time."

"That's not a very reassuring answer."

Bernadette snorted and shook her head.

"You're serious about knowing some midwives here, though, right? Not just something you said to make her feel better?"

"She doesn't need *me* to make her feel better." The breeze whistled through the palmetto fronds around them, followed by that hollow clicking of so many reeds against themselves. Leaves and moss on the spreading live oak branches swayed and added their own music to what had been the background of her life, so long ago—so many years before Bernadette left it all for very different sounds. Not the least of which was the sound of her own beat.

"Bernadette."

"Yes, Brad. I know a few midwives, and I will make a few calls." She couldn't help but smile at the sight of Mirela pausing beneath the first of the outstretched branches hundreds of years older than any of them. The woman's head would be tilted slightly back as she let herself take in the fresh air and what hope she could within their limited possibilities here. "Cell reception's shit down here, but I'm heading into town tonight. So I'll do it then."

"You mean Charleston."

Bernadette nodded. When he didn't seem to get the message behind her patient silence, she glanced at him and pointed into the trees. "Now quit buzzing around me and go take a walk with your wife."

Brad ran a hand through his ruffled red hair, took a breath like he had one more thing to say, then left the woman who still owned part of this property and headed toward the woman who'd be giving birth to his child any day now.

She watched them together from a distance. Moving slowly gave them more time for the privacy they'd had very little opportunity to grasp until now. Bernadette didn't mind a moment or two to herself, either. With the wind picking up and carrying the muggy heat behind her toward the cabin, she pulled out a smoke and turned downwind to light it. The first drag, and a deep, pensive sigh.

If this land hadn't belonged to her family, if it hadn't carried so many memories and reminders of why she'd abandoned all of it, Bernadette had to admit it was a damn fine place to have a baby.

"Oh, wait. Wait…" Mirela lifted her hand, signaling to her husband that she had to stop, and stared with wide eyes at the closest live oak.

Brad froze. "Babe?"

"Just—" She put a hand to her swollen belly and bent forward the slightest bit.

"Oh, my God. Is this it? Oh, shit." Brad gripped his fiery red hair with both hands and spun around in the grass. "Bernadette! I think something's wrong."

Her immediate reaction was to start laughing. Then Bernadette pushed herself forward on slow legs. "I don't think anything's wrong."

"Yeah, look at her. She just stopped walking, and she can't talk—"

"I can talk just fine, Brad." Mirela straightened fully again—as much as she could with a whole person inside her ready to come out at any minute—and took a deep breath. "Maybe you should try *not* talking for a while."

Bernadette snorted.

"You're okay?" He reached out for his wife and gently set his hands on her shoulders. "Mirela."

"I'm fine." His wife shot him a tired, apologetic smile. "This kid's kicking around in there and messing everything up. Just gas or something."

Bernadette lifted her fingers to her lips with a small smile. "Or labor."

The young couple both turned toward her with wide eyes. It was hard to tell, but she thought she saw the man's already pale face drain of what little color it had beneath his bright-red beard. "*What?*"

11

THE LOW RED light made almost every single one of these girls look like a fucking goddess. Bernadette didn't waste her time anymore wondering if she would have looked just like them up on that stage. It had crossed her mind a few times—the kind of money she could make if she stripped off just a little more of her limitations by stripping off just a few more articles of clothing. But Pete didn't like his dancers to be running around with one man and one man only, and everyone at Lookie Lou's knew about Darrell. She'd made that perfectly clear from the beginning.

"Plus, you make more dough than any other cocktail waitress I've ever seen," Grace had told her after her second week. "Don't give up a good thing if you don't have to, Bee-bee."

So she hadn't. Beebee wasn't a very good stripper name anyway, and the regulars knew her well enough by now that she couldn't just up and change it. Bernadette's regulars. That was what the other girls called the string of half a dozen men who each came in at least twice a week to ask for Bee-bee by name. Not for a strip dance. Not for a private show. Just to sit down in the privacy of a round booth in the corner and get their rocks off by listening to the magic in Beebee's words.

She didn't really have a name for it yet, so they all stuck to calling it *a story*. And as far as she knew, she was the only girl here who could tell the kind of story these regulars came in to hear. She could've walked in wearing overalls and a straw hat, reeking of manure and sweat, and they sure as shit would've still paid the fee at the door and asked for a story from Beebee. After six weeks, they'd proven that much just as sure as Bernadette had proven to herself that she could keep hiking the price whenever she wanted, and they'd pay right up.

Pete hadn't added anything to the proverbial menu to advertise for an extra little kick in the pants by his newest cocktail waitress, who gave his customers more bang for their buck without laying a hand or an ass or naked tits on anybody. Bernadette actually preferred it that way, mostly because she'd learned that all the other girls now knew the prices Pete had set. But when the regulars came in and asked for "one of them special stories", bypassing the other girls altogether, Bernadette could tell them fifty, one-fifty, two hundred bucks, and they didn't bat an eye. And she didn't have to tell Pete or give him a proportionately higher cut, either.

Tonight, she leaned back in one such private booth in the corner and lit one of the cigarettes she'd taken up smoking since she'd gotten the job. It wasn't so much for her as it was for the men who kept coming for her words; that thought made her smirk as she took a drag. These guys opened up their wallets for a *friendly conversation*, and they seemed a lot less itchy about it when she seemed like she'd gotten something out of the deal besides their money. The dancing girls could offer light caresses or a whispered word of encouragement or gyrating, mostly naked hips. Bernadette wasn't actually serious about using her body for a gig at Lookie Lou's, so if smoking a fag made her regulars more comfortable, she'd light up a couple a night and smoke them halfway down until the last guy pulled himself together enough to stand and show himself out.

The man sitting across the booth from her now said his name was Bill. Just Bill. And every time, he sat in that booth with his arms wrapped around his middle like someone had dragged him through the doors in a straitjacket. He never looked at her, didn't open his eyes once after she started, and after the first two times, he'd taken to gently sliding a crisp hundred-dollar bill toward her across the low table before she even opened her mouth. Bernadette had taken to leaving it there until she was done.

A thick, heavy breath escaped Bill's slack-jawed mouth as he waited for the coup de grâce. Bernadette took a drag, turned away from him, exhaled.

"Like that song, right? 'Put the lime in the coconut and mix it all—'"

The man grunted and snapped his mouth shut with an audible click; she was convinced at this point that he wore dentures, if only because that sound, every time he finished, made her think more and more of two cracking pieces of porcelain. Bill leaned forward over his lap, still holding himself around the middle, and shuddered. For a few more seconds after that, he didn't move at all.

Bernadette took another drag and glanced up at the ceiling.

"Jesus." The man chuckled, let out another thick grunt, and finally sat up again. "If my wife talked like you half the time she opens her mouth, we'd both be a lot happier."

She lifted the smoke away from her face and shrugged. "You know that song?"

"Heard it once or twice."

"Maybe you should play it for your wife. See what happens."

When he looked up at her, smoothing a hand back across his bald head, Bernadette just raised an eyebrow. Bill snorted. "Lime in the fucking coconut, huh?" Then he nodded at the hundred on the table and quickly stood. "I'd say don't work yourself too hard tonight, but something tells me you got it pretty good in this joint."

"I do what I can." She crossed one leg over the other in her short, pleated skirt—just short enough to make it perfectly clear she worked here but not short enough to confuse a cocktail waitress for a stripper.

"Sure ya do." Bill grabbed his jacket off the booth and wadded it up in both hands. "You working Friday?"

"I'll see you then."

He didn't look at her when he nodded and stepped out of the booth, mumbling about fucking coconuts on his way across the club toward the front door.

"Yeah. Fucking coconuts." Bernadette let herself have a little laugh about it on her own now as Pete told the room to give it up for Kitty and that Ginger would now be taking the stage. Kitty stopped to collect the rest of the dollars bills she hadn't already stowed away somewhere, picked up the clothes she'd taken off, and made way for the next dancer.

"Beebee." Grace stopped just in front of the private booth in the corner and stuck a hand on her hip—naked except for the thin black band of a thong and a matching bra that was always just as thin.

Bernadette looked up at the first friend she'd made at Lookie's and smirked. "Oh, you finally want a turn now, huh? Shouldn't we wait 'til after we're both off?"

The stripper snorted and gestured toward the front of the club. "Your man came to see you."

"Yeah?" Bernadette stubbed out the half-smoked cigarette and left the other half propped up in the tray. "Pete see him yet?"

"Yep." Grace shot her an exasperated look—not at Bernadette or even Darrell but at the owner of Lookie Lou's who always managed to find something amiss in his little kingdom of flesh and booze. Every girl who worked here had perfected that look, and it just made Bernadette laugh.

"Okay. If he asks, I went on break." She stuffed the hundred she'd just made into the waistband of her skirt.

"Sure." Grace turned back toward the front of the club as Bernadette stood and gave Darrell an approving glance.

But Darrell Wilkins didn't see it. He hadn't seen Kitty walking off the stage, and he didn't see Ginger step up onto it. Bernadette left the corner booth and headed across the half-full club toward her man standing there just inside the front doors with both hands in his pockets. He didn't even look *her* over in her short skirt and low-cut tank top. The man's eyes were glued to Bernadette's while the rest of him showed only a bored apathy for everything else in the room. She didn't worry about what he thought of her, whether he had a problem with her working as a cocktail waitress in one of the few strip clubs around. If he did, he would've said something about it, and they'd be having a completely different kind of conversation.

When she reached him, Darrell's lips turned up in a tiny smile as he pursed them and tried to cover it up. "What's going on?"

"I got a call, B." Those lips twitched again, and Bernadette turned toward the MC stand beside the bar—one of Pete's many thrones in his palace. The club owner used it now to glare at his newest cocktail waitress and the man who never stepped through those doors to spend any money. Not for a Heineken. Not for a dance. Not even on his girl.

"A call from who?"

"Ronnie. Half an hour ago." Darrell kept his hands in his pockets, but he finally eyed Bernadette up and down, then raised an eyebrow.

"I'm on break, babe. Let's… step outside."

"Mm-hmm."

No doubt Darrell felt Pete's gaze on them as he turned around with Bernadette to step out through the front doors of the club. But he didn't once look up to shoot the owner a warning glance or even something like acknowledgment. Darrell always knew when people were looking at him, what they wanted, what they didn't. And even then, he rarely made a move to change it. That was just one more of the many things Bernadette knew made them such a perfect fit. Her man knew, and his confidence was strong enough all on its own that no one ever thought he just didn't care. No one thought he turned his back out of cowardice or some kind of ingrained complacency. That kind of intelligence mixed with a lack of anger, jealousy, or even insult was more powerful than the man's fist, and only an idiot would be stupid enough to fuck with it.

Bernadette pushed on the outer doors, and they stepped out together into the muggy, sweltering evening heat of September in South Carolina. That was when she took Darrell's hand in hers—just as he pulled it out of the pocket of his royal-blue slacks—and she led him around the side of the building in Lookie Lou's parking lot.

His other hand came up to cup her cheek, and he bent down to press his lips against hers as her back pressed against the smooth brick wall coated a dying shade of gray. Darrell pulled back after only a few seconds and shook his head. "You taste like smoke again."

She shrugged. "Just a few drags after a good story, baby. I go through two a night, maybe. If it's a good night."

Darrell huffed through his nose and tucked her hair behind her ear. "I'm thinkin' you won't have to pretty soon."

"Won't have to what?" She grinned at him and cocked her head. Her man talked in circles when he was excited, and she let him. But she thought she already knew where he was going with this one anyway.

"Smoke that nasty shit, for one." They both chuckled, and he stuck a hand against the wall beside her head, leaning toward her. "Or hope for a good night at this sad sack's excuse for a club. Or tell any more of them *good stories*." He licked his lips and stared at hers. "If you don't want to."

"Because of some phone call you got half an hour ago?" Bernadette's back arched away from the wall as she grabbed his hips, his blue-and-white-striped shirt tucked into his blue slacks.

"That's just the start, B." He let her pull him toward her a little, though his hand never left the wall by her head. "Ronnie says they're ready to go. The whole goddamn crew. Benny, Chuck... Jimmy Woodson—"

"Jimmy Woodson? Are you serious?"

With a little chuckle, Darrell pulled his head back and stared down at her with those deep brown eyes beneath thick lashes. "Don't I look serious, girl?"

"Uh-uh. You look like you're about ready to jump me in this parking lot."

"Any other parking lot, maybe."

Bernadette bit her lip as she grinned up at him, pulling his hips closer. "So the whole *goddamn crew* is ready, huh?"

"Yep."

"Are *you* ready?"

Darrell pressed his lips together, obviously trying not to laugh. "See, now you're just confusin' the conversation. Are you talkin' about this gig, or you talkin' about yourself?"

She pretended to consider it like it was a valid question in the first place. "I might be able to answer that if you tell me when they want you."

"Next week, B. They already have the setup. Got at least four big shows booked out and some smaller jams to fill in. Got a place for *us*, too."

"Wait a minute." Pressing the back of her head against the wall, she gently poked a finger into his chest and turned her head away from him to shoot him a sidelong glance. "I thought I was getting out when you brought me home with you. We've been up here six months, and now you're telling me we have a week to pick up and head all the way back down to Charleston?"

He licked his lips again, and this time, it was with a little more uncertainty than Bernadette ever meant to dredge up. "I was thinkin' more like we'd step right outta this mess tomorrow. Go back down, settle in."

"Settle in." She raised an eyebrow.

"Break in the new place. I heard that's how you make a home, ain't it?" Darrell's eyes narrowed, then he leaned toward her again and brought his lips right up to her ear. "Don't make me beg you to come with me, girl. 'Cause you know I will. And then you'd really owe me one."

A little shiver ran down her spine when he kissed her neck just below her ear. Breathing in his scent—earth and a little sweat and the clean tang of slightly scented soap—Bernadette closed her eyes and focused on the warmth of his body pressing her against the brick wall and of his lips pressing against her skin. Finally, she whispered, "You just want a live-in groupie."

Darrell chuckled through his nose and dropped his forehead onto her shoulder in defeat. "Ain't nothin' wrong with a man who wants to come home to his biggest fan. 'Specially after a night of playin' his soul out for everyone else."

"Nothin' wrong with it." Her fingers slid up along the back of his neck before he kissed the dip beside her shoulder. She played with the thick hair at the back of his head, which he'd let grow out just a little over the last few months. "I just wanna make sure you still have somethin' left for me after you spend all night with that shiny piece of sax."

He paused for a split second, then pulled away just enough to meet her gaze again and hold it. "I'm gonna play my heart out with those cats in Charleston, B. Takes a lotta soul to get anywhere near them. Where you think I get mine from, girl?"

That was more than she'd been looking for. Bernadette had just been playing around; there was never a doubt in her mind that she'd pick up and go with him wherever he wanted her to go. She'd already left her entire life behind—all twenty years of hypocrisy and strangled, shuttered, swept-under-the-rug hatred and more resentment than any of the people who called herself their family were capable of recognizing, even when it hit them in the face. She would have picked up and left anywhere, gone anywhere, with Darrell Wilkins, and he knew it. To her, that was all just wrapped up in one final truth. That she belonged with him. But she'd had no idea how long she'd just been assuming it meant the same thing to him. It did. And now he was flat-out saying it to her face.

She ran her hands over the soft cotton of his collared shirt, up his chest, around the back of his strong, sturdy neck bending hopefully toward her. He hadn't begged her yet, but this was as close as she was willing to let him get. "I'm not sharing a bed with that saxophone."

"You—man…" He let out a short laugh and shook his head. "Now, you tell me why the hell I'd want a cold piece of metal in my arms instead of this." Darrell's wrapped his arms around her and pulled her roughly against him before laying on her the kind of long, slow, deep kiss he'd been working up to when he started under her ear.

Bernadette gripped the back of his neck and kissed him even deeper, his collared shirt and her low-cut tank top already damp with the Southern humidity and now growing sticky between them. And neither of them cared.

Darrell pressed her back against the wall again and pulled away with a crooked smile. "Any other parking lot, girl."

She laughed. "We still have a bed in Columbia. Unless you already took care of that too."

"Naw. I ain't gonna hawk our bed when we still got business in it. You lose your mind tellin' all them *special stories* and draggin' on cigarettes in this dump?"

"Probably."

Darrell just shook his head and smirked at her. His hand trailed down her ribcage and fell to the waistline of her skirt. He slipped a finger beneath it against her skin and stopped before looking down at her hip. "What's this?"

"Oh." She laughed and pulled out the hundred-dollar bill from Bill. "Been a good night already, I guess."

"Shit…" With another chuckle, Darrell rubbed his fingers over his lips. "You know what? You wanna keep tellin' them stories in Charleston, you do your thing. Hundred bucks for a story." He puffed out a sigh and slowly shook his head.

"A *good* one."

"Ain't they all."

Grinning, Bernadette grabbed his hand and led him quickly across the parking lot of Lookie Lou's toward Darrell's Monte Carlo.

He frowned at her and jerked his head toward the club. "What about them? I thought this was your break."

"Fuck 'em."

Darrell burst into low, deep laughter and pulled his car keys out of his front pocket.

That laugh was rare and more contagious than the plague. Bernadette walked around the car as he unlocked the driver-side door and spread her arms. "I don't need this place. I got the new saxophonist with Woodson Blues."

They opened the doors and climbed inside. Darrell started the engine and clicked his tongue against his teeth. "Forget new. You got the best."

"Damn right I do. And he's takin' me back to Charleston."

"See, you got this whole thing backward."

"Oh, yeah?"

Darrell shifted the car into drive and shot her a sideways glance before looking her up and down. "Nobody takes you anywhere, B. You always headin' exactly where you wanna go."

"Good thing that just happens to be with you, then, huh?"

"Better be. Once I get you in that bed, you ain't leavin' 'til we're on the road."

She laughed again and rolled the window all the way down. "And then you'll sell it."

His laughter hissed out through his teeth as he drove them across the parking lot and away from Lookie Lou's forever. "Somebody's trippin' if they even *think* about payin' us for that thing.".

12

I CAN'T BELIEVE you're going back, Bernie. I mean, I get it. Sounds like D's got some serious talent. I hadn't heard of Woodson Blues before, but Donna says they're major. Which is so rad. I can't even tell you how stoked I am for both of you.

You know I'm not trying to step on your toes or anything, but I just have to write it down anyway, so you know that I'm not. I'm glad you're out of that strip club. I mean, sure, a cocktail waitress isn't a stripper, but that's not where you belong. You're so much better than that. I hope you find something back in Charleston that treats you the way you should be treated.

And that's something else totally bogus about people like us. People who can do what we do. If we want a place where we can be ourselves, use this ability we have with our words and not give a fuck about who sees or hears or what anyone else thinks, we gotta do it in the dark. You feel me? Like, all I wanna do is sit at home in my silk robe (Donna got it for me and insists it's a kimono. I think she's crazy, man. It's just a robe) and paint all day. I mean, yeah, I could do that anyway. But Donna goes on and on about how we have this responsibility *to the other people like us out there. That we have to get up off our asses and find them, bring them in under our wing, show them that there's hope.*

Except that the kinda places Donna and her crew bring these new people to are just more of the same places we're trying to get out of (the way she puts it, too). Dark, hidden, secretive. There aren't any huge rallies out in the streets. There's nothing in legislation—yet. Somehow, I feel like making laws about people like us is only gonna make things worse. Apparently, we're fighting this fight to be seen and heard, to be recognized and not judged for this thing we can do that nobody understands. But it doesn't really make sense that we're doing it where no one can see or hear us.

I don't know. I can't really say that I actually want this whole movement of hers to go any further than a few meetings a week in some nightclub or dude's basement or out in the boonies where there's nobody to see us anyway. Donna's the one calling it a movement, by the way. There's a little more than fifty of us now, I think. Besides those guys from California and Florida who came up last year, we have people from Louisiana, Illinois, and New York. Crazy, right? Honestly, I don't even know how she's finding them, but they're really starting to roll in and "hop on the beat." That's what everybody's saying around here. I think it sounds like "let's jump some cops." Pretty fucking stupid. But it caught on, and they're all saying it now. Whatever.

Anyway, I was talking about you and D moving back to Charleston! And he's playing saxophone with Woodson Blues! I seriously can't believe it, and I hope everything turns out the way you two want it to. For real.

Also, if it ever doesn't turn out the right way... I want you to know that you have a place out here with us in Alabama. Always. And Donna doesn't turn anyone away. Yeah, I'm probably a little annoyed about that, but what can I do? She's heading a movement, whatever that means. Doesn't apply to you, though. I actually know you. You know I've told her about you, Bernie. She's read our letters, and something tells me you don't really give a shit. I hope you don't. After the last time you wrote, though, Donna said I should have you come out here and join us. If you were anyone else, I probably wouldn't have even said anything. But how fucking rad would it be to have you up here? To talk in person after all the time we've spent writing to each other? Hey, I might even do your portrait (no pressure. I'm only halfway decent).

Think about it? If Charleston doesn't work out, just know that you always have somewhere to go. I got your back. Sure, Donna might try to get you to "hop on the beat" with the rest of her crew, but I have a feeling tearing down the system and stickin' it to the Man aren't on your list of things to never, ever do. Things get crazy around here sometimes. But there's some peace, too. I'm just trying to enjoy the peace while I can, 'cause I just can't shake the feeling that something else is coming. Soon. Something big that's *gonna change everything. Damn, it would be really good to have you here when that happens.*

Be safe out there, Bernie. Tell D I hope this gig with Woodson Blues really pans out. And forget about your family. If they can't see what's right in front of them—how incredible you are, no matter what you can do or who you love—they're not worth it. You are.

Write me back if you have any time between all D's shows and moving back home and whatever else you have going on. Someone like you doesn't just sit around doing nothing. Just maybe stay out of strip clubs. Ha!

Love and peace from Alabama,

—Janet

13

MIRELA LOOKED LIKE she wanted to hit somebody. Maybe Bernadette for having even said the most likely possibility out loud. The older woman shrugged and gestured toward the open land around them. "Keep walking for a bit. See how you feel. If that bit of gas comes back again at least two times in the next fifteen minutes, I'd say it's probably not gas."

"Oh, boy." Mirela blew out a long, slow breath through tight lips and nodded. "Let's keep going."

"What? No. If you're in labor, babe, shouldn't you be, like… lying down or something?"

Bernadette burst out laughing, which brought a genuine smile to the pregnant woman's lips and another baffled look from her husband. "If she's in labor, Brad, her body knows exactly what it needs. This is just the beginning. She can walk around in the fresh air for as long as she wants."

"And that won't… you know." Brad raised his eyebrows with a conspiratorial nod.

"I'm afraid I don't, no." It was all she could do to keep from laughing at him again. Either the man would figure out what his role was for the next twenty-four hours—give or take—and step into it with as much grace as he could drum up, or he'd keep flailing around like this while his wife did what women had been doing since the very beginning. It wouldn't really matter once that child was born and they both got a good first look at what they'd created together. At the entire person who would belong to them completely only for a little while before sailing off into the unknown of a life they would never know as intimately as they knew it now. But it would help everyone if Brad ripped his panic out by the roots. Soon. Right now, it looked like that panic was about to shatter him.

"I mean…" He scratched the back of his neck and briefly glanced at Mirela. "You know."

"Brad, I have no idea what you're talking about." The frustration seemed to have dissipated from her completely, now that she recognized what was most likely happening. A small, sympathetic smile bloomed across her mouth, and she held her hand out toward him. "But I don't need a worst-case-scenario kinda guy right now. Which, by the way, isn't what you do, remember? I need *you*."

With a crooked smile, Brad stared at her hand and took it. "Yeah. Yeah, I know, babe. You have me. Anything you need, I got it."

"Good." She laced their fingers together and shot Bernadette a look that said it all—*If I'd known it was this easy to pull him out of that spiral, I would've done it a long time ago.*

Bernadette smirked and wanted to tell the woman to just wait until that unborn child became a toddler. Not much different than dealing with a teenager. Not that much different than dealing with a man who didn't know how to deal with the birth of his first child. Until now, maybe.

"I just wanna keep walking, okay? So let's walk."

Brad leaned toward his wife and placed a gentle kiss on her temple. But he didn't say another word as they took off again through the crabgrass and around the next cluster of palmetto fronds between where they stood and the spreading canopy of centuries-old live oaks rising everywhere across the flat, open, marshy land.

"Y'all give me a call if you need anything," Bernadette called after them.

Turning halfway around to look at her over his shoulder, Brad almost slipped back into that flailing panic. "Where are you going?"

"I'm gonna find the best midwives in the low country who owe me a favor or three." Bernadette just nodded slowly and gave him a look she hoped he understood. The man didn't need to pay attention to an old woman with more than a few bad habits and a goddamn never-ending ache in her knees. "And they'll take care of the rest."

"We're *walking*, Brad. After everything we've been through, please don't pick now to start *not* trusting her." Mirela tugged her husband along beside her as she waddled through the grass, her other hand pressing against her lower back.

And that seemed to snap the man right out of his apprehension. At least as far as what Bernadette did with her own time was concerned.

The woman was right, though. How could anyone who'd been through what the seven of them had been through together not trust each other like their small chapter of Sleepwater did? They'd watched their friends and family get snatched away from them, no matter what time of day or night. They'd seen those same people returned to them as mere shadows of themselves—if they returned at all. They'd been hunted by a government wanting to silence them, eradicate them, spread fear and loathing and dissension through the country in pursuit of those who could do what Bernadette and her friends could do. They'd broken others with the beat out of research facilities, armored vans, holding cells, their own goddamn lives falling apart all around them. And they'd brought one after another of these people into the fold, giving those lost, confused, terrified souls a place to call home when every other home had either shut its doors or been wiped off the face of the Earth.

Most of them stayed, as long as they could, and added whatever they had to offer to Sleepwater's world. Some moved on from Sleepwater altogether, like Leo and John, trying to make a life for themselves that didn't involve so much constant running and so much loss. Even Louis had done enough, in his own way. It would've been fucking hard to come back to the same world as empty as that man had been when he finally got out of that place. Whoever those fuckers were, they'd taken Louis' beat too, after everything else that had been taken from him. Tony was going through the same thing, though with his brother around, helping to guide him back home, Bernadette felt it even in her locked-up joints that Tony wouldn't go the same bitter, resentful route as the owner of the Purple Lion—the man who'd sin-glehandedly pushed this faction of Sleepwater into fucked-up Robin Hoods for people with the beat. Just like so many other Sleepwater groups had done before them.

Some didn't make it, like Karl. A sharp pain of longing and regret shot through Bernadette when her mind turned to him and his swift, unexpected death; none of them had been given the time to grieve him or to truly come to terms with the fact that he was gone. That he would never loaf on in with his wild beard and shining eyes and mask of stoicism he wore to hide all that love in his heart. That he would never give her one of those looks they all came to know like a code phrase or some secret password—*This one's all right. Let's bring 'em in. Let's help 'em be the person they don't even know they can be yet. Let's give 'em a place to rest and re-member that not everyone wants to either shoot 'em or lock 'em up.*

Bernadette watched Brad and Mirela moving slowly be-neath the wide, sprawling live oak branches draped in grand-father moss. At least they had each other. At least this one pair of connected souls who'd come to Bernadette and Sleepwater together had managed to stay that way.

Cameron and Kaylee had come to them together too, in a different way, and now Kaylee was…

With a short gasp, Bernadette pressed a hand against her heart and turned around to walk back toward her family's abandoned cabin. She hadn't thought of Richard, Mary, and Candace as her true family in so very long. They weren't anymore. Not really. The family Bernadette had now, she'd built for herself. More fathers and mothers, more sisters, even brothers she'd never had—all of them brought together by the one thing that made them different than everything else. The family she'd been born to had hated so many differences, hers and everyone else's. And maybe, in some ways, the family she'd made before Sleepwater—the family of her own flesh and blood, the family she'd given life to in her womb and tried to protect the best way she knew how—hated her too. Olivia had every right to feel that way, after what Bernadette had done. Still, she'd thought she'd found another daughter within this hidden world of so many people living in the shadows, spinning beats in secret, just trying to stay alive and help a few others do the same. She'd thought the girl might have felt something of that bond, that what Kaylee had gotten from Sleepwater and nowhere else might have made a new type of family out of them. Even if it had, it wasn't strong enough to keep the girl from turning on them all before she walked off into the night almost seven months ago. Before she broke Bernadette's heart and didn't even say goodbye.

When she reached the screened-in porch, Bernadette had to steady herself with a hand against the outer railing. This was all just part of it, wasn't it? When the whole world wanted them gone so much, just because they were terrified of this power in so many people's words, those like Bernadette were bound to lose what they loved. If they were lucky, they wouldn't lose themselves along the way. So many already had.

Sleepwater's world had changed so much in the last fifty years, and now it seemed things had finally come back around full circle. Bernadette didn't know how safe it was to show her face around a town where, once, almost everyone knew her name. Charleston had changed, she was sure, and the people were different. But if anyone from that old life of hers still remained, she could only hope they hadn't changed so much with everything else that she wouldn't recognize them.

He might not even be happy to see her, given the gaping chasm of time and distance between them. He might not even be willing to help, however small the request might seem. But if Bernadette had built a life for herself—a life of constant upheaval and never-ending movement but a life all the same—with mothers and fathers, sisters, brothers, a few children she might have loved as her own along the way, she'd still never found a damn soul to fill in for what Darrell had given her. When it came to someone who knew the core of another person, who saw through the games and the doubt and the misplaced desires, Darrell was all she had.

With a deep breath, Bernadette straightened and grimaced at the deep ribbon of pain creaking up her back like a tire crunching over broken glass. Her hand fell away from the railing, bringing a small shower of chipped paint and rotting wood with it.

"Suck it up and do what you need to do, girl. He'll get a kick out of it."

She opened the screen door and forced herself up the two steps onto the porch just as the closest door into the cabin opened as well.

Randall stood there in the doorway, his upper lip squashed beneath his long nose as he shot her a goofy grin. "Got the swamp coolers up."

"No kiddin'?" Bernadette nodded in approval, and the man stepped aside to let her into the cabin.

"Probably won't take too long to cool the whole place down, but I don't know how well-insulated things are in here."

"Doesn't matter." Bernadette shook her head and moved through the kitchen toward the main room of the cabin. "Any bit of cool air we can pump into this place is gonna be better than that sauna outside. Mirela's gonna need it."

"She having a hard time sleeping still?"

Bernadette paused inside the living room and turned to shoot Randall a wide-eyed gaze. A little chuckle escaped her. "Well, I don't think she'll be sleeping very much at all tonight. Or at least not longer than a few seconds at a time."

The lanky man standing there in the kitchen with both hands in the pockets of his Bermuda shorts frowned. Then his eyes grew wide, and he pushed the center of his glasses back up on his nose. "Is she…"

"Yep."

"Tonight?"

"Well I sure as hell hope so." Bernadette laughed again and shook her head. "She'll be fine. We'll be having a few more friends over later, though. If I can find 'em. The rest of y'all might have to lay your heads down somewhere else tonight. We'll see what she says."

"Holy shit." Randall flashed her another wide, goofy grin and blinked heavily. "How are we gonna handle a baby on the road with us?"

"We'll handle it. Just like we handle everything else." She gave him a knowing smile and waved him off to head across the living room. "We have a bit more time, and I'm gonna use it to—"

The other door into the cabin opened up ahead on her left, and Cameron stepped inside, rubbing his hands on his cargo pants. "We got the swamp coolers up."

"So I heard." Bernadette cocked her head at the man in his early thirties with the shaggy hair and the barest hint of a smirk. "Good to see you fixin' something again."

Cameron snorted. "Guess how many dead animals I found in that thing."

"How many dead—" Bernadette stuck a hand on her hip and dipped her head. "Are you serious?"

"They were dumb enough to get stuck in the first place. Not my fault." He shrugged. "Found a tiny bird must've dropped out of a nest or something. Two squirrels."

Bernadette took a tentative sniff of the air and shook her head. "Well y'all seem to have cleared that right out. We all appreciate it." She headed through the living room toward the bedroom in the back she hadn't even used the night before. "Where are the twins?"

Cameron picked dirt out from under his fingernails, his eyebrows raised in apathy. "Swimming."

"Swimming."

A half-smile lifted one corner of the man's mouth. "Just dropped trow right there on the bank and dove in." He looked up from his fingernails and scanned the much emptier-feeling cabin. "Brad and Mirela?"

"Out taking a walk. They'll be back." Bernadette took the opportunity to remove herself from any more conversation before she fell over right then and there.

Just before her fingers closed around the iron-latched handle of the back bedroom's door, she heard Randall mutter, "She said Mirela's about to have her baby."

"No shit, man. Riding in a car with her all this time, you think I don't know she's about to pop?"

"Tonight."

Bernadette opened the bedroom door and turned around just out of curiosity. Most people wouldn't have pegged Cameron as a man who'd grin like Randall when hearing their friend was going into labor. And he didn't. When she settled her gaze on where he'd stood, all she saw was the door shutting firmly before Cameron stalked off across the porch and right out the swinging screen door.

Randall shrugged.

"When Mirela gets back from her walk, make sure you ask her who she wants here and who she wants gone." Bernadette pointed at the man and nodded. "That's up to her. Now I'm taking a nap in this air conditioning so I don't age twenty years in the next five minutes."

14

"CAN'T BELIEVE WE'RE doin' this." Darrell shut the driver-side door of his Monte Carlo and stuck his hands in his pockets. He took in the sight of the upper-middle-class neighborhood in Vincent, Alabama with the same careful, calculated consideration with which he studied everything else he didn't know inside and out.

Bernadette smirked and stepped up onto the sidewalk, her moccasin shoes crunching across a few scattered pieces of mulch from the landscaped yard. "See? The drive wasn't all that bad."

"Yeah, you could just keep drivin' and drivin' forever, couldn't you?" He walked around the front of the car and joined her on the sidewalk. "Wouldn't surprise me if you just kept drivin' on without me, B."

She feigned insult and let her jaw drop, then laughed and hooked her arm through his. Those hands never left his pockets. "I would never do that. What's the point of going… wherever without you?"

Darrell shrugged a little as they moved up the sidewalk beside the long line of cars parked at the curb. "Just to go, I bet." When he cocked his head and turned it just a little toward her, they shared a subdued laugh.

"Well as long as you keep making drives like this with me, I won't have to go drivin' off by myself. And you're gonna freak when you see what these people are up to."

"Yeah. That's what I'm tryin' to forget about." They passed the first house at least three times the size of their Charleston apartment, and he cleared his throat. "You sure I'm even supposed to come to one of these things, B? I ain't… working with the same kinda words as y'all. If they're tryin' to keep it low, how's somebody like me gonna fit into a shape I ain't got?"

Bernadette's eyes widened, and she looked up at him. The man stared straight ahead, pursing his lips a little.

"Hey." When she tugged on his arm, he sniffed and turned his head, his gaze lingering down the street as if he were only halfway listening to her. She knew he just didn't want her to see in his eyes what they'd already both heard in his voice. Then he met her gaze with a raised eyebrow, which he'd always failed at passing off as indifference. At least with her. "You coming here with me is just like me walking down the street with you to Benny's for a cookout. Are you gonna try telling me I didn't belong there however many times we've gone?"

"Naw, that ain't the same."

Bernadette tried to hold back her laughter and managed to squish it down into a quick exhale through her nose. "Then go ahead and tell me how it's different."

"Those boys love you, B."

"So do their wives and little Jackson. Monique."

"Uh-huh. Yeah. Everybody loves you." Darrell snorted and rolled his eyes back toward the end of the block, searching for something neither one of them understood. "But it's different is all."

"How?"

"See, now you're pushin'."

She did laugh this time. "I'm not pushing."

"Now, don't go—"

"I'm not *pushing*." Grinning up at him, Bernadette grabbed his bare arm beneath the t-shirt sleeve with both hands, one of her elbows still linked through his. "But if you want me to understand what you're tryin' to say, you have to actually say something."

An indignant sigh puffed through his loose lips, and his dark-brown eyes swept across the street from one house bordering on intimidatingly large to the next. "We just chill at Benny's."

"We're chillin' here too."

"No, I mean where a brother can bring his woman and hang and not give a shit about what anyone else is tryin' to *do*."

Bernadette raised her eyebrows and nodded, though she knew they hadn't gotten to the heart of what made his whole body cringe on this sidewalk. Darrell hardly showed any of that discomfort just looking at him, but she could feel the tension in the flexed muscles and twisted sinews of his bicep beneath her hands. "This isn't one of *those* kinda parties. No one's trying to *do* anything. They wouldn't have invited us—both of us—if there was somethin' else going on."

"See, and then that just means it's for show, don't it? Y'all sit around and talk, like you do, and all those people get to see what you can do and everyone else. How am I gonna be in all that? Just stand in the back like someone's payin' me to wait there while y'all take y'all's sweet time with the rest? I got no business showin' up here, B."

"You think you're too different for anyone to want you in that house?" Bernadette nodded toward the next house over, with the white siding and the navy-blue shutters and trim. Darrell just jerked his eyebrows up and pressed his lips together so tightly, they all but disappeared. "Okay, go ahead and tell me I didn't have any business sittin' in a chair on Benny's back porch."

"That's not—"

"Fine. I'll make it easier." Bernadette slid a hand up his arm and pressed herself against him, craning her neck to look up at him despite the fact that he was busy staring at nothing down the street again. "If you can tell me that a white girl who left everything to be with you, without a second thought, doesn't belong at a cookout with no other white faces, then okay. I'll tell you you don't belong at a party where you *might* be the only person who can't do something *special* with their words. Go ahead and tell me that's the truth, and we'll get back in the car."

Darrell cleared his throat. "They're not the same, B. The folks at Benny's already know you."

"Not before I met them. *At* Benny's." A stunned, reflective silence hung between them. Cicadas droned in the background. Muffled, fast-paced music flared up from the house just down from where they stood. When Darrell took a deep breath and finally met her gaze full-on, she knew she'd hit a mark inside that quiet, calculating mind. "Benny invited both of us that first time, and we were invited *together* to this thing too. This isn't any different than one of those cookouts, got it?"

He studied her gaze and blinked slowly, like he still couldn't believe he'd let her talk him into this. "'Cept for the size of these houses. I mean, damn."

That was it. That was all either of them needed to keep moving forward. Bernadette snorted and gave his arm a little tug as she moved down the sidewalk toward the white house. He hadn't completely relaxed, but his elbow had a little more give to it now, and she couldn't ask for anything more than that. She didn't have to.

Without another word, they turned onto the cement walkway up to the house with navy-blue trim, which was now clearly the source of the muted music on the other side of that navy-blue door. Bernadette stared at the dark paint before reaching up to press the doorbell set in the brick wall, also painted white. A round of laughter bubbled up from inside the house, then the doorknob turned, and the door opened.

The woman on the other side of it looked everything and nothing like what Bernadette had expected—skin the same light-brown as the sunset reflecting off Folly Beach, black hair falling in tight ringlets around her shoulders, shining eyes that wavered somewhere between hazel and amber. Her lips parted in a wide grin, and she glanced from Bernadette to Darrell and back again. "Bernie?"

"Hey. This is—"

"Darrell, yeah. Janet's told me all about you. I'm Donna." She stuck out a hand toward Darrell first, who accepted the handshake and blinked quickly a few times. The corner of his mouth twitched up into an approving smile when Donna reached out for Bernadette's hand next and pulled her inside. "Wait 'til we show her y'all actually showed up. I swear, that woman's gonna kill me with how much she worries 'bout everything. Damn, though. It's good to finally have you up here with us. Both of y'all."

With her arm around Bernadette's shoulder, Donna turned back to shoot Darrell a crisp nod. He chuckled and dipped his head, and the only thing Bernadette could do was offer him a playful, just-go-with-it shrug.

Their hostess led them into a huge living room that looked like something straight out of *House Beautiful*—all neon colors and geometric patterns. Donna's arm slid across Bernadette's back before the woman raised both hands and clapped once. "Listen up! Y'all aren't gonna believe who decided to finally come check out Vincent. Bernie and Darrell, y'all. All the way from Charleston."

It wasn't quite a cheer—more like at least twenty people all calling out to Bernadette and Darrell like they'd met before and wasn't this the damnedest surprise?—but it made her laugh all the same. She raised a hand, grinning, and all

Darrell could do was jerk his head back in acknowledgement, failing to hide a surprised, disbelieving smile of his
own.

"See?" Bernadette bumped her shoulder against his arm
and nodded toward the room and everyone in it who'd gone
back to their previous conversations. "Literally with open
arms."

Darrell finally took a hand out of his pocket and settled
it on the small of her back, then leaned in to mutter, "We'll
see. S'long as you don't go gettin' us into too much trouble."
Despite the way that could have sounded, if he were saying
it to anyone else, she just rolled her eyes and still couldn't
get rid of that grin. Darrell chuckled and kissed her temple,
then a woman in tight black spandex practically ran toward
them.

"Holy shit! You made it!" Janet was at least five years
older and a lot less uncertain-looking than the last picture
she'd sent in one of her letters, but she had the same straight
brown hair so dark it was almost black, same strikingly pale
skin even lighter than Bernadette's, same gray-blue eyes and
lopsided smile.

"I'd be a total airhead to pass *this* up. Stayin' in y'all's
house, getting to finally meet everybody."

"This is... wow. I mean, yeah. You're really here." Janet's surprise bloomed into a grin, though she stared at Bernadette with an unexpected intensity that just made Bernadette want to laugh. And it lasted long enough to make Bernadette think there was something else going on. Then Janet
blinked quickly and shook her head with a little chuckle.
"Well hurry the hell up and come here."

Bernadette stepped into the other woman's arms and in no way expected such a warm, tight, almost desperate embrace. But it felt right, after almost ten years of writing each other at least once a month, sometimes twice. She already knew everything there was to know about Janet Hammel and the life she'd spent those ten years building for herself here in Vincent. Except for just what, exactly, that desperation in Janet's hug was really trying to say.

Then the woman pulled back, tucked a strand of Bernadette's blonde hair behind her ear, and laughed at herself for doing something like that without even thinking about it. "I just can't believe it. You're actually here. Oh, and *Darrell*. I can't even tell you how good it is to finally meet you."

Janet leapt away from Bernadette to spread some of her oddly focused attention elsewhere. "That's a big deal, man. Making the drive out here with her to meet a bunch of folks you don't even know."

"Yeah, long drive." Darrell smirked and held out his hand. "I'm guessin' you've heard all about me too."

"Enough to not be insulted by a damn handshake." Janet slapped the back of his hand and spread her arms. "Put that thing away. I only do hugs."

He hissed out a sigh through his smile and leaned in for a quick, slightly awkward embrace from the woman who only knew everything about him through hundreds of handwritten letters. Meeting Bernadette's gaze with wide eyes, he muttered, "She only does hugs."

"Damn straight I do." Janet patted his back a few times, then stepped away and stuck her hands on her hips. That lingering gaze of hers found a home again on Bernadette, only this time it covered the woman from South Carolina from head to toe in approval before Janet laughed and shook her head. "Come on. Y'all need to meet everyone else. This is... ah!"

She waved them after her, and when Darrell raised questioning eyebrows, Bernadette lifted one shoulder in half a shrug and slipped her hand into his. They followed Janet farther into the living room than just the first few feet and got introduced all around.

Phil from Houston dipped his head, his eyes crinkling as he grinned, both thumbs stuck through the beltloops of his jeans. All he was missing were a giant, shiny belt buckle and a Stetson.

Alice and Tom had stopped by from their visit with family just outside Birmingham. The blonde-haired, blue-eyed couple looked so much alike, Bernadette wondered if they were siblings until they moved on and she saw Tom's hand slip into the back pocket of Alice's high-waisted jeans.

Jiyun's pitch-black hair hung in a shimmering bob around her golden-toned face, straight bangs hovering just over her slowly dipping eyelashes. Her lips never parted as she smiled at the newcomers and shook their hands with thin, cold, limp fingers.

They met Tiffany from Chicago, Andrés from Brooklyn, Raymond with a five-inch mohawk from much closer in Atlanta, Marcus and Damien from San Francisco who looked nothing alike but were definitely a couple, and wasn't it a trip that those two had been in the Golden State with Charles at the same time he was still in Oakland?

Darrell looked a little more relieved, just a little more comfortable, when Janet brought them around to shake hands with Charles and Anton and Latisha. The man about ten years older than everyone else here nodded at Darrell and stuck out his hand. "Charles."

"Darrell."

The shake was firm and quick and over with in a second. "Good to have you here, brother."

"Yeah, man."

"Real good." Charles slapped a hand on Darrell's shoulder. "Donna was just talkin' 'bout a brother playin' sax with Woodson Blues. That you?"

Darrell hissed and dipped his head to scratch the back of his neck. "Been about a year, now. Yeah."

"No kiddin'. You bring that horn up with ya from Charleston?"

Laughing, Darrell just barely shook his head. "Didn't think it was that kinda party, man."

Charles let out a sharp bark of a laugh and readjusted his black leather jacket over his black button-up shirt. "That's fine, man. You breakin' it down with Woodson Blues. Real fine. I've heard good things."

"'Preciate it, man."

"Not that kinda party..." With another laugh, Charles lifted his head and turned around to call out to the room, "Donna. You didn't think to ask the man if he wanted to jam a little at one of these things?"

From the other side of the room, Donna flung a hand into the air. "Not that kinda party, baby."

"Not that kinda party." Charles laughed, cleared his throat, and cocked his head, jerking his finger up and down not directly at Darrell but at least toward him. "I tell you what. Maybe it's not that kinda party, but I might just do a whole lot to see Woodson Blues up close."

Bernadette squeezed Darrell's hand. "Come down to Charleston. They're playing all the time."

"That right? You ever get outta the state?"

"Once or twice." Darrell stared at the floor and nodded slowly. "Went out to Atlanta couple weeks ago."

"Well, you make it over just a few state lines, and you might see my face. Excuse me." With another pat on Darrell's back, Charles stepped back and disappeared somewhere else in the house.

A loud, unabashed explosion of laughter came from behind them, where Donna had her arm around Janet's shoulders now, pulling her partner closer and shaking a playfully warning finger at whoever had made her laugh like that. Then the women steered themselves back toward Bernadette and Darrell, their heads bent toward each other. Janet grinned as Donna muttered something fierce and quick and obviously meant to be private. Then they reached their newest guests, and Donna shoved her free hand into her pocket. "What do y'all think so far?"

Bernadette smirked. "Y'all squeeze a lotta people into this house."

"Aw." Donna chuckled and tipped her head toward Janet. "She's so new. This is nothin', Bernie. Come back when we got people gathered around for something a little more… productive. Then you'll see. This is just for fun."

Janet met Bernadette's gaze and offered a little smile through pursed lips, her eyes slowly widening. "That's how she gets ya."

"What's that?" Donna stared at her partner, feigning surprise.

"It's all fun and games at first." Janet lurched forward just a little, like she'd just swallowed her own laughter, and lifted two hands with curved fingers. "Then the claws come out."

"What?" Donna clicked her tongue and shook Janet a little by the shoulders. "Girl…"

"Just sayin'."

"Mm-mm." Shaking her head, Donna looked up at Bernadette and winked. "Somethin' to think about. Hell, Darrell, you come too. See what we're all about when we get down to business, huh?"

"You don't have to answer that," Janet added with a nervous-sounding chuckle. Maybe even apologetic.

"*He* knows that. Don'tcha, D?"

The man just cleared his throat and slipped his hand back down to the small of Bernadette's back.

"See? He's got the right idea. Just say nothin'." Donna pointed at him and turned her head away in a warning sideways glance. "Don't go provin' me wrong, now. Can I get y'all anything to drink? We put water and tea out so far. The rest comes later."

"Hey, let the man have a drink, babe." Janet gestured toward him as her partner leaned away, getting ready to head toward wherever these drinks had been put out for the guests. "He's not sittin' down to tell a story."

"Huh." Donna looked him up and down, then chuckled. "I wasn't even thinkin' about that. You a whiskey man?"

"If that's what y'all got, I am."

"You know, I like him." Donna shook her finger at him again, stepped away, then stopped herself and leaned back in, slapping Darrell's arm with the back of a hand. "Don't let any of these other fools know what you got in your cup, yeah? Then everybody's gonna want to start *breaking the rules*." Her head moved in an exaggerated swerve as she spoke, her tight curls bouncing back behind her shoulders. Then she let out another unabashed laugh and darted out of the living room.

"You hear that?" Darrell dipped his head toward Bernadette and looked like he might actually prefer to stand in the back while everyone else did what they'd come here to do. "You brought me to a party with *rules*."

Before Bernadette could come up with something smart enough to say back, Janet leaned toward them, shaking her hand back and forth. "Y'all can just ignore whatever she says about rules, okay? And Darrell, you're pretty much exempt from all of them, even if we took 'em seriously."

"Huh." He seemed on the verge of laughing beneath the confused frown he sent her way. "First time someone's given me a free pass."

Janet's next chuckle, embarrassed and apologetic and self-critical, sounded a little too out of place for the high energy filling her living room. "No, I just mean… you know. Donna likes to get everybody together and have like a… story time."

He leaned back and brought his hand up from Bernadette's back to her shoulder. "You hear about this?"

"Nope." It was all she could do not to laugh at the obvious layers of confusion being tossed between the three of them like randomly flung darts. "There's a *story time,* Janet?"

"Uh... well, yeah. You know, the special kind. That we..." She gestured to herself and then Bernadette, biting down on her bottom lip. "Booze makes it impossible to do anything with our words, so we wait until all the... *stories* are over. And Darrell doesn't have a—"

"Naw, I get it." Now Darrell was trying not to laugh. "Sure. I can't do what y'all do, and that's fine. Means I get a drink, and I ain't gonna try askin' for anything else."

The fact that Bernadette honestly couldn't tell if he was put out or put at ease by the whole thing surprised her. Darrell just shook his head and rubbed his hand back and forth across his mouth, which made figuring out what he was thinking that much harder.

"Oh, don't... We definitely want you here." Janet's brows drew together in concern. "Please don't think that's even a thing. It's incredible that you both came—"

"Hey, it's chill." Darrell swallowed and spread his arms. "I'm good. Just get a"—he chuckled through the words—"little liquor in me, I'll be all smiles. 'Cause we about to sit around and get told all kindsa crazy shit, ain't we?"

Janet's eyes widened again at Bernadette, then both of them burst out laughing. Their hostess ran a hand through her straight, nearly black hair and shrugged. "Something like that, yeah."

Glancing at the ceiling, he pulled Bernadette toward him until she wrapped her arms around his waist, still laughing. Janet looked them over, smiling, then her face lit up when Donna stepped back into the living room with two red plastic Solo cups. "Okay, get ready."

"For the whiskey man." Donna thrust one cup toward Darrell so quickly, it almost splashed all over him and Bernadette both. He took the cup, and Donna laughed when she extended the other one toward Bernadette. "Y'all just made the drive, so I figured it was safer to go with, uh... sugar and caffeine for you, honey. We'll get to the good stuff. Don't worry." She winked when Bernadette took the cup from her, then walked past all of them, smacking Janet's ass on her way toward the rest of their guests.

Janet's mouth fell open in a shocked smile, and she turned to watch her partner lift both arms into the air to grab everyone's attention.

"All right, y'all. We're done talkin', but we're not done talkin'. Know what I'm sayin'?" The separate conversations died down into small, knowing chuckles. "Y'all get your asses into a seat or a lap or whatever the hell you're least likely to fall out of. We'll kick this off the way we do, huh?"

"Amen," someone called from the other side of the room.

Donna cocked her head and pointed. "Aw... not yet."

"Grab a seat," Janet said, gazing back at Bernadette over her shoulder. Then she nodded and headed across the living room, where Donna pulled her down into her lap and leaned toward the man sitting beside her to say something that made them all laugh.

"Where do you wanna sit?" Bernadette found Darrell staring into his red Solo cup, expressionless but for his incredibly wide eyes.

"Woman's tryin' to get me wasted. Shit."

"What?" She stood on her tiptoes to peer over the rim of his cup, which was in fact filled over halfway with whiskey. "Oh, man. Is that just straight whiskey?"

He took a sip, swallowed, licked his lips, stared straight ahead at the opposite wall. "Uh-huh."

Choking back a laugh, Bernadette pulled him around the few extra chairs dotting the living room, all of the seats more or less arranged in a circle with only the black coffee table with neon-green stripes left in the center. "You'll be fine. Just maybe set it down once someone starts talking."

He let out a low whistle and kept staring into the cup.

The only seat left was a purple armchair with orange armrests and room for one person. Darrell slowly lowered himself into it and pulled her toward him with a hand on her hip until she opted instead to sit sideways on the armrest.

"Why you wanna sit up there when you got the best seat in the house right here?" Darrell gestured toward his lap and almost had her convinced that she'd hurt his feelings.

"I don't want you spillin' that drink all over me when it drops outta your hand. I'm serious. You should put it down. At least until you hear whoever's first."

Darrell clicked his tongue at her, took a surprisingly long pull of whiskey, and set the plastic cup on the carpet. A quick, sharp sigh escaped him as he reached for her hips again with both hands. "The things you make me do for you, girl. I swear."

"I didn't make you do—" She shrieked when he yanked her backward off the armchair and into his lap, then she burst out laughing. His lips on hers smothered the laugh. Darrell tasted like way too much whiskey and a little of the po'boys they'd picked up on the drive, but she kissed him back and slung an arm around his neck.

"Hey, South Carolina!" Across the room, Donna clapped her hands and leaned forward, chuckling. "We didn't invite y'all out here to put on a show. That comes later."

Laughing through her nose, Bernadette pressed her lips even harder against Darrell's and held his face where it was before finally letting go. He cleared his throat and tried to lean over her in his lap. "Where's that drink?"

"No."

His smirk gave him away, though he stared at the coffee table now and sat back in the armchair, his hand sliding up onto her thigh. Donna started talking, but the only thing Bernadette heard was Darrell's voice whispering in her ear. "You ever been to something like this?"

She licked her lips and shook her head, forcing herself not to react to his hand.

"Then if I get all fucked up from whatever kinda stories these people got comin', I'ma need you to fix me." His hand kept moving slowly up her thigh, then he pinched her.

She slapped his hand, making him chuckle, and leaned back to look up at him; she could only see his lips without twisting her neck so far around that it hurt. "I'll break you first if you don't stop."

"Mm-hmm. Trouble."

"Shut up."

Darrell's mouth twitched into a tiny, secretive smile while he stared at the coffee table. Though she tried to split her mind and use half of it to focus on Donna's introduction to whatever they'd just sat down to do, she could only focus on those lips.

15

I DON'T KNOW if I should actually write this down, Bernie. It's been, what? Three weeks? And no matter what I do, I can't stop thinking about what happened. I don't blame you for any of it. Please don't think that. It's not even about blame, really, because I'm not mad. I might use the word "confused", but I've heard that tossed around so many times, mostly at me, that it's more like a hate-hate relationship. But I'm just… reconsidering things? Maybe.

I want you to know that nothing's changed. Between you and me. I'm pretty sure you already know that, but it feels so wrong not to at least give voice to it, you know? To make sure I write it down in this letter, just so I can turn my brain off once I know that you've seen it, read the words. That you understand. I hope.

Donna's been acting like the whole thing's just hilarious. Maybe it is. Maybe it would've been for me if it had happened to someone other than me and I was just there, watching like everyone else. I can see how she might feel that way and just blow it all off like it didn't mean anything. I mean, I don't even know if it did or not. Did it?

Fuck, I've been thinking about how to write this letter for weeks, and I can't even get it out the way I want it. You ever have anyone else get so… wrapped up about it, I guess? I know it's just what you do. I know you tried to pick someone else. I know you kinda had no choice in the end, and maybe you felt pressured into it when Donna just wouldn't let up. Most people do. That's just how she is. I know all these things and what they mean or don't mean, but I can't stop thinking about it. About you. About what things would look like if we'd met each other in person five years ago. Seven. Eight. We haven't talked about it, and we don't need to.

I'm still glad you made it that night. I'm glad both of you came, and I really hope D wrote the whole thing off just like Donna did. If he hasn't, if that night made anything weird between you guys, I am so, so sorry. Sure, I didn't actually do anything, but seeing as Donna doesn't really apologize for anything, I'll say it for both of us. It won't happen again. I don't know, Bernie, there might not even be a next time, but if there is, I promise I won't let it happen again.

The point is, I don't want you to think that I'm avoiding you. (I know, right? How do we avoid each other through letters?) I don't want you to think that you can't still tell me about what's going on in your life, even if it has to do with me now. Seriously, I can't tell you how much these letters have saved me from some pretty fucked-up places, and I don't really know what would happen if I didn't have you to talk to anymore.

Things are... tense around here. With Donna, anyway. Somehow, I know it's not even about what happened when you and D came out here. Maybe she doesn't even have the time to give two shits about any of it. I'm pretty sure it's just more crap with her damn "movement" bringing out all her anger. More of it, anyway. Something broke out the other day. I don't know exactly what happened, but one of their meetings got busted up. It wasn't really a raid. I mean, it's not like any of us have anything that can actually be taken. Not like they were doing anything illegal the other night. But the fuzz don't actually need an honest reason to break up somebody else's party and start cuffing people, do they? That part hasn't changed, at least.

Donna's pissed, obviously. They didn't take her, but they took a few others. Probably because those people had a record for some tiny thing in the past. Over and done with, but it was enough of an excuse to send in some uniforms with guns drawn and handcuffs out. Two of the people at that meeting got out yesterday. Because the cops couldn't make anything stick. But now we have this to deal with. And Donna's been pulling her hair out trying to find a new place where the meetings won't be so easy to find. Plus, she's kind of obsessing over how the cops found them in the first place. She thinks someone ratted us out. But now we know we're being watched, either way. Again, not like this "movement" has done anything illegal. Yet. You wouldn't believe some of the crap I've heard them talking about. Making plans. I don't know. But everything I knew was coming is starting to happen, Bernie. This is just the beginning, and I'm starting to wonder if I even wanna stick around to see the end, you know? Fuck, even the middle.

But that's not really what I wanted to write to you about anyway. I guess I already got to the most important parts. Please write back and let me know what you're thinking. If I'm just running myself around in circles for no reason, tell me that too. Write me a giant slap in the face from South Carolina. I might need it. Maybe I'm just looking for some reassurance, because everything I thought I knew is starting to unravel.

Donna just came home from another one of her meetings, and that always means a few hours of her pouring out everything she couldn't say in front of everyone else. It just gets dumped out onto the floor between us, and I think she expects me to pick up the mess every time. Man, but I'm stuck in my own mess right now. Is it even possible to be there for someone when you're not even sure that what you're doing for yourself is working the way it used to?

I'm out of time. Hope I hear from you soon.

—Janet

16

THE NAP HADN'T given Bernadette nearly as much relief as she'd been hoping for. Still, it was enough to get her back on her feet and headed out the door.

When she'd left, Brad and Mirela were back inside the cabin, Mirela propped up on the couch with a bottled water in hand. And Brad had finally taken some initiative, apparently already well into a foot massage that had his pregnant wife groaning a lot louder than the contractions coming closer together. Bernadette had left them with a kiss on Mirela's sweaty temple and a smile on her own face. Cameron, Randall, and the twins hadn't looked too comfortable about the whole thing, but apparently Mirela had wanted them all there.

Of course she did. Bernadette readjusted the van's rearview mirror and shook her head with a little chuckle. That woman wanted everyone to be a part of everything, to feel needed and appreciated and at home at all times. Even when she had much more important things needing her immediate attention. Like impending childbirth. But they still had a few hours yet before things got a little more complicated, and Bernadette had a little more time to look for a few friends in a city she hardly recognized anymore. If those friends were even still here.

She parked the van on the corner in the Bee Street Garage, then got out with a grunt and hoped her back would quit crying all on its own. The city smelled exactly the same as she remembered it—salty air straight from the Atlantic, old stone, more five-star restaurants than she thought could have popped up in such a tightly packed city even after a few decades, and the occasional whiff of pluff mud. She'd forgotten about the hay-sweet stink of horseshit on the cobblestone streets, but it wasn't anything new. All of it was familiar and smelled like home. It smelled like the last place in the world she wanted to be.

The walk to Mr. B's on Line Street didn't take long— not anywhere near the miles she'd put in around this city on her own two feet. It felt more like walking from and through and into a dream, really. The lights looked brighter and felt bigger. The heavy traffic made her feel a little more claustrophobic than it used to, because it never used to be so bad. But the missing chunks in the sidewalks, the long, narrow houses and apartment building stretching way up Norman and Ashton, and the sight of that single unmarked door in the corner of the building brought her right back. So many nights spent at Mr. B's, talking the night away with the regulars out on the back patio after closing, but a speakeasy never really closed. So many shows and drinks and hours spent dancing in the tiny space in front of the stage. So many goddamn memories that had no place assaulting her, especially now.

She opened the door and stepped into her dream, her past, her whatever. The place hadn't changed a bit.

Strings of thin, glittering ribbons hung from the ceiling, some of them tying off silver paper stars at the end. The tables to the left of the door were already filled up, bodies in seats forming a row all the way up to the entrance. A blues guitar cried out from the stage on the right, where a few more people sat at the high-top tables on tall stools covered in red pleather. Bernadette was actually glad to see that damn pole was still there, almost right in the middle of what Mr. B's turned into the dancefloor during live shows.

What she hadn't expected was to be noticed at all. Bernadette didn't know why it surprised her. An old white lady walking into this place alone with her gray hair all piled on top of her head and her long dress that held all the secrets of what her body had become over the years. And her damn loafers. It wasn't like she had the time or even the supplies to try dressing herself up. To look more like she used to the last time she'd been here. And that would've been a cruel joke to play on herself, wouldn't it?

Still, there was something about the feeling in the air, the looks she knew she was getting—even from the people who had five or ten years on her at least—that made her stomach turn a few flips. And she couldn't put her finger on it.

The bar stretched out in front of her on a sloping incline, and she crossed the small space to step up onto the ramp-like floor and head right for the bar. She thought she recognized the curve of those shoulders as the man behind the bar wiped down the bottom of the liquor shelf. Bernadette set her hands on the chipped wood and waited for him to turn around. He didn't, so she leaned forward a little, fighting not to laugh. "And I thought *I* looked old."

Her voice carried above the music onstage just enough to make the man freeze. Then he turned slowly around and raised a bushy eyebrow in a dark face lined with wrinkles. And still, it looked so much the same, even after twenty years. He had to have thought the same about her in the two seconds before those eyebrows drew up toward a receding hairline going gray around the edges. "B?"

"Hey, Ronnie."

"Well, goddamn." The man's face wrinkled even more in a lopsided smile, and he smacked his hand down on the bar between them. "You just… Girl, what you doin' all the way out here?"

"Just passin' through. You know. Stoppin' by to see a few old sights. And old friends."

Ronnie clicked his tongue against his teeth and drew in a hissing breath. "Yeah, man. You got that one right. Old." A little chuckle escaped him, though it was whisked away beneath the music. "Hit me real hard. Just like the damn arthritis." A crooked hand lifted from the other side of the bar, then he settled it back down where most people couldn't see it again.

"You're still kickin'."

"And proud of it. Look at *you*, B. Can't run away from time, but shit. Looks like you're faster'n me. Still lookin' good, girl." Bernadette shot him a skeptical frown above a smile she couldn't keep down below the surface, despite the way he flicked his gaze around the bar and over everyone sitting in it. Like he was either way too interested in who saw them talking or looking for someone to save him from the conversation. "You, uh… you wanna drink?"

Fuckin right she did. "Whiskey ginger. Please."

"Uh-huh." Out came the small cup of translucent-white plastic. In went the whiskey and the ginger ale straight from the gun. The thing nearly spilled all over his crooked hand as he slid the cup across the bar.

"Still no ice, huh?"

Ronnie snorted. "White girl and her *ice cubes*. I swear."

"I like it better this way."

"Course you do." He smirked at her and shook his head while she took a quick sip to keep it from spilling over. The last thing this old white lady needed now was to be walking around with a stain on her dress and smelling like Hansen O'Malley on a good night.

"Prices still the same?"

"Naw. I got you, B." He studied her for a few seconds, glanced at the stage, then dipped his head toward her and sniffed. "You know, I don't give a hot goddamn about what any of these folks say when they spoutin' off. Whole buncha people got somethin' ridin' up their jimmies. I'm glad you stopped by. Don't forget that, got it? It's good to see ya."

"You too, Ronnie." She took the cup and turned slowly away from the bar, wondering what the hell the man was talking about. It didn't feel real that people would still be talking about her after all this time. That a city that had changed so much and held so many lives wouldn't have let go of the hole Bernadette Manney left behind her when she left everything else. Taking another sip of the drink stronger than she'd expected, even from Ronnie, she scanned the faces under Mr. B's low lights and for a second wanted to chug her whole fucking drink.

People were looking at her now. Openly, without trying to hide it. And she recognized what it was that made this place feel so different despite the fact that nothing was different. She hadn't expected to be looked at like this, especially not here. Not looked at like she didn't belong but watched like she wasn't *wanted*. Like the people in here, shooting her dirty looks over the rims of their own plastic cups as they stopped bobbing their heads to the blues onstage, wanted her out. But none of them were about to stand up and just say it. None of them would say a thing until they figured out just what the hell she was doing here and what she wanted in *their bar.*

She recognized the looks, all right. But for the first time, they were directed at her instead of around her. The same look in her father's eyes and behind her mother's fake smile. The same look redirected through her and piercing a straight line to the light-brown hand peeking over the stroller's padded bar or the dark brown hand in her own. As if Bernadette herself had never existed in those moments except as the magnifying glass focusing sunlight onto an anthill no one wanted in their back yard. It made her head pound a little to realize that now she was the anthill. Or maybe it was the whiskey, which would have made a lot more sense right now.

"Hey, Ronnie."

"Yeah."

Bernadette turned to face him fully at the bar again and couldn't believe she was about to come right out and ask it. "You know where I can find him?"

They both knew she didn't have to say the name out loud. It had to have been written across her face as surely as it was reflected in Ronnie's dark, shimmering eyes. With a tiny smile lifting the corner of his mouth, Ronnie nodded toward the stage and turned slowly around to shuffle down the bar toward the woman stopping by for another drink.

That woman could've been Mia Jones; the perpetually high arc of her eyebrows had apparently kept up their shape through the years. And despite the fact that Bernadette saw the woman's nostrils flare just before she leaned in to mutter something to Ronnie, Bernadette didn't have enough room inside her to feel anything about it.

Her heart had already broken wide open, filling every part of her with more longing, shame, joy, regret, and a perversely persistent self-doubt than she'd ever experienced all at once. She froze at the end of that bar she'd leaned against so many times, too afraid to turn around and face the source of that sweet, mournful saxophone rising over the low conversation buzzing through Mr. B's. Which now, apparently, included quite a few things people had to say about her. She couldn't hear the words, but she could *feel* them prickling along her face and neck, like the tip of a razor drawing along her flesh lightly enough not to pierce through the skin but still deeply enough to feel. Just deeply enough to hint at a warning and a threat—*don't make any sudden moves, and you might get through this.*

Bernadette hardly felt the hot tears welling in her eyes. That razor drawn along every part of her body and the pain of everything once possible but eventually rejected over the course of twenty-odd years made her weak, sick. Alive and dying at the same time. Just like she always had been.

Slowly, her body moving as if those sailing, crying notes pulled her along by invisible strings of fate, she turned toward the stage. It almost made her cry out right there to see him standing at the far end of Mr. B's, one brown shoe occasionally tapping against the black floor as his fingers moved up and down over the keys. She didn't recognize the other musicians playing up there with him. Even if she had, it wasn't like they held any more weight in that moment than Ronnie behind her. Ronnie who'd said he didn't give a hot goddamn about what anyone was saying. What they were bound to say now. What they *would* say if Bernadette gave in and moved against that razorblade of warning and contempt. She wondered who, in fact, actually held that razor and for a few moments considered the fact that it might have been her.

She sipped at her whiskey and ginger ale and wanted a cigarette. At this point, not even a real razor held against her throat would make her turn her back and walk away from him again. Not now. Not yet.

She stayed through the entire set, which might have lasted an hour and a half, but she would never know. The plastic cup in her hand was empty, but she still held it poised against her chest, waiting for the next excuse to lift it to her lips again. Only she hadn't noticed the emptiness in that bit of white-translucent plastic. Just her own.

"That's it, y'all. Thanks for comin'." The guitarist nodded, raised a wizened hand toward the crowd, and lifted the strap over his head.

Darrell spoke to the band for another minute—the band Bernadette didn't know but that had most likely become like another family to the man who used to be hers, just like she'd built her own family away from every home she'd ever known. So many of them, and none of them like this place. She watched him intently, trying to find some discrepancy in the way he lifted the saxophone strap over his head; in the way he turned and squatted there on the floor to place the instrument he'd kept with him all this time into the scuffed, dented black case; in the way he passed his hand over his lips before pushing himself to his feet again and turning toward the bar. Maybe if she found something that didn't fit, that didn't sit right with the man she'd known and loved and broken, she could convince herself that it wasn't really him. That maybe she'd made a mistake in thinking anything still breathed within the space between them that had shrunken with an overwhelming suddenness. That maybe she was still dreaming and always had been.

When Darrell looked up at the bar and met her gaze, she both hoped and feared that he wouldn't recognize her. He did. Of course he did. How could he not? Twenty years wasn't nearly enough time to erase the marks left on each of them by who they'd once been. As he moved across the small impromptu dancefloor toward her, Bernadette's strength somehow returned. She set the empty plastic cup on the bar behind her and folded her arms, preparing herself for the shitstorm she'd created all on her own.

The man didn't look nearly as old as she'd expected. Not nearly as old as she'd become since the last time they stood face to face like this, staring at each other. He had the same soft brown eyes, the same full lips diminished only a little with so many more age lines, the same breadth to his shoulders, though his shirt hung off his frame a little more than she remembered. Darrell's eyes narrowed for a second when he stopped in front of her, and Bernadette lifted her chin. She wasn't about to let him see the pit of quicksand inside her, desperately swallowing her up while she couldn't yet decide if she wanted to fight it.

"Hey, B."

Just two words, and it was like the last thirty years hadn't even happened. "Hey, yourself."

She expected him to look her up and down again, to appraise the changes she'd seen in herself every day and hadn't given a damn about until now. But those eyes bored into hers and didn't move away from her face.

"What're you doin' here?"

"Just makin' a few stops and a few calls along the way." She shrugged and pressed her lips together. "Figured I'd make this one in person."

"So you're callin' on me now, huh?" Darrell tilted his head and ran his tongue over his teeth. "Yeah. Looks like you are."

Bernadette nodded behind him without breaking away from his gaze. "You still sound as good as ever."

"Naw, that's just 'cause you haven't heard me in a while. You, uh… you stayin' here in the city?"

The only thing she could do was shake her head. If she ever did tell him where she was—where she'd brought the hobbled-together semblance of her new family, right back here where the old one had started—it wouldn't be now. "Hell of a drive to get here, though."

An airy chuckle puffed through his nose, and he leaned down toward her. Her heart leapt like a terrified, panicked squirrel that couldn't decide whether or not to cross the other fourth of a busy road or turn around and race back to the starting line. But he only muttered, "You probably shouldn't be here right now."

The razorblade returned. "I hear you, and I can tell most people in here feel the same way. But nobody's said a damn word about why."

He studied her some more and chewed on the inside of his bottom lip. "You don't know why."

"No, Darrell. I don't know why. If you can clear that up for me, I'll be happy to step right on out." Goddamnit, it was so easy to fall right back into the way they used to speak to each other—the way she'd promised herself she'd never speak to anyone. That was before unbearable mistakes had become less bearable consequences. Darrell raised an eyebrow, and Bernadette slowly shook her head. Her gaze slid down the side of his dark neck to the even darker black t-shirt beneath his slate-gray sports jacket. "I'm sorry. I really just came to talk. Even for a few minutes, if you have some spare time for me."

"For you. B, you know how hard it is to tell you I ain't got it in me?"

She hummed in acknowledgement. "Pretty hard, I imagine."

"Uh-huh. That's what I wanna tell you. But I never could lie to you, so I won't." Finally, Darrell lifted his head, leaned away from her, and glanced at something behind her. Maybe Ronnie. Maybe everyone else who still frequented the same damn bar as they had in their twenties with the whole world laid wide open all around them; in their thirties with the whole world bundled up in a pink blanket right in front of them; in their forties with the whole world closing in around Bernadette until she couldn't find a molecule of air in this city to pull into her own lungs.

"I'll tell you why you shouldn't be here, B. Seein' as you really don't know. Let's take a walk, then, huh?" Without out waiting for a reply, he stepped around the corner of the bar before walking down the sloping incline. Darrell tapped his knuckles on the old, chipped wood, the thick silver ring on his right hand clicking over the low murmur of a few dozen voices and the faint music coming over a fading sound system overhead. "Tell Max to stick the gear in my car, yeah? I'll be back around."

Ronnie looked up at him, impassively pressing his lips together. "Yeah, man."

"Thanks, Ronnie."

Bernadette finally found her heavy, aching legs and moved them. She couldn't help but glance at Ronnie, who offered a small smile from behind the bar. "You take care of yourself, B. Ya hear?"

"You too, Ronnie." Then she was walking toward the sliver of yellow streetlight slicing through the front door of Mr. B's. For a moment, her entire being reached out for the tall, broad-shouldered silhouette standing in that doorway—a palimpsest of the man in his prime, both covered and washed away by the pieces of himself still clinging to every possible future, even through time and emptiness and what he'd been forced to build from them. Alone.

The world picked up and moved again, Bernadette followed, and the door clicked shut behind her with a muted echo of thick metal.

17

THE TWENTY OR so guests gathered in Donna and Janet's home sat silently and listened to the words of the fifth person asked to give a little presentation of the power in their words. Jiyun finished telling her *story*, and while Bernadette couldn't for the life of her focus on the actual words filling the living room in that gentle, lilting tone, she knew what she felt.

She hadn't realized she'd been scratching at her whole body, brushing frantically at her skin and moving sporadically from forearm to knee to head to chin to thigh every few seconds. Some memory of thinking she felt the crawling all over her skin—ants, maybe, or even spiders—faded away as quickly as the lightly settled fog of hearing someone else, like her, use their own *special story*.

Taking a deep breath, Bernadette lowered her scratching hands into her lap and felt Darrell shudder beneath her.

"Damn," he whispered, the words barely loud enough to rise over the uncomfortable shifting and rearranging of the other guests coming back into their own awareness. Another shudder pulsed through him. "That shit was creepy."

She could only nod and lean back against him, keeping her hands in her lap, as if she expected the crawling tickle to come back any minute and might scratch them again preemptively. The memory of it was almost enough to make her do just that.

Someone else in the room let out a low whistle, and a few others laughed in tense appreciation. Charles cleared his throat. "That one would actually be useful for a good number of things."

Jiyun flashed him a small, closed-lipped smile and dipped her head. "I'm glad you think so."

"Ooh." Donna shook her head vigorously and wrapped her arms a little tighter around Janice sitting in her lap. "Makes me wanna strip down and burn these clothes."

Almost in response, Janet's hand smacked down on her own thigh before the rest of that white, foggy screen of hearing a story like *this* disappeared from her eyes completely. She let out a nervous chuckle just like a few others and ran a hand through her hair. "Not my favorite. But Jiyun, it's strong."

"That's all anyone can ask for, right?" The woman who'd just finished with the power in her words cocked her head. "I don't mind not being the favorite if at least it makes people feel *something*."

"Ain't that the truth," Anton agreed from where he sat cross-legged on the floor, his back to the entrance into the living room.

"We could use some of that for sure." Donna nodded and patted Janet's thighs a few times with both hands. "For sure. Okay. Who wants the next five minutes of fame and glory?"

A few people laughed again. Before Jiyun's apparent ability to make them all feel like their skin was literally crawling off their bodies, they'd listened to the others' words—words that made them feel like they were drowning, that made everyone else in the room look like the storyteller, that had seemingly dropped the floor out from beneath them and left the whole party floating in the black expanse of space. The man who'd gone before Jiyun—Bernadette thought his name was Willie—had made her feel like she'd suddenly gained eighty pounds. Also not her favorite, but it was better than the nonexistent things skittering up and down her limbs and across her face.

The living room fell into a hushed, expectant silence as Donna and Janet's guests gazed at each other. The others had volunteered themselves, and Bernadette figured there was some kind of process to the whole thing. Seeing as it was her first time to one of these gatherings, she hadn't even considered the fact that she'd be included in more than sitting around the circle just to listen. She hadn't even thought it was a thing to volunteer someone else or even to call them out in front of the entire living room of people and ask if they wanted to show what they could do.

But when Donna's gaze settled on her and the woman flashed Bernadette a wild grin—like a large, predatory feline who'd just caught sight of her next meal—all Bernadette's nonexistent expectations turned on their heads.

"Bernie."

"Yeah?" She smiled right on back at both of her hostesses. Donna wouldn't actually *call* on her to share her kind of story, would she? That couldn't be how this worked with someone so new sitting in on this for the first time. Then again, Bernadette had absolutely no idea how this worked.

"Why don't you go on ahead and show us what you got, girl."

"What?" Bernadette laughed. If Donna was serious, she obviously didn't know exactly what Bernadette's words did to another person. She might not have read the letters between her newest guest and her own partner—at least, not those that went as far back as Bernadette's confession of her own strange magic with certain types of words.

Janet leaned away from Donna just enough to shoot the woman a surprised and not entirely approving look.

"Sure." Donna gestured toward Bernadette and Darrell in the armchair. "Why not?"

"Oh, I… No, that's okay." When Bernadette looked at Darrell—searching, maybe, for an indication that he cared one way or the other—she only found him staring at her with raised eyebrows, just like everyone else. Would she take the opportunity? Would she refuse? No one here could make that choice for her, and yet Donna seemed entirely too eager to do just that.

"Don't be shy, South Carolina." Donna's grin widened even farther, her nose crinkling below her glistening hazel-brown eyes. "You didn't drive all the way out here just to sit around and listen to a bunch of us who've already seen what everyone else here can do."

"More than a few times," Marcus added, smirking like he was about fed up and done with the repetition, his arm slung casually around Damien's shoulders as they shared the far end of the second couch. His partner shot him the same exasperated look and whispered something about leaving the poor woman alone.

"You want me to say please?" Donna asked, leaning forward even with Janet in her lap. "Okay, I'll say please. Give us a story, Bernie. Pretty, pretty please."

Bernadette laughed again. What else was she supposed to do? It wasn't like she had anything against her own words. Not after how many times she'd used them for reasons too varied to count. And after almost six months working at Lookie Lou's, she had no problem telling a special story for strangers. But those had been private stories. One on one. Not out in the open for everyone else to watch, because it only worked for one person at a time. Tailored, she might have said. And Donna wasn't paying her, either.

"Well, it's…" Bernadette brushed her hair away from her forehead and looked at Darrell one more time. He just tilted his head, impassive as ever, and waited for her to make up her own damn mind. "It's not really the kind that hits everybody the same way."

"Even better." Donna looked absolutely delighted, tinged with an underlying glint of either malice or just more of a mischievous streak than seemed fitting for a woman living in a house like this—living a life like this—with a partner like Janet.

Bernadette immediately chastised herself for even having that thought. And everyone stared at her with open invitation, maybe even pleading—the same hunger for a new kind of story they'd never heard before burning behind their eyes.

"I mean, I don't think anyone here's gonna complain about a little bit of a different experience, huh? Then we can swap versions after." Donna laughed and bobbed her head, gazing around the room and definitely collecting on the approval and general agreement she so clearly wanted to see in their faces.

"Not *that* kind of different." Now it was Bernadette's turn to search their potential new friends. There was no way to know how they'd react. To any of this. "It, uh… it only works on one person at a time. You know, like, tailored to someone specific. Nobody else gets to feel the…" And just what the hell was she supposed to call it? All the words she might have used were ridiculously blunt and would just make her sound like a tool. "You know. The effects."

"Seriously?" Alice asked, her hand settled firmly on Tom's thigh beside her. "Just one person at a time."

"Yeah. Kinda crazy, right?"

"Wait, so you can aim it? Like decide who you want to hear, and everyone else can just buzz off?" That came from the man who'd transported them all out into the middle of space, with no floor or ceiling. Just in their minds. He squinted at Bernadette with his head half-turned away, like he really thought she was full of shit.

"Kinda, yeah." Now that the interest came from a few other people besides Donna, Bernadette started to think maybe she really had something here. The indecision melted away, and she shrugged, spending a few seconds on each intent gaze staring at her from around the circle before moving on to the next. "It's more like I can pick up on the specific words that'll make it through to different people. Most of the time I can pick those words out on the first try."

"How?" The question came from another woman who hadn't shared her own story yet or even her name with the suddenly interesting newcomer.

"Just part of the whole thing, I guess."

"Uh-huh." Donna's gaze shifted quickly to Darrell, who gave nothing away, and back to Bernadette. "Bernie, I gotta say the way you're talkin' about your story makes me think you don't really wanna share."

"No, it's not that—"

"And that only makes me wanna hear it more. So go on. Who you gonna pick to get some extra-special attention?"

Darrell snorted, and Bernadette fought back her own laugh; the other woman had no idea how ironically close to home she'd hit with that description.

"Yeah? That's funny?"

Donna still grinned at them, but now Bernadette understood only too well what Janet had been writing in so many of their letters. Donna was charismatic, bright, funny, gorgeous, passionate, and like a stick of dynamite with an extra-short fuse just waiting to be lit. That made it especially easy to write about being in love and scared of it all at once.

"A little funny, yeah." Bernadette shrugged and returned the grin, though hers was scrubbed clean of the underlying animosity flaring up in her hostess' entire expression. "You just summed it up kinda perfectly. But I don't know if what I can do is something everybody wants to see, you know? Like, not the kinda thing I wanna just spring on somebody I just met."

"No, you're not backing out of this one *now*." Donna tightened her arms around Janet's waist and smiled up at her partner. "You know what kinda story Bernie has, don't you, baby?"

Janet stiffened and blinked at the freshly vacuumed carpet. "I know, yeah." Her voice was barely above a whisper.

"Right on. Then she can show us how things work and focus it on you. Y'all been writing each other for years, huh? I wouldn't buy it if y'all said you were still strangers."

The few seconds of silence stretched interminably long, then Janet's gaze flicked up to fall on Bernadette.

How was that supposed to make this any easier? Bernadette gave her long-distance friend a reassuring smile. "You don't have to do this."

"She knows that. She's a big girl, Bernie. Makes her own decisions and everything." Donna's arms tightened a little more around her partner's waist as she leaned to the side and shot Janet another winning smile. "So how 'bout it, beautiful? I really, *really*"—another laugh escaped her—"wanna hear what this woman can do."

Janet just sat there on the woman's lap with a smile half excitement and half humiliation. But she wouldn't take her eyes off Bernadette, and Bernadette wasn't the only one in the room who noticed. They'd all picked up on the near-instant flip in Donna too, the transformation from fun and going with the flow of this whole gathering to simmering rage and resentment hidden behind a very thin mask of etiquette. And the woman was on the verge of tearing right through that, too.

"I don't mind." Janet said it slowly, almost numbly, like she'd hardened herself already to the implication behind all Donna's false and forced charm. "I'll do it."

"Yeah, girl." Donna slapped the side of Janet's thigh and laughed. "Let's hear it."

"You sure?" Bernadette held Janet's gaze and wanted to scream at Donna to quit being such a cunt. The only thing that stopped her was the unwavering determination in her friend's eyes passing itself off pretty damn convincingly as guilt.

"Yeah. Why not?" Janet's small smile bloomed, and she lifted her chin, drawing all that determination from the inside out. "That's why we're all here, right?"

Maybe. Or maybe Donna was on some kind of power trip that extended beyond all this party business. That blended with her meetings and her "movement". Maybe she was looking for new recruits. Maybe she just wanted an excuse to see how far she could push someone into something, even if that person was her own partner. Or maybe they were all just here to tell special goddamn stories and make themselves feel as useful and normal about it as they could.

"I guess so." With a quick breath, Bernadette nodded once and got herself ready to make things weird. Darrell shifted beneath her in the armchair, as if he'd forgotten the woman sitting in his lap before trying to get up. She leaned down to pick up the still mostly half-full Solo cup of whiskey and handed to him. He took it and looked up at her with expectant eyes. "You cool with this?" she whispered.

"Aw…" He cocked his head, more than a little amusement turning up the corner of his mouth. "I'll tell you what *I* think later. You ain't gettin' outta this one."

Yeah, she didn't think so, either.

He nodded toward Janet again, though he was watching Donna now, and brought the plastic cup to his lips for a long sip.

"Okay…" Bernadette spread her arms in a shrug, then slapped her hands down on her thighs and rubbed them up and down a few times. "Here goes."

Janet didn't move a muscle, and Bernadette could so clearly read everything in her friend's upright posture, hands folded in her lap, chin lifted a little while she stared straight through Bernadette into some other level of reality where they didn't need words—*Do it. Make it good, and if you can, make her feel like an asshole for pushing so hard. I can take it.*

The sentiment was so perfectly clear, so direct, that Bernadette couldn't figure out why the hell she felt so guilty for the first time about doing what she did. What she did so well, men had been willing to pay her more than enough to build a life for herself just by popping into a dumpy strip club twice a week.

Leaning forward just a little, Bernadette shut out all the eyes she felt on her grasping for the next thrill, and focused on Janet. It shouldn't have surprised her, really. That it was so easy to find the words to turn the tumblers in the lock of Janet's self-control. Maybe she'd wanted it to take a little more time, to be a challenge. Then this might not have felt like such a flippant jab at everyone here.

"I found this old box of nails."

Still, Janet didn't move but for a slight tilt in her head that might have been confusion or a challenge or both. It didn't matter what exactly had caused it. Knowing wouldn't change how the rest of this went down.

The words burned hot up Bernadette's chest, through her throat, between her lips. "Huge box, with hundreds of old, rusty nails inside."

That was when Janet took a sharp breath, her lips parting slightly as she held Bernadette's gaze and most likely still tried to fight it off. That wouldn't last long.

"There were more of those long, skinny ones than any other kind," Bernadette continued. "Like the nails I'd hammer into the wall to hang a picture. They all rolled around in the box, metal scratching up on metal. Clanging around when I shook it just to see what would happen."

Janet's fingers curled into tight, white-knuckled fists in her lap. Behind her, Donna squinted with a smile of disbelief, looking slowly back and forth between her partner and the newcomer here to tell them a different kind of story. Odds were, Donna had no idea what was happening to the woman sitting in her lap. That wouldn't last long, either.

"Then I reached into the box." Bernadette took a deep breath and pushed on, tasting heat and metal on her tongue. "Pulled out just a single long, thin nail. The point sharp enough to scratch a thin line into my finger. The flat head on the other end not that much wider around than the rest of it."

With a gasp, Janet's eyes fluttered closed, her held tilting back farther, farther, slowly. Donna raised an eyebrow and eyed her partner up and down.

"One nail from that box just wasn't enough." Bernadette couldn't think of anything else now but the magic burning through her and what it was doing to her friend. "I took some more, held all three of them between my fingers. Rolled them back and forth."

A long, low moan escaped the woman for whom these words about rusty nails were uniquely strung out just like this. One of Janet's clenched fists slid down her own thigh, back up again, her fingers opening and closing like a dying spider's last, undecided twitch.

"All that steel fit into so many of the same shapes."

Slow, shuddering breath quickened into a light, breathless panting. Donna licked her lips and watched her partner writhing on her lap under the spell of Bernadette's words.

"I grabbed a whole handful from that box."

Another moan not unlike a shriek now.

"Let them fall through my fingers one by one. They bounced off the floor of the garage. Nothing like the sound a nail makes when it hits cement."

As if invisible hands pushed her down now, Janet fell back against Donna's shoulder and slid down on her partner's lap, arching her back. Donna let out a hoarse little chuckle and bit her lip. So many more words of nails and steel and rust, and Janet's mouth opened all the way in slackened, overpowered ecstasy. Her thighs drew apart as all that unseen force—the caress of invisible hands attached to no one and nothing but the power behind Bernadette's story—pushed her back farther on Donna's lap and the couch's armrest. Janet's own hands moved up her body until she'd raised them all the way above her head. Fingernails scratched along the wall behind her. Donna kept biting her lip.

Whatever words Bernadette said next were drowned out by the rising moans floating through Janet's open mouth, her heaving chest, as her hips moved up and down right there on her lover's lap. A lover who hadn't laid a finger on her but was now clearly fighting an urge almost just as strong to do it anyway. Janet begged with her body, with the rising pitch of each wordless, pleading cry ending in another shuddering gasp. It was slow and languid, oddly graceful for having been put on the spot like this and for having known exactly what was coming. But there was no denying it most certainly wasn't an act. Especially when Donna seemed to realize it too after her surprised amusement faded. She glanced up at Bernadette with a tiny smirk, like she and Bernadette had been in on this together from the beginning. Like Donna knew some secret Bernadette hadn't yet discovered while Janet writhed on her lap under the spell of another woman's words.

Bernadette hardly paid attention to what she said once she'd started this kind of story. But she always knew just when to end it. "No room for any more in my hands, so I stuck the last few nails between my teeth—"

Janet's so far rather admirable composure, given the circumstances, broke completely. She screamed in release, nearly lifting herself all the way off Donna's lap before collapsing into herself again, shuddering and heaving one heavy, trembling breath after another. Her head rolled to the side toward Donna, though her eyes remained closed. Finally, Janet pressed her lips together as the rest of her melted into the pleasure of the moment and everything leading up to it. A small, satisfied smile spread across her lips, then she opened her eyes and stared at her partner.

"Well." Donna raised an eyebrow, her lips pursed in not quite disapproval. It was more like vindication, and that made the whole thing feel even more wrong than when Bernadette had started. "That looked like fun."

Janet blinked in surprise as the rest of the world came rushing back into her awareness. With a sharp breath, she pushed herself up off the back of the couch and looked right at Bernadette again with wide, terrified eyes. Her mouth worked soundlessly, opened and closed, before she rose swiftly from Donna's lap and hurried across the living room. "Excuse me."

Then she was gone, where no one could see her, and a door closed somewhere else in the house. It was soft and gentle, as if the woman preferred nobody knew where she'd gone or that she'd shut herself away. But the living room was so infected with stunned silence, not only did everyone sitting in that circle hear the door shut, but they also heard the water rushing from the faucet and the sharp, startled bark of laughter behind it.

"Well done, South Carolina." Donna leaned forward to dig an elbow into her thigh. Then she propped her chin in her hand and grinned that deviously feral grin one more time. "That definitely wasn't anything *close* to what I expected. But hey." She sat back up again and spread her arms. "I'm just one of those people who really likes surprises."

"Surprise." Bernadette tried to laugh, to make it sound like none of this mattered. It wouldn't have if she'd used her words on anyone else. What were the chances that anyone else would have responded the way Janet did, suddenly overcome by their own desire and the fulfillment of it through an invisible, disembodied caress? Especially when they wouldn't have known what to expect? Pretty fucking slim chances, she knew. Most people didn't take to it the way Janet did. Come to think of it, the only person who ever openly enjoyed her *stories* like that was Darrell, because he knew it was coming. Because he knew it was coming for him, on purpose, from his woman who used her words like they were just another part of her body between the sheets. Because he *wanted* it from her. And Janet…

Janet had wanted it too.

Forcing her smile to grow so that was all any of them would see, Bernadette shook her head and shrugged again. "Now you know what I can do."

"Wow." Damien shook his head and let out a strained laugh. "That was *incredible…*"

"Oh, thanks." Her laugh was genuine this time. So much for putting on a show *later*. "It's not very useful, though."

"Mm." Donna cocked her head and sat back again, throwing one arm over the back of the couch and scanning the faces of all her guests—stunned, embarrassed, awed, confused, perhaps some even a little jealous. "No, I'd say that's *very* useful. I don't even have room in my head for all the possibilities coming to me right now. Darrell."

She pointed at him, and the man just lifted his chin in response.

"You think your woman's stories are pretty damn useful, don't you?"

He looked up at Bernadette and didn't say a word before raising the plastic cup to his lips again for another long drink.

"Yeah…" Donna bared her teeth and sucked in a hissing breath, drawing her shoulders up toward either side of her face like she just couldn't contain herself. Hopefully that wasn't the case. "Of course you do. You won't say anything, but you seem like the kinda brother who holds onto a good thing when he's got it. Huh." The woman laughed, nodding at the carpet in front of her. "So it's not like anybody wants to follow that one up, is it?"

A few other people around the circle laughed and murmured their assent, running hands through hair and down cheeks and up arms. Donna clapped her hands, rubbing them together as she stood from the couch.

"Who wants a fucking drink?" The words rushed out of her in a casual chuckle, so overly casual that it also sounded like spite. And anger. The start of some unnamed storm brewing inside the winning smile and all the sarcastic charm. If Bernadette hadn't read so many letters from the woman who knew Donna better than most, she would have believed the act. "It's an open bar, y'all. Make yourselves at home. Hey, not too much at home, though, okay? We only have four bedrooms, so don't get any ideas."

Then she brushed out of the living room, her long legs moving with purpose and an unwavering intent toward wherever she kept that bar of hers. That broke the spell of tension in the living room, and everyone else stood from their chairs and couches and from off the floor. Twenty people didn't seem like too many when they were all quiet, but all the tiny conversations now made it feel like there were at least twice that many.

Jiyun approached the armchair where Bernadette still sat on Darrell's lap. A hand settled on Bernadette's shoulder, and the other woman leaned in just a little. "Really amazing."

"Oh." Bernadette's wry surprise and the chuckle sighing out of her went completely unnoticed. "Thanks."

"Just... very well done." Jiyun gave her that same small, demure smile, patted Bernadette's shoulder lightly, and headed out of the living room with most of the others.

"Okay, now, is Bernie short for something?" Marcus stopped in front of her next. He lifted a palm toward her and bounced it up and down to emphasize his words. "Or is there something else you'd rather go by? Because I really don't want to call you by a name you just don't like."

"I don't mind Bernie at all."

Darrell readjusted his arm around her and leaned to the side a little, propping his massive cup of whiskey on the armrest.

"Fantastic. Listen, Bernie, that absolutely blew me away."

Just behind him, Damien rolled his eyes. "Really? You feel like making puns about this?"

"What? That wasn't a—oh. Oh, that *is* a little bit of a pun, isn't it?" The men shared a giggle of realization before Damien playfully slapped his partner's arm so Marcus would continue. "Okay, okay. But seriously, Bernie. One-hundred-percent fantastic. *I* am going to... just a second." The man pulled a shiny silver card case from the front pocket of his slacks, opened it with a self-conscious smile, and slid out the top card before handing it right to Bernadette. "There. Now you have my card. So. If you end up looking for some other way you can use that gorgeously brilliant storytelling of yours, even if you're just curious, okay, my number's on there. You give me a call, and I will hook you up with some of my contacts who would pay you *whatever* you asked just to show them a good time. Like what you just showed us, okay?"

"Good God, don't say it like that." Damien linked his arm through Marcus' and shot Bernadette an apologetic smile. "That makes you sound like a pimp."

"What? I'm not a pimp."

"*I* know that."

Marcus turned back toward the newest couple among Donna's guests and shook his head. "I am *not* a pimp."

"He's really not a pimp."

Bernadette took Marcus' card and couldn't keep the smile off her face. "Never even crossed my mind."

Darrell buried his face in the plastic cup of whiskey.

"Oh, good. Because I'm not." Marcus lifted both hands in surrender and let out a nervous laugh. "I definitely don't want you to think that's what this is. My God, that would be awful, wouldn't it?"

"We need to get you a *drink*." With an exaggerated smile and nod, Damien tugged his partner toward the entrance to the living room. "But really, Bernie. That was terrific. We love it that you both made it out here this weekend."

"Love it," Marcus whispered, only half-fighting against Damien's growing insistence. "Just think about it, okay? Give me a call. We'll have a little chat. I'll tell you all about it. Do you want a drink? Can I get you a little something?"

Damien rolled his eyes and dropped the other man's arm. "I give up."

"I'll grab something in a bit," Bernadette said through her restrained laughter, flipping the business card over and over in her hand. "But thank you. Y'all go ahead."

"Right." Grinning, Marcus turned back toward his partner and let out a sigh that was probably meant to be a little more private than it actually was. "Oh… she says *y'all*."

"She says—of course she says y'all. We're in the *South*, Marcus."

"I'm in love. I *love* her."

"I'm pouring you a double, okay? And you better drink all of it, or I'm gonna end up having to pull you out into the…"

Their voices faded away beneath all the other conversations receding from the living room toward somewhere else in the house like the surf at low tide.

With a deep breath, Bernadette lifted her arm to wrap it around Darrell's shoulders and had to dip her chin almost all the way down to her chest to look him in the eye. "What are *you* thinking about this whole thing?"

He slowly shook his head, staring at the cleared coffee table in the center of the room. "You mean other'n all these folks trippin' all up and down themselves?"

Well, that was one way to put it. Bernadette certainly hadn't expected to get such a wide range of reactions after her *story*. Really, without having planned to share her own words here, she hadn't expected any reaction at all, let alone the simmering volatility beneath Donna's energetic charisma or what was basically a job offer from a man who had to say at least three times that he wasn't a pimp.

"Yeah, honey." She ran her hand up the side of his neck and trailed a finger along his hairline. "Other than that."

Darrell cocked his head, then all his well-maintained stoicism—his own personal mask that was far more effective than Donna's attempts to be the exact opposite—shattered. A grin broke through his pursed lips, and he hissed out a laugh. "Shit, B. *I'd* pay to see that exact same thing all over again."

His low, rumbling laughter filled the now-empty living room when she smacked his chest. Then she plucked the red Solo cup—still heavy with nothing but whiskey—from his hand and took a long sip. That made him laugh even more, which in and of itself made the last ten minutes more than worth it. Still, even the whiskey going right to her head before she slipped off his lap didn't completely wipe out the feeling that she'd just opened a huge can of worms tonight.

She just didn't know exactly what those worms looked like or if she'd find them somewhere she least expected.

18

I DON'T KNOW how you do it, Bernie. I mean, like we all saw that night, you have a kind of power in your words that goes so much further than what most of us can do. So much deeper. And then you end up writing a whole different kind of words in your last letter that makes you so dangerously easy to love.

Thank you. I'm not gonna talk about it anymore, I promise. That's just one tiny part of why we've been doing this for so long. Writing these letters. But I have to just tell you it was a huge weight off my shoulders to hear you say I don't have anything to worry about. That that night didn't change anything. I didn't even realize how worried I was about that until you gave me every reason to stop worrying. And holy shit, I feel so much better. You didn't have to say everything you did, but I'm really, really grateful.

And yeah, even after I wrote you last, Donna's been acting like everything's just another day in the life around here. Maybe she really doesn't care, and if that's true, then I'm the only one who thought there was something else going on that night. Call me crazy, right? Sometimes she does. She calls me crazy. But I know she doesn't always mean everything she says. That would be impossible. Or if it's not, maybe I actually am *crazy for sticking around.*

Get this, though. Right after I sent you that last letter, she's been hounding me about you. Not in a bad way, just really *all over me about getting you to come back out here. It started with just a few little random things, you know? Like what you've been up to, if you had any plans for whenever, if I'd talked to you at all about coming back up and putting your words to use. I honestly thought for a while she was just trying to get back at me. You know, that she'd spun things around somehow and blamed me for the whole thing because I didn't* tell *her what your stories do to people. Yeah, I know. It's a ridiculous thing to think, but it wouldn't be the first time she's pulled something like that. The woman gets excited and intense, and sometimes I think she doesn't even hear what she's saying. Like it just comes out, and she's got some kind of amnesia about it. Anyway, that's not the point.*

She finally just came out and asked me straight up if I thought you'd come meet us and her crew here for this thing she's got planned. Seriously, Bernie, she's calling them "missions" now, and I still can't tell if it's supposed to be a joke or if she really thinks everyone's banding together, uniting for the cause or some shit, and we're gonna storm in, guns, blazing, and... what? Spray some graffiti on a few buildings? Go fight crime? It's not exactly like we have anything to actually fight *at this point. Not yet. I can't shake this feeling that all Donna really wants is to start a fight, just to see if she can win. Because she always wins. Now she wants to go bigger. Messier, maybe.*

She just wouldn't let up on asking about you. Bernie this, and Bernie that. I finally had to ask her what the hell she wanted you up here so badly for, and you know what she told me? You'll die when you hear this. I can't believe I'm actually writing it all down. She said, "A woman like that can get to anyone. *We need to blackmail someone powerful like a rich guy or a senator or anyone with enough leverage to be useful for what we're trying to accomplish? Bernie's our girl. You don't even have to find out what these old fat dudes sitting up in their towers are actually* into, *right? What gets 'em off. Doesn't matter with her. She'll get to anyone we need."*

And I'm over here like what the actual fuck? She thinks she's some kinda lesbian James Bond or something, and I have absolutely no idea what kinda "mission" she's trying to plan. She keeps telling me it's important. That I need to ask you and see if you're on board or not, but I can't get her to tell me a goddamn thing about the rest of it.

I can't lie to the woman, Bernie. Now that you've met her, you have to know how hard that is for me. Donna sees right through everything. So, just to get her off my back, I'm sitting down to ask you if you wanna take another little trip back to Alabama to come talk to her about ... hell, whatever it is. I have no idea. Not sure if there's anything in it for you other than "knowing it's the right thing and standing up for the cause with our own people". Literally, that's how Donna says it. It's 1987, Bernie. What lunatic goes around saying stuff like this? Or am I just blowing this way out of proportion? Honestly, I can't even tell anymore, and you're the only person I know I can ask and not have to worry about you going back to Donna to tell her everything we talked about. There's been a lot of that going around, lately.

And hey, if you don't think you're that into running around with Donna's "movement" and being called to go seduce a senator or some other dumbshit idea, maybe you could still come down to see us, huh? It was so great to have you here last time, and I wish we'd had more time to hang out together. Things aren't that ... busy here, normally. I mean in our house. Donna's always busy doing something and acting like the whole world's gonna implode if she doesn't get it figured out right now. It's not a problem if you don't wanna be a part of that. Trust me, I get it. But at least if you came back to see us for a little while, you could tell Donna no thank you to her face, and then you and I could sit down and actually talk to each other for longer than ten minutes. If you wanted. That's what I was hoping we'd be able to do when you and D came down the last time, but there was way too much going on then.

There's no pressure or anything. Of course there's not (and Donna would just say I'm full of it and need to grow a spine if I'm trying to ask for something I want). But I'd really like to see you again. Get to hang out a little more like we still haven't gotten to do. And yeah, Donna might actually loosen up a little if she heard it straight from you one way or the other. So, just let me know. Either way, you're always welcome here, whenever you want, for any reason.

—Janet

P.S. I heard a little rumor that Woodson Blues might actually be making it to Alabama this year. Is that for real? That would be sick. Send my love to D too, okay?

19

OUTSIDE THE FRONT door of Mr. B's, Darrell stuck his hands into the pockets of his jeans and nodded down the sidewalk on Line Street. "Let's walk."

This was how he wanted to start their conversation, after all this time. Bernadette's short, dry chuckle felt as humorless as her own displacement. "Right down memory lane, huh?"

"For you, maybe." His shoulders inched slowly up around his neck before dropping with the same languid, undecided speed. "I'm still here."

"I know." Her ankles were swollen now from so much standing. She should've been used to the standing, the walking, the half-assed running, when she had to push herself, and that still happened from time to time, even living out of a van with six other people. "I'm glad you are."

Darrell shot her a sidelong glance. "Uh-huh. Makes me pretty damn easy to find, don't it?"

She couldn't even begin to guess whether the bitterness in his voice, just slightly lower and a little raspier than she remembered it, was aimed at her or the fact that he'd made the choice to stay. The man couldn't blame either of them for seizing their own free will, no matter how much they'd torn each other apart. "Did you *want* it to be hard?"

"Naw, come on." Shaking his head, he glanced up at the yellow streetlight up ahead and the glinting silhouettes of dull, faded cars lining the street. "I got nothin' against where I am. Just don't seem like you can say the same."

A sharp laugh escaped her—much sharper than she'd expected. Maybe not as sharp as she'd intended. "I can't even begin to guess what that's supposed to mean."

She could, though. She just didn't want to. There wasn't any rule against standing by one's decisions, knowing they were right, and regretting them at the same time. Nothing was that simple, and he knew it.

With his head bent low, Darrell turned the corner onto President, his long legs lifting his feet just enough that any-one watching would have expected to hear the soles of those brown work boots scuffing against the concrete. They never did. Once they rounded the corner, the man let out a long sigh and stopped. He looked down the street at the rows of crowded, narrow houses, those that had once looked on the verge of collapse now having been lifted, reshaped, re-formed. And right there beside them in comparison, the nic-est houses here thirty years ago now looked as if they'd been abandoned completely. Anyone who knew the street and the houses and the people in them also knew abandoned was the wrong word. Those houses weren't empty, and they weren't broken. Just old. Untended. The lowest item on an over-whelmingly long list of priorities and minor irritations.

One hand lifted from his pocket and moved slowly up toward his lips. He rubbed them back and forth a few times, and the old, self-conscious gesture made it almost too hard to breathe. Bernadette just stood there, immediately dropped right back into their old pattern of his intense thinking and her willingness to wait until he was ready. It wasn't like she had anywhere to be, at least for the next few hours. Not un-less someone called her cell phone and told her to get her ass back down to that cabin, she was needed.

"I ain't gonna pretend I know what things are like for you, B. One time of tryin' it was enough to convince me it just ain't possible." Darrell stared at the massive crack in the sidewalk a foot away from his shoe. Was that hand at his lips starting to tremble? "What I meant was are *you* glad to be here? To be back for however long—"

"Darrell, I'm not *back*."

"Sure, I know. I know." Dark fingers, just a little more twisted than she remembered, moved from his mouth to his far-more-than-receding hairline and what was left of that hair, now all but completely gray. "Call it passin' through, then. Like you said. Are you glad about it even a little?"

Bernadette's nose burned just before a new wave of tears stung her eyes, but she blinked them back and reached into the pocket of her cardigan. Amazing she could even wear a cardigan now, on a summer night, without breaking a sweat. Or maybe it was just the conversation keeping her cold.

"Honestly, honey, I don't even know how to answer that." She pulled her cigarettes and a lighter from the pocket, slipped one out to light it before everything else went back into the cardigan.

"See, I think you do." Darrell watched her with his head tilted a little, not reacting at all to the first puff of smoke as she lit the cigarette or the thin stream of it rising from the cherry-red tip and disappearing into the night sky. "I know you still *feel* things, B. I know you still got so much inside you, and I'm willin' to bet that's what's killin' you right now."

Her gaze flicked back up to settle on his dark eyes beneath a brow wrinkled with concern. Just like that, the threat of tears was gone. For now. "What do you want me to say?" One more drag, one more exhale that felt shaky but didn't make a sound as it wafted up into the muggy heat. "Any kind of answer I give you is just gonna be the wrong thing to put into words, no matter what it is. Darrell, I can't fix any of it. And I'd be stupid to think I can."

"I know." That sad, pitying smile was worse than if he'd told her to fuck off and never try to find him again. "Just thought you might like to get all that off your chest. I see it pressin' down on you."

She huffed out a humorless laugh and took another drag. "You always could."

"Mm-hmm." He nodded slowly and finally released her from the heavy burden of his full attention. Turning more directly down the sidewalk, he started walking again.

Even with how easy it was to match his slow, leisurely pace, Bernadette still felt rushed. Pressured. Scrambling for something she couldn't name but knew wasn't there in the first place. So she shoved the frightened animal back down into its hole with an overly experienced hand and told it to stay.

"Tell me what's going on at Mr. B's." Her head turned toward him, but she couldn't look up from the crooked, fractured sidewalk that had seen fewer repairs than most of the houses around them.

"Not just there. It's everywhere." Darrell cleared his throat. "Whole damn city. Probably everywhere else, too. Don't know how much actually starts down here these days. If it ever did."

She had to ignore that. Otherwise, it would send her to her knees on the cement glittering under the streetlights. What a self-centered thought, that he could have possibly been talking about her, them, their life. But she was always making the connection between things that really had no business being drawn together like this, wasn't she? Everywhere she went, every piece of her followed.

"Please, Darrell." Another drag made her throat burn a little more and the supplication sting a little less. "Just lay it out for me. Maybe you're not too old to talk circles around me or anyone else, but I'm too old to try keepin' up."

"Naw, you're keepin' up just fine. I'm the one trippin' all over myself."

That sort of confession was new. People said wisdom came with age. Experience, knowledge, understanding all came with age. Bernadette felt like a child trying to piece together the broken bits of conversation as they launched out of the grownups' mouths and right over her head.

"You don't trip."

"Well, my balance ain't what it used to be, either." It brought silent, strained chuckles from them both. A tiny dog barked through an open window down the street, even after the two cars driving way too fast had disappeared from view. "I'm guessin' you've watched the news at least once in the last year."

"At least, sure."

"All that shit floatin' around about your kinda folks out there."

Bernadette sighed. "TV. Radio. We saw a flyer pinned up at a gas station on our way through Mississippi."

He coughed. "You got more of your people with you?"

"Not surprising, is it?" Bernadette caught his shrug from the corner of her eye. "There aren't a lot of people I can be around these days if they're not *my kinda folks.*"

"Sure. Yeah, I get that. Makes it safer, some ways. Might make it harder to keep goin', some ways, too."

"Because my people are all over the news?"

Darrell's head dipped in hesitant agreement. "All over the country too, ain't they? And the whole damn country's finally payin' attention."

"Well, that kinda thing was bound to happen." Bernadette lifted the cigarette to her lips again and paused to watch a young mother drag her two buoyant, bouncing kids behind her from the car to the front door of their home. If Darrell had seen it too—and how could he not?—he didn't seem to have a reaction. Then again, why would he? He'd said it himself; he was still here. She lowered the cigarette again without another drag and kept walking. "I guess it just took longer than any of us thought before *my kinda folks* got any widespread recognition."

"Naw, see... see that's where you're missin' the whole point." Darrell's voice—the voice that never rose above normal speaking volume, no matter the conversation; the voice that could soothe or rebuke with the exact same intensity behind each—was just loud enough to bounce back at them from the wooden fence lining the yard of one of the nicer houses on the street. Bernadette shot him a quick glance, and the man sniffed. When he spoke again, the composure and calculated lucidity had fully returned, as if he'd never spoken that last sentence aloud. "I don't think you understand what's happening 'round here. Maybe in other parts too, but I can't speak for anywhere else. It ain't recognition spreadin'. It's fear, girl. Hate. Rage. You hear what I'm sayin'?"

She finally took that drag she'd missed in lieu of watching the doubled echo of her past pulling children indoors after a late night out. And it was long. So long, she expected to cough out the hot, searing smoke and then cough some more after that. That might have even been better than the crackle of the cherry tip and the soft, whispering steps as they moved through the neighborhood. She heard him all right, and somewhere in the back of her mind, she'd already known the truth of it when she felt so many eyes on her inside Mr. B's. Hearing it from this man's mouth cracked open

KATHRIN HUTSON

the seal of her own denial and let loose all the other certain-
ties she'd forced into a box much too small to keep them
there for long.

"Bernadette."

A little hum of regret and heartache seeped out of her.
Maybe three times she'd heard her full name from Darrell's
lips, and each of those times was sewn to a day and a place
she would've given what remained of her sanity to forget. "I
heard you. I hear you."

"Sounds to me like you ain't listenin', though. Now,
just the other day, I walked past the Harris Teeter and heard
two white men talkin' to each other with some real venom
on their tongues. White men who'd just as soon pretend they
didn't see me steppin' past to walk inside and buy my own
damn groceries. You know what they were sayin'?"

There was literally no way to guess at this point, but she
knew Darrell didn't want a guess. Now that he'd started this,
he wanted to be heard out all the way to the end. She tilted
her head in a small gesture of interest, and that was enough.

"They were talkin' 'bout stringin' folks up as a lesson.
Goddamn 2031, B, and they were talkin' that shit like they
took a goddamn time machine and slipped back into the city
when my daddy was runnin' 'round naked in the front yard.
And sure, I got angry. Sure, I can't stand hearing that kinda
hate come from anybody's mouth, and I damn near let it eat
me up 'cause I thought they were talkin' 'bout me. Can you
guess what they did after that?"

"Go on and tell me, then." She didn't bring the cigarette
to her lips again, didn't want to run the risk of dropping that
smoke onto the sidewalk, didn't want him to see how much

her fingers trembled now as she tried to hold them steady at her side.

"Now." Darrell stopped and gently grabbed her shoulders, forcing her to look up at him because she would have felt ridiculous staring at his black t-shirt. "They didn't ignore me. These folks were lookin' for someone, anyone, and I just about had a heart attack right there when one of them came joggin' up behind me. 'Excuse me, sir. Excuse me. Just a moment of your time, please.' That's what he said to *me*. Like I was some buttoned-up suit with a lot better things to do with my time. He asked me if I'd heard of these *beaters*. Said it like I've heard too many other violent words said to my face or otherwise. Said these *beaters* can't be trusted. Can't be allowed to come on into our city, our home, tearin' things up from the inside when they got this special *ability* the rest of us just ain't got. You say you saw a flyer tacked up on some gas station, B. I was *handed* one of them goddamn flyers by a white man who didn't see the color of my face. He saw another man who might hate someone else just as much as he did and pass it off as self-preservation. Or patriotism or courage and some fucked-up sense of duty. I don't know what kinda shit he was thinkin'. And I…"

Darrell's throat clicked when he swallowed again, this time dry and heavy and cutting off everything he had left to say. Bernadette just waited, her cigarette forgotten but still dangling at her side between her fingers.

"Christ, B, I wasn't even mad after that. All that anger just washed right outta me, and I… I was just plain scared. Terrified deep in my bones like nothin' I ever felt." A heavy sigh escaped him, and he searched her gaze for something neither one of them could name.

"Nothin' wrong with bein' scared, Darrell."

"Naw, I know. I don't give a damn about feelin' it, but—aw." His hands slipped off her shoulders and slapped back down against his dark jeans. "But what I did… God help me, B. What I—" The closest thing to a sob she'd ever heard burst from between his lips, and he took a quick step back. As if Bernadette had drawn a gun on him or held up a mirror to everything he so clearly wanted to hide but so desperately needed to tell her. When his lower lip trembled and he raised his hand to his mouth, barely covering it with shaking fingers, she knew something more had broken inside him than he would ever find the courage to tell her. "All that fear, and I just smiled and said, 'Yessir,' and I… I *took* that goddamn flyer from him—"

Another shuddering breath ripped through Darrell's lungs, another sob of self-loathing and a pain so deep, Bernadette couldn't reach down far enough to touch it. So when he drew his hand down his mouth, over his chin, and let it drop, she reached out and touched that instead. Gave his fingers a little squeeze.

Finally, he somehow managed to look her in the eye again. "So much of myself, B. I just tossed it away 'cause I was afraid. And you know, part of me was relieved, too. That I ain't… that I ain't one of y'all. That I ain't got headin' toward me what you got chasin' after you. I can tell you this. I know it don't change a thing, but how am I supposed to look at our—"

He'd almost said it. They glanced away from each other, neither one of them all that interested in drawing more pain from the never-ending wellspring they'd built of it. Bernadette rubbed his arm a few times as Darrell collected himself with a long, slow breath into lungs strengthened by a decades-long career spent using them.

"Now, she's a grown woman," he added. "I know that. She don't need protectin', neither, but how's it gonna be for her in a place like this? It's like we gave her the best of our own damn selves and the worst of both worlds. I can't look at her straight and tell her what I did."

"No. There's no need for that. Doesn't make you better or worse for telling her, either. So I'd say just let it go."

"Right." Darrell sniffed and shoved his hands back into his pockets, nodding slowly. "Right. She don't need that from me."

Pressing her lips together, Bernadette shook her head too, mirroring him in that if not in any other way.

"You hear what I'm tryin' to tell you, huh?" His brows drew together tightly enough to deepen his eyes, to bring all the lines of so many years folding in around them, enclosing them in memory and doubt and an urgent plea that made Bernadette want to turn away.

Now, she thought. Now he looked as old as she felt.

"It's not safe for you down here, B. Not where folks know you. What you can do. Reasons that took you away for so long." Darrell rocked back and forth a little on his heels, grimacing now as he stared down the street again. "Strange times, and I can't see nothin' turnin' out good. Especially not for a woman who refuses to keep her damn head down, no matter what comes after."

She closed her eyes and shook her head a little. He had no idea. "Let me tell you something, honey. I've seen things you wouldn't believe when it comes to my kinda people. Things that would just keep twisting you up inside. A little bit of fear down here? Yeah, it's scary. It's hateful. We've both seen what that can do to somebody."

"Uh-huh."

"You know what's worse?" Dipping her head, she looked up at him from beneath her darkening brow and just went for it. He needed to hear it, and she needed to tell someone who hadn't been through the whole goddamn ringer right there with her. "There are people out there who do the same hateful, Godawful things to people like me. But what they do isn't done out of fear or hatred, Darrell. They're doing it because they can. Because we exist, and now they've made a goddamn law that says they can lock us up just for being who we are. It's just about as good as making it illegal for us to exist at all. I know you understand that."

Darrell hissed out a sigh and shuffled around the sidewalk a little, like he wanted to walk right back down the way they'd come and forget her altogether but was tethered to this section of cement by an invisible leash.

"No, look at me." She stepped in front of him and pointed to the space just between her temple and her eyebrow. "You see this? Two men broke into my house seven, eight months ago. Tried to take me with them, is my guess. Just took a piece of my forehead instead, and then I got behind the wheel and drove my Jeep into a ditch."

"Aw, come on, now. You ain't gotta tell me all about that business."

"I do. You need to hear it, and I need to tell it. That was just a warning. For me, for all of us. The people who did that to me are fucking powerful, Darrell. And it turns out they… they made some of us even more powerful than them. I don't know everything about what they're doing. What they want. I have some friends who might. But I'll tell you this much. Handing out flyers—hell, even *taking* flyers—doesn't even scratch the surface of what's coming. I've spent the last twenty years keeping as many of *my kinda people* safe from that growing storm as I could. I'm not stopping now." Bernadette's hand lifted all on its own, brought the filter of her cigarette up to her lips before she even realized the thing had gone out. "Damnit."

She jammed her hand into the pocket of her cardigan, brought the lighter to her cupped palm, and couldn't for the life of her get the damn thing to light again.

"Hold up." Darrell produced a lighter from his own pocket and waited for her to lower her hand before his flame ignited at the burnt tip of her cigarette.

Bernadette stared at his hand with wide eyes, sucking the filter again on autopilot despite the cold knife plunging through her chest. "Jesus."

Yanking the cigarette out of her mouth, she exhaled and turned away from Darrell. Darrell, who was different in so many ways than the man who'd been lighting her cigarettes for her like that for so many years. Until the bastard who'd killed Karl's wife killed Karl too in an alley across the street from Sleepwater's cheap motel that night. No wonder she and Karl had gotten along so well. No wonder they'd recognized each other the first time they met. He was so much like Darrell too, and she hadn't seen it until the flesh-and-blood ghost of her past had lit her cigarette like no one had in the last seven months. Tiny details. Just one more piece of her heart sliced away and tossed aside to wither.

"You all right?" Darrell seemed to have come back to himself, either because of her own sudden upheaval or in spite of it.

"I'm fine. You just..." Bernadette took a real drag this time and let all the smoke back out before she turned to face him again. "You just reminded me of someone the way you pulled out that lighter."

"*I* reminded you of someone *else*." His disbelieving chuckle sounded so out of place as he scratched his cheek— a dry rasp of calloused fingers over day-old stubble. "That's a new one, I tell you what."

"Yeah, well, must just be one of those nights. Full of surprises."

"Man..." Darrell shook his head, smirking at the broken sidewalk and scuffing his shoe back and forth against the concrete. "Anyone I know?"

Bernadette snorted. "I seriously doubt it. The two of y'all would've gotten along just fine, though."

"Who is he?"

She blinked and found that now she'd taken on the role of staring off down the street at nothing, searching for what she couldn't name and would never find here or anywhere else. Who was Karl? The man who'd put his life and his pride on the line to bring Sleepwater together, the way they'd been for far too short a time before things crumbled beneath them. "You know, if I'd ever had a son, he might've been it."

"Might've."

A sharp breath filled her lungs, and she forced herself into a bitter smile five sizes too small for all the grief it was meant to hide. "He died."

She couldn't very well use a euphemism for that. Not with Darrell. For them, to say *gone* or *never coming back* meant something else entirely. Bernadette had cemented those definitions in both their minds a long time ago. Never say never, though, right? Here she was.

"Oh... I'm sorry."

"Thank you." Shitty words for a shittier topic. She shook herself out of the last few minutes and cleared her throat. "I wouldn't mind being walked back to my car now."

He looked genuinely surprised at that. Because of course he expected her to dive deeper and ask more. To try gleaning something from a silence left unbroken for too long not to make it heavier than anything else. But Bernadette was tired, and it felt like the door to that opportunity had just been slammed shut in her face.

"Sure, B. Yeah, I gotta head back that way anyway." They turned together on President Street and headed over the sidewalk they'd already traveled before stopping in that little bubble of mutual confession.

The conversation died too until they turned the corner onto Line again.

"Just tell me." She took a deep breath and turned her head toward him without looking. "How is she?"

"Still can't say her name, can you?"

Taking another drag, Bernadette cocked her head and wasn't willing to answer that question, either. She didn't owe him an answer anyway. Then again, neither did he.

"She's doin' fine. Smart. Real smart." Darrell chuckled. "Strong. Knows how to stand up for herself. You taught her that much."

"And you taught her how to not run away."

He glanced at her, then quickly looked away, like he'd had to make sure she was still there and was only disappointed to find the truth of it. "Don't say it like that."

"I'm serious. It's a *good* thing. Roots. Home. Head down and pushin' through in the same place for as long as it takes."

The only response she got was Darrell tipping his head back to stare up at the clear, cloudless night. Only a few stars were bright enough to shine through the haze of light blooming from the streetlamps and restaurants and cars of the oddly crowded city Charleston had become.

"Just like you said, honey. The best of ourselves."

"Hmm." They slowed on the sidewalk until he left the emptiness of the sky and scanned the other side of the street. "Where'd you park?"

"Over on Bee Street."

"All right, then." And he walked her all the way.

When she stopped at the driver-side door of the white van, Darrell didn't quite manage to hide his amusement. "You drivin' around in this piece?"

"Hundred thousand miles and still purrin'."

"Sure, like a fat lion."

Bernadette rolled her eyes and unlocked the door, swallowing her laughter back down. If she started laughing with him too much now, she'd start crying, too. She reached for the door's handle and froze beneath the pressure of his hand on the small of her back. Funny, that term. Nothing about her felt small these days. Except maybe her conviction in that moment.

"I got it." Darrell grabbed the handle instead and opened the door for her, and it seemed for a moment that he'd just stand there, fingers curled around the open door, and never take his hand off her back.

So she turned around to face him and didn't leave either of them with a choice. "Can I have her number?"

His head dropped toward his chest—in defeat, in surprise, in whatever else made him unable to keep looking at her. "I don't know…"

"I get it, Darrell. I do. I gave up the right to ask, but I'm asking anyway."

"Damn." He let out another heavy sigh. "You know, I spent too much time askin' myself how I'd answer that question. Couldn't for the life of me settle on one way or the other. Didn't think we'd actually be standin' here like…" His dark hand swept across the space between them before lifting to scratch his cheek again. "I couldn't even tell you no in my own head."

Bernadette leaned back against the side of the van while the man who could never tell her no pulled his phone from his pocket and poked at it for a few seconds, squinting at the screen lighting up the parking lot. Her own phone came out of her cardigan's other pocket, and she waited.

"You ready?"

"Of course I am."

Darrell shot her a quick, halfway-interested glance, then narrowed his eyes even more. She couldn't tell him how much time she'd spent wondering about this moment, too. That it hadn't seemed remotely possible until the last few months had forced her and her other family—not of blood or commitment or her own body but bound to her just the same—to seek somewhere else they could put up their feet. Just for a little while. All the meaning and memory seeping out of that place be damned.

A flutter of terrified hope made her dizzy when he read out loud the number on his phone. But she typed it into her own, maybe just a little slower than the sound of the numbers left Darrell's lips. When he finished, he waited patiently for her to add the name she hadn't spoken in so long before last night, as she foolishly told a woman about to have her first child that Bernadette hadn't spoken to her own daughter in twenty years. Olivia. The name looked painfully foreign on the tiny screen of her cell phone, but it was there, at least. It was something.

She swayed on her feet and sidled toward the open driver-side door. "I need to sit down."

"All right." Darrell closed in on her as she lifted herself up into the driver's seat.

Bernadette sighed at the sudden and still painful relief of getting off her feet after at least two hours of being on them. She tossed her cell phone into the passenger seat and gave herself a few more seconds just to breathe.

"You gonna be okay?"

"Oh, sure." Blinking heavily, she looked up at the man standing so close to the side of her seat and smiled warmly. After all this time, they still understood each other, and neither one of them could pretend they didn't care. "Aren't I always?"

"I mean to drive." Darrell raised an eyebrow and dipped his head. "You talkin' all that nonsense 'bout head wounds and drivin' into ditches has me a little worried 'bout you, B."

She waved him off. "I didn't say all that to worry you. I'll be fine."

"Uh-huh." He gripped the doorframe and leaned a little closer, studying her face. "It's all worth worryin' 'bout a little. Even you, girl. 'Specially."

What was he trying to do, saying something like that? At least she'd already gotten off her feet before the next crushing wave of loving regret and an overly simplistic uselessness pushed her down even farther into the upholstery. "Would it make you feel better if I said I don't worry about you at all?"

A secret smile of understanding passed between them, and Darrell dropped his head again with a sigh. "Naw. Not really."

Bernadette didn't see it coming when he leaned inside the car just enough to press his lips against her temple. She wasn't prepared for that kind of gesture from him, not today, not ever again, and maybe she leaned into it a little because it was so agonizingly familiar and crucial that she knew it was real. That she could let herself believe this whole day had been real. None of it felt like her life, and here was her life coming right back at her like a soft, warm hand brushing her awake.

Then Darrell stepped back, nodded slowly, sniffed because he didn't have more to say than, "Go on, now."

She stared at him from the driver's seat of the van, across empty air as he stepped back, through the pollen-dusted window as he shut the door, across space and time again as he lifted a hand in farewell and walked back across the street. By the time he'd disappeared, she might as well have been dreaming all over again. The last few hours might not have happened at all but within the fading memories she could have hoped to cover with the reality of the present.

The only proof she had was saved in her phone on the passenger seat. And Bernadette hoped the strength she'd carried with her through all these years would be enough to use it.

20

THE SECOND TIME Bernadette and Darrell decided to make the drive back to Alabama, they were greeted by a lot fewer people and far less tension. Which was quite honestly a relief. Bernadette didn't want to keep making these trips only to find herself at the center of the kind of attention Donna's friends liked to give. She was, of course, still close to the center of Donna's attention, once more inside the house the woman shared with Janet. But this time felt a lot more casual, with far less to prove and enough time behind them for all parties to have loosened up a little.

At least, that was the vibe Donna had been giving off for the last two hours at her long kitchen table, all six chairs filled with people now—Donna and Janet, Bernadette and Darrell, Marcus and Damien.

Someone had had the bright idea to order Chinese take-out to eat in the privacy of their host's home instead of all going out to a restaurant. That made the dinner cheaper over-all too, especially because the bottles of wine had therefore been bought at liquor-store prices instead of paying the same amount to be served by the glass.

And Bernadette had now had four of those glasses. She thought. The Kung Pao Chicken and Mu-Shu Pork had been reduced to smears of sauce on plates and a few straggling noodles. The wine was still flowing. It seemed endless, re-ally.

"You're empty, Bernie." Donna pointed at her wine-glass, then waved down the table at Marcus until he passed her the closest open bottle. "Yeah, I had a feeling you like breaking the rules. Can't let this one fly, though. No empty drinks."

The woman poured another massive glass of wine, and Bernadette just stared at it, feeling chased—or drunk—into a corner by so much insistent hospitality. "I don't think I can drink any more."

"I don't care if you *drink* it." Grinning, Donna finished pouring and refilled her own glass first before emptying the rest of the bottle into Janet's beside her. "The rule is no empty glasses. You do whatever you want with the wine."

Swimming through the haze of alcohol—not unpleasant but definitely thicker than she'd been expecting coming into this meal—Bernadette reached for the glass and muttered, "Yeah, but if it's in front of me, I'm gonna drink it."

Darrell chuckled, tried unsuccessfully to squash it down when she shot him a warning glance, and the rest of the table burst into laughter.

"I think you only have yourself to blame for that," Damien said, leaning forward over the table to shoot her an incredibly fake grimace of apology.

"Well, you know what? I wasn't actually trying to blame anyone for anything." Bernadette lifted her glass for another sip and nearly knocked the whole thing over again when she set the base down on the end of a chopstick. Darrell caught it for her and slid the chopstick out of the way without a word.

"Of course not." Marcus laughed. "Not explicitly. That's obvious."

"Not int—implicitly, either." Bernadette rolled her eyes at the man and shook her head. "So y'all just leave me alone and let a woman drink her wine."

Through another round of laughter, Janet looked up across the table at Bernadette and shrugged. "Or not."

"Ha!" Donna ran a hand over her partner's thigh and gave it a little squeeze. "Or not. See? I'm not tryin' to make anybody do anything. But rules"—she pointed at Bernadette again, then at Darrell, almost as an afterthought—"are rules. And y'all are in *my* house."

Janet lifted her own refilled glass to her lips and took an abnormally long drink that caught everyone's attention.

Laughing again, Donna patted Janet's thigh and shook her head. "Our house. *Our* house." She leaned toward her partner, kissed Janet's cheek, and muttered, "You know what I meant."

Though she didn't say anything, Janet's smile wasn't completely invisible above the rim of her wineglass.

"Okay, so we've been dying to know." Damien stuck his elbow on the table and tossed a finger back and forth between Bernadette and Janet. "How in the world did you two meet?"

"Huh." Janet propped her chin in her hand and stared at the ceiling. "First time anyone's ever asked me that."

"Oh." Bernadette swallowed another sip of the wine she couldn't *not* drink and paid very careful attention to where she set the glass down this time. "It was a... just one of those school projects, wasn't it?"

Marcus' eyes widened. "Oh, so you're from Alabama, then? Originally?"

It had to have been way more than four glasses of wine; Bernadette couldn't settle her spinning head enough to sift through that odd question and recognize what he meant by it. "No..." She sat back in her chair with a little frown. "I was born and raised in South Carolina. Never left."

"Huh." Damien frowned at his partner, and whatever silent conversation was happening around the table, Bernadette couldn't even try to follow it. They could talk circles around themselves all night. She wouldn't be sitting in this chair much longer anyway. Not feeling the way she felt now.

"So what was it, then? Like some kind of... out-of-state project, or..." The man shook his head and waited for someone to fill in the blanks. He might have even looked at Darrell for an answer, but Darrell sat back in his chair with folded arms and heavy eyelids. Get enough booze in the man, and all he did was sit there like that, smirking constantly, until something worth his much duller attention pulled him out of it. Marcus' questioning gaze definitely wasn't one of those things.

"Somethin' like that, yeah." Bernadette meant to put her hand on Darrell's shoulder but only managed to smack his arm instead. "Didn't I tell you where... how that whole..."

Damn, she couldn't even fake her way into sounding coherent.

"Just a pen-pal project," Janet added quickly. She didn't sound nearly as drunk as Bernadette, though it wasn't too far out of the question that Janet had been drinking a lot more than Bernadette recently. Maybe even for a good reason. And who could fucking tell anymore, right?

"Pen pal." Marcus glanced at both women again, let out an unsure little laugh, then blinked rapidly and set his chin against the back of his hand this time. "Well that's cute."

"One of the dumbest homework assignments I ever had." Bernadette snorted, and the laughter spread across the table. "Some shit about the importance of meeting people outside our *comfort zone*, wasn't it?"

Janet shrugged. "Something like that."

"Out of your comfort zone, huh?" Donna flicked around the broken pieces of her fortune cookie, then tossed one into her mouth. "They really failed y'all on that. Two white girls living in Southern states, writin' to each other out of their comfort zones."

Darrell barked out a laugh and finished the rest of it in a much quieter, hissing breath as he dropped his chin toward his folded arms. Apparently, Donna thought that was pretty funny too.

"I mean, what were y'all supposed to learn from each other that neither of y'all couldn't figure out from lookin' in the mirror?"

Damien let out a little hum of consideration, which was just about as close as most people got to telling Donna she was walking on thin ice. Not that anything she'd just said wasn't true, but she'd left out a few very real differences between her lesbian partner and the woman across the table who'd cut ties with her family to love a man they hated. A man who was, in fact, the only person sitting at this table without the type of magical storytelling everyone else here possessed.

"Yeah, I don't think that was the point, though," Marcus added, jumping on the carpet his partner had laid out to stop this train before it wrecked their entire dinner. "I had something like that too in high school. Right?" He turned back toward Damien for backup.

"Oh, yeah. I definitely remember having to do something like that. And the dry, awkward, *boring* responses I got from some kid in Ohio. Who lives in *Ohio*?"

"Dry, awkward, boring people." Marcus tried to hold back a laugh, and then they were cracking up together as Damien tried to finish his point.

"Right? Well that's what—" He broke again into a laugh of disbelief. "That's what I'm saying. And we had to write a letter a week to our *pen pal* for the whole semester. It was awful."

"I think that happened with most people." Janet took another sip of her wine and lifted her shoulder, dismissing every other high school student over the course of whatever that assignment was supposed to do. "But I didn't get a single letter like that from Bernie."

"Oh, yeah?" Donna crunched on more fortune cookie. "She was a real eloquent, hormonal teenager?"

"I don't know about eloquent." Janet snorted and leaned across the table toward Bernadette, her mouth hanging open in mock surprise at her own confession. Bernadette just grinned and rolled her eyes. "Not Shakespeare or anything. Just… funny."

"Funny." Marcus pointed at her. "That's what was always missing, right? Everyone was always too chickenshit to let themselves be funny."

"Funny's good." Damien offered a crooked smile, nodding slowly. "Everyone likes funny."

"Funny." Donna just raised an eyebrow.

"Yeah, like…" Gesturing across the table, Janet apparently wanted to give Bernadette the opportunity to jump in with something to add. Anything. Bernadette could hardly follow the conversation as it was, and her eyes felt way too heavy. So she just sat there and smiled, folding her arms in an unconscious echo of Darrell's posture beside her. "Okay, like I think the first thing Bernie sent me, after that ridiculous introduction letter we had to send first that was basically copied from a piece of paper the teacher passed out— at least at my school—was this whole story about a fishing trip. Right? Bernie's dad took her and her sister down to… I don't know what y'all call the water down there. Was it the ocean?"

Janet laughed at her own ignorance, and Bernadette nodded. "Russell Creek."

"Russell Creek. Okay. She kept sticking worms in her sister's pockets, and her dad thought Candace was just wasting the bait the whole time. 'Cause she was already so awful at fishing anyway."

"Who's Candace?" Donna leaned away from her partner with a raised eyebrow.

"Bernie's sister. The way she told it in that letter, though, I was—"

"You know her sister's name too?"

Janet turned to look at her partner, the smile of fond memories fading from her lips just a little. "Well, yeah. She's—" She let out another laugh, this one much more self-conscious under Donna's scrutiny. "I mean, she didn't *only* write about her sister, but a lot of the time she did. It's not weird when you send letters back and forth with somebody for... what? Ten years, Bernie? Eleven?"

Bernadette widened her eyes and tried to focus on one thing that wouldn't keep spinning away from her gaze. "Eleven, maybe. I don't know. I don't mix math and wine."

Damien and Marcus burst out laughing at the other end of the table, and Darrell unfolded his arms to lay one of them gently over the back of Bernadette's chair. She didn't realize why he'd suddenly changed his posture until she looked up at Donna, grinning, and was met with a surprisingly hostile smirk in return.

"Sorry." She tried to meet Donna's gaze, kept sliding away from it, and finally gave up. "That's just one of *my* rules."

Janet lifted a hand to hide a shocked smile behind it. Marcus and Damien stopped laughing, but just barely. "Anyway, I thought it was a really funny letter when I got it." The wineglass lifting toward Janet's mouth wobbled a little in her hand until she finally steadied it against her lips, gazing intently at Bernadette and very obviously ignoring the overly suspicious woman she called her partner sitting beside her. "And we just never really stopped after that."

"Pretty good deal." Bernadette sighed and dropped her head back against Darrell's arm behind her, just to let him know she knew he was there. "I didn't know I was that funny."

"Huh." Donna picked the pile of fortune-cookie crumbs off the tablecloth and sprinkled them onto her empty plate coated in thick, syrupy sauce. "So now I'm just curious. Which one of y'all stepped out their comfort zone the most with this cute little pen-pal thing?"

"You're still on that?" Janet finally shot her partner an exasperated look. "That's not the point of—"

"Hey, it's the point *I'm* trying to make, okay?" Donna's laughter sounded like it could slip into a growl at any second. "I'm serious, here. I really wanna know, 'cause I just can't figure it out." She lifted her arm and jabbed her finger—as much as she could jab with all the alcohol in her system, which now just fed whatever fire had already been burning behind her flashing grin—back and forth between

Donna and Janet. "Which one of y'all had the most uncomfortable life when you started writing letters to each other like a couple old biddies, huh?"

"Donna…" Janet had turned almost all the way around in her seat now to stare at her partner. "Can we just drop it—"

"What? No. I'm not gonna drop it." Donna's grin widened even farther as her eyes burned into Bernadette's face. "It's a pretty simple fucking question, don't you think? And I don't see why somebody can't just give me a goddamn simple answer."

"Baby, that's not really something we can just decide—"

"Sure it is. I already know what things were like for *you* growing up, and I guess other than you being too much of a pussy to do anything about it until you met me, it really didn't look that bad. So I just wanna hear if Bernie can shed a little light on what kinda *comfort zone* she was supposed to try getting out of, exactly." The words were all venom now, spitting out of Donna's mouth despite how well she kept herself together. At least for how much rage there was burning through her with all the wine.

The dining room fell painfully silent. Janet turned slowly back around in her chair to face the table and rested her hands in her lap, staring at the tablecloth scattered with open, empty takeout boxes. Damien and Marcus sipped their wine. Darrell let out a long sigh through his nose as he eyed Donna carefully, most likely waiting for her next outburst to see whether it required him stepping in. For a second there, it had seemed like someone might have had to step in.

Maybe someone should have, even without the woman taking her tirade to a physical level. But now Donna just slumped sideways in her chair, propping herself up on the armrest, and shot Bernadette an intent, sickeningly sweet smile.

"So how 'bout it, South Carolina. You step out of all your comfort to make a half-assed friend with Janet? Or did you just drag her through the mud out of hers?"

"All right, now." Darrell removed his arm from around Bernadette and leaned forward. The hand he placed on the tablecloth was quiet, subdued, but still balled into a fist.

Bernadette grabbed his forearm and shook her head. He knew it meant she didn't want this to go any further, that it was okay, she could handle someone talking to her like this—someone like Donna who didn't know the first thing about stepping into someone else's shoes if she couldn't get something tangible out of it in return. "I definitely had too much wine."

"Ha." Nodding, Donna ran her tongue along the edge of her teeth and looked about ready to bite a chunk out of something. Or someone. No doubt the woman could rip apart anything, if she had enough will to do it.

Bernadette didn't have enough will to stay in that chair and try to correct anything that was said when she could hardly think. So she pushed her chair back and stood.

"Come on, B—"

Her hand tightened around Darrell's arm, then she released him and bent down to press a quick kiss against the corner of his mouth. "If I don't get into a bed right now, I'll pass out at the table. Nothing about that sounds fun."

"All right." Darrell braced his hands on the armrests. "Lemme help you get—"

"I got it. I'm fine. Y'all just keep talkin' about… whatever. I can't even understand myself right now." Not exactly true, but if Bernadette had a chance of righting the things Donna had so clearly gotten wrong, she'd tossed that chance out when she started tossing back the wine. There was nothing smart about trying to argue with a woman who didn't actually want to understand. The woman across the table with the glistening grin and the fire behind those brown-hazel eyes only wanted to fight, and she was bound to make that happen one way or another. Kind of hard to fight somebody when they were passed out drunk in the guest room.

Darrell eased himself back into her chair, giving her hand a little squeeze when she settled it on his shoulder. That was just to keep herself from falling over as she turned toward the back of the house, but she didn't need to tell *him* that.

"Whoever brought the second, third, whatever bottles of wine, well done. And dinner. Dinner too. That place knows how to food their… cook it… yeah…" Bernadette waved herself off. She couldn't even make a goddamn coherent sentence anymore, which was her cue to get the hell out. "'Night, y'all."

"Good night, Bernie." Marcus and Damien both shot her sympathetic looks glazed over with wary concern.

"Yeah, you gon' have to sleep that off." Donna's head bobbed up and down, and she laughed even as her eyes held steady, perfectly focused, on the swaying Bernadette moving down the back hallway.

"Second door on the left, Bernie," Janet called behind her.

"I got it." The wall serving as the entrance to the hallway almost hit her right in the face before she avoided it. Someone sucked in a sharp breath behind her.

"Here, let me help you—"

"Sit down, girl. She said she got it. She'll be all right. And you can drink the rest of her wine, huh?"

Bernadette's fingers fumbled with the doorknob, but she finally managed turning and pushing in at the same time. Stumbling into one of three guest rooms—apparently the one made up for her and Darrell for the next two nights—she heard a few whispers and some hushed laughter from the dining room.

"All right, then," Donna shouted. "Grownup time, now. Darrell, how's your poker face?"

"You tell me." His voice was low, much more effectively hiding whatever animosity he might or might not have held behind it.

Bernadette would bet on Darrell any day of the week to hide more behind his steady gaze than Donna would ever manage with her overstepping intensity. She had no problem leaving him out there without her, and if Bernadette had told him she was fine and didn't need his help to end her night, he had no problem letting her take care of her own damn self.

"Naw." Donna laughed again, followed by her chair scooting back across the dining room floor and her quick, excited footsteps across the room. "Let's see how well you do once I deal you a hand. Marcus. Damien. You in?"

Marcus and Damien murmured something together.

"Baby, you wanna play?"

Bernadette's hand found the edge of the open door in the dark bedroom, and she shut it behind her before she ever heard Janet's reply. Then she staggered toward where she thought she'd seen the bed and fell into it. Maybe if she passed out right now, she'd forget about the questions she'd refused to answer. Then maybe everyone else would too.

It couldn't have been more than half an hour later when the bedroom door whispered softly open across the carpet. A thin sliver of muted yellow light spilled inside from the hallway, burning Bernadette's eyes through closed lids. She groaned a little and tried to turn away from the light before it all but disappeared again into the thinnest line of the cracked-open door. Definitely too much wine.

Footsteps padded softly across the carpet. A silent but absolutely physical weight settled on the edge of the bed, just barely brushing up against the curve of Bernadette's back as she curled into her own inebriation and the tantalizing promise of sleep. A warm hand came down on her shoulder.

She'd already told Darrell she was fine, that she didn't need him or anyone else to put her to bed. As Donna was apparently so fond of saying about almost everyone, Bernadette was a big girl. Her choice to drink so much, her responsibility to deal with what happened because of it. And whatever had been said at that dinner table could sure as hell wait to be discussed until the world stopped spinning and her guts rearranged themselves into something resembling where they belonged.

The body at the edge of the bed shifted closer against Bernadette's back—a question, a challenge, a call to rise to it. What did he want?

It was impossible to know whether the near-complete darkness in that guest room made her churning, wine-addled head harder or easier to bear. But Bernadette rolled over halfway onto her back just the same, willing, at the very least, to find out what the hell was wanted from her right now.

It wasn't Darrell. The booze made a good excuse for not having realized that sooner. Booze made good excuses for a lot of things, until it didn't anymore. Apparently, the booze calling Bernadette's body a temporary home had given Janet the excuse to remove herself from the card game at the table, slip into the guest room of her own house, bring herself physically—and maybe more than that—closer to Bernadette by sitting at the edge of this bed than they'd ever managed until this moment.

The fact that Bernadette saw two, then three, then two versions again of her friend didn't necessarily mean Janet wasn't there.

"What's goin' on?" At least, that was what she tried to ask the woman she'd been writing back and forth for the last eleven years but had only met in person a few months ago. The sound worming its way through Bernadette's lips came out nothing like the words she'd intended and everything like a thin, diaphanous moan that could have meant anything. Bernadette couldn't even be sure that *that* wasn't what she'd intended, either.

"I actually thought she'd be different with you," Janet whispered. "Kinda crazy, right? Like maybe she'd see how much you don't try to be like everyone else, or anyone else, and then she'd appreciate you that much more. Like I do."

Bernadette shifted a little more toward her friend, trying to keep her eyes open. Trying to be sure this conversation was actually happening. The needle-thin sliver of light spilling through the crack in the door seemed impossibly bright now.

"I *want* to, Bernie." Janet scanned Bernadette's face. "But I can't actually bring myself to apologize for her. I don't even know what's stopping me anymore."

Another little shift in the bed, and Bernadette's hand slid from where it had dangled over her own hip before it slipped into Janet's lap. Against Janet's hand. Warm fingers closed around other fingers Bernadette wasn't even sure she could feel.

"I have to tell you before it kills me." A small smile flickered at the corners of Janet's mouth, then she leaned down over Bernadette's half-turned body, pressing harder against Bernadette's hip and thigh. A sudden weight of confusion and unexpected anticipation made Bernadette's body heavier than anything the wine could claim as a consequence. Janet's warm hand disappeared from around her friend's fingers and reappeared at Bernadette's neck, below her jaw, at her cheek. "Donna can say whatever she wants. You'll always be my first, Bernie. For everything."

It shouldn't have made sense, but it made all the sense in the world. The pieces fell together in Bernadette's mind faster than she could see the shape they took in the blink of an eye. Even when her own heavy lids—so heavy with drunkenness and a surreal understanding and was that relief, too?—closed and took forever to open again. When they did, all she saw was Janet's face, colorless in the mostly dark room, glowing from some internal place because there wasn't enough light in here to be the true source of it.

Closer. Heavier. Janet's lips on hers. Janet's fingers in Bernadette's hair. Janet's breath fluttering against Bernadette's cheek. Janet, like eleven years of paper and pen and agony, sorrow, shame, hope molded into a body as warm and real as Bernadette's own. Janet without any secrets now, because she'd given them all to Bernadette to do with them as Bernadette saw fit.

What were either of them supposed to do with that?

Then the lips that tasted like four more glasses of wine—or maybe just the four Bernadette should have left in that glass—were at her ear, whispering again with what could have been a need for more. It could have been an invitation. It could have been an apology, or a brazen lack thereof. It could have been the end.

"Now you know."

The heaviness and the warmth faded. The weight at the edge of the bed disappeared, seeping back into the carpet and the darkness, back into Bernadette's consciousness that didn't know what to do with itself now. She fumbled in the darkness of the room, of her mind, of her body that had moved and responded and risen to that challenge simply because she hadn't been able to withstand it. Or maybe in spite of her own knowing that she could have stopped it. If she'd wanted to at all.

21

PEOPLE SAY THERE'S a fine line between genius and insanity. You've heard that before, right? I swear to God, Bernie, there's a fine line between everything else right now too. Love and hate. Freedom and imprisonment. Tenderness and cruelty. The truth and so much fucking bullshit.

I'm surrounded by people who think they're fucking Albert Einstein and Karl Marx and Martin Luther King, Jr. all rolled into one. Without any of them stopping to consider how fucking insane that is. And it's starting to make me think I'm *the one who's going crazy.*

It's gotten even worse over the last six months. Everybody waiting around for this slow-ass system to finish the hell up with the Rodney King trials, right? That's all anybody's talking about anymore, and I've been having the *weirdest fucking daydreams about stabbing out my own god-damn eardrums so I just don't have to listen to it anymore. Not their rage over what those pigs did to the man. That makes sense. That's real, and anyone who isn't disgusted and fired up by it is either lying to themselves and everyone else or was just born without a soul. I feel it too. But Donna's crew isn't just getting fired up about Rodney King and the system and the goddamn wrongness of the way things are. The shit that makes my skin crawl. They're twisting it into something else. Like they're trying to turn the man into some fucking poster boy for their fucking cause. Like what happened to him, what's still happening to so many people we don't even hear about, is the fucking excuse they've been waiting for to start ripping the world apart.*

They say it's because we have to protect ourselves, Bernie. People like us who can do what we do. The storytellers. They say it's gonna be exactly the same for us, and our kids, and whoever the fuck else has this thing we have if we don't "rip it out by the roots first". They're using these trials as a goddamn platform for the wrong fucking thing, and I can't take it. It's almost just as disgusting, almost just as hateful as what this country's been looking at with our own eyes. That's not the way to handle it. It's not right, no matter how hard they try to twist it around their own fucked-up reasoning. It can't be. I can't wrap my head around any reality where what they're talking about is even a little bit okay.

There's not a goddamn thing I can do to stop it. Or them. I feel like one of my own paintings, Bernie. A conversation starter. A centerpiece. Something pretty to look at, maybe even more meaningful sometimes, maybe with some real value. But a painting never gets people to fucking stop with the bullshit and listen to the truth. To reason. To what has to be better than what Donna and her people are trying to do. I'm just hanging here on the wall, without the ability to say a goddamn thing. Just watching it all crumble to pieces in front of me.

Donna says it's my white privilege trying to get between us. And okay, maybe that's part of it. I'm not above my own ability to see that I can't separate that from everything else. I'm a white lesbian who can tell the kind of stories the world is gonna lose its shit over when people find out what we can do. Three outta four minority groups right there, and I fuck-ing know *they don't cancel each other out. I* know *it's not a competition. I* know *I shouldn't feel like people are keeping score. But Donna still can't tell me why it's okay for her and her people to do serious harm to others, no matter what they look like, all for her fucking cause. Why I'm the idiot for being terrified, every day, that the woman I built my life with is gonna get herself killed and take a whole bunch of inno-cent people with her. Why me hoping for a different solution, something better than making everyone else suffer now just to avoid our own suffering later, means I've given up. That I'm not committed and never really was. That I don't love her enough to be proud of who we are, what we can do, and how she wants to "change the world".*

Or maybe I'm just a fucking coward.

Maybe that's all this is. Maybe it's all I've ever been and there isn't a goddamn thing I can do about it because I just don't understand shit. Maybe I should just be grateful for what I do *have and quit holding onto the pain of every-thing else. Maybe I just wasn't cut out for any of this.*

Donna's pain makes her stronger. Gives her a reason to act, to push, question, fight back, fuck shit up, make some noise and not give a damn about who hears it. Yeah, she's a little rough around the edges, but who isn't? Show me one fucking perfect person in this world, and I'll go jump off a cliff right now. Donna's pain saved my fucking life. And mine? My pain almost ended it.

I don't know who I am, Bernie. I don't even know who I want to be. *How I want to change. What kind of person doesn't know that shit about themselves?*

What's wrong with me?

22

THE SIGHT OF a beat-up, faded tan truck and a shiny black Range Rover parked in front of her family's cabin in the middle of nowhere sent a momentary flash of panic through Bernadette's racing heart. Then she remembered the calls she'd made and the favors she'd asked at the end of them. Some friends came and went over the years, and some friends went so far back, they could always be counted on. If not to help Bernadette herself, then at least to be there for the woman laboring for the first time just on the other side of that front door off the screened-in porch.

The van crunched to a stop on the gravel, still rocking a little when Bernadette shoved the door open and stepped out onto the drive. The entire property plunged into a deeper shade of night without the van's headlights spilling huge pools of bright white all over everything. As she headed toward the screen door onto the porch, the three figures emerging around the side of the cabin from the darkness nearly gave her a heart attack.

"Oh, Christ!" Bernadette leapt back and slapped a hand over her heart. "What the hell are y'all doin' lurkin' around like that, huh?"

Only half of Cameron's face was visible beneath the single bulb spilling dull light over the porch. But it didn't lessen the effect of his smirk as he folded his arms. "How come you didn't pick up some Midwestern accent when we were out in Colorado?"

A baffled laugh escaped her. "What are you talkin' about?"

"You say y'all now." Cameron's smirk faded into a deadpan gaze. "It's freakin' me out."

"You know what?" Bernadette shook a finger at him and glanced briefly at the closest door into the cabin. Soft voices and the occasional low moan rose from inside. "I grew up sayin' y'all since way before you were born, kid. Guess I just lost the accent somewhere along the way."

Randall stepped up beside Cameron, his hands in the pockets of his shorts, and shrugged. "I heard it's pretty easy to slip back into."

"Yeah, well, easy or not, it makes you sound like an old lady who spends all day in a rocking chair drinking iced tea." Scoffing, Cameron turned back toward the third figure still shrouded in the thick darkness all the way out here. Only his thin outline was visible outside the direct ring of dampened light. "Right, Tony? We were just talking about how weird she got since we pulled up to this dump."

Tony didn't say anything, which none of them really expected anyway. But when he stepped into the light, one eyebrow was already raised, his nose wrinkled and his lips twisted to one side in both agreement and apology. He shrugged at Bernadette, and Cameron punched him in the shoulder.

"See? This guy knows what I'm talkin' about."

Bernadette eyed all three of them for a few more seconds before pulling her cigarettes from the pocket of her cardigan again. This time, she had no problem lighting the smoke on her own. And she couldn't take much offense to Cameron's *freak-out* about the way she sounded down here. At the very least, the conversation had brought an actual expression to Tony's face, which was more than he'd given anyone in a long time.

"Well sorry it's throwin' you off your groove." She smiled around the cigarette, pulled it away, exhaled. "When did the midwives get here?"

"Oh…" Randall scratched his head and glanced at the truck and the Range Rover. "Maybe an hour and a half ago."

The clock on the dash had shown just after 11:30 p.m. when Bernadette finished the drive back down here that felt a lot longer than the drive up into Charleston. That sounded about right. "Good. You ask her what she wanted all y'all to do with yourselves?"

"Yep." Randall pushed his glasses back up along the curved bridge of his nose. "Apparently, she doesn't want us in the house."

Cameron's eyes darted around the outside of the porch. "Like any of us were gonna fight her on that one."

"All right. Well, it's her call, and it's our job to get her what she needs." Bernadette shrugged, wondering what Mirela might have said about her, if anything. "Let me just grab a few things outta the back, then y'all can take the van and go find a hotel somewhere, I guess."

"Uh..." Randall chuckled. "She also told us not to go anywhere."

Bernadette puffed out a laugh through her next drag on the cigarette, followed by a little cough. "She doesn't want you *inside* the cabin, just around it?"

"One point for the y'all lady." Cameron snorted. "Does everybody want messed-up shit like that when they're having a baby, or is it just her?"

Bernadette tilted her head from side to side, rolling through the handful of births she'd attended—to watch, to learn, to offer support to more than just those laboring mamas. And that was a different time she'd rather not think about right now, either. "In their own way, sure. Every woman's got a different version of what she wants. Trust me, this isn't the weirdest thing. Kinda funny, though."

"What the hell are we supposed to do, though?" Cameron's frown wasn't hiding anything behind it this time. It was all disapproval and annoyance, and Bernadette almost laughed again.

"What've y'all been doing since she kicked you out?"

"Just... standing around. Some sitting." Cameron shot her a blank look. "Staring at nothing."

She pointed at him with a pert smile. "Then that's what y'all get to keep doin' until Mirela decides she wants something else."

Tony let out a long, heavy sigh, hunching his shoulders and tipping his head back in overly dramatic aggravation.

Cameron shot him a sidelong glance and said rather dryly, "Right there with you, dude."

Bernadette took another drag on her cigarette and listened a bit more to the subdued tones inside. "Okay, I get why Brad's in there. But Don?"

Randall snorted. "Yeah, she was *really* specific about that. No clue why she didn't send him out with us."

Leaning forward, Tony spread his arms and stared at Randall with wide eyes.

"What? She did. That's what she said."

Tony turned to Cameron next, obviously hoping the guy would come to whatever conclusion the silent twin seemed to think was so clear. Cameron eyed the guy up and down, and his brows flickered toward each other. "Yeah, I got nothin'."

The member of Sleepwater without his beat slapped a hand against his forehead and stalked off around the back of the cabin again, shaking his head.

Bernadette pressed her lips together, took another drag of her cigarette, then stepped toward the porch to put the thing out on the old, rotting railing. She stamped out the fallen cherry-red coal and stuck the half-smoked cigarette back into the box. "All right. One of y'all can come help me bring these things in from the van. I mean, if you're not too busy."

That made Randall laugh harder than seemed necessary, and Cameron rolled his eyes again. "Not like I have anything better to do. Hey, you pick up any bug spray while you were out running around without telling us?"

"Must've slipped my mind." She opened the trunk of the van and let it raise itself the rest of the way before gesturing at the lid-less boxes she'd filled and stuck behind the back row of seats before her little walk down memory lane with Darrell. "You gettin' eaten up out here already?"

"Not yet." Cameron slapped at his neck and checked his hand for the evidence. "But if we have to spend all night out here, it's gonna get worse. Right? Someone told me it always gets worse."

As Cameron reached for the largest box, leaving the smaller one for Bernadette to drag toward her across the back of the van, she stuffed down more bitter laughter. "Yeah, that sounds like something I'd say."

"What?" The young man readjusted the box in his arms and blinked at her.

"It's nothing. Never mind." Bernadette pulled down the trunk and headed toward the screened-in porch with the box of salves and tea and a few random miscellaneous medical supplies she was more than willing to pick up. It was the least she could do when old friends were willing to drive down at a moment's notice for one long-overdue favor.

Just before she crossed the porch, the door into the kitchen opened. Brad stared at the box in her arms with wide eyes, then glanced at the larger one Cameron carried and let out a short, hurried sigh. "That all the stuff they asked you to get?"

"As far as I know."

"Okay. Okay, yeah. Come on in."

Bernadette didn't even bother to mention the irony of the red-haired man inviting her into a building that by all rights still belonged to her. Unless she'd been cut out of inheriting it, which wouldn't have surprised her in the least. She'd never bothered to check. For all intents and purposes, though, the cabin did in one very big way belong to Mirela, Brad, and their baby on the way. The old woman who'd brought them here had no issues with loaning it out for as long as they needed it.

Brad took the smaller box from her, then nodded at Cameron. "Just, uh… stick that one right outside the kitchen, huh?"

Without waiting for an answer, the man hustled back into the main room of the cabin to deliver Bernadette's deliveries for her. Cameron shot her an unamused glance and shuffled with his slow, almost careless gait toward the edge of the kitchen. A long, low moan—airy and loose and very much like Bernadette remembered during her own child's birth—rose from the living room. After that, Cameron hustled like she didn't know he could. The box dropped with a soft hush onto the floor beyond the step into the kitchen, and it seemed like the front door was closing behind him almost immediately.

Without any knowledge of whether she was wanted here, one way or another, Bernadette stood just in front of the pocket door into the living room. There was a certain inherent privacy needed for an event like this, and she hadn't exactly been given an invitation. But she wanted to be close by, just in case.

A few heads bobbed slowly from in front of the couch, and a woman in a long, draping skirt and sweater pushed herself up off the floor with a grunt. She turned toward Bernadette, and a slow, tired smile spread across her lips. Bernadette had to return it, of course, as she leaned against the doorway off the kitchen. That was what friends did, wasn't it? Even after so long without speaking or catching a glimpse of one another. But Hellen had never turned her old friend away, and she most certainly hadn't turned away the call of her profession to come walk another expectant mama through the kind of physical, mental, emotional work every other woman in the cabin had experienced herself.

Hellen muttered something to the bobbing head of dark hair streaked with gray in front of the couch, who Bernadette could only assume was Loretta. Then the woman headed toward the kitchen, and Bernadette stepped aside so they could have whatever conversation was coming without disturbing Mirela in the next room.

"Look at you," Hellen said, her voice soft and low and still as soothing as Bernadette remembered it. "Lord, Bernie. It's been too long."

It wouldn't have necessarily been Bernadette's first choice to embrace her old friend right here in the kitchen— not with Mirela doing the only thing that qualified exclusively as *women's work*. But she wrapped her arms around Hellen anyway and let herself take a short moment of comfort from it.

When they pulled away, Hellen's dark, slate-gray eyes roamed over Bernadette's face, up and down her cardigan and dress, then up to the hair that had definitely been blonde instead of gray the last time they'd seen each other. "You look good, lady."

Bernadette snorted. "You haven't gotten any better at lying."

They shared a silent chuckle, then Hellen glanced back again into the living room, just to be sure she had enough time for a quick step away from the only thing she could do at this point—just be there. "Has she seen an OB? Any other midwives?"

Shaking her head, Bernadette pressed her lips together. "She hasn't really had the opportunity to see anyone."

Hellen raised her eyebrows, then blinked away her surprise and most likely her judgment. "Well, working with what we've got now, I can say that baby's positioned exactly where she needs to be. Good strong heartbeat. No distress, and hopefully there won't be any. Mama's only at five centimeters, so she's still got a ways to go."

"I know. Thank you for coming all this way down here. Hell, thanks for answering my call."

Hellen shrugged. "I can't say I wasn't surprised to hear your voice. But I'm glad you thought of me instead of trying to deliver this baby by yourself with one very nervous daddy and those men out there who look more clueless than a catfish outta water."

That made them both laugh quietly, neither of them wanting to disturb what few moments of peace Mirela might snatch from the empty spaces between each new wave of pain and effort. "I'd hoped the man might've settled down a little by the time they got to this point."

"Oh, he's doing fine." Hellen nodded and took another glance over her shoulder. "Better than fine, really. He's been ready and willing to jump on any task we give him. I might've already run through all my options, though. He's holdin' it together, but barely and for who knows how much longer. You know I can feel these things, Bernie."

Bernadette sighed and lifted a hand to the long, gray hair piled on top of her head. "Well, at least he's trying. Trust me, it's a lot better now than it has been."

"That other one in there." The midwife stuck a thumb over her shoulder toward the living room. "The one with the twin."

"Don. Yeah."

"He said y'all have been driving around this whole time. Mentioned a few states between here and Texas before I told him never mind. Is that the truth of it?" The woman's brows drew together in concern, though Hellen had had close to fifty years perfecting the art of showing just enough concern to be taken seriously and stashing all the rest of it away.

"Mm-hmm." Bernadette knew some form of this conversation was bound to happen. A pregnant woman these days didn't just drive around the country with her husband and five other people, not stopping long enough in any one place to pull together a plan for the birth of her first child, without some very good reasons for it. Reasons Bernadette figured Hellen could very easily guess. But the midwife had more sense than to act as if she'd already figured it all out.

She had the courtesy to ask, at the very least. "We've been through a few things, Hellen."

"I'm sure you have."

"And we'll go through a lot more when everything's said and done, you understand?"

Hellen tilted her head a little and blinked. "You know I do."

"Which is why I called you." Bernadette set a hand on her friend's shoulder and gave it a gentle squeeze. "And I appreciate it more than I can say."

"Well, I hear that plenty." Hellen nodded with another subdued, understanding smile. It faded after a few seconds, and the low tone of her voice filtered even more into something just above a whisper. "I wouldn't say too much about it to Loretta."

That warning lodged a wrench between the gears of Bernadette's confidence. She couldn't have expected everything and everyone to be the same after thirty years, to feel the same way about her and what she did and what her life had become. That was too long a time to hope for consistency, but she really hadn't expected the kind of changes Hellen was implying existed within a woman who'd been both their friend for some time.

"You think she'll take issue with it?"

Hellen couldn't seem to find the right gesture with which to fully respond. Her head wobbled side to side. "I know she already does. Now, nothing's been mentioned so far. At least, nothing that you and your young friends can't return from."

"My young friends." Bernadette chuckled.

"Well, honestly, Bernie. What else should I call them?"

"No, that's fine. You and Loretta can be my old friends."

Though Hellen clearly tried to look unamused, Bernadette's lighthearted jabs at all three women in the cabin who had at least twenty-five years on Randall—if not more—was apparently too much to write off altogether. "I suppose we've earned that title, haven't we?"

"Damn right, we have." Licking her lips, Bernadette forced herself to dig just a little deeper. She didn't want to, never looked forward to it, but it was necessary. Seven months ago, that role had settled squarely on Karl's shoulders—the digging, the questions, the finding of information before he brought it back to their little Sleepwater faction so they could all pitch in with new plans. With so many of their unlikely family gone now, she'd had to step up herself to take the man's place in that, among so many other things. It almost made her choke before she pushed herself through it. "Is Loretta gonna cause any problems for us? I wouldn't have called her if I thought that was possible, but now…"

"As long as everyone with that little something extra keeps their mouths shut that way, y'all should be fine." Hellen's eyebrows drew together again, and she folded her arms. "How many of y'all riding in that van can do it?"

The meaning of *it* was self-evident enough. The same *it* Hellen strongly recommended be kept away from Loretta. The same *it* that had scared and enraged so many people that they'd nearly broken a man named Darrell Wilkins in half just by inviting him to help them fight *it*. Turned out coming down here to a cabin in the middle of nowhere in the low country wasn't as safe as she'd hoped. "Used to be all of us at one point."

Hellen's eyes bulged like that sentence had lodged itself as a bone in her throat. "*All*."

"At one point. Tony's the only one who can't now. Got taken right out of him like a stolen kidney." Bernadette knew she'd hit the mark when her friend cringed.

"Which one's Tony?"

"The silent twin." Bernadette nodded toward the door off the kitchen. "Hasn't said a word since it happened. Nothing in months."

"Well." Hellen had rarely been at a loss for words, back when Bernadette was driving around with the woman visiting new and almost mamas having babies in their living rooms or bedrooms or back yards and definitely not hospitals. Bernadette had a feeling the woman still always had something to say, except for now. Just another one of those nights, apparently.

"Well," Bernadette repeated. Such a simple way to tell the woman she understood, that it wasn't Hellen's fault for not knowing who all these strangers were or why they'd come back here to a town and a life the old woman among them had forsaken. That she wouldn't possibly be blamed for whatever might be going through her own head, as long as it stayed there. "I'll pass along the advice. Don't worry yourself about the rest of them."

"I'm not worried about anyone but Loretta. The woman's one of the best when it comes to her work, but with everything else, she's… well, she's the type of person nowadays I'd hesitate to call my friend in some circles. For her own safety, you understand. Maybe sometimes for mine. Radical opinions."

"I understand." How interesting that that term could be twisted into so many different shapes. Radical. Radical opinions. Radicalized hatred. Radical terrorist group. Radically violent mutations. That last one had been tossed around on the television and through the radio one too many times—more than that—to not have cemented itself in Bernadette's memory. All those other phrases could be used now to describe the rest of the world who thought people like her were more of a threat than any of them truly wanted to be. But that last one? That last one she'd only ever heard applied to her kind of people. To Sleepwater in general. And yes, once or twice or more, to Bernadette herself, to Brad and Mirela, Randall, Cameron, the twins. At one point even to Leo and John. Karl, too, God love him. Kaylee, though … that girl might have just been the only one of them who deserved the label and embodied it all on her own.

The next low moan rising from Mirela through her next contraction pulled Bernadette from her thoughts like peeling masking tape off a freshly painted wall. Hellen was giving her an uncharacteristically funny look, so she smiled and imagined she had to look a lot more tired than she felt. "Is there anything I can do? In a professional capacity, I mean."

"Nothing more to do than stick around, for now. It's gonna be a long night still."

A long night for all of them, not just the laboring mother in the next room. That was just the way of it.

"You still up in Awendaw?"

Hellen nodded with one slow, tired blink.

"That's a long drive home in the middle of the night. Y'all are both more than welcome to stay here instead." Bernadette nodded across the living room at the bedroom in the back. "Two beds back there, freshly made up. Neither of 'em slept in, either."

"Thank you. I might just do that. I want to keep an eye on her for at least another hour, most likely. See if she starts moving along any quicker. Then I'll let you know."

"Okay. If you need anything else—"

"I'll be coming straight to you for it, believe me." Hellen let out another soft chuckle and glanced back into the living room at one of the two twin beds nestled up against adjacent corners.

Don had apparently laid claim to that bed, sitting on the edge of it with his sneakers just brushing against the floor, his hands in his lap and head bent low. Bernadette hadn't seen him once look up from that position, but she knew the twenty-something-year-old well enough to see he was clearly uncomfortable. Being asked for by name to stick around inside right now, without any comprehensible reason for it, would likely make anyone uncomfortable.

"Randall told me she wanted Don in there specifically."

Hellen shook her head and her short, thinning hair—cut in the style Bernadette swore to herself years ago she'd never adopt, if she even made it long enough in this world to consider the convenience of it—and the puff of it at the top rustled with the movement. "I don't know anything about that. He was already sitting on that bed when I got here. Hasn't moved."

"Hmm." And that made it even more strange. What would Don have to do with any of Mirela's experience right now or for the rest of the long night ahead? A sliver of understanding entered her mind, but it was blocked out by the movement from the other side of the couch.

Both women turned to see Brad all but tiptoeing toward the kitchen, an empty water bottle in hand. He gave them a strained smile, but beyond the obvious drain of the last ten hours, he seemed to be just fine. Good for him.

"Thanks for picking up those straws," he whispered, setting an absent hand on Bernadette's shoulder before passing her for the fridge. "Gotta get more water."

"How are *you* doin'?" Bernadette waited for the man to turn around with a fresh, cold bottle of water in hand.

Brad scratched through his already disheveled red hair and shot her a blank, numb look. "I have no idea."

The women almost twice his age chuckled. "That sounds about right."

"I told her you were here, though. She said come say hi, so..." He cocked his head and took that vacant stare with him back into the living room.

"None of them have ever gone through this before, have they?"

Bernadette shot her old friend a crooked smile and shook her head. "Just me. You. Loretta."

"Well, I guess that's all she needs. Go on in there. I'm just stepping out for a quick breath."

"Uh-huh. Hey, mind the boys out there who know even less about what's goin' on, okay? They're feelin' pretty useless right about now."

"I can imagine." Hellen winked at her old friend, then stepped through the kitchen and out onto the front porch.

Bernadette moved slowly out of the kitchen and across the living room, which honestly felt like she'd just walked right into a completely different world. The two couches facing each other beside the empty fireplace had been pulled even farther apart to allow for the little nest of labor Mirela had made for herself. They'd taken the thick comforter off the king-sized bed in the front and spread it out across the cold wood floor. And there was Mirela, on her hands and knees, completely naked. Bernadette glanced quickly back at Don sitting on the edge of the bed, only his side turned toward them, and wondered why the hell he'd been asked to stay, out of everyone else, to sit through keeping his eyes off the naked, laboring new mama on the floor. Don didn't even seem to notice anyone was there.

Mirela's head hung between her shoulders as she hissed out a long, slow sigh with tightly shut eyes. One of those hands both clutched Brad's fingers and smashed them against the comforter beneath her weight. Then she sighed, fully relaxed, and leaned sideways into the huge mound of pillows stacked beside her.

"Good." Kneeling just behind her, Loretta gently rubbed Mirela's sweat-slickened back. She looked up at Bernadette's approach, smiled a little, and nodded.

It was hard to think of this woman as Hellen had described her now. Loretta, as Bernadette had known her, was free-spirited, compassionate, willing to do whatever she could to lend help where it was needed. Maybe she'd forgotten that Bernadette was part of the alleged problem, as far as this new *radical mindset* was concerned. Maybe she just figured a woman in her seventies had been out of the game for long enough now to not be an issue. Or maybe the woman had gotten a lot better than even Hellen at hiding her opinions. Whatever explanation Loretta's smile carried with it, Bernadette just couldn't look at the woman in the same light now. It was foolish to think she could depend on the consistency of people with not nearly as much to lose.

Brad grimaced a little at the sight of his red fingers temporarily released from his wife's grasp. Then he watched Bernadette lower herself onto the floor at the edge of the rumpled comforter and looked entirely relieved.

"Look at you," Bernadette said, keeping her voice soft and low so as not to startle anyone.

Leaning sideways on the pillows, Mirela lifted her head and gave the woman an exhausted half smile. "Here we are."

"Here we are." Everyone in their own way adding to the twenty-four hours leading up to the most important moment of a new mother's life. At least, she hoped Mirela would see it that way. Bernadette had, thirty-five years ago, though some people would say she was lying to tell it that way, after everything she'd done since then. That didn't matter right now. This did. "You're doin' great, honey."

With another slow sigh, Mirela reached out for Bernadette, her arm trembling a little under the effort. Their fingers gripped one another with enough force to prove both women were aware of the gesture's meaning. Bernadette patted the back of that hand in hers a few times and nodded slowly. A few seconds of that, then Mirela heaved herself up off the pillows and returned to all fours on the sweat-pooled comforter. She nearly dragged Bernadette flat onto the floor with the force of her grip, now clenching both Bernadette's and Brad's fingers with the same force. Another long, drawn-out moan escaped the woman's open mouth as Mirela rocked back and forth mere inches on her knees.

When it was over, she released both hands in hers and collapsed as gracefully as anyone could collapse on a pile of pillows. "Sorry," she whispered.

"You have nothing to be sorry about." Bernadette rubbed her crunched fingers and just kept smiling. "Still doing great."

Brad lowered the new bottle of water toward his wife's lips and offered her the straw poking out of the top. "Thanks for these. Again." He nodded at the straw. "Makes this a lot easier."

"That's what they're for." She studied the man's face, still pale beneath his bright-red beard and the darkening circles under his eyes despite the fact that he looked more attentive than exhausted. Which was the point. "Have you been sitting here the whole time?"

"Since we came back from our walk, pretty much." He smoothed a few sweaty strands of dark hair away from Mirela's mouth as she took one more tiny, sustaining sip from the straw. "Other than, you know, more water."

Nodding, Bernadette leaned toward Mirela with a low sigh. "How 'bout I take over for him? Just for a few minutes."

The woman swallowed, gazed up at her husband, and closed her eyes. "Sure. As long as he comes back."

"I'm not leaving, though." Brad shook his head, silently pleading with Bernadette not to make him go. "I'm staying right here."

"Okay, now." Bernadette reached out to pat his knee where he sat cross-legged on the floor. "You're working as hard as she is, honey. Just a different kinda work. Go take a few minutes. Eat whatever's left in the fridge. Step outside. I promise we'll be right where you left us when you're ready to come back."

Brad just stared at his wife.

"I'm fine," Mirela whispered. "Go. I'm fine."

Loretta gave him the same reassuring nod, and finally, he handed the water bottle to Bernadette and struggled to stand. But at least he had enough sense in him to take the advice and do something with it.

Bernadette scooted into his vacant spot and offered Mirela more water. It was rejected, but that was fine. They still had a long way to go.

Mirela's next contraction and crushing grip pressing Bernadette's hand into the floor made Brad freeze before he spun around and stared at his laboring wife like he'd just walked into a murder scene. Bernadette shooed him away with a quick nod, and then he staggered into the kitchen and out the door.

Once Mirela returned to her momentary lounging on the pillows, Loretta apparently interpreted this short moment of rest as the best opportunity to talk about what was better left for later. Or never.

"Finally decided to come back around, huh?" The woman's short, sectioned black hair added an air of edginess

Bernadette had never known Loretta to possess. It went right along with her stretchy black nylon leggings and some attempt at business-casual with a fuchsia suit jacket that wasn't actually a jacket.

What the woman really needed was to pick the age she wanted to portray and stick with it. Something about what Loretta had going on—especially coming out to a natural birth all the way down here in Hollywood, even for a friend—brought Hellen's warning back with a new flavor Bernadette didn't quite understand. She'd been around enough to think she knew what *certain circles* Hellen had meant, but now the strange mix of pity and suspicion behind Loretta's gentle smile brought even more possibilities to light. Of course, Bernadette couldn't possibly account for all the things she just didn't know. That she'd missed after so long moving from house to house, state to state, motel to garage to safehouse.

"Just passin' through, Loretta." That was all she could manage to say without starting something that had no business being spoken on the floor between these two couches. "And it turned out to be pretty good timing."

"I'll say."

Right on cue, Mirela lunged for Bernadette's hand again before lifting herself off the pillows to wait out another contraction on her goddamn hands and knees. One might have expected the opposite get-up-lie-down pattern, but if Mirela found what worked for her, nothing else mattered. Except for maybe the ache now shooting up Bernadette's wrist and forearm as the other woman ground that clenched hand down into the floor. Then it was over. Mirela's grip released.

Bernadette blew out a long, slow, silent breath through a tiny hole in her lips and rubbed her hand. And to think, Brad had been doing this every few minutes for a couple hours at least. Based on what she knew and what Hellen had told her, they were only halfway there.

"Why now, though?" Loretta's large brown eyes regarded her old friend with a refocused intensity. "Something else bring you down this way?"

"Nothing in particular, no." If it hadn't been for the naked woman lying on a pile of pillows between them, Bernadette would have told the other midwife to mind her own goddamn business. She hadn't called Loretta down here to offer an opportunity for personal interrogation. She'd called the woman because Loretta was one of the best, right up there with Hellen and a few others, though Bernadette had found how to contact these two and figured they were enough. They should have been. But now her intentions were being jeopardized by Loretta's questions so obviously lacking in innocent curiosity.

"Ah." Loretta nodded. "Any idea how long y'all are stayin' for?"

That smile had once been attractive and energetic and highly contagious. Twenty-five years later, it just looked stained. Or maybe it was just because the smile was aimed at Bernadette specifically.

"We'll move on when we're ready." Bernadette offered the straw and water to Mirela again, who was still so consumed by the natural courses of her own body that she hadn't seemed to notice the precarious line being walked on her behalf. She just took another sip and closed her eyes. "When was the last time y'all checked dilation?"

Loretta's nostrils flared despite her unwavering smile. "We still have time."

Sure they did, but Bernadette didn't have enough patience to sit here and clumsily dodge so many goddamn questions. Now just wasn't the time.

Loretta seemed to know this too, and Loretta seemed to just not give a shit. "Lotta people to be driving around in one van for so long."

"Okay." Bernadette closed her eyes and kept her voice level enough not to startle Mirela out of her rest or her concentration. She hoped. "There's a better time for this conversation, Loretta. I'm more than happy to have it with you. Later."

The midwife pursed her lips and glanced at Mirela lying once more on the pillows stacked beneath her ribs. "Mm-hmm."

Then they stopped talking altogether, because there really wasn't any room to start up something else. Not with Mirela right there, and not with a door so succinctly closed between the two older women who used to leave all doors open with each other. Most of them, at any rate.

There was no doubt in Bernadette's mind that Mirela would keep doing just fine until she was holding that baby in her arms and calling the whole thing more than worth it. But she did wonder if her own patience would make it through even the next hour if she had to sit across from Loretta on this floor beneath the burning accusations of an old friend's gaze.

23

THE CROWD PACKED inside The Flying Dutchman on Dorchester Road erupted in cheers, applause, and more than a few loud whistles as Woodson Blues finished another song. Bernadette just leaned back against the bar, the glass of soda water in her hand dripping condensation all over the floor. She brought it up to the side of her neck, grateful for ice-cold drinks despite how quickly the ice in hers was melting tonight.

"Thank you," Ronnie said into the microphone, his voice raspy with too much smoking and not a lot more cardio than professional bass-playing afforded. "Thanks for comin' out tonight, y'all. Kind of a special night for us too, now, you see?"

"Ain't it always?" The shout rose from somewhere on the far side of the crowd, where people had been dancing for the last two hours to the standard of funk and soul Woodson Blues had been shelling out since the very beginning. A round of laughter and more cheers rose up.

"Yeah, yeah. We know we're good." Ronnie's half-concealed smile lit up a room, when he actually used it, and he readjusted the black pork pie hat on his head. "But for real, y'all, this is a big night. If you've been followin' us for at least a couple years, y'all remember when we got ourselves a new master on the sax over here. Darrell Wilkins." Ronnie stepped sideways away from the mic to gesture beside him at the man standing there with a hand on his saxophone, the strap hanging heavy around his neck. Darrell, for all his musical talent and for how much he lost himself when he played, didn't seem to know what to do with being called out like that. More cheering and whistles rose from the crowd. He just chuckled a little and gazed at the stage beneath him, rubbing the back of his neck. "Yeah, yeah, and we all know how good he is too. I ain't talkin' 'bout that now, just for a minute. I'm talkin' 'bout a different kinda music, y'all. Darrell, my man, just found out he's gonna be a daddy."

For a bunch of people who came to groove to some blues and funk and forget their own excitements or worries for a few hours, the crowd made more noise for that announcement than they had for any of Woodson Blues' jams.

"Oh, jeeze." Bernadette laughed and rubbed at her hairline. Nobody had told her this was coming, but the way Darrell stood up there on that stage, staring at her with his dark eyes and the barest hint of a smile, convinced her he knew.

Maybe he hadn't put the guys up to it, but he sure as hell hadn't talked them out of it, either.

"So now—" Ronnie laughed when Darrell's composure broke into a wide, flashing grin. "So now, y'all, Woodson Blues gets to add one more tiny member to our own little family. Ain't that right?"

"Maybe even our next new saxophonist," Benny chimed in from behind the drums. The microphones didn't pick up on it all the way, but the venue was so small, the words weren't lost on anyone.

Darrell pointed at him. "Yeah, if y'all even live that long."

"We ain't talkin' 'bout that tonight, neither," Ronnie shouted. "But the resta y'all need to show this man some love. And his woman standing all the way over there against the bar. You done a number on him already, B. I'd buy you a drink, but…"

Laughing, Bernadette spread her arms and shrugged and people turned to see who she was, laughing and clapping and throwing out a few whoops just for fun. Most of those faces didn't hold anything remotely close to the distaste she knew she would have found so clearly in her own family's eyes. A few of them were surprised to see that *she* was the saxophonist's woman, as Benny had so eloquently put it. All of them looked genuinely happy—in various shades of actually expressing it.

Ronnie stepped back from the microphone and counted off. Woodson Blues launched into the end of their set, and Darrell shook his head. He shouted something to Ronnie as the bass-player laughed again. Then, clutching his saxophone against his black t-shirt, Darrell jumped off the stage.

The crowd gave him plenty of room to move through, standing back to watch where the hell he was going. Darrell made a straight line toward Bernadette, moved his saxophone aside with one hand, and reached for her with the other. Just as she set the sweaty glass of soda water on the bar, his arm wrapped around her and pulled her toward him for a fierce kiss.

Laughter broke out all around them, punctuated by a few whistles. Somewhere in all the noise, Bernadette heard one woman shrieking in amusement. Another woman just down the bar dragged out a loud, long, "Uh-*uh*." The only thing Bernadette cared about at all was the back of Darrell's sweat-slickened neck beneath her hand, the way his lips moved against hers, the way the edge of the saxophone dug just a little into her ribcage as he held her tightly. She might have even enjoyed that stab of pain; at the very least, it convinced her she wasn't dreaming up any of it.

When he released her, he let out a little laugh again, winked, and spun around. Right on time with the rest of the band, Darrell launched into a solo before he'd made it halfway back toward the stage. He leapt up onto it between notes and stood there beside Ronnie, playing away like his life depended on it.

Maybe it did, Bernadette thought. They had to do everything now like their lives depended on it, didn't they? One life already depended on every choice they made from here on out, and it wasn't either of theirs.

Her cheeks already hurt from grinning, but she fell into dancing with everyone else as Woodson Blues put everything they had into the final jam of the night. The way Darrell moved up on stage made her laugh—not because it was funny but because this was what she knew had always been inside him. Not that calm, calculating indifference he showed the rest of the world while he saved the best of his humor, his passion, his unending strength for her. The only time anyone else got to see it was when he made music up on that stage with the four other guys who *had* become family over the last four months. Far more of a family than Bernadette's had been to her. Far more than they would have ever been to Darrell. Or their child.

But the fact that she didn't care about any of it at this point made her all the more certain that she was headed down the right path for all three of them. Bernadette had wondered if she'd end up feeling guilty over not having felt a single ounce of guilt yet. If she hadn't so far, she didn't think she ever would.

24

SHE'S DOING IT, Bernie. Actually doing it. I can't even begin to imagine where she got the stupid fucking idea that she and her people could actually pull this off. And I'm just... I don't even know. I don't think scared is even the right word. No, you know what it is? I'm fucking pissed.

Donna's taking her stupid fucking crew down to this rally. I shouldn't say where it is. Not to protect her goddamn secrets anymore. Just to keep you safe. But just take a minute to think about that MOVE bombing in Philly, then stick Donna's face all over the fucking thing. That'll give you a better picture, won't it?

I don't think I can keep this all locked up anymore like she wants me to. Last week, she came up to my studio and told me to put the paints away, she had something more important to show me. Forget how insulting it was. I thought something really amazing had happened, the way she was grinning and pulling on me. Or maybe some kind of surprise she'd cooked up. She does that sometimes. I never get an apology, Bernie. Not one in nine years of being with this woman. The next best thing is some kinda gift, like buying me something and surprising me with it is enough to make an apology completely useless. And hey, I get plenty of gifts.

But it wasn't even that. We came downstairs, and I actually let myself get excited. Feed off her enthusiasm. Like a goddamn kid on Christmas morning, only there weren't any presents. No. She'd just spread out all these newspaper clippings and photos and transcripts. All of them covering one story after another about gang activity and crimes committed by a group of people nobody could find. Some stupid fucking blue lines drawn all over the place. She just kept pointing and asking what I thought, saying it was time I got my head in the game 'cause now shit was getting real. Her crew was making moves. And what did I have to say about her movement now?

She thought I'd actually appreciate that bullshit. Not even a little bit of concern or apology or, "This is what we have to do if we want to make a difference." Even then, a difference with fucking what? Nobody knows who we are! Nobody knows what we are. But this wasn't about choosing the lesser of two evils, Bernie. This was about showing off her fucking trophies.

I'm serious, I've never been so glad to hear the phone ring when it did. She went running after it, and I just barely made it to the toilet without puking all over myself instead.

All this time. Jesus Christ, all this time I kept thinking some-thing awful was heading toward us, and she was already running around out there doing *those awful things. Bringing it down on herself. On us. On all the people who follow her and believe what she's saying just because she says it really well.*

Who knows how many people she's hurt with this? Vio-lent stuff. Shit I can't even write down on this paper, 'cause then that just means it's completely real.

I'm done. I have to be done. I can't sit in this house anymore, by myself, knowing she's out there with all the people she brainwashed into thinking they're fighting for something worthwhile. Knowing she's doing the same kinda things she showed me in all those articles. Next time she leaves, Bernie, I'm leaving too. I mean it. I should've left this fucking mess a long time ago. I know that now. It's all coming together. Donna's not the problem. She never was. It's me. I'm the fucking problem. I let this happen. I failed to do everything I should have because I love her. I do, and I probably always will. But I can't love her enough to turn what she's done into something that even looks *right, no matter which way I turn it.*

I'll call you. The next time she leaves to go tear some-thing else down, I'll let you know. I haven't figured every-thing out yet, but I will. And I swear, Bernie, I'm never com-ing back to this.

Stay safe out there. You see any fucking blue lines stuck up anywhere, just stay away. You have a lot more to think about right now and a hell of a lot more to lose.

Cross your fingers for me.

—Janet.

25

"THAT'S IT. HOLD it right there, Mirela. Just a few more seconds. You can do it. Breathe."

Bernadette sat on the edge of the bed in the cabin's living room, right across from where Don lay on his back on the bed opposite her. He had a forearm flung over his eyes, one hand resting on his chest. Lying there like that, he could've been sleeping through the whole thing. Except for the fact that he held his breath every time Mirela let out another grunt of effort and the occasional jarring shriek.

The woman was on her back now, propped up with pillows and the comforter beneath her on the floor. Twenty hours of labor, Hellen and Loretta taking shifts to let the other catch a few hours of sleep in the back bedroom. Bernadette had stepped in herself once or twice over the course of that long night, which was undoubtedly longer for Mirela than anyone else there with her. And now, it really seemed like that child was almost here. Maybe just an hour away from taking its first breath while the rest of them could finally relax and settle into something that wasn't tense waiting under an inability to do anything while Mirela worked all on her own. She was the only one who could do anything now.

Brad knelt beside his wife's head, holding her hand and smoothing the hair back away from her sweaty forehead, over and over. The cabin had all but transformed into a giant refrigerator with the swamp coolers turned up all the way without a single break during the night. And still, Mirela was covered in sweat, flushed, trembling, straining to do what the midwives told her despite what her body so clearly wanted to finish *right now*.

"You're almost there, babe," he whispered, leaning down to kiss her forehead. The man looked like shit, but they all did. It wasn't called labor for nothing.

"Okay, with your next contraction, Mirela, I want you to push just a little. Only a little, then stop. Okay?"

Thankfully, Hellen's body blocked the entire view of what she was doing to help Mirela along bit by bit, but Bernadette didn't need to see any of it to know what was happening. She remembered her own homebirth all too well, and while everything had gone exactly the way it was supposed to, she found herself more than happy to step aside and let the women whose job it was to birth babies birth this one.

Without a word, Bernadette stood from the bed in the corner just off the kitchen and shuffled toward the door by the master bedroom. The wave of muggy August heat washing over her when she stepped out onto the porch—even at eight thirty in the morning—almost blew her back against the door. She pulled out a cigarette instead and opened the screen door to give herself a minute.

Randall, Cameron, and Tony had set up makeshift beds on the porch. Cameron sat up from the ruffled pile of blankets on the floor when the screen door closed behind Bernadette. He rubbed his face and groaned. "They done yet?"

"You know, they'll be done when they're done, and there's nothing any of us can do about it." With a snort, Bernadette lit the cigarette and stepped a little farther across the grass away from the porch.

"Hey, what's with that one lady?" Cameron's yawn was so loud, it was probably exactly what woke up Tony and Randall. They both stirred in their own temporary beds. Tony thumped a fist down on the porch's old floorboards.

Bernadette blew smoke away from the cabin. "Which one?"

"Short hair. With the stick up her ass."

Of course he meant Loretta. One more drag, and she asked, "What about her?"

"She was asking a bunch of stupid questions every time she came out here last night." Cameron lowered himself onto his back again with his hands behind his head. "Like she was trying to get some big secret out of us. I don't like her."

"I can see how you wouldn't." A strangled cry rose from inside the cabin. Bernadette frowned. "Y'all actually get any sleep out here?"

"Best option we had, wasn't it?" Randall let out a heavy sigh. His hand dropped over the side of the long bench where he'd slept, his feet propped up on the opposite armrest because none of the furniture in or around this place was long enough for him to sleep head to toe and make everything fit. "Now I know I really *can* sleep through anything."

"Hmm." Bernadette listened to the muted, murmuring voices coming from inside. The words were completely lost, but she figured they were still enough to drown out the conversation happening out here. "Hellen told me she'd had a little talk with y'all last night."

"Little talk? That's what she called it?" Cameron's laugh was devoid of humor and left no room for interpretation; mostly, Cameron's laughter was just his way of being pissed off. "Would've been easier and faster if she'd slipped a fucking coded message under the door and called it good."

"She was trying to be discreet." Randall cleared his throat a few times and grunted, blinking heavily against the sunlight not quite yet pouring onto the porch. "But yeah. She was clear enough."

"Good." Bernadette nodded and stepped a few feet to the side, readjusted the way she held her cigarette so the smoke wouldn't blow right up onto the porch. "As soon as this baby gets here and the midwives finish up, we won't have to worry about being extra careful. But until then, at least while Loretta's still here—"

"Yeah, we know. No beats. No talking about beats or blowing up buildings, human experimentation, how much everyone wants us dead or locked up or—"

Tony whipped a pillow out from underneath himself and chucked it at Cameron's head.

"Oh, yeah?" Cameron's chuckle sounded more like a growl. "You got something to say about it too, man? Go ahead. Say it."

Scowling, Tony just ruffled his dark hair and shook his head.

"Yep." Bernadette eyed the silent twin a few moments longer through the screen around the porch. "That about sums it up, boys. I have half a mind to send one of y'all out to the market to stock up on food for the rest of the day. Maybe even tomorrow too."

"Mirela gonna have an issue with that?" Randall pushed himself fully up to sit on the too-short bench.

"Trust me, she won't be paying attention to anything but that baby. Not even one of y'all gone for groceries. And it'll be a lot better for everyone if we already have food by the time she remembers she can and needs to eat something after the last twenty-something hours." Stubbing out what was left of her cigarette, Bernadette went to the other screen door of the porch closest to Randall and stepped inside again. She stopped just in front of where Cameron still lay sprawled out in his makeshift bed, pulled the van's keys out of her cardigan pocket, and dropped them onto the porch by his head. "Brad took the last run, but he's not leavin' that living room any time soon. Feel like gettin' outta here for another well-rounded shopping trip?"

"Actually, yeah." With a groan, Cameron snatched up the keys and pushed himself to his feet. "Any special *requests*?"

The kid—and she had to remind herself that just because they were all so much younger than her didn't mean they were still *kids* at all—made a face like he'd just been commanded to go clean toilets instead. Bernadette gave herself a few seconds to shoot Cameron an equally mocking gaze hinting at surprise, as if she just couldn't believe he'd put himself so far out on a limb to ask what anyone else wanted. "Just make sure you bring back something from every food group, yeah?"

"Uh-huh." He stuck the keys in his pocket and brushed past her to step off the porch, barely concealing a smirk.

"And I don't have to remind you that fruits and vegetables *are* actually one of those food groups, do I?"

"Not anymore." Cameron gave her a dismissive wave and stepped behind one of the trees on the other side of the van to relieve himself.

Bernadette chuckled, patting her own belly, and turned back toward the other virtual campers on the screened-in porch. "Do I need to send one of y'all with him?"

Tony just hung his head between his bent knees and vigorously scratched through his hair. Randall blinked furiously as he cleaned his glasses on the hem of his shirt before sticking them back on. "Well, we're not sending him out alone to go plant half a dozen explosives…"

That brought a small laugh from everyone on the porch; even Tony let out a soundless, airy chuckle as he shook his head.

Then Randall looked back up at Bernadette with wide eyes as he seemed to have fallen right into the hole of his own logic. "You don't think he can do the same kinda damage just going out for groceries, right?"

Bernadette looked over her shoulder to see Cameron pulling his leg into the van before shutting the driver-side door. The engine turned. The kid backed the vehicle across the gravel drive just slowly enough to hint at his own capacity for caution. "He acts like he just doesn't give a shit. But you know he does."

"Yeah, I know." Randall's tired, crooked half smile just made him look more bewildered than anything else. "Man, I still can't wrap my head around—"

"Bernadette?" Brad's face poked through the narrow crack in the door off the kitchen. It seemed a little odd that he wouldn't just open the door right in front of her from off the living room, but that was probably more for privacy's sake than anything else. "She's, uh... she wants you in here."

"Everything okay?"

"Fuck if I know." The man looked pale again beneath the red beard. "I'm just doing what I'm told at this point."

"Okay." Bernadette nodded at Randall—who looked like he couldn't decide whether to burst out laughing at Brad's dishevelment or jump in and ask how he could help—then crossed the porch toward the kitchen door and followed Brad inside.

"I think this is it, though," he whispered, turning quickly to flash her a wild-eyed glance before spinning back around toward the entrance into the living room. "They said she could start pushing soon. I think. They said that like twenty minutes ago too."

"Soon's pretty relative right now." If she said anything else, she knew she'd just end up embarrassing the man or worrying him even more. Or both. So she just followed him into the living room and waited to be needed.

"Oh, Bernie. Good." Hellen turned briefly from where she knelt between Mirela's legs. The laboring woman still hadn't moved from her nest of sweaty comforters and pillows in the widened space between the couches. "Come over here."

Bernadette skirted around her friend and between the edge of the blankets and the front of the couch. Fortunately, someone had pilfered one of the couch cushions and set it on the floor beside Mirela's pile of pillows. It was as good a seat as any of them were likely to get right now. The oldest member of this Sleepwater faction lowered herself onto the cushion on the floor and took Mirela's outstretched hand. "Hey, sweetheart."

"I'm almost done, right?" Mirela's voice was just above a whisper, her once-fierce grip now clammy and offering only a little pressure around Bernadette's fingers.

A quick glance up at Hellen—who gave Bernadette a perfunctory nod as Loretta sifted through the box of supplies the midwives had brought themselves—told her now was one of those times when the truth most certainly couldn't do any harm to anyone. "Yeah, honey. You're almost done."

Another contraction overwhelmed the woman just as Brad knelt between Loretta and the pillows piled beneath and around his wife's head. Mirela's face twisted in a grimace of effort. The next second, that effort morphed into wide-eyed surprise and the kind of pain any mother who'd given birth like this would remember only too well.

"Just hold it right there, Mirela," Hellen cooed. "Don't push yet. You're almost there. I'm just helping things—"

Mirela let out a wild, tortured grunt and finally seemed to find enough life in her hand to squeeze Bernadette's mercilessly. Bernadette bit back her own cry of pain. "Oh, my *God*!"

"I know, honey." With her free hand, Bernadette wiped more sweat-matted hair away from her friend's face. "You're doin' so well."

"What the—" Another groan escaped Mirela.

This one turned into a growling scream of exhaustion and frustration, nearly overpowering Hellen's not-quite-shout of, "Don't push yet, Mirela. Hold it back. You got this."

The midwife did her best to time things well enough that both mother and baby would come out of this as safely as possible; easier said than done when the person with the most control over *timing things well* was the woman who wanted this whole thing over with more than the rest of them. "Just hold it through one more, Mirela. Okay?"

Mirela's shriek ended in a harsh, breathless gasp, her mouth and eyes reflecting the same wide O of surprise and agony. All Brad could do was lean down and kiss his wife's damp, sticky forehead, running his hand over and over through her hair. When Loretta handed him a soaked, folded washcloth and nodded, he seemed to do a lot better with an actual task and settled that rag on his wife's forehead with gentle, urgent care.

"Okay, honey." Hellen looked up with a tired smile and nodded. "You can push now."

"I can? Right now?"

"On your next contraction—"

Which came the very next second. Mirela grunted and seemed to double over even where she lay on all the blankets and pillows.

"Woah!" The cry of surprise came from everyone else gathered around the birthing woman; none of them had expected that baby to come out so quickly and all at once like that.

Hellen moved faster than Bernadette would have been able; the midwife caught the newborn heading toward her with so much force behind Mirela's one push and redirected the warm body the best she could onto its mother's chest. "Would you look at that."

Loretta and Hellen glanced at each other in surprise and relief and more than a little amusement. Brad clutched at his wild hair with both hands, his jaw dropping at the sight of his child so suddenly now in his wife's arms.

Mirela made a sound half sigh and half cry of amazement. "Hi, baby. Oh, hi." She held the baby to her breast and all but melted into the floor beneath her. "I thought you'd never get here."

The only thing Bernadette could do was laugh and wipe the tears from the corner of her eye with the back of a hand. "Would you look at that."

"You did it, babe. Holy shit, you did it. I—" Brad's strangled laugh cut off as he reached down and gently touched the top of his child's head. Then the last twenty-four hours caught up with him, and a sob escaped him before he pressed his lips against Mirela's sweaty cheek. "I love you so much."

"I love you." She turned to kiss him back and didn't seem to notice at all when Loretta settled a thin blanket over both mother and child. "Look at this."

"Perfect baby girl." Hellen grinned up at the new parents, then shot Bernadette a quick glance of surprise.

Bernadette hadn't been to a birth in countless years, but she'd attended enough—with Hellen and Loretta, even—to know that most women didn't deliver their babies like that, with that much conviction and only one push. Especially when it was their first. But leave it to Mirela, with all her silent strength and willingness to do whatever it took so everyone around her had what they needed, to get through the home stretch of childbirth without messing around.

The hardest part of it all was behind the new mother now, but she wasn't by any means finished. And while Mirela and Brad gazed at their daughter with more wonder than either of them had thought was possible, her body did what was needed to complete the hard-earned task of bringing her daughter into the world.

Five minutes later, Bernadette found herself feeding armfuls of towels to Hellen. She wouldn't say a thing about it—that was for the midwives to decide, to draw the line between practicality and panic—but something was definitely wrong.

Hellen nodded at Loretta. "Give her that Pitocin right now. Bernadette, there's a bottle of Vitamin K supplement in this box. Mirela needs two of those." The woman pressed gently on Mirela's abdomen and shook her head.

Bernadette had seen this only once before—the body's inability to shut down its own system that had done its job to perfection. Except at the end. Her sore fingers fumbled inside the box for that bottle of Vitamin K, she somehow managed to tap two out onto her palm, then she leaned toward Mirela. "Okay, honey. You need to take these."

Brad's smile faded as he finally noticed the three much older women moving quickly, succinctly, almost as if they could read each other's minds. "What's going on?"

Loretta pressed a syringe into Mirela's thigh and rubbed the area quickly. Mirela didn't even seem to notice.

"Is something wrong?" The man's eyes were wide with the first hesitant rushes of fear now as he waited for someone to tell him he had a good reason to let it consume him wholly.

"She's bleeding too much." Hellen lowered another bundle of towels beneath the new mother and shifted toward Bernadette to get Mirela's attention. "You did a fantastic job with that baby girl, Mirela. And your body hasn't quite caught up with the rest of it. Time to close up shop now, honey. I need you to turn all your focus to that now, okay? You tell your womb it did its job, and it's time to close everything on up, now. You hear me?"

"Yeah. Yeah, okay." Mirela's nod was weak, her eyelids fluttering in tandem with her shallow, shuddering breath. "Am I okay?"

Bernadette gently slid the wet washcloth off the woman's forehead. "You're doin' great, honey. Just get your body to wrap things up, huh?"

"I can do that. Yeah. I'll just…"

The sight of so much color draining instantly from her friend's face made Bernadette's heart flutter in her chest. "Come on, now, honey. Mirela. You're not quite done yet."

Mirela's head barely moved in assent, but she mumbled something under her breath and gently patted her daughter's back beneath the thin blanket covering them both. The newborn let out a high, thin whine—the first sound she'd made at all in this world—and it seemed to snap Mirela right back into the moment. "I'm trying. I'm just…"

"Shut everything down, Mirela." Loretta pressed down tentatively on the new mother's abdomen, and Bernadette had to turn away from the result. "You're almost there."

"I'm so—" A violent shudder wracked Mirela's body, her teeth chattering now and clacking together. "I'm so *cold*. Am I supposed to be cold?"

"You just spent twenty-something hours sweatin' everything outta you. Now you're just goin' the other way." Bernadette gave her a reassuring smile despite knowing how much of the truth she'd left out of her words. Mirela was losing too much blood, and if the medication didn't work, if willing her own body to do what it should have done inherently didn't work, they'd have one hell of a time trying to get the woman to the closest hospital at least an hour away from this cabin.

"Can we build a fire in there?" Loretta pointed toward the dark, empty hearth behind Brad and Mirela.

"Not fast enough." Bernadette shook her head. Who built up supplies to get a full fire roaring in the middle of a Southern August?

"Babe…" Mirela's limp hand swung back toward her husband, and Brad took it in both of his. "I don't know—"

Their daughter let out another tiny, shrill cry on her mother's breast, and Mirela's attention turned fully toward her baby once more. "You're okay, little love. We're both okay." A flash of realization flared behind her eyes, and Mirela looked quickly up at Bernadette. "Get Don."

"Don?" Bernadette stretched her arm out behind her and motioned toward the twin sitting—still, after all this time—stoically on the edge of one single bed in the corner. "He's been here the whole time, honey."

"Bring him"—Mirela shivered and let out a small whimper—"over here. Please."

"Uh-huh." Frowning in confusion, Bernadette couldn't very well find it in her heart to tell the woman there were slightly more important things to spend her energy on now. But Mirela wanted Don, and it was a small favor to ask. "Don, honey."

The young man blinked and slowly turned toward the midwives gathered on the floor around Mirela, Brad, and their new baby. He'd gone pale at this point too, though he obviously tried incredibly hard not to let his gaze settle on anything but Bernadette's face.

"She's askin' for you over here, now."

With raised eyebrows, Don slid off the bed and shuffled toward the nest of women and Brad in front of the stone hearth on the floor. He looked like he'd been half asleep this whole time, which was most likely true if he really hadn't left the living room since Mirela had asked him to stay nearly twenty-four hours before. His thin frame slipped easily behind Bernadette until he sat on the couch's remaining cushion and gazed at the silent, pink bundle wrapped up in Mirela's arms. "She's beautiful."

Mirela's dangerously pale lips twitched in a weak smile, just as dangerous for both of them. "I need you now. Please."

His dark eyes studied her, glinting in the morning light spilling through so many windows of the cabin's living room. "Yeah, sure. Okay."

As Don bowed his head and gathered his thoughts, Bernadette had only enough time to look up and meet Brad's gaze, only enough time to see the same surprise bordering on panic reflecting in the man's wide eyes. They'd thought they'd covered their bases with a few whispered warnings of how important discretion was right now. For all of them. In that moment, both Bernadette and Brad realized too late that no one had thought to tell either Don or Mirela that none of them could truly be themselves right now, at least not while Loretta was still here. But Don had already started to spin his own beat.

26

BERNADETTE'S HEART RACED as she pulled up beside the motel in Darrell's Monte Carlo. This was it. This was the place. She couldn't believe she was fucking doing this.

She got out of the car as quickly and quietly as she could in the darkness, which wasn't really all that dark with the motel's yellow streetlights in the parking lot and the buzz-ing, flickering neon Vacant sign on the marquee. There was the van, too, parked just a few spaces down from her. Janet had said there would be a van, and it was their job to drive that van and finish what Donna and her people had started.

Was there supposed to be this much adrenaline shooting through her now, when all she'd done was drive across state lines and pull up at a cheap motel right across the border from Mississippi into Arkansas? Her hands flashed with hot and cold and hot again, and she wiped them on the black jeans she'd bought just for tonight. Good luck ever trying to wear them again after what she was about to do wearing them now.

The room number Janet had given her was easy enough to find, right there on the ground floor between that black van and Darrell's car. Bernadette pulled her blonde hair up into a ponytail, twisted it into a bun, figured that was the best way to keep it out of her face and her out of trouble. Who was she kidding? This whole thing was trouble.

One brief knock on the door. She was going for two, but the door jerked open before her knuckles could make contact a second time. Then she was staring at Janet's wide, dark eyes, her face framed by straight black hair. Looking wild. Looking on the edge of jumping out into oblivion with Bernadette right beside her, pushing each other on, finally taking action after so long of hiding in the dark, and how could they ever go back to *normal* after this?

"Hey." Bernadette broke into an eager grin, not quite sure what the rules were for something like this.

Janet peered around her to scan the motel parking lot and the adjacent rooms where who knew what kind of people were doing who knew what kind of business on a night like tonight. The only certainty was that none of them could possibly be doing what Bernadette and Janet were about to do. None of them could possibly have a job as crucial or as dangerous as the job these women had been given tonight.

"Come on. Hurry." Janet snatched Bernadette's wrist and yanked her into the motel room, swiftly shutting the door again. The deadbolt turned. The second lock clicked into place. The little security chain that would be completely useless if anyone really wanted to knock this door down was slid into the little latch. Janet sighed and hung her head.

Still grinning, Bernadette turned around to face her friend, bouncing a little on her heels. "Everything ready?"

"Yeah." Janet's voice was short, sharp, distracted.

No fucking wonder. They had to sit here and wait for the designated time to go out and do their thing. Janet's thing, maybe. Not Bernadette's. Not yet, anyway, but she was here to make it her thing, to make herself a part of this, because fuck the silence and the hiding and constantly looking over her shoulder for no reason. She'd much rather have a reason.

"How you doin'?" Janet's eyes glistened in the low light spilling out from under two—no, three—dusty-yellow lampshades. They only settled on Bernadette's face for a few seconds before darting away again, searching for something else in the motel room paid for by the hour.

"I'm fine. I'm—" With a quick, breathless laugh, Bernadette lifted her hands. "I'm fucking shaking."

"Yeah, that happens." Janet turned around again and peered through the peephole in the door, then ran her fingers through her black hair and nodded. "How's Darrell? Olivia?"

"They're good." This was just small talk, wasn't it? Something to take their minds off the waiting and the fact that their hearts were about to burst right out of their chests with that waiting. At least, Bernadette's might. Janet looked a lot calmer, somehow. Calmer, sadder, a little more avoidant. But it wasn't that strange. Nerves got to everyone in different ways. Bernadette's made her feel more alive than almost anything else in her life. Almost.

The way Janet was looking at her—wide-eyed, a tiny smile curving her lips, a brief, encouraging nod—made it clear that maybe just *good* wasn't enough.

"Really, really good," she added, and that just sounded moronic. "Darrell's been playing around with a few new guys. Couple shows a week. It's going really well. And Olivia just started kindergarten."

The mention of Bernadette's daughter made Janet recalibrate her focus even as she paced back and forth across the motel room. Her eyes lit up. Her smile widened. Her roiling anxiety and readiness to do what had to be done dampened just enough to settle on the right distraction. "Oh, yeah? Man, I can't believe she's that big already."

"It's pretty crazy. Smart as a fuckin' whip, too."

"That's great. Yeah, that's really great, Bernie." Janet turned again in her pacing, marched across the room. Turn. March. Stop. "Does he know you came out here tonight?"

"Of course he knows."

"Does he know *why*?"

Bernadette gave her friend an unsure smile. "You know I tell him everything."

"What'd he say?"

"He said exactly what I knew he would. That I had to go do what I had to do. That this was my thing, and he couldn't follow this time, but if I was standing up and getting involved in something, it was good. He's behind this a hundred-percent, Janet. Come on. I'm not sneakin' around." The words hit her with a heavy dose of irony, and she let out some kind of giggle. A fucking *giggle*. "Well, not with him, anyway. Sneaking around here is a whole different story."

"Yeah, well… it is what it is, huh?" Janet sniffed, rubbed a hand over her mouth, and kept up the pacing.

The woman was really taking things to a whole new level. Then Bernadette realized the differences in their different kinds of nerves. She was pumped, eager, ready to be a part of this kind of change and finally make a difference. Just like Donna and her crew had been talking about for years. Just like Janet had been talking about too, in a different way. But when the talk had started to align, Bernadette figured the women had learned to make things work. That they'd come to a different kind of understanding, and now she herself could be a part of it.

But Janet wasn't pumped. Janet wasn't eager or ready to be a part of this at all. Janet was frayed, standing on the brink, yes, but of an entirely different cliff. Janet was scared, like she didn't want to be here at all. Like she didn't want to stick around for the aftermath of whatever went down once she did what she came here to do.

Very suddenly, Bernadette didn't think she and Janet had come here to do the same thing at all. So she had to break the tense, heart-pounding silence in that motel room, or she'd end up screaming something that made no sense at all. "You said she gave you a time to be there with the van."

"What?" Janet stopped pacing long enough to remember one of her oldest friends stood right in front of her, between the door and the outdated patterns of the bed's comforter. "Oh, yeah. Yeah, she gave me a time."

"Well?" Bernadette watched the other woman move back and forth, footsteps jerky now, a thin sheen of sweat appearing at her dark hairline. "It's eleven-thirty. When are we supposed to be there?"

Silence. Pacing. Complete avoidance of Bernadette's gaze now.

"Janet."

"It's fine, Bernie. It's fine."

"Hey. When are we supposed to be there?"

Finally, Janet stopped pacing and turned toward her friend. Those eyes wouldn't lift far enough to Bernadette's face. The woman swayed from side to side, then ran both hands down her cheeks and stared at the stained carpet between them. "We're not going anywhere."

That was definitely just the nerves talking now. Bernadette laughed. "Listen to you. We already came this far. There's no going back now. You made a promise. Hell, *I* made a promise, and your partner and all the other people like us that she's got rallied behind this thing are waiting for us to show up and get them out when they need to get out. That's all it is, Janet. Just a getaway van."

"It's too late."

"What?"

"Bernie, it's too late. It's over."

Bernadette's gut sank with a cold, stony heaviness. She wanted to sound firm, to snap her friend out of this over-thinking, over-anxious funk. But it was just a soft, hesitant question, daring itself to be heard at all because the answer—the real answer—was already forming itself in her mind. "When are we supposed to be there?"

"Half an hour ago."

Neither of them looked at each other. Bernadette could

only stare up at the popcorn ceiling above their heads, and wherever her friend's gaze fell … well, she didn't really give a shit now. "You mean eleven."

"Yeah."

"We were supposed to be there with the van at eleven o'clock?"

"Yeah."

"Janet, what the *fuck*?"

The black-haired woman groaned and lowered herself onto the edge of the bed. "It's over."

"You told me to be here at eleven-thirty."

"I know."

"You said I'd be early. That we'd have a little time to get ready." Bernadette's chest and shoulders felt like they were on fire now, the whole world of her understanding and expectation crashing down around her. "You told me to be here now, and I got here *now*. How could you fuck up the timing like that? Are you high?"

"Fuck, that would really help me out right now—"

"Janet!"

"No! No, I'm not high. I didn't fuck up the timing, Bernie. I didn't forget. I didn't accidentally tell you eleven o'clock, okay? This was… I made a choice."

Bernadette took one step toward the bed and had to stop, afraid that if she took another, her knees would buckle and she'd lose all the support she had left. "Janet. Aw, fuck… They were *waiting* for us."

"I know."

"They needed us to be there. To get them out of the shit." A dry, bitter laugh of disbelief escaped her, because it was easier to laugh when the world fell apart. Otherwise, she'd end up falling apart with it. "They were supposed to be in the back of that van outside. *Your* van. And now—" She laughed again, a humorless, biting sting. "Yeah, they're in the back of a van all right. In handcuffs. You know that, don't you? You just fucked everybody."

"Bernie, I *know*!" Janet leaned forward over her lap and buried her face in her hands. She took a long, shuddering breath, then sat back up again. "I told you I was done, didn't I? I told you I was gonna leave, that I was stepping out and dropping all Donna's crazy shit behind me. I *told* you—"

"That was like four years ago!" Both hands went up to Bernadette's blonde hair, and she spun in a slow, shaky circle. "Four fucking years, man. You know how much changes in four years? You said all that shit, and then you never left. You stayed. You kept up with Donna, you hung around. How the fuck was anyone supposed to expect this from you now?"

When she'd finished, it barely registered in the back of her mind how hard she was breathing, how tightly she'd clenched her fists by her sides, how far toward Janet and the bed she'd bent at the waist, looming like storm clouds and fuck the threat of rain and thunder and hurricane winds; this was a *promise*.

"Why?" That was all she could think of to add when Janet didn't say anything else. "Why'd you let me think I was finally ready to be a part of something?"

"Because this is the only way to make it stop." Janet's voice broke when she said it, over a decade of a life spent with a woman—whom she hadn't really sacrificed tonight so much as failed to save—shuddering out of her more and more with each short, trembling breath. "This whole fucking thing went on way too long. She's hurt too many people. She's hurt *me* too many times. I can't... I had to *do* something."

"This isn't *doing* something, Janet. This is doing *nothing*. This is..." Bernadette ran both hands over her hair, glanced at the ceiling, and dropped her hands against her thighs. "This is making promises and then doing absolutely fucking nothing."

"Maybe that's just all I can do, huh? Maybe I'm only capable of just *nothing*."

"I'm not even... I mean, why the fuck did you ask me to come if you already knew this was gonna happen?"

The other woman stared blankly at the stained motel carpeting, her eyes glazed over with a vacant erasure. Like disappearing inside herself was the only way she'd learned how to survive. To be protected by someone, at least, even if that someone happened to be her. Which it probably had been for a long, long time, knowing Donna. "I didn't want to be alone for this, Bernie. I still don't."

With a sigh, Bernadette stopped her own momentary pacing and sat beside her friend on the edge of the bed. "You had me come all the way out here, thinking I was heading into the craziest night of my life, just because you didn't want to be alone."

Janet lifted her gaze from the floor and slowly turned toward her friend. "I need you, Bernie. You're the only person I want with me to not be alone."

The words hung between them like a veil, like one of

those rice-paper doors, thin and almost transparent; they could see the silhouette of the person in the other room, watch the movements, imagine the clarity, and all they had to do was slide that door aside to confirm what they already knew was there.

It was definitely unexpected. So was Janet's twitch of a smile as she held Bernadette's gaze. So was the small movement, the leaning in, as if the woman reconsidered even that much before going all the way to whisper into Bernadette's ear. So was the fact that Bernadette didn't give her own ear a chance to hear it, that instead she turned toward Janet— just to be sure, was that it?—and the whisper that had never been a whisper at all pressed against her lips.

This time, it didn't feel like a dream. Bernadette's heart still raced—some combination of expectation and surprise and the remnants of anxious anticipation she'd carried from all of five minutes ago when she still believed she'd be spending her night doing something as far from this as she could have been.

"You go take care of your own business," Darrell had told her. *"Go do what you gotta do. We'll be here when it's over."*

Bernadette's business just over the line between Mississippi and Arkansas had changed, all right. And while Donna and her crew—Charles, Jiyun, Marcus and Damien, Latisha, the dozen other people with magic in their words and a fire stoked by Donna's inability to back down from any of it—were pinned down and handcuffed and tucked into the hard plastic seats in the back of so many police cars,

Bernadette let Janet pull her down on the bed in a cheap motel room rented by the hour.

27

From j.hammel@aol.com
Sent: January 17th, 2001

Bernie,

Email's probably best right now. I know someone could probably find this on the internet if they really wanted, but it's better than somebody snatching up an envelope out of the mailbox. And honestly, I wouldn't even know what kind of return address to put on a letter. Seeing as I don't technically have an address right now.

I'm sure you know Donna told me to leave after they got out last week. I'm sure you're not surprised. She's got someone in her back pocket with enough money for bail and lawyers, but it doesn't really matter. I wanted out, and I guess this is how I get out.

The choice was all mine. Can't blame anybody else for what happened. But I thought I could put a stop to everything. Or at least keep it from going any further. I was wrong. So it might just be the best thing for everyone that I'm out. And Donna's just gonna keep ... doing whatever she's doing.

I never meant to hurt you, *though, Bernie. You have to believe that. Maybe I'm the pariah now, but at least I'm smart enough to know this won't keep up for very much longer. I have a cousin in Illinois, so I'm heading out there. He's telling me they're starting to get rough with people like us. What Donna's doing is just the start, but it's not making anyone listen. It's just making people scared. Maybe even more scared than they would've been if Donna's people weren't trying to make a statement with bombs and kidnappings.*

I shouldn't say anything else. Just wanted you to know I'm okay and that you can email me any time you want at this address. It's kind of hard to find places on the road that have AOL, but I think my cousin has his own computer. Pretty cool, right?

Take care of yourself, Bernie. Give my love to D and little O.

—Janet.

28

THE MINUTE DON started talking, the magic in his beat filled the living room of Bernadette's family's cabin like a smoke bomb.

"Everything's gonna be okay," he said softly, his voice sailing through the room. Though he'd turned toward where Mirela lay—shivering and taking slow, shallow breaths with her daughter in her arms—he hung his head between his shoulders and stared at the floor. Bernadette could only imagine how awkward the kid must've felt, being asked specifically to sit there through Mirela's labor, while he most likely just wanted to skip on out of there and be relegated to the front porch with the others. But now it was perfectly clear why Mirela had asked for him, and Don wasn't about to shy away from this one job he'd been given. Not when he spun a beat for one of their own. Not when they were all still in this together. "You got that baby now. And she needs you. We all do. Whatever happens, you still have a job to do."

It was a sweet message, really. Something that didn't sound at all out of place. But there was so much more floating beneath the surface of what Don said.

Bernadette glanced up quickly to meet Brad's gaze, both of their eyes wide. They couldn't stop Don now. Not with Loretta right there. Not after Hellen had warned them that the other midwife who'd just helped birth this brand-new baby was the kind of person who'd turn them in for being who they were. Who'd turn on them without a moment's thought.

Brad looked a hell of a lot like he was sharing her thoughts right now, and neither one of them said a word. Then the force of Don's beat hit them head-on. Bernadette saw that glassy, foggy screen clouding Brad's normally bright eyes. A second later, she felt it in herself. The slackness. The low, humming buzz her body had more than grown used to after so many years listening to so many beats from all the people she'd met and loved, saved and lost and left behind.

Don's beat took over. She wouldn't have been able to say what the words were after that, but the actual words never mattered. Not unless it was Bernadette's beat, and this one was far from it. The first taste was just a warm pressure settling around her shoulders, like a thick woolen blanket tossed on by a friend. Then the heat grew, spreading down her arms, over her legs, making the back of her neck prickle as it washed up into her hair and across her scalp. The swamp coolers had been pumping in cold air for almost twenty-four hours, filling up an oasis from the August heat outside. And now Don's beat was undoing all of it.

Without really being aware of it, Bernadette lifted a hand to the top button at the collar of her dress and slipped it open with quick fingers. Sweat beaded at her hairline. The flush of standing beside a fire that had never been lit bloomed in her cheeks and down her neck.

Beside Mirela, Brad gazed blankly down at their new-born child and pushed his sleeves up his forearms. Hellen wiped her glistening forehead with the back of a hand. Loretta let out a little sigh and fanned at her own face, frowning at the sudden heat in such an unexpected moment. Mirela herself took a deep breath and let it all out slowly, in a gentle sigh, like she'd just lowered herself into a hot bath after the last twenty-something hours of such hard work—just the beginning of all the hard work a new mother had ahead of her. The infant in her arms let out a little mewl, but it seemed more in satisfaction than anything else.

Bernadette took in all of this, knew what it was, felt it and saw it and couldn't do a damn thing about it. Don's beat wasn't the strongest or most interesting, but it was useful. And it had done its part to calm the woman who needed to focus not on how afraid she was of being so cold, of losing so much blood, of something gone wrong in that moment. She was warm and didn't feel anything else but his beat and her love for that baby.

The infant let out another squealing cry, and that one sounded more urgent. Don's head jerked up from where he hung it, his words stopping short. Then he looked quickly away to give the woman lying on the floor the privacy of not being stared at—at least not by Don.

Loretta, though, sat back on the floor where she'd been kneeling and fanned furiously at her face. Glistening beads of sweat ran down her wrinkled temples and the hollowing cheeks, taking her makeup with it. Her recovery time once Don's beat stopped and the power of it started to fade was a lot longer than for Bernadette, Brad, and Mirela. Because they'd spent a lifetime listening to this kind of power in words. Because it was a part of them, too, and maybe that was the reason. But while Loretta struggled with the internal burn of Don's beat, trying to loosen the collar of her shirt around her neck and gasping a little at the receding warmth, Bernadette caught Brad's eyes again.

So far, it seemed safe. They still seemed safe.

"Oh, *hey…*" Mirela cooed to the baby. She'd definitely stopped shivering now. "That wasn't so bad, was it? Just a little one. Just before I show you what your Mommy has to offer, huh?"

Hellen slightly turned her head to look up at Bernadette. The same warning was written all over her face—*Not in front of Loretta.* The woman puffed out a sigh as the magic of Don's beat fully cleared away from her eyes too—that disappearing of what was once there, like steam on a bathroom mirror fading after an open door. Then she returned her attention to the work that still had to be done with the woman who'd done most of the work of childbirth already.

The baby squirmed a little on Mirela's breast, and she sighed, taking in every tiny detail of her daughter's features. "You listen to me, little one. This is where you come from."

"Uh… babe?" Brad leaned down and kissed his wife's sweaty temple again. His hands came down on her shoulders. "Maybe we should wait a little for that, huh? You know, once the midwives—"

"I'm lying here naked on the floor, Brad." Mirela's voice was soft, already taking on that nurturing quality of awestruck relief now that their daughter was finally here. "Don't tell me everyone here couldn't use a little comfort. And we talked about this. It's the one thing I care about. A first impression."

"Babe, maybe you both just need some rest…"

Shaking her head, Mirela started talking anyway, spinning her own beat in the way that had been born into her. Brad met Bernadette's gaze again, this time with far more fear than the last. His wife's beat wasn't anywhere close to dangerous, but where Loretta could easily have written off Don's beat as an aftershock of working hard through the night to bring a child into this world, even as a midwife, the woman most definitely wouldn't have an explanation for the way Mirela's words would make her feel. For the way it would make them all feel.

"Honey, I don't think that's the best…" Bernadette's words faded away, slipped out of her control beneath the rush of emotion sweeping over her that most certainly didn't belong to her. Everything was fine, wasn't it? Everything was so beautiful. She glanced at the baby in her mother's arms, and *fuck*, that was the most beautiful sight of all.

Mirela crooned to her child, the words of her beat lost beneath their own power.

Bernadette turned toward Hellen beside her with tears

in her eyes. It was so damn good to see a friend like this after so long, wasn't it? Friends really meant something, even after so much time and space between them. Hellen returned the gaze, her eyes fogged up with the veil of losing herself in Mirela's beat and her own shimmering tears. The woman reached out for Bernadette's hand, and when Bernadette grabbed it, they leaned toward each other for a strong, warm embrace damp with sweat.

Brad lowered his cheek onto the top of his wife's head and blinked huge tears of joy and love and complete disregard for the secret they were supposed to keep right now. The secret too dangerous for Loretta to see, but Mirela didn't know.

Don slipped down off the edge of the twin bed in the corner and shuffled toward Bernadette and Hellen hugging each other right there on the floor. He dropped to his knees and put his arms around both women almost old enough to be his grandmother. Bernadette felt the added weight around her shoulders and felt her own tears slipping down her face.

On the other side of Bernadette, Loretta let out another airy sigh, this one out of pure joy and comfort and love for everyone in the room affected by a beat she had no idea existed. Not yet. The woman leaned forward with wide eyes, reaching out to touch Brad's shoulder. Two pairs of fogged-over eyes met each other, and the midwife who shouldn't have found out about any of them—not like this—shook her head in awestruck amazement.

They were this short of stripping down into a goddamn love fest, and as Bernadette melted under Mirela's beat and couldn't control the way she felt or the fact that she hadn't hugged anyone like this in years, a small awareness at the back of her mind still existed. Everything was happy-slappy now, sure. The minute Mirela's beat ended, they were fucked. Maybe they already were.

Then the living room of the cabin fell silent again. Mirela's beat was over. The magic was fading. It left those with their own beats much faster than it withdrew from the midwives. Don patted Bernadette's shoulder and stood. When he reached the twin bed in the corner again, he lowered himself onto it with a sigh and lay all the way down on his back. Bernadette slowly pulled herself away from Hellen. She could only hope *this* friend of hers wouldn't say or do anything blatant while they waited for the other shoe to drop. Loretta's shoe, specifically.

Hellen pulled away from Bernadette and took in a sharp, halting breath. This wasn't supposed to happen. She'd told them not to spin a fucking beat where Loretta would hear.

And Loretta, who'd been gazing at Brad and Mirela and their child with glazed eyes and a fabricated oneness that lasted only slightly longer than the new mother's words, slowly began to blink away the fog of her own susceptibility. As far as any of them knew, there were only a few people out there who didn't have to protect themselves from another's beat with technology and the filtering of another's words through it. And none of those people were here.

"There..." Mirela let out a small, satisfied laugh as her daughter stared up at her from the cradle of her mother's arms. "You feel that, little one? This is the family you've been born into."

Loretta quickly withdrew her hand from Brad's arm. He so obviously tried to pretend like he hadn't even noticed, but Bernadette saw his jaw working steadily beneath his bristling red beard while he forced his eyes to stay on his daughter. Like if none of them acknowledged what had happened, that might just erase it from the truth of things. A truth Loretta quickly realized all on her own.

"I..." Her breath quickened as she sat back on her heels. The woman's short hair and her fuchsia-and-black outfit suddenly made her look like she'd been dropped right into this cabin from another world, baffled and terrified to find herself surrounded by strangers in a world that meant nothing to her but fear and mistrust and consequently hatred. She cleared her throat. "I have to go."

"Everything okay?" Hellen asked, playing it off well enough. Mirela was still clueless of the danger, of course, but Brad forced his gaze up toward Bernadette again. She slowly shook her head.

"I just remembered I have... something important." Loretta pushed herself to her feet with surprising speed for being a few years older than Bernadette. "I have to go."

"We still have all the post-partum to cover—"

"You don't need me for that," Loretta hissed. She shot Mirela and that perfect new baby a scowl of pure disgust, and then she stormed out from the space between the pushed-back couches and headed swiftly up the one step into the kitchen.

Don pushed himself up on the bed. "What happened?" Everyone ignored him.

"Hellen," Bernadette muttered. She had to reach out for

the couch beside her just for an extra boost up off the floor. And why couldn't her aching joints give her a goddam fucking break already? "Help me talk her down out of this."

The midwife shook her head, her attention already returned to the work of cleaning up and checking both mother and baby now that Mirela had in fact stopped bleeding. It would have taken so much less time with her professional partner there like she was supposed to be. Probably ex-partner now, if Bernadette was reading all the signs right. "I don't wanna get involved," Hellen muttered.

Bernadette froze, staring down at her old friend and wanting nothing more than to slap some sense into the woman. It sounded just like something Janet Hammel would have said thirty years ago, twenty, hell probably even today. All she could do was snort instead and take off into the kitchen as the door to the screened-in porch slammed shut. "Nothin's really changed around here at all, you know that?" she muttered. "Everyone's still a fucking coward."

"What's up now?" Don asked, glancing quickly back and forth between Brad and Bernadette.

"Something like Plan B."

"*What*?" Don launched himself off the bed and almost jogged after her into the kitchen, past the wobbly table, toward the door. "Why?"

"Because a baby makes everyone lose their shit." It was the only thing she could think to say before she yanked open the kitchen door and stepped out onto the porch. It wasn't Don's fault. He didn't know. And Mirela had been and still was too caught up in the new-baby bubble to notice Loretta hightailing it out of that living room like they'd all pulled a gun on her instead. Which Bernadette might have, if they hadn't left everything in the back of that goddamn van.

She pushed open the screen door off the porch in the middle of it swinging back at her and gritted her teeth against the flare of pain shooting through her knees and down her legs. Too much time sitting on the floor, being there for the people who needed her most. Now they needed her even more, and she was just one more old lady with a washed-up history finally being used against her.

"Loretta," she called, huffing a little as she pushed herself faster down the gravel drive toward the Range Rover parked beside Hellen's faded truck. "Hold on, now."

Loretta whirled around on the gravel, her eyes widening when she saw Bernadette Manney stalking after her. "No!" Her arms pumped at her sides in that fuchsia blazer. It would have made for a good laugh under better circumstances.

Fuck better—*any* other circumstances but these.

"You can't just go runnin' off like this," Bernadette added as Loretta reached the Range Rover and fumbled with the handle on the driver-side door. "That baby and her mother still need your help before this is all over. I know how you and Hellen do things, remember? I've seen what they still need in there—"

"Don't!" Loretta whirled away from her car and shoved a crooked finger in Bernadette's face. The only thing Bernadette could think was how much that manicured fingernail in the same fuchsia as the woman's blazer looked like a claw. "I don't owe those animals a thing."

"*Animals?*" Bernadette blinked. "That's a mother and her child in there—"

"I know what I saw. What I… felt." Rage and emblazoned hatred radiated from the midwife's squinting eyes, her jaw opening and closing while her lips puckered in a wrinkled O like a fish with a hook stuck through the cheek. "It's disgusting."

"They're *people*, Loretta." Shit, this was going so badly.

"They're *not human*. As God is my witness, I should have taken that abomination right out of that room with me and gotten rid of it myself. They're… they're *breeding*—"

"You watch that foul shit." Bernadette's voice was low now, warning, furious. "Do you hear yourself right now?"

The midwife hissed through her teeth and poked that finger against Bernadette's shoulder. It did actually feel like a claw. "Don't you think for one second that I've forgotten about *you*, Bernadette Manney. You're just like the rest of these ungodly freaks. Just you try to deny it."

Bernadette glanced at the acrylic nail digging into her shoulder and gritted her teeth. "I'm not tryin' to deny anything."

"No…" Loretta sneered at her, her eyes wild with condemnation. "The devil took you years ago."

"Maybe." Bernadette swallowed. "This isn't about me, though. It's about that new family inside and a mistake that couldn't be helped. Now I'm asking you, Loretta, please. Let's go for a walk. We can talk about this."

"I'm not going anywhere with you." Loretta spun around again, finally managed to slip her fingers under the handle, and jerked open the door.

"You best think long and hard about what happens

next." Despite how calm she sounded, Bernadette was trembling. "There's no reason to go makin' a big deal out of things. Nobody got hurt. Nothing bad happened."

The midwife let out a bitter shriek of laughter and climbed up into the SUV. "You were lucky thirty years ago, Bernadette. When no one could say exactly what you were or how to handle it. Things have changed around here. You'll get what's coming to you, all right. You and this entire freakshow of Satan's agents. I'll sleep like a baby when I know all y'all are burning in Hell where you belong!"

"Satan? Are you—" Bernadette wrenched the door back open before Loretta could close it and cut her off. A zap of pain flared through her shoulder and wrist, but she ignored it. "Are you *crazy*, woman? You're a good person, Loretta. I've seen it. Whatever kinda hate's been drilled into you isn't who you are."

"Take your hands off my car."

"Not until you tell me where you're going." Bernadette felt like a fucking earthquake on the move with all the anger coursing through her; she shook now like she really was possessed, like the bullshit the people like Loretta had cooked up all on their own to explain the beat-spinners in this world had taken form in reality. "You tell me where you're going. Tell me you're not about to do something stupid you won't ever be able to take back."

The other woman's nostrils flared, and she drew her head back before spitting in Bernadette's face.

It would've been better for Loretta if she'd punched Bernadette instead. That kind of reaction she understood. That kind was backed by force and challenge and a readiness to engage on a level playing field. But Loretta was up there in her goddamn Range Rover, eyes burning with revulsion and pure, undiluted loathing. And Bernadette was forced down to a lower level of payback she hadn't inhabited in decades.

If Loretta thought she was an ungodly animal, some spawn of Satan, fine. Bernadette could be those things and all the rest of it. Fuck it.

She took a deep breath and felt the burn of her own words rising up through her chest, burning up her throat toward her mouth. Call it the fires of Hell, sure. She'd already pinned this woman's story down decades ago.

"Those fingernails are dirty. You don't know how they got that way, all that dirt and grit jammed up under there..."

"What are you doing?" Now Loretta just looked like she'd been stabbed in the gut, doubling over a little toward the steering wheel.

"Washing won't work on all that grime. Oh, no. You need something sharp, something to slide between the nail and the skin and dig out everything that slipped in there when you weren't paying attention."

"Stop it," Loretta spat and gasped despite herself. "You stop it right—"

"A toothpick does the job. Small enough to scrape out the first line of dirt under those perfectly manicured fucking nails."

"You can't—" The other woman's shoulders drew up toward her ears, like she'd just been doused with a bucket of cold water. But she wasn't feeling *cold* now, was she? And the heat of Don's beat had nothing on the fire Bernadette's words stoked now in this dried-up joke of a fucking bigot.

"One steady scrape. One nice big chunk of grit. And there's your clean nail afterward. That little crescent of white at the tip."

"Oh… oh!" Loretta gasped again and almost threw her face against the steering wheel, her body shuddering within the goddamn blazer. "Our Father, who art… w-who art in heav—"

"And look. There's a napkin right there. Someplace to wipe off all the dirt and grit. The proof that life just gets downright fucking messy, isn't it? The dirt you just can't stand. You wipe that toothpick clean."

"Heaven!" The midwife gasped and threw herself backward in the driver's seat. Maybe hard enough to give herself a nice big headache after this. Wouldn't that just be fucking peachy?

"And then you pick the next fingernail and slip that tiny wooden point right… back… underneath." Bernadette spat the last word like a curse, condemning everything about Loretta and people like her. She'd tried to be reasonable with the woman. She'd tried to make this work, to salvage what she could of one massive oversight on her part. But the patience she'd spent so long stockpiling away had all burned up. "You just have to get out all that dirt."

Loretta shrieked behind the wheel and spasmed in release. Probably for the first time since she'd had to start dyeing all that short, spikey hair to cover the gray. Then she pushed herself back upright, panting, and grabbed the inside handle of the door. "You'll pay for that, you fucking bitch!"

"You're welcome." Bernadette glared at her old

friend—now just one more bigoted coward trying to find her own worth by snatching it away from others.

Loretta slammed the car door and started the engine. The Range Rover's tires churned through the gravel almost at the same second, the engine revving dangerously. Then the car jerked against found traction and kicked up off the gravel and onto the grass beside the cabin. Loretta almost drove herself right into a palmetto tree before correcting enough for a tighter turn, and the SUV sped back down the gravel drive toward the main road, spraying up rocks and dust and sand.

Bernadette lifted the collar of her dress enough to wipe the woman's spit off her face. It wasn't an efficient attempt—she was too riled up to pay much more attention—but at least it wasn't running down her jaw anymore. She stood there glaring after the quickly disappearing black vehicle, her chest heaving, and felt nothing in her aching, ageing body but the searing fire of her beat in her chest and her racing heart beneath it.

"What the hell was that?" Randall asked as he stepped up behind her.

"That was me buying us as much time as I could." She turned stiffly around and didn't miss the surprise and concern in the man's eyes. He must have seen her fury. He must have thought she'd lost her mind. "And it just ran out."

29

BERNADETTE OPENED THE back door into the kitchen of their long row house in Charleston, thinking she'd catch them watching a movie in the living room on the other side of the house. It felt like the time for a few good surprises, especially after the hell of a night she'd just had. So she didn't even bother to look up into the kitchen when she closed the door behind her and dropped her keys on the counter.

"Mom!"

She jumped a little and whirled toward the kitchen table. A grin broke out across her face when she saw her daughter at the kitchen table. "*Hey*, baby. I..." A surprised laugh escaped her. "I did *not* expect you to be sittin' right here."

Olivia shrugged, her thick, dark curls pulled back into

pigtails exploding from the hair ties over her shoulders. "I'm almost done."

"Almost done?" Bernadette stepped toward the round kitchen table across from the stove and bent to press a kiss to her daughter's cheek. She pulled Olivia's face just a little closer, squishing the girl's cheek against her lips and breathing in the smell of that ridiculous Blue Raspberry body wash the girl loved so much. "Mm."

Olivia patted her mom's cheek a few times, waiting to be released, and stared at her notebooks spread out on the table. Finally, Bernadette released her and straightened, grinning even wider when the girl flashed her a proud smile. "Yeah. Just a few more problems, then I'm done with *everything*."

"How long have you been sitting here?" Bernadette glanced at the clock on the stove; it was 11:13 p.m.

"Since I got home." Olivia shrugged again and twirled her pencil between her fingers as she leaned back over her notebook.

"From *school*?"

"Yep."

With a little chuckle, Bernadette ran a hand over the top of her daughter's head and studied all the textbooks and papers scattered across the table. "Honey, it's Friday. You don't have to get all this done today."

"Yeah, I know. But this way, I have the whole weekend to do whatever I want."

"Huh. You might just be the only fifth-grader I know who doesn't wait 'til the last minute on the weekend to do all their homework."

Olivia turned to look up at her mom, those light-brown eyes shimmering with mischief and a knowing most ten-year-olds didn't carry with them. "How many other fifth-graders do you even know?"

"How many—hey…" Bernadette gave her daughter's shoulder a playful little shove. "I know Jackson and Courtney, don't I?"

"Yeah, just because they're my friends." The girl rolled her eyes and turned back toward her work, but a small smile lingered at the corners of her mouth. "I know Jackson gets all his stuff done first too. He's faster than me."

"Not for long." Smirking, Bernadette folded her arms and tried to figure out what the heck kind of math problems her kid had almost blown completely through. None of it made any sense, but it didn't matter. Olivia didn't look anywhere close to asking anybody for help with a single piece of this mess. "They sure did give you a lot to do."

"Not really. Some of this isn't due 'til Tuesday."

Bernadette blinked. "Are you serious?"

"I tried to get her to take a break." Darrell leaned against the doorway into the kitchen, his arms folded beneath his usually impassive expression. He raised his eyebrows. "Einstein turned down a movie *and* popcorn. Bought this whole box of Skittles, too. Didn't make a difference."

He jiggled the box back and forth, the pieces rattling around inside.

"And you'd rather do your homework than be a part of that?" Bernadette raised an eyebrow at her daughter, who just shot her notebooks an exaggerated blink.

"Tonight, yeah. Are y'all actually *trying* to distract me

right now?"

"Um… a little. Uh-huh." Bernadette glanced across the kitchen at Darrell. The man pressed his lips together to smother a laugh. Shaking her head, she crossed the kitchen and didn't quite whisper it as softly as she could have. "She'd rather do homework than watch a movie on a Friday night."

"Girl's got some different priorities."

"She's *ten*."

"Nothin' wrong with startin' early, I guess." Darrell unfolded his arms and reached for her when she got close enough.

"Oh, sure. She's startin' early. And apparently, we can't even bribe our own kid into having a little fun." Bernadette laughed and tipped her head back to meet his kiss.

"I can still hear y'all, by the way." Olivia didn't look up from her notebook again, and her parents smothered another laugh.

"We're too distracting, aren't we?"

"Can't get in the way of genius." Darrell smoothed his hand over Bernadette's hair and chuckled. She'd pulled it back in a tight ponytail hours ago when she'd set out for Donna's little shindig tonight. Most of it had come undone somewhere between running around that distribution center and getting back into her car to make the few hours' drive home.

"Better let the genius work, then." With a final glance back at their daughter, whose attention seemed fully returned to her oh-so-important schoolwork, Bernadette even tried to chuckle in a whisper.

"How did it go?" Darrell settled his hands on her hips and pulled her closer against him.

"It was… You know what? It was wild. They had more of that"—she lowered her voice again—"that awful *shit* than I thought was possible in one place."

"Pointera?"

"Mm-hmm." She wrapped her arms around his waist and clasped her hands behind his back. Only now, as she craned her neck to look up into his dark, curious eyes, did she realize just how sore her neck and back really were after the night she'd had. Most likely, she could blame the whiplash, among other things.

"And?" Darrell raised his eyebrows, the lightheartedness hardening now into something else. Something she'd expected, but planning on having to face that when she came home didn't make seeing it now any easier.

"And we did what we had to do." Bernadette looked over her shoulder just to double-check they weren't being overheard. Too hard to tell where Olivia's attention was now anyway. The girl could multi-task in her sleep.

"B…" He dipped his head toward her. "Come on, now. Tell me y'all did something worth the trip down there."

"Of course it was worth it." She shot him a playful frown and tried to brush him off. "You know what we're trying to do."

"Uh-huh. You told me you talked to Donna about snatching up all that shit instead. You told me she thought it was a good idea."

"She *did* think it was a good idea, babe. We had the talk. Brought it up to a vote with everyone else." A cold knot of anxiety twisted a little tighter in her gut. She'd done her part to bring up an alternative, and then she'd done her part once the decision had been made. "They voted the other way."

"Aw, see?" Darrell's hands dropped from around her waist, and he lifted his head to scan the opposite wall of the hallway. "How am I supposed to sit around here feelin' good about you bein' gone after this? Y'all can't just keep blowin' shit up whenever you feel like it—"

"Hey, watch it." Bernadette nodded into the kitchen.

"She's gonna figure it out one way or another, B." He ran a hand over his closely buzzed hair and ended up rubbing his neck in frustration. "Either she hears it from us first, or she hears it from the goddamn news. Or her teachers and the other kids at school."

"We were careful. We always are. Nobody knows what's goin' on, and somebody has to do something about that shit they're about to pump out into the world for everyone to pick up whenever they want."

"Yeah, and maybe there's a good thing can come of it. You ever think of that?"

"That's not what's happening." She stepped away from him and leaned back against the wall of the hallway. "Archie has a doctor friend, babe. The guy says that drug's gonna backfire and hurt way more people than it helps."

"How's that any different than what y'all are doin' right now? Playin' goddamn James Bond when nobody asked y'all to take this shit on."

"Who else is gonna stop this?" She'd raised her voice now, despite the lingering awareness in the back of her mind that Olivia sat at the table on the other side of the kitchen.

"You want our daughter to grow up in a world where she can just walk right into a pharmacy with a script for meth? Or heroin? Look at how much she cares about getting ahead. Being faster and better at everything she does. She's exactly the kind of person they're trying to hit with this shit."

"Nobody's selling meth out of a CVS, B."

"Well not *now*. Now they don't have anything to sell. Because of *us*."

"That ain't the *point*!" Darrell closed his eyes and let out a long sigh. "Y'all are wastin' your time on somethin' that just doesn't matter. Those companies'll keep comin' back, poppin' outta the ground every time you think you buried 'em. Y'all should be tryin' to help the people who actually need help instead of playin' games with somethin' way bigger than Donna thinks she is."

"We *are* helping people."

"Looks like y'all are just causin' headaches, is what it looks like."

"You know what?" Bernadette lifted her hands and stepped sideways down the hall. "I don't need this shit right now. I came home wanting to see my family and spend some time forgettin' about all that. If we have to talk about this later, fine. Not now."

"Naw. We're talkin' about this."

She turned down the hall, shaking her head. A huge, warm hand clamped down around her wrist and stopped her. Bernadette stared at Darrell's dark fingers, then slowly looked up at him. He let her go just as quickly and spread his arms.

"This needs to be talked about, B. 'Cause there's

helpin' people, and then there's just bein' hooked on all Donna's kinda craziness. Y'all could be doin' somethin' *good* for people right now."

"Like what?"

"Shit, you know how many people been' comin' on down here since Katrina? What about helpin' them?"

Bernadette let out a bitter laugh. "I don't think my beat's gonna have anything to offer people who lost their homes."

"And those special words of yours do a lot when you're blowin' up a warehouse full of drugs, huh?"

"Darrell…"

"I'm serious 'bout this. Donna's got connections all over the place. People who know people. What you *could* be doin' is using that beat or whatever y'all are callin' it now and get someone to pass some better laws around here. Like a trade, right?"

"What?" She leaned toward him, her eyes wide as she tried so hard to keep her fucking voice down. "Are you seriously tellin' me to go pimp out my beat for legislation?"

"Come on. It's not the first time you told those stories to get somethin' done. I remember hundred-dollar bills in your hand for fifteen minutes in a strip club—"

"That was different."

"No it ain't. I had no beef with it then, B. I don't give a damn if that's what you gotta do to get people to listen to what we need around here."

"Don't tell me what I need!"

"Mom?"

Bernadette whipped her head toward the kitchen. Olivia

sat up in her chair now, her eyes wide with concern. The pencil had been abandoned on the table, and the girl now rubbed her chest, looking worried and confused and a little ashen.

"We're just talkin', honey. Go on and finish your home-work."

"Y'all are just tearin' down when y'all should be buildin' up, B." Darrell stepped toward her, looking worried now too and softened by some unvoiced need he couldn't quite express. "I've seen too many things torn down for no reason. Takin' all kindsa people with it. We both have."

"It wasn't my choice to make."

"Then find someone else makin' different choices. Donna's people aren't the only ones like you out there. You find *them*, and you make it a point to start *buildin'* somethin' with what y'all got."

"Well it's not like I can just go around South Carolina asking if people have some freak thing inside them they can't explain. You *know* what's about to happen with that anyway. They're about to make what I do..." Bernadette shook her head and forced herself to whisper. "They're about to make it a goddamn felony, Darrell. I saw a draft of that new bill. Nobody's gonna just start steppin' up and claiming they can do this, all proud and brave."

"Come on. Destroyin' government property ain't ex-actly legit, either."

"Mom... Dad?"

They both turned toward their daughter, who looked like she'd gotten something stuck in her throat. Olivia's hand had moved from her chest to her neck now, rubbing at something there none of them could see.

"What's wrong, baby? You need to get a glass of water or somethin'?"

"I don't…" Olivia blinked and stared blankly at the table.

"Go get her some water." Bernadette nodded into the kitchen. "We shouldn't be talkin' about this right here anyway."

"Oh, sure. Just keep brushin' me off like every other time I try to have the real hard conversations with you." Darrell smacked a hand down on the doorway into the kitchen. "Damnit, B, I don't even know when you're gonna be home half the time. We ain't sayin' what needs to be said when you're gone, and I'm not interested in pretendin' you can't do better with that thing you've been given."

"You think I'm just wastin' it, do ya?" Bernadette patted her own chest and stepped toward him, her neck craned back so she could hold his gaze. "Think there's some perfect job waiting out there for me where I'm *not* doin' somethin' folks would generally frown upon? I'm not gonna sit behind a desk all day and kill myself for somethin' I don't believe in—"

"Yeah, you're gon' kill yourself, all right. Y'all are just as bad as—"

"Stop it!" Olivia lurched up from her seat, sending the chair clattering back against the wall behind the door. "Stop yelling at each other. This isn't what y'all do! I know y'all love each other, so can't you just act like…"

Her daughter's words fizzled away somewhere in the back of Bernadette's mind. As Olivia shouted at them from behind the kitchen table, Bernadette found herself focusing only on the tightness in her chest. Her throat closed, like some invisible hand had wrapped around it and squeezed. She tried to take a breath and choked on the effort. Her own hands went up to her throat, trying to free it from the sudden pressure. The burning in her lungs now was nothing like her own beat and everything like suffocating right there in the hall. When she staggered backward and thumped against the hallway wall, she looked up to see Darrell doubled over, holding himself up with a hand against the doorway while he coughed and tried to suck in a full breath that just wouldn't come.

He dropped to one knee, and Bernadette's awareness scrambled to find an answer. The carbon monoxide detectors would've gone off a long time ago, right? And what about Olivia?

Bernadette pushed herself off the wall, gasping and wheezing, and found herself on her hands and knees a second later. She looked up into the kitchen, reaching for her daughter. If this was it for her, fine. But she had to get Olivia outside. She had to get her child out of this before all three of them were—

"What's... W-what's going on?" Olivia stared at them and lurched out from behind the table. "Mama?" The girl froze there in the middle of the kitchen, her lower lip trembling as she stared at her parents falling over themselves in the hall.

The grip around Bernadette's throat let off just enough for her take in a raw, searing, desperate gasp. Behind her, Darrell fell into a fit of coughing and sat back against the wall. Now she could breathe again. Now she could think, and the light in the kitchen seemed brighter than ever.

"Are you okay?" Olivia's voice cracked, her eyes quickly filling with tears. The curls bursting from her pigtails shivered as a wave of trembling washed over the ten-year-old girl who'd just done what none of them had expected. What none of them could have ever known until it happened, just like this.

And that was exactly what it was. Bernadette was certain of it. She stared up at her daughter and for a moment just couldn't move.

Olivia's shaking hand returned to her own throat, as if she had to double-check that she was still inside her body. Still there. This was real. "Mama, I... I didn't mean to—"

"Oh, baby." Bernadette leapt to her feet and raced across the kitchen toward her daughter. The girl's tiny, solid frame fit right into her arms, and Olivia let out a strangled sob.

"I couldn't stop it—"

"No, no. Shh. It's okay." She wanted to squeeze her daughter tighter than she ever had, to press the girl so closely against her that it would suck all that horror and shame right out of Olivia and into Bernadette herself. "You're okay. We're all fine."

"I'm sorry, Mama..."

"You didn't know. We didn't know, baby. Everything's okay." She stroked those dark, shivering curls and felt two small hands clutching at her jacket. Olivia bucked in her arms with silent tears, her entire body still trembling with all the reactions Bernadette had had to teach herself to rein in.

But no one in Bernadette's family had known what to do with a child who could make them feel something just because of the words she'd spoken, whether in rage or terror or spite or just because she fucking could.

But Olivia didn't have that problem, did she? Bernadette might have considered her daughter lucky on that count and that count only. The girl wouldn't have to go through this alone, because Bernadette was there, and Bernadette knew what this was.

A shadow passed over them in the living room, and she looked up to see Darrell standing behind them. Tears swam in the dark pools of his eyes too, and he bit his bottom lip as he studied his child and her mother—two-thirds of their family who now belonged to a world he accepted but could never fully understand.

She didn't need to explain to him what had just happened. He already knew, and he didn't have to say that he still stood by them no matter what. Darrell set a hand on the back of Bernadette's neck. Olivia lifted her head for a gasping breath, her light-brown cheeks flushed and glistening with a layer of her own tears. When she saw her father standing there, the pain on that face—a face too young to have to feel anything like this—broke Bernadette's heart. It was a pain that started right here with hoping her daddy still loved her, despite what he'd just watched her become. And no matter what Darrell did now, that pain would stay with Olivia for the rest of her life.

"Come here, baby." That was all he had to say, and the girl threw herself against him. He lifted her up into his arms and ran his hand down her tight curls before burying his face in them. When he met Bernadette's gaze again, everything he might have said but didn't was right there in his eyes. They'd get through this too, just like they were getting through everything else. But where the rest of the world could see them and make their own judgments—a white woman and a black man raising their daughter in the South in the twenty-first century—no one would ever see the other legacy Olivia carried with her until it was too late. And how the fuck were they supposed to make sure that things never got that far?

Darrell sniffed and turned away, carrying their crying child out of the kitchen. Olivia had looked so damn grown up sitting at that table with her head in her books and a sharp, witty defiance against anything that got in her way. But in her daddy's arms, she was still so terrifyingly small.

Bernadette stepped back against the counter beside the kitchen sink. Her own body trembled now too, and she clapped both hands over her mouth so they wouldn't hear her crying beside the fridge. But her hands just weren't strong enough to keep it all down.

30

From j.hammel@aol.com
Sent: March 24th, 2007

Just in case you haven't seen this little news clip. I'm not sure how widespread it is right now, but it's from last night. One of my friends was holding the camera. Those aren't cops, Bernie. I don't know who the hell these people are, but they're watching us. Didn't identify themselves, and none of the beat-spinners put up a fight at all. And these ass-holes just... Well, you'll see.

I know you want to protect O too, but maybe showing her some of this is just another way of keeping her safe. You stay safe too, Bernie.

—Janet

From j.hammel@aol.com
Sent: December 3, 2008

Federal Law Declares "Powerful Stories" a Punishable Of-
fense

    Can you believe this shit? Especially now, *with what's*
happening in this country. We just elected the first black
president (I sure as shit voted for him), and I thought things
were about to start looking up. I guess not. Not for us, any-
way.
    This is fucking bullshit.

From j.hammel@aol.com
Sent: June 27, 2010

Topper and MindBlink Roll Out One-Minute Infodeos For
Faster Learning

Pointera Is "The Gold Standard" in Information Technol-
ogy

Social Media Corporations Claim the "Miracle Drug"
Pointera Saves IT Industry

    What the fuck is this shit? My neighbor's already
hooked on this poison, Bernie. And the whole world's eating

lies like candy.

I haven't left my house in two fucking weeks. No way they're telling us everything.

—J.

31

"RAN OUT OF time for what?" Randall apparently had no problem on those long legs of his keeping up with Bernadette's pace. And she felt like she was almost running.

"This safehouse isn't a goddamn safehouse anymore, Randall. That woman's lost her mind, and she's about to bring down some kinda hell on us. We need to move."

"Wait a minute. What?"

She stopped and whirled on the man. Randall blinked in surprise, his eyes large behind his glasses. "What part of Plan B don't you understand, man? Loretta found out who we are. Time to go."

"But we already talked about it. No beats while she was here."

"Yeah, and we were stupid enough to forget about passing the message to Don and Mirela too."

He stopped. "Both of them?"

"Yeah." She just stormed on up to the porch, flinging the screen door aside and letting it fall behind her with a bang. Tony jumped up out of the rocking chair and spread his arms, his eyes wide. "Back on the road. It's time."

The kid shot Randall the same confused look, and Randall just shrugged before he followed Bernadette into the kitchen. "Bernadette, what about Mirela and the baby?"

"Them too. Hey, call Cameron. Tell him to get his ass back here right now. I don't care if he's not done. Tell him we hit trouble." She threw open the door into the master bedroom and closed it swiftly behind her. Then she sat on the edge of the king-sized bed and finally let herself take a deep breath. She should never have sent Cameron out with that van while the midwives were here. Hellen was fine, sure. Maybe she didn't agree with what they were doing, but she didn't hold anything against Sleepwater or people with the beat in general. But Loretta? "Fuck."

She couldn't have known that Loretta would get sucked up in some kind of hate group disguised as law-abiding citizens. How could someone really change that much in twenty years? Only when the world changed first, wasn't that right? Only when the powers that be decided to toss all reason and justice out the window. And then good people did bad things, and those bad things turned them into someone Bernadette didn't fucking recognize.

"Me and my goddamn temper." She closed her eyes and sighed heavily, then pulled the cheap phone out of the pocket of her cardigan. For a few seconds, all she could do was stare at it. She didn't want to make the call like this. Not with so many other lives quite literally on the line. And now one more life in all their hands, not just her parents'. Loretta didn't bat a fucking eyelash before spewing all that shit at the *child* she'd helped deliver herself. No, for that woman, this was black and white. And that was how Bernadette had to see things now. The hard choices were always easier to make when there were only two. When she'd already seen the consequences of the choice she just couldn't make again.

She had to make the call.

Flipping open that cheap phone, she pulled up the contacts list. Not as long as when she'd had a phone plan and a semblance of stability. Not as short as the last phone she'd left somewhere in Kentucky. Then the phone buzzed in her hand, and the pain in her chest made her wonder if this was it. Bernadette would have a heart attack right here on this fucking bed in her family's fucking cabin, and no one would know.

Olivia. She'd saved the number herself just last night, but seeing it come up all on its own was an electrifying reminder of how long she'd gone without seeing the word in front of her at all, let alone speaking it. She thought she'd find her fingers trembling when she pressed the button to accept the call, but they didn't.

"Hello?"

A few seconds of silence greeted her. Maybe her daughter had butt-dialed her somehow. Bullshit. Until yesterday, Bernadette hadn't given this number out to anyone.

"Hi, B."

A quick, sharp laugh escaped her, much sharper than she thought possible. Of course she wasn't Mom anymore.

Hard to think of her as Mom when she hadn't been one for twenty years.

"How did you get this number?" And what else was she supposed to say? *How are you? It's been a long time, huh? Hope you're doing well.* That was useless.

"Dad gave it to me."

"He did, huh?"

"I let him have his moment. Honestly, I didn't think I'd ever make this call, but I—" Olivia took a sharp breath, and a few muffled voices in the background cut off entirely. "Something happened."

It didn't matter that they hadn't spoken for more than half her daughter's life. Bernadette heard the uncertainty and fear in that voice like she'd just tuned into a private station. "What's goin' on?"

"They…" Olivia sighed, and the sound of a car blinker came through the line. "A lot of people are really pissed off that you came back to Charleston."

"Loretta's friends?" She was going out on a limb with that one, assuming Olivia even knew who the woman associated with these days. And there was no way Loretta had made it back to the city yet. But the woman had a phone, and she was definitely one of those pissed-off people.

"No, I don't think so. A lot of people I've seen around Mr. B's at Dad's shows. Mickey Anderson. Whitt Palmer and his brothers. Shandra Bryan."

"You're kidding."

"I wouldn't call you just for a joke, B."

"No, no. I know. Guess the cat's outta the bag on this one, huh? Surprise. I'm back."

"Yeah, well, it was one hell of a way to find out." Olivia sighed again, and somewhere in the background, a car honked.

"Listen, I was just about to call you." Bernadette's hand went automatically to her heart. This was it. Give nothing for over two decades just to ask for a favor out of the blue.

"Oh, yeah? Why?"

The words sent a dagger through her heart. Why would a mother call her own child? Why hadn't she until now? "I need a favor, honey."

"Ha. *You* need a favor. I just... Fine. What is it?"

Olivia sounded scattered, short, off-balance. "Loretta wasn't very happy to see me back in town, either. I thought we could trust her, but I made a mistake. I was hoping you might have a safe place for us to come lay low. Just for a night or two while we figure out our next moves."

"We?" Olivia cleared her throat. "B, how many do you have with you?"

"Me and six others. And a baby."

"A *baby*?"

"'Bout an hour old, give or take. And I'll be damned if I hang around here just waiting for Loretta to come back with whoever she went off to talk to. We're stayin' at the cabin in Hollywood."

"Oh, my God. You... Yeah. Yeah, of course."

The relief washing through Bernadette at those words made her think for a moment that she would fall over right there on the bed and pass out entirely. "Thank you. I know it's a lot to ask—"

"Y'all have a baby with you. It's not that much to ask."

Olivia sniffed, and something rustled against the phone.

"Just text me your address, then? We travel light, so as soon as our van gets back—"

"No, you can't come to my house." Her daughter's voice broke for a second, and a shaky breath burst out of her. "I'd bring y'all inside if I could, but my place isn't safe."

"What?"

"That's where they found me. Screaming about you and how I was just as—" Olivia blew out another long breath. "I can't go back there, either."

"Did they hurt you?"

"No, I'm fine. If anyone got hurt, it was them." The wry amusement in those words left them both breathless and silent for a second. Then Olivia barked out a laugh, which was quickly muffled again. "I can't believe I just did that. I, uh… I might still be in shock. I don't know. I have a friend up in Aiken. That's where I'm heading. So I'll text you that address, and y'all can come there."

Bernadette's gut twisted all over again. Those mother-fuckers had taken all their hate and their fury and probably what they thought was a sense of justice to her *daughter's house*. And all of it was meant for Bernadette instead. All of it. And she couldn't think of anything to say but, "Are you sure you're okay?"

"No, B. I'm not sure. But I'll just… Look, I have to get off the phone. I'll send you the address."

Then the line went dead, and Bernadette was left staring at the phone lowering into her lap. That was the call. Their first conversation since Olivia was still in high school, and that was what they had to say to each other. Why had she even called Bernadette in the first place? Mickey Anderson and the Palmer brothers and Shandra Bryan and whoever the fuck else thought they could storm through Olivia Wilkins' front door just to get at Bernadette, and Olivia should have been more pissed off than anything else. Right?

For the life of her, Bernadette couldn't figure out if that call had been a warning or a condemnation. Or maybe a cry for help. And that possibility hurt more than all the others.

She shoved the phone into her pocket and pushed herself off the bed. They still had another hour and a half, maybe two, before Loretta brought another posse of infuriated, terrified idiots all the way back down here with her, depending on how fast the woman drove back up 17. That wasn't very long at all, but it was more time than this Sleepwater group usually had when they were being chased out of one house and right back onto the road again.

The tricky part now was getting the message across without throwing Mirela into a panic. The woman was strong; that had been clear from the beginning, when she and Brad joined Sleepwater and made it their life by choice and nothing else. But a baby changed things. It always did.

When she pulled open the bedroom door again, Randall and the twins were gathered right there in the kitchen. They all turned toward her with their full attention, ready to do what had to be done. And looking to her for direction on just what exactly that was.

They were all used to jumping into action at the last minute. But the threat coming after them hadn't reached their door yet, and where was Cameron with that goddamn van?

"Did you talk to him?" she asked Randall.

"Yeah, he was already on his way back. Should be here any minute."

"Good. Start packing up. We need to be out of here five minutes ago." Bernadette took off toward the step down into the living room. The twins nearly leapt out of her way, and she swore she could feel their silent gazes ripping right through her back. Brad looked up at her as she approached him and Mirela and their child. This family shouldn't have had to do what she was about to ask, but not asking was even more dangerous for all of them.

Bernadette sat on the couch—if she got down on that fucking floor again, she'd need a crane to pick her back up—and leaned forward toward Hellen. "How are they doin'?"

"Everybody's healthy. Baby's doing great. Mama did a pretty damn fine job too. The worst part's over."

What a euphemism for *'We almost had to drive her an hour to the hospital, and how fucked up would that have been?'*

"That's good." Bernadette nodded slowly and hated herself for the next words not yet out of her mouth. "Healthy enough to travel?"

Hellen's jaw dropped. "What?"

"*What?*" Brad slid his hands off Mirela's shoulder and stared at Bernadette. His wife cradled their baby and slowly lifted her gaze as well.

"Just answer the question." Bernadette swallowed.

"I wouldn't recommend it, no." Hellen sat back on her heels and dropped her hands into her lap. Her gloves were off now, tossed aside into the cardboard box she'd turned into a trashcan. "They need rest—"

"I know. But is getting into a van for a few hours gonna hurt either one of them more than they can handle?" More than Mirela could handle, really. But the woman had regained almost all of her color, and she was remarkably calm for the fact that Bernadette even had to ask this question right there in front of her. She hoped that would last at least until they got to this other house in Aiken.

Hellen's eyes narrowed. "No, but—"

"Thank you." Bernadette turned to Brad and Mirela. "I am *so* sorry."

"What happened?" Brad's eyes burned into hers, his jaw working again and making his red beard ripple like a fur coat.

"I couldn't talk her down is what happened. And believe me, she'll be back."

"Jesus," Hellen whispered and put a hand to her mouth.

"Bernadette, where are we gonna go?" Brad settled a hand back on Mirela's shoulder. "She just had a baby—"

"I know, Brad. I was here. And now we *really* need to not be here. Especially with that sweet child. Mirela, honey."

The new mother nodded, her eyes clear and determined and fully aware of what was being asked of her. "It's fine."

"Babe, it's *not* fine! You can't just get up and start running. What about—"

"Brad." Mirela leaned back on the pillow and tipped her head back to look at her husband. "Do you know how many shootouts we were in while I was pregnant? If I can run from a helicopter falling out of the sky and get hit by Kaylee's—" She stopped; none of them had done much talking about what had marked the end of one insanely dangerous chapter of Sleepwater's work before this endless running began. "If I made it through all that, I can walk to a van. We'll be fine."

Brad ran a hand through his hair and stared at her. Then that hand went down to stroke the top of their daughter's head and the tiny patch of dark fuzz covering it.

Tires crunched across the gravel outside, then a door opened and closed before they heard Cameron shouting, "What the fuck happened this time?"

Bernadette nodded. "Get her up. We need to go."

Then she pushed herself off the couch and fought back an echo of the groan coming from every joint in her body.

"Bernadette." Hellen stared at the woman who'd gone from prodigal pariah returned to this person taking charge and making inconceivable demands. "You can't be serious."

"Watch me." Bernadette didn't look at her old friend from a time when she herself had tried to make the right decisions, to settle into her role and find a purpose guiding new life into the world instead of eventually taking it. More than anything in this moment, she wished Karl were here. The rest of Sleepwater had come to understand that her decisions were worth listening to every time. But if Karl had given her only one thing, it was the reassurance that she could trust *herself*.

She headed for the back bedroom where she'd been sleeping, where Hellen and Loretta had slept in shifts overnight through the long process of sharing Mirela's labor, where she and Candace had spent so many summer nights in a reckless sort of childhood ignorance until they'd come to hate each other very well. When she packed up her small overnight bag with everything a woman needed and couldn't find on the road, she knew she was never coming back.

It wouldn't have surprised her if this little abandoned cabin down in Hollywood made the news—*Vacation Shack Burns Down. No Casualties. Authorities Still Investigating.* Except for they wouldn't investigate. Not really. Because the rest of the world had finally heard of the beat and what beat-spinners could do, and the rest of the world thought they knew what it meant. For Bernadette, it meant nothing more than who she was and what she'd passed on, but that form of simplicity never made for good headlines, and it sure as shit wasn't strong enough to divide a nation and sow all the hate so crucial for control. And that type of lie wasn't anything new.

Sleepwater and those with the beat were most definitely not the first with this kind of target on their backs, and they certainly wouldn't be the last.

She stormed back through the living room with her bag slung over her shoulder and nodded at Brad helping his wife to her feet. Hellen held their daughter while the woman who'd just birthed the child slipped back into some semblance of clothing. Bernadette settled a hand on her old friend's back and muttered, "Whatever you can send with us to help these two would be very much appreciated."

The midwife turned toward her, that tiny pink head covered in tufts of black hair so very small in her arms. "They need aftercare, Bernie. Someone who can follow up and make sure everything's working the way it should."

"They'll have it for the next few days, at least. Thank you for being here. I'm sorry this is the way things had to be."

Tears shimmered in Hellen's eyes beneath the strands of gray hair worried loose from their place. "I'm sorry too."

"Well, you tried." Bernadette glanced one more time at the child, but the babe would be with them the whole way. And she'd be safe, even if it was the last thing this old, washed-up beat-spinner could do for a new generation whose futures she was too old to see. But not too old to touch.

The twins walked into the kitchen from the porch just as she stepped back up out of the main room. Don's face had taken on a bright-red flush. "Bernadette, I'm sorry," he muttered. "I didn't know."

"Not your fault." She laid a hand on his bony shoulder. "We didn't cover all our bases, and someone should have told you."

"Mirela said she had a feeling she'd need my beat. That it might save them—"

"Don't." Bernadette squeezed his shoulder. "No one's blaming you, and no one ever will. Now I need you two to get on into that master bedroom and clear out all their things. New parents have enough to worry about on a good day. This is what you can do for them, yeah?"

She left the twins standing in the kitchen and headed for the door out onto the porch. Don just stared blankly at the counter until Tony thumped him on the back and took off into the bedroom. His brother followed, struck with just as much silent bewilderment as his identical other half who hadn't said a word in seven months.

The kitchen door whispered shut behind her, then the screen door onto the porch. Randall and Cameron stood in front of the van that had carried them all across the country and then some, arguing about whatever the hell needed arguing in their minds. Cameron caught sight of her huffing toward them and flipped Randall the bird, cutting the man off mid-sentence. "You said we were safe down here."

"We were." Bernadette headed straight for the back of the van and opened the trunk with a quick jerk.

"You shouldn't have sent me out for fucking grocery shopping," Cameron added, stalking toward her. His mop of dirty-blond hair fell across his sweaty forehead in the mid-morning heat. "I have no problem pulling old ladies out of their cars. I could've stopped her. At least made her too fucking confused to get behind the wheel—"

"And then what?" She turned toward him and folded her arms. "Then we'd have a confused old lady tied up somewhere around here with an even more fucked-up idea of who we are. We don't kidnap people, Cameron."

"We don't fuck around, either." The man jammed his hands into his pockets and scowled at her, looking every bit as brooding as the day Randall had brought him and Kaylee to her front door—as the day three months ago when he'd finally said it out loud that Kaylee was probably dead in a ditch somewhere and deserved every bit of it for what she'd done to them. Nobody had argued, but nobody believed he'd really meant it.

Scanning the bags of groceries piled haphazardly around the black duffel bags full of what she hoped they wouldn't have to use—not in South Carolina—Bernadette nodded at him and stepped back. "At least we're stocked up. You did your part. Make some room in here for the rest of our things. As soon as Mirela and that baby are in this god-damn van, we're outta here."

Cameron rolled his eyes but did what was asked of him anyway. Just like the rest of them. They had to, if they wanted to survive this. Just like they'd had to before and survived one narrow escape after the next. They looked after their own, and the questions could wait.

Randall stepped toward her and dipped his head to mutter, "We're driving around with a newborn? For real?"

"Yes, Randall. Unless you wanna start building a barricade right now to fight off the villagers when they show up with torches and pitchforks, we're driving with a newborn."

He grimaced and pushed his glasses back up his hooked nose. "They need rest, don't they? Food. Sleep. A doctor, probably?"

"They'll have all that in a few hours when we get where we're going." Bernadette held his gaze and raised her eyebrows, really hoping he wouldn't keep pushing. The man didn't push unless he thought it was absolutely necessary, unless he figured no one else would do it first.

"Another safehouse?"

"Sort of. While we need it, yeah."

The man pressed his lips together and tilted his head, skepticism and doubt written all over that awfully bird-like gesture. "How do we know it's safe?"

Jesus Christ, he was really fucking drilling her *right now*.

"Because I got a call from someone who has too much of a conscience to sell us out." She pulled her pack of cigarettes and the lighter from the pocket of her cardigan and turned away from the van and the breeze to light it.

"You heard from Leo and John?" There it was—all that hope written across his face that they'd been carrying with them for months. All the hope she now had to crush one more time.

"No."

"Then who the hell would call you out of the blue to give a safehouse right when we need it?"

Bernadette took a long drag, wishing now that she'd taken that guy in Louisiana's offer when he'd opened his hand and told her she could have the four thin joints he'd rolled that morning. And she'd thought she wouldn't want them later. She'd thought she wouldn't need it. Her breath shuddered through her lips, dragging all the smoke out with it.

"Bernadette. Who's got our lives in their hands this time?"

She glanced up at him with a frown, then had to look away before she said it. "My daughter."

32

"MOM, I'M HOME!" The kitchen door shut with an enthu-
siastic bang, followed by the thump of a backpack on the
table and quick, carefree footsteps.

Bernadette's heart pounded heavily in her chest. How
the fuck was she supposed to have this conversation? How
the fuck had she not seen this coming?

"Mom? Where are you—oh. Hey." Olivia grinned at
her in the entrance to the living room, but Bernadette
couldn't even look up at her. "You okay?"

"Take a seat." She patted the couch cushion beside her,
her hand flopping limply like a dead bird. "We need to talk."

"Okay…" Olivia took a few halting steps into the living
room and slowly lowered herself onto the couch. She sat
closer than her mother expected—closer than either one of

them would want to be in the next few seconds. "What's going on?"

Bernadette brushed her finger across the mouse pad of the laptop on the coffee table to wake it up, then turned the whole thing toward her daughter. "I really hope you can tell me this isn't what it looks like, but I don't think that's possible."

The girl's light-brown eyes widened, then she slammed the laptop closed and pulled it into her lap. "You went through my *email*?"

"Olivia—"

"I seriously thought you trusted me enough not to spy on me like a fucking helicopter mom—"

"Watch your mouth." She didn't raise her voice, but the level sternness in it—the steady, warning seriousness she'd adopted over sixteen years of parenting with a man who'd spoken that way his entire life—made her daughter swallow hard. "Honey, I'm not spying on you. My computer died, and I needed to check a few emails, so I figured I'd just use yours real quick and be done with it. You left that open for anyone to find."

"You could've just used your phone," Olivia whispered.

"That's not what matters right now, is it?" Finally, Bernadette found the courage to look up and meet her daughter's gaze. She was so beautiful—those light-brown eyes like looking through dark glass in the sunlight; her skin the color of the last bit of sunset reflecting off the beach, and hadn't Bernadette thought that same analogy of someone else once? So many dark, tight curls framed Olivia's smooth face, thicker than her mother's hair and not quite like her father's. She saw the wheels turning behind the girl's eyes. There wasn't panic behind them, not yet, if it ever came at all. Just a cool, calculating awareness of how the game had changed now and a quick inventory of all her options. That was how this brilliant girl navigated the world, like one giant, endless game of chess against whatever opponent sat down on the other side of that infinite table, even when she played against herself. Right now, Olivia pondered how to make her next move against her own mother.

"Then what matters right now?" It was a bold move for sure, handing it right back to Bernadette and forcing her to come right out and say it if she wanted to move them past this point at all.

"Tell me you're not goin' with them." Bernadette's nose stung, warning of the tears she wouldn't yet let form. Not until she knew if they'd be in fear, anger, or relief.

Olivia slowly tilted her head, like *she* was the one who'd caught Bernadette red-handed. Like *she* was the one justified in her condescension. "I thought you never wanted me to lie to you."

"Honey, *not* telling me about this is just as much of a lie—"

"No it's not. She invited me down. Said I was old enough to come take a look for myself and make my own decisions." The girl tossed her dark, tight curls back over one shoulder. "I'm definitely old enough."

"For a lot of things, sure. But not for this."

"Are you kidding me? I could test out of high school right now and score higher than anyone else in the state. And you know it."

Bernadette sighed and shifted her body toward her daughter. "And if that's what you wanna do, baby, we can talk about that later. But this won't test you out of anything. This is Donna willingly putting a minor in harm's way, and she has no business trying to drag you into it."

Olivia pushed herself away from her mother to put another foot of space between them. "I'll be fine, Mom. I can take care of myself. Trust me."

"I trust *you*, honey. Of course I do." One more shaky inhale, and fuck, she wanted a cigarette. "When it comes to you, I do *not* trust Donna—"

"Oh, that's such bullshit."

"Language."

"No, Mom. If you really didn't trust her as much as you suddenly don't trust her, why would you stay friends with her for so long? You don't take your family every summer to visit someone you don't trust."

That statement should have been true, and how in the world was Bernadette supposed to explain the fallacies and all their nuances to a sixteen-year-old with the entire world at her feet? "As a friend, yes. Donna's been a friend for a long time, and she loves you."

"Then why is this such a big deal?"

"Because I've seen what she does to people she loves, Olivia." Now she'd reached the point where she couldn't corral her voice back into its pen of self-control where it belonged. "Time after time, I've watched that woman care about people and bring them into her world. And I can tell you right now that those people are the first ones she throws right under the bus."

The girl's frown made Bernadette feel even more like an idiot than her daughter's next words. "Do you hear how crazy you sound right now?"

"I'm not crazy, baby. I didn't get this far in life by blindly trusting everybody who says they care about me."

"Oh, my God." Olivia scoffed, blinking furiously to clear the fog of bafflement from her own senses. If it was even real. So many layers of things to unravel with this girl since the day she turned three. "Just because you gave up on fighting for people like us doesn't mean you get to choose for me."

"I didn't give up fighting—"

"You stopped working with Donna to be a midwife, Mom. Not even a midwife. You're just an assistant with a training certificate. Come *on*."

"And that is one of the best decisions I ever made," Bernadette shot back. "I don't like what's happening in the world right now any more than you do. I know I can't shelter you from it, baby, and I stopped trying to do that a long time ago because you're just too damn smart to let me get in your way." She thrust her finger toward the laptop in Olivia's arms. "But I *won't* let you be the next poster child for Donna's insane campaigns. I've been down that road, and it doesn't make nearly as much of a difference as she wants you to believe."

The girl stared at her, her nostrils flaring, and Bernadette saw her daughter make the leap even before the words came out. "At least Donna believes in something."

"Sweetheart…"

"At least she's willing to fight for it. And what are you doing? You just threw away all your power to go be someone else's *assistant* while they deliver babies. Why? 'Cause you think it's cute? Does that really make you feel better about yourself?"

Bernadette tried to breathe through the rush of … she couldn't put her finger on anything she felt now. It was all mixed up, all dumped together into a boiling pot, and her daughter just kept tossing more shit into it before Bernadette had a chance to taste it the way it was. "I did what I had to do to keep you safe, baby—"

"No, you did what you had to do to convince yourself that you're not a fucking coward just like everyone else." Olivia leapt from the couch, shaking her head and sending all that disgust and condescension right at Bernadette with a knifelike intensity that didn't miss its mark. And maybe her mother deserved it. Maybe the girl saw right through all Bernadette's attempts to make this life mean something more than who she wasn't and who her family would never be allowed to become. And that could have been the end of it before her daughter took it further than Bernadette hoped it would never go. "I'm going, and you know you can't stop me. Whatever you do, I'll just find another way."

"Don't you dare." Bernadette grew rigid on that couch cushion. She knew what was coming next—knew it and hoped with everything inside her that this girl didn't keep going.

"What are you gonna do to stop me, huh?" Olivia's chest heaved with anger and teenage righteousness and the words her mother knew were just now burning in her chest.

"You can't do anything."

The pressure came down around Bernadette's throat like it had only three other times in the last six years. She swallowed and tried to fight it off.

"Unless you wanna start living the rest of your life listening to everyone through a pair of headphones, you don't have anything to—"

"Stop!" Bernadette leapt from the couch and shoved a finger toward her daughter, cutting off Olivia's beat before it even had a chance to bloom. "You don't get to use those words on me, girl. I have done *everything* I can to keep you safe in a world that wants to tear you down and leave you there to rot. You wanna know why I gave it all up?" Her chest was on fire now, and she really, truly thought it was the fire of her own heart breaking. "I've seen more destruction than you can even imagine. Explosions and burning buildings. People running for their lives. Screaming. People who weren't fast enough and lost the ability to run at all because their goddamn legs had landed three feet beside them."

The girl let out a small, startled gasp, and Bernadette knew she'd hit the mark of shock and fear now. She knew she could drive her point home.

"I've seen people like us beaten to death by cops who didn't give two shits because they think we're all animals. I've seen brilliant people waste their beat and waste so much potential because they'd rather slit their own wrists than fight this thing you think Donna is so capable of overcoming."

"Mom…" The laptop almost slipped out of Olivia's

arms as she staggered forward, her eyes wide and her cheeks more than a little flushed.

"Love doesn't mean a goddamn thing to that woman or any of the others like her. Don't spend your life idolizing monsters."

"Stop it—"

"The only thing that matters to them is violence and inflicting pain and blaming it on everyone but themselves!"

"*Fuck*!" The silver laptop clattered to the floor as Olivia dropped to her knees with a raw, terrified gasp. She caught herself with both hands on the rug and knelt there on all fours, her body wracked with one relentless spasm after another.

Bernadette's chest heaved, the burning, metallic remnants of her beat fading off her tongue and back down her throat again, but it was too late to take any of it back. She sucked in a trembling, mortified breath and whispered, "What…"

A sob escaped her daughter doubled over on the floor. When Olivia looked up at her again, there was no trace of the horror or the fear or the realization that she'd been wrong—all the things Bernadette had fully expected to see after she'd finally opened her daughter's eyes to reality. But that wasn't what had happened. Not really. Olivia hadn't heard reality in her mother's words. There'd been no room for it beneath the magic of Bernadette's beat that had set her own daughter ablaze in a very different kind of way. The worst way imaginable. And now the only thing existing behind those light-brown eyes the color of damp brown leaves was the same kind of hatred Bernadette had been trying to hold at bay for the last sixteen years. To keep it from Olivia, and now she'd just made it a part of Olivia.

A hand rose quickly to Bernadette's mouth, but she didn't let herself touch her own lips for fear that it would break whatever was left of her after this. "Sweetheart, I didn't—"

"Yeah." A sharp, cruel laugh of disbelief burst from the girl's trembling lips. Humiliated tears spilled down those flawless cheeks—flawless even beneath the blush that should never have been put there by the woman who birthed her into this world. "Fuck you."

"Olivia—"

The girl snatched up her laptop and clutched it to her chest as she stormed out of the living room. Her footsteps thudded down the hall, across the house, up the stairs and back across again until her bedroom door slammed shut with a bang.

That was the sound of the end. It was the sound of Bernadette's heart slamming shut just the same.

How had she not known? Sixteen years of giving more time and energy and love than she ever thought she'd have to give, and how the fuck had she not known the words that would tailor her beat to her own fucking daughter?

Bernadette choked for her next breath of air, not because of Olivia's beat this time but because she'd done the unthinkable, and now her body had initiated a self-destruct command discovered only by what she should never have been allowed to do. That was how she would pay for her proud blindness, wasn't it? She would drop right there on the rug in her family's living room and never get back up again; she'd give her life as the only reparation that would mean anything after crossing a line that never should have existed. And it would never be enough. Bernadette could let go completely, right now, and for the rest of Olivia's life, it would never be enough.

Her knees buckled beneath her, and she almost did crumble to the floor in that moment. Somehow, by the grace of some unseen force—or was it a curse?—Bernadette managed to keep her footing, even as she stumbled forward toward the back end of her home. With unseeing eyes, her head reeling, this body that had seen too much already and had finally done more than could be absolved shuffled across the worn wooden floors toward the kitchen.

A hand that wasn't her own reached up and slid the keyring off the hook by the kitchen door. That hand just kept moving all by itself, curved around the dented brass doorknob, twisted just the right amount. The door swung open, and it didn't matter now whether that hand remembered to shut it again or if it had simply had other plans in mind.

If Bernadette wasn't meant to drop dead in her own living room after this, maybe that was where her feet took her now. Maybe once she slid dumbly behind the wheel of Darrell's Monte Carlo, that phantom hand would steer her toward her final resting place. The James Island Connector or the Arthur Ravenel Jr. Bridge were plenty high enough above the harbor to get the job done. Or maybe she'd find herself down in Hollywood again, back where it all started, her lungs filling with saltwater brine and pluff mud and the scent of the best clusters opening up before the harvest for oyster season, wondering how she got there until she stopped wondering anything at all.

The only thing she knew for certain was that there was no going back after this. No apologies. No forgiveness. No stepping through that door to be met with smiles and open arms and a love she'd given to the wrong people for half her life before realizing who the right people really were. Before carrying one of them for nine months in her own womb only to reach this point sixteen years later. The point where she'd brought it all crashing down around her with a few fiery words the true meaning of which she'd been too fucking stupid to recognize. She'd given her own experience—her own vague play-by-play of the horrors she'd seen and the horrors meted out by her own hand, indirectly and sometimes far less so. And with a kind, loving, gentle, brilliant child who thought herself a woman already, *those* had been the undiscovered words Olivia's mother had used against her.

No, Bernadette could never go back. And somehow, miraculously—though she'd convinced herself years ago that she didn't believe in miracles—Bernadette just kept moving. She never stopped.

33

From j.hammel@aol.com
Sent: December 19, 2011

I got a call from Darrell. Olivia reached out to me too, Bernie. I've never heard her so upset. They want you home. They're worried about you. No one knows where you are, and I'm really hoping you're still checking your emails, at the very least.

Whatever happened, it can't be worse than leaving everyone behind. You don't have to run away from anything. I know you'd probably say you're just doing what I did, but I was actually asked to leave. And I'm still in contact, obviously.

I told your family that I'm sure you're fine, that you just need some space to breathe, and then you'll come home.

That you have to work through whatever shame and fear you're going through but that they're still the most important thing in your life and you wouldn't just let that slip through your fingers.

Everyone knows you can handle your shit, Bernie. Honestly, I didn't even think twice about it until fucking Donna called me next, asking if I've heard from you. Now I'm worried too.

Reach out to someone, okay? Darrell and your daughter. Me. Donna. Hell, even knowing that you talked to Loretta or Hellen would make all of us feel a lot better. Just to know you're safe. I hope you are. Don't forget that we all love you, no matter what happened. We'd be a bunch of fucking hypocrites, otherwise.

—Janet

From brushandfemme@gmail.com
Sent: April 3, 2018

It's Janet. New email. Feels like a necessity with all this other shit rolling around. People have already been going crazy with this social media monster I'll never understand. Topper. Twitter. MindBlink. Everyone plugged into their goddamn phones all the time. Fucking scary that this Pointera shit is actually out on the market. I remember when they were making it, when they hadn't finished the "drug trials" yet and hadn't gotten federal approval. I heard back then that someone tried to take out the warehouse where they were storing everything. Maybe you know something about it.

And now we have this giant, racist orange toddler in the White House, and I can't even sleep. I'm not painting. Seriously, it feels like I spend eighty-percent of my time just sitting around and shaking, waiting for the ceiling to cave in. Trying to stay busy. I've found a new group I finally feel at home with, though. Same kinda friends as you have, Bernie. Different people. Different place. I'd be dead without them. I'm fifty-nine years old, and I feel like I'm fucking ninety.

If people find out about us the way things are now, I have no doubt in my mind that we'll be getting a fucking wall built around us too.

This feels like being with Donna all over again, and it looks like fucking Nazi Germany.

I hope you're laying low. If you change any of your info, don't forget to send it my way.

—J

From brushandfemme@gmail.com
Sent: July 27, 2024

Jesus fucking Christ. Guess there actually is something that can stand against us, huh? The beat doesn't work through technology, B. Headphones, speakers, cell phones, radio, intercom. Just fucking kills it. We had three of our people snatched right out of our meeting the other night, and now these fucking assholes have a way to protect themselves. Now it's gone military, and I feel like I'm right back where I started.

Sleepwater will find a way, won't we? We always do. Keep your people safe. I'm glad you have them, at least. Shit, I'm glad they have you.

—J

From brushandfemme@gmail.com
Sent: August 23, 2027

They've got eyes on us. And they're taking us out, chapter by chapter. Members disappearing all over the place, and when they come back, if *they come back... Fuck, B. They're empty. Used up. This is what zombies look like in real life. Our people used as fucking experimental pincushions and tossed back out like empty banana peels.*

Don't let them find you. Tell your chapter to lay low. I wish any of us knew how long this is gonna last.

—J

From brushandfemme@gmail.com
Sent: November 13, 2030

Salco Genomics Research Facility Targeted by Radical Ter-
rorist Group

Was this you?

From brushandfemme@gmail.com
Sent: February 20, 2031

I wouldn't have believed what you told me if I hadn't
seen it myself. We already knew they could take our beat.
Looks like shit really backfired with Frankenstein's monster,
doesn't it? They made some of us invincible.

I didn't tell anyone that you have Marcus Tieffler's
daughter with you. That's her business and yours. But fuck.
Can't imagine what it's like in that girl's head.

I'm so sorry about Karl. He was the kind of man every-
one wants on their side. We lit a candle for him out here.
Call us if you need another safehouse. You know we got each
other's backs in this.

Plans are rolling down the line for something huge.
They really poked the bear this time. We're stronger than
they think. Keep checking your email.

34

IT FELT LIKE Bernadette had held her breath the entire drive up to Aiken. Despite the van's AC working just fine, she was covered in sweat, her dress clinging to her body like she'd just gone for a swim. And at her age, she couldn't even blame it on hormones.

When they pulled up in front of the massive Victorian-style house just off some golf course, the first thing through her mind was how lucky they were to have enough space for everybody after so long. Then she remembered who'd given them the address and felt like she'd suffocate all over again anyway, no matter how many rooms were in that house.

"All right. This is it." Randall shifted the van into park but left the engine running. His hand went up to readjust the rearview mirror before he looked back at the other five people in their little Sleepwater chapter on the run. Five and a pint. "Everybody good?"

The twins both shot him two thumbs-up from the back seat. Beside them, Cameron just thumped his forehead against the window, staring at the house. Mirela hummed something like assent, her three-hour-old daughter nestled tightly in her arms. Brad had his hand on her knee and nodded slowly.

When Randall looked at Bernadette, she knew he'd see her shaking. But then she looked down at her hands in her own lap and saw they were calm, steady, trained over a lifetime of building and strengthening and reforging her own damn mask. She only glanced at him for a second before staring back out the windshield with a curt nod. "Let's go."

Her aching knees did their job and held her up when she slipped out of the passenger seat. The door felt way heavier than it should have when she pushed it closed, then she jerked on the handle of the sliding side door and pulled it aside.

"You got it?" Bernadette reached out toward Mirela as the woman rose gingerly from her seat, pressing her daughter against her chest.

"Oh, yeah." With a little wince, Mirela took Bernadette's offered hand and let the woman help her down out of the van. Brad quickly followed behind her, taking his wife's arm almost before his feet landed on the asphalt.

"That is one happy baby." Bernadette's small, tight smile was hard enough to give.

"Of course she is," Mirela said softly, lifting the child higher against her chest with both hands now, Brad at her elbow. "She has everything she needs."

It wasn't untrue. That child had what she needed, all right, and then some. What she didn't need was to spend the first few hours of her life sardined into a getaway van with her mother and six other people. Still, for how unsavory the circumstances, they'd all done remarkably well on this drive. Minus the baby, they'd had plenty of practice.

"I'm just glad that thing didn't start screaming," Cameron muttered, stepping through the seat in the middle row and ducking to climb out through the side door.

"She's not a *thing*, Cameron."

"Baby. Whatever."

Tony and Don followed right behind him. "Dude, you know you're gonna get put on babysitting duty eventually."

Cameron glared at Don as the twins jumped out of the van. "Not if they're smart. I don't do babies."

He slid the door shut again, and Don snickered. "Man, you can't handle anything that breathes and has a pulse."

Tony mimed strangling himself, which just made Bernadette frown and shake her head. If a few guys in their twenties had to joke around about some shit she didn't understand just to deal with what they all dealt with together, there were definitely worse things.

She stepped around the back of the van and pointed to the trunk as Randall headed on up the walkway after Brad and Mirela. "Grab everything out of the back, will you? Duffel bags and everything."

The twins' eyes widened in tandem, and Cameron scratched the back of his head. "Just in case, huh?"

Nodding, she patted him on the shoulder and raised an eyebrow. "Just in case."

Then she shuffled herself up the walkway after that brand-new family and the man who would no doubt turn out to be the steady, easygoing, silent-smiling uncle for their child. Pretty necessary when they had these three jokers hanging around too. But they weren't really the jokers they'd been seven, ten, twelve months ago, were they? Too much had happened to make humor—even the sharp, bitter, sarcastic kind—much of a salve for anyone now. Maybe a baby would change that.

Bernadette seriously hoped Brad and Mirela would find a way out of this before that child was old enough to grow used to this kind of life but still too young to recognize that it wasn't normal at all. That no one deserved this. Well, almost no one.

Her insides quivered and sloshed around the closer she got to that front door. It didn't matter whose house it was or where they came from, what they might think of this dwindling Sleepwater chapter showing up at their front door on nothing but the word of a woman who didn't know any of them at all. Not even her own mother.

The door opened when she was halfway there. A tall, broad-shouldered man with short brown hair and an unmistakable reserve of compassion stood behind it. His eyes softened when he saw the baby in Mirela's arms. After one quick glance around the neighborhood, he ushered Randall and the new family inside and left the door open.

For Bernadette. So she could force herself up this walkway all on her own, stand at the open door, make the decision to face all the demons she'd created by trying to outrun the others. Because the other option was to flee again and leave behind so much more than the man she'd chosen as her own and the daughter he'd given her.

The front porch offered the first bit of shade and the barest relief from the midday heat. Cool air sifted through the open door and out onto her face, against her sweat-soaked dress. The inside of the house was so dark compared to the brightness of the day, but she did it. With all the strength left in her, she actually fucking did it and stepped up into the entryway despite knowing just exactly who was waiting for her on the other side. Somewhere.

She peered around the corner and took a few steps to her left. The broad-shouldered man turned around toward her just as a head of tight black curls disappeared around the corner into the hallway, Randall following closely behind. Words murmured in low, soft voices receded after them. Then Bernadette found herself face to face with their next host in a long, seemingly endless string of so many others who'd put up this Sleepwater chapter for a few days or a few weeks, however they could.

"I'm David." The man extended his hand, blue eyes shining beneath the hallway light with just the barest hint of laugh lines at the corners. He couldn't have been much older than Brad and Mirela.

"Bernadette." She took his hand and tried not to glance around at the walls and the hallways and the open rooms as if she expected ghosts to pop out at her from everywhere all at once. In some ways, that was exactly what she expected. "We really appreciate you opening your doors, David. Been a rough time."

"Don't worry about it. Seriously. If Olivia can vouch

for a few friends needing a little extra help, that's all I need to hear."

A few friends. Had she even told this one just who exactly was heading up to Aiken with a van full of outlaws running from the government and private corporations and now their own fucking neighbors, too?

David gave her a tight-lipped, empathetic smile and nodded. "Y'all with Sleepwater, then?"

Her eyebrows shot up at that. "A small part of it, yeah. You?"

"No, ma'am. I checked it out a few times way back when. Then I met my wife, and our son was born a few years after that. Settled down for family life and pretty much kept things quiet after that. You know how it is."

The words pierced through her, and how could the man have known the way she envied his decision that had apparently been so easy to make? How could he have known that at one point, Bernadette might have given everything to settle back down for family life and keep things quiet after that? No, Olivia clearly hadn't told him who she was. The only thing she could do was force on another smile. "Sure. I know."

"Well, come on in." David gestured toward the living room but didn't yet step aside. "I know y'all just made the long drive, but you're welcome to have a seat. Make yourselves at home."

"Thank you."

"You got a few more friends out there?"

"Yep." Bernadette turned around and pulled the door closed behind her. "They'll be in with a few armloads, if that's all right."

"Absolutely fine. Not sure if we have enough actual beds for everyone. I put a mattress on the floor in the kid's room. He can sleep with us for a few nights. Got another guest room upstairs and the one down here. Olivia took your friends with the new baby into that one. How old's the little one?"

She licked her lips and followed the man out of the entryway and into the living room. "A few hours."

David glanced at her over his shoulder as she caught up to him, blinking heavily. "Oh. Wow."

"Like I said. Bit of a rough time."

"Uh. Yeah." He ran a hand through his hair. "Well hopefully, staying here for a bit gives y'all a chance to cool down a little. Regroup, so to speak."

"That's a fine way to put it…" They'd made it into the living room now, and Bernadette's gaze fell on the man she most certainly did not expect to see sitting in the cream-colored armchair beside the empty fireplace. His dark eyes widened when he saw her, then he peeled himself up out of the chair and just wouldn't look away.

35

"HEY, I'M SORRY." David sidled across the living room toward the armchair. "Bernadette, this is Darrell—"

"We know each other, David." The words trickled out of her like water, rattling in her throat the way a whisper rattled but somehow coming out loud and sure enough to stop their new host mid-sentence. "Thank you."

"Oh." The man let out a nervous little chuckle and looked back and forth between the two people in the living room who probably had a few years on his own parents. "Small world, huh?"

"It's a lot bigger than you might think." Bernadette shot David a quick glance but felt herself pulled back into the magnetism of Darrell's eyes burning into her skin, clutching at her, concerned and accusatory all at once.

"Right. Well, I'm just gonna grab something to drink. Y'all want anything? Water? Tea? Something stronger?"

"Water would be wonderful. Thank you."

Darrell shoved his hands into the pockets of his tan slacks. "Have any sweet tea?"

"Yes, sir."

"Sweet tea'll be fine. No ice."

"Sure. Sure. Yeah, I'll be… right back." David took one step toward the entryway, paused, then reassured himself that he'd picked the right time to step out and did just that.

With their host's footsteps still thumping across the floors toward the other side of the house, Darrell's hands remained in his pockets even as he lifted and lowered his shoulders in a slow shrug. The olive-green polo shirt ruffled across his chest like a drape against an open window. "Twice in two days. What's goin' on, B?"

"Well I only planned one of those ahead of time." Bernadette took a deep breath through her nose. If she looked away from him now, she'd fall apart like one of those wooden figurines made of so many broken pieces. For now, apparently, Darrell was the string pulling them all together. "She called you too."

"Yep. I was already on the road. Detour's not too bad. She was real shaken up."

When she nodded, it was slow and heavy and seemed to take forever. "And you gave her *my* number."

One dark, slightly graying eyebrow lifted and settled back into place. "Had a feelin' she might wanna use it. You weren't gonna give it to her, and I didn't know how long y'all were stickin' around."

"Not as long as I'd meant it to be." Another wave of heat flashed through her. This time, she couldn't pretend to know why. "When did you get here?"

Darrell nodded at the door. "'Bout half an hour ago. Right before she did. I ain't seen her rattled like that since—well. Long time."

Bernadette swallowed. "At least you were here for her."

"Yeah, you might be too." His dark, wide hands slipped out of his pockets as he walked slowly toward her. She couldn't move, trapped in his gaze and this house and knowing that her daughter was somewhere inside it. In the same fucking house. A slow, shattered breath leaked through her lips no matter how hard she tried to hold it back. Darrell's brows flickered together as he reached up and touched her shoulder. "Aw, you're shakin', girl. Come on."

"It'll pass." Maybe she was shaking. She might never stop, with this much of everything flowing through her all at once.

"You ain't gonna fool both of us with that, B. At least sit down."

She shook her head just the tiniest bit, and only with the movement did she start to feel like one of those bobblehead dolls stuck to the dashboard. "I won't get back up."

His other hand somehow found her fingers, wherever she'd put them, and he stood there so close in front of her, holding her trembling hand and gently squeezing her shoulder.

The front door whispered open, followed by Cameron's frustrated grunt. "Fuck."

Then the silence of the house was ruptured by Cameron and the twins lugging everyone's things into the house.

"Coulda used a cart or a… wagon or something."

Don snorted. "Bet they have a wheelbarrow. This looks

like the kinda place with a wheelbarrow."

"Dude, I have no fucking clue what you're talking about."

All three of them hefted their stuff into the living room, apparently by instinct. Don was loaded down like a pack mule with backpacks, totes, blue and red and green duffel bags. Cameron had the long, heavy black ones made even heavier by all the gear Bernadette's conscience would never have allowed them to bring into the same house with a baby around. Until today. Tony's face was barely visible above all the brown paper grocery bags piled high in his arms.

The warning wasn't nearly long enough for Bernadette and Darrell to react. Cameron stopped just inside the living room and stared at them standing a few feet away from the armchair. The black duffel bags in each of his hands thumped to the floor. "The fuck?"

Bernadette and Darrell released each other, and his hands went right back into his pockets as he took one small step away from her.

The last vinyl strap was ripped over Cameron's head, and he tossed the final bag onto one of the others before wagging his finger back and forth between the two senior citizens caught in the act of comforting each other in private. "What's all this?"

The bags of what few personal items they'd brought with them sloughed out of Don's arms and off his shoulders. He made a lame attempt to catch the first ones as they slid against him toward the floor but quickly gave up and leaned against the doorway into the living room with a sigh. Tony just stood there buried in grocery bags, silent and unmoving as usual.

Darrell lifted an eyebrow and leaned his head down toward her to mutter, "You drivin' around with a buncha white boys now, huh?"

She nudged his arm with her elbow. "And Mirela."

"Kaylee was Asian," Don added with a shrug. "Chinese, maybe. Japanese? Dunno."

Cameron glared at him. "She's Chinese-American, you moron. And quit talking about her like she fucking died or something."

"We don't know…"

"Shut up." Lifting his feet high over the duffel bags to step aside, Cameron puffed his hair out of his eyes and backed up toward the other side of the living room, like he wanted to get a good look at Bernadette and her friend from a different angle. He jerked his chin up at Darrell. "This your house?"

"Nope."

David appeared in the entryway with three glasses balanced in his hands. "It's mine, actually."

Cameron pointed at him and raised his eyebrows as he watched David step over the bags in his front entryway to bring Bernadette and Darrell their drinks. "New guy."

"Here we go. That one's the water." David nodded as Bernadette reached out to take the closest glass in the triangle of them between the man's hands. "And sweet tea. No ice."

Darrell took his glass and nodded. "'Preciate it."

Then David turned quickly and moved right across the living room to extend a hand toward Cameron. "David. Y'all are the new guys."

"Fair enough. Cameron." They shook, and the normally gloomy thirty-something-year-old nodded with an impressive display of courtesy. At least he could pull it out when he needed to use it. They'd had plenty of practice with that too. "Thanks for letting us crash."

"No worries, man. You want a drink? Got some sweet tea. Probably a few beers in the fridge."

"Naw, we're good." Cameron nodded toward the standing stack of grocery bags in Tony's arms. "Pretty sure there's a bottle of something in there. Or maybe that's still in the van."

The bags shifted a little, and Tony stepped one foot back to compensate. A red apple toppled over the side of the top bag and thumped to the floor before rolling down into the hall. Don snorted. "You bought apples? Nobody asked for apples."

Cameron shrugged. "Food groups, right? And I heard they were good for babies or something."

"Apple*sauce*, maybe." Ignoring his brother, Don passed right by Tony to chase after the apple. "And not for a baby who was literally just born. Seriously, dude. How dumb do you have to be to think—"

He froze right there in the hall where he'd bent over to snatch up the apple. From where Bernadette stood, she couldn't see what he'd found there, but she saw him straighten quickly again before he cleared his throat. "Sorry."

Don whirled around again and stormed toward his brother with wide eyes before chucking the apple back down in the bag. Tony grunted. "David, you got a... kitchen counter or a table or..."

"Oh, yeah, yeah. Come on back this way." David took off toward the twins, skipping a little over all the bags on the floor. "Didn't expect y'all to come in with a bunch of groceries, but that's great."

"Give me that." Don hefted the top bag out of his brother's arms, shooting another wide-eyed glance into the hallway as the twins turned around together to follow their host into the kitchen.

Cameron folded his arms and leaned back against the wall with a thump.

Bernadette hardly noticed. She stared at the dark entrance to that hallway gaping like the mouth of some eternal beast that had waited for twenty years to swallow her up. She felt it coming for her too, despite the fact that she stood right there beside Darrell, motionless, hardly daring to breathe. It seemed too much even to think that she *wasn't* dreaming this moment. That every cell of her body didn't fear it and long for it in equal parts.

A shadow appeared at the end of the hall, emerging from the darkness but still growing shorter before its owner stepped out into the light.

Olivia's hands were shoved into the back pockets of her jean shorts, a stethoscope hanging casually around her neck and looking no less fitting above her loose white t-shirt with the Roper Hospital logo stretching in purple and red across the front. All those dark, tight curls were pulled loosely back into some kind of clip that managed only to keep all that hair away from her face before it broke free again to spill over her shoulders and down her back.

Bernadette's heart stopped. Her daughter, thirty-six years old, looking everything and nothing like the sixteen-year-old she'd betrayed and abandoned without a word. It hurt somewhere in the back of her mind to think that now, standing there like that just inside the living room, Olivia looked more like Donna at that age than anyone else. Except for the dark split on her lower lip and the swollen skin around it, not quite bruised yet but still darker than the rest of her smooth, light-brown jaw and cheek.

The woman's eyes traveled across the room and landed on her father first, as if she were pleading with him to save her from what was coming next. Or maybe she was looking for some reassurance that this was nothing, that she'd handled so much more in her life than the presence of a woman who hadn't even been there for more than half of it. Then those bright pools of her liquid-brown eyes shifted just a little to fall on Bernadette. "Hey."

It was flat and cold and unattached, completely emotionless. However long it had taken Olivia to make the switch from calling Bernadette Mom to calling her B—to thinking of her only as B—had obviously been enough time to prepare her for the apathetic flatness of that one word.

That one word meant everything to her mother.

Bernadette swallowed. "Hey."

"Holy shit." With a surprised chuckle, Cameron leaned forward, his tailbone still pressed against the wall. "Bet that hurts."

Olivia turned her head toward him and just raised her eyebrows. "I hurt them even more. And yeah, before anyone asks, I *did* take an oath, and I still did what I had to do. Callin' it self-defense."

She whipped the stethoscope down from around her neck and folded it in half, holding it with both hands as she stepped past Cameron toward the couch.

He followed her with curiosity and a crooked smile. "You got a beat?"

Olivia only spared him another quick glance before she dropped onto the couch with a little sigh. "Just like you."

Cameron's nose wrinkled as his smile widened. "You Sleepwater?"

Bernadette's daughter looked up at her again and this time said a lot more with that gaze than she could have with just one word—*Well, we're here now, so we might as well get this over with.* She held Bernadette's gaze even as she answered Cameron's question. "Not even close. I'm just a friend."

"Right on. A doctor friend who can take a punch and hit right back. What'd you have? A baseball bat or something?"

"Just my words." Olivia let each word out in a long sigh. "That's all I need."

The guy looked up at Bernadette too and pointed at her daughter. "Remind you of someone?"

The tension erupting in that room between the family Bernadette had broken and never tried to fix filled her with a slow, steady shock of ice. Darrell stood rigid beside her. Olivia leaned forward over her lap, sliding her forearms down her thighs, and closed her eyes.

Either Cameron was smart enough to ignore the reaction or just thick enough not to notice it. It could have gone either way, really. Especially when he and Bernadette both knew that he'd really been talking about Kaylee—the other person they knew who could take down any number of people with her beat and hurt them far more than they'd hurt her. But Kaylee hadn't limited her beat to self-defense before she'd turned on them. Cameron seemed to have forgotten that part.

He smirked and leaned back against the wall. "I like her."

Out of all four of them, he was still the only one completely comfortable with the silence and the thickness of unsaid things and so much buried time hurtling across the room between that couch and the cream-colored armchair. Finally, Olivia clasped her hands together over her bent knees and looked up at her parents. "Y'all gonna sit down, or are we just gonna keep pretending this isn't weird as shit?"

36

WITH A SNORT, Cameron folded his arms again and studied Olivia from his perch on the couch's armrest. "This is gonna be fun."

Fortunately, Bernadette was saved from having to answer her daughter's not-so-subtle question when Randall stepped out of the hallway. He offered everyone a small, tight-lipped smile and apparently hadn't picked up on the buzzing tension crackling across the room. "They're settled in pretty well. Given the circumstances, I guess."

"Thanks, Randall."

"Don't thank me. *She's* the one who looked them over and gave the all-clear to relax a little." He nodded at Olivia and crossed the living room to sit in the middle of the couch between her and Cameron. "Kinda nice to have a doctor around. That's a new one for us."

Olivia just nodded at him, her lips pressed tightly together for a smile that had very little to do with positive emotions in general. "Better me than someone else who has no idea what's going on. And it's my job."

"I know they appreciate it." Randall clasped his hands together, resting his forearms on his long, lanky thighs. "We all do."

When he looked up at Bernadette, the man's smile faded. A flicker of realization passed across his brow, and he shot Olivia one more confused look before staring at the floor.

It didn't take a rocket scientist to put the pieces together. Bernadette would've been surprised if he *hadn't* realized who Olivia was by now, and it was her own damn fault for never having said a word about it until they'd left her family's cabin for the last time. Somehow, Randall's new appreciation for the underlying dynamics in this room didn't make it any better.

"They're doing okay, though?" That was the only thing she could think of to say. An important question about a few of her people who weren't even in the room—a neutral party in comparison—was a hell of a lot better than asking Olivia about herself.

"Yeah. They're okay." Olivia stared at the coffee table and nodded slowly. "That's about as far I'm willing to stretch it without lying to anybody. She really shouldn't have picked up and made the drive as soon as she did. They need to rest. Mirela could probably use a big meal in a few hours, and an iron supplement would go a long way. Might be too much at this point to think peace and quiet, limiting stressful situations, and a few days spent in that bed are even a possibility."

Now, Bernadette couldn't stop staring at her daughter's face. She knew it wouldn't last if Olivia looked up from that coffee table, but she'd take every opportunity she had to memorize all over again the features that had changed so much and still not at all. "How many days?"

Olivia raised her eyebrows. "Brad said she lost a lot of blood."

"Yeah. Hellen pulled out a few emergency stops. Clotting agents. Pitocin."

With a sigh, Dr. Wilkins leaned back in the couch again, drawing her hands up her thighs. "Then I'd say she needs a week of bedrest, at least."

Randall's head drew back in surprise. "Woah."

Bernadette's fingers moved back and forth across her lips. "We can handle two days, maybe three, without things getting too tight. In more ways than one."

Darrell took one step toward her in the armchair, his hands still in his pockets. "B, y'all need to—"

"Okay. I figured we'd just bring the whole thing out here, and y'all can help yourselves." David stepped into the living room with a tray of crackers, some kind of almond-cheese spread, pickled okra, pimiento cheese, and olives. Behind him, Don carried a pitcher in each hand, and Tony's arms were loaded down this time with a stack of plastic cups, a package of napkins, and small paper plates. "This should stick until we can figure out what to do for lunch. Or even an early dinner, I guess. I'll wait for the boss to get home so she can start passing out jobs for everyone."

He was the only person who chuckled at his own joke

as he set the tray down on the coffee table. Then he straightened, looked over everything one more time, and rubbed his hands down the sides of his shorts.

"Jeeze." Cameron slid off the armchair and reached for the olives while the twins set the drinks and everything else down on the table too. "How come we don't get a spread like this everywhere we stop?"

"That's just Southern hospitality." David took another step back and nodded. "Y'all help yourselves. There's plenty, and hors d'oeuvres are just about the only thing I can do in the kitchen."

"Thanks, man." Randall stood from the couch, still bent halfway over, and grabbed himself a plate. He snorted and thumped the back of his hand against Cameron's chest. "Come on, man. Use a plate."

"Why?" Cameron puffed out a laugh around a huge mouthful of cracker and cheese spread. "It's right in front of me."

"You just literally don't know the definition of *for everyone*, do you?"

"Hey, I don't care who uses a plate. What I'm doin' is better for the environment, anyway. You ever think of that? You're just making more trash with all this paper crap you don't even need."

The twins glanced at each other, shrugged, and each grabbed a plate, napkin, and paper cup.

"Jesus Christ. Nobody cares." Shaking his head, Cameron stuck an entire pickled okra into his mouth whole and lifted his hands in surrender. Then he backtracked to the couch and slung a leg over the armrest again.

"Sorry." David swallowed his own mouthful of crackers. "I didn't think it would be such a big deal."

Randall eyed Cameron, who just stared at the twins picking through the hors d'oeuvres tray like a pair of starving chickens. The man pushed his glasses back up his aquiline nose and muttered, "Yeah, that's new."

Tony looked up at Olivia and froze, even with a mouthful of half-chewed food. With wide eyes, he nudged his brother's shoulder and nodded toward the doctor.

"Oh." Don barely managed to keep an olive from popping right back out of his mouth. "You want some of this?"

Olivia snorted and shook her head. "No. Thanks. I'm not hungry."

"'Cause it hurts?" He gestured to his own jaw, and she didn't even try to cover up or explain the swelling and what would most definitely be a nasty bruise around her lip and the side of her jaw in the morning.

"Sure. That's one reason."

"You know, Karl could've taken care of that for you in like ten seconds." Don shoveled more food in his mouth, completely unaware of the sharp looks cast his way from the other Sleepwater members in the room. "Just with his beat, you know? Made the guy a walking bottle of morphine."

Cameron puffed out a sigh. "That's what he told us, anyway. Never actually used his beat. Not around us, at least."

"Really?" Olivia looked back and forth between them with a curious frown. A skeptical smile bloomed across her parted lips. "Why the hell not?"

In the armchair, Bernadette's breath had become a wheezing struggle in her chest. The girl—no, she was a woman now—had always been beautiful. Was still beautiful. But when Olivia smiled, even just the slightest bit like she did now, she lit up the room like a damn sparkler. It was all Bernadette could do not to launch herself across that living room and wrap her arms around the woman she hadn't spoken to or seen in twenty years. The daughter she hardly knew, and yes, it was definitely for a lack of trying.

Cameron shrugged. "I dunno. Something to do with his dead wife, I think."

"Dude." Randall cocked his head at the guy and spread his arms. "Show a little respect, huh?"

"What? *Karl* didn't kill her. It's not like I'm making this shit up just for fun."

"Just pick a better way to talk about it, all right?"

"Hey, at least I'm *talking* about it. It's been seven fucking months. At least. Don't you think it's just a little shitty to go that long without talking about *anything* that happened?"

Randall shook his head and set his paper plate on the edge of the coffee table.

Bernadette's next breath came out in a little choke of a sob, quick to escape and just as quick to get sucked back behind the hardened wall of her own composure. The wall she'd built around herself out of so much necessity, over and over again, another piece of her shriveling away with each new brick. And wasn't that just the best fucking joke in the world? Hiding behind that wall of cowardice and failure and calling it strength. Letting everyone else call it strength and not saying a fucking thing about it.

Her hand moved all on its own toward her chest, and

Darrell leaned toward her, one arm slung over the back of the armchair. "B?"

"I'm fine."

"Not from where I'm standin'."

She shook her head and waved him off.

"What happened?" Olivia's unsure smile widened just a little. No doubt she felt like she was just on the verge of being let into their world—a world she'd wanted to be a part of but had chosen to turn away from, and with good reason. She'd always been smart enough to know when to turn away.

Don swallowed. "What happened with what?"

"With Karl. And whatever else seven or however many months ago."

"With Karl?" Cameron raised his eyebrows, took a deep breath, and was momentarily lost for words. "Uh… Well, he—"

"Excuse me." Clearing her throat, Bernadette launched herself out of the armchair, ignoring the screaming protest from her knees and that goddamn hip now too, ignoring the sudden silence in the room, all eyes turning toward her as she made a clumsy but essential exit.

"You okay?" Randall called after her as she staggered toward the hallway.

"Just fine. Y'all don't mind me." She waved them off, shuffling away from the group toward the darkness and solitude waiting for her in one of those rooms. She'd been here before, stumbling away from a party thirty-eight, thirty-nine years ago while everyone else kept up with whatever they'd started. That time, Bernadette had been drunk on too much wine and probably not enough Chinese food. Now, it was grief and the overwhelming shame of impotence making her head spin.

"Oh, uh… Bathroom's on the right," David called after her. "Second door."

"Yeah." She fumbled with the doorknob and cursed when her fingers wouldn't work the way they'd been trained. Was it too much noise for Brad and Mirela and the baby across the hall? Would anyone come out, follow her toward this door, tell her she was falling apart and making a mess of herself and it was time to fucking pull her shit together because they needed her?

The door finally shoved open with a little click, and she quickly slipped into the bathroom before closing the door again as quietly as she could manage. Her hand shook when she removed it from the doorknob, and it still shook when she turned around and almost fell against the counter, when she reached out to turn on the faucet. The rushing water echoing through the bathroom sure as fuck cut off the sound of the conversation picking back up in the living room. At least she didn't have to listen to *that*. At least she didn't have to hear the other Sleepwater members—her family away from home, without a home—tell her daughter in their own words about the man she'd loved like a son and had failed to protect. The man to whom she never got the chance to say goodbye.

With a shaky sigh, Bernadette looked up at her own reflection. Her fingers brushed over the scar above her right eyebrow. The scar left by men with guns in unmarked fatigues jumping out of nowhere as she'd pulled into the driveway with a few bags of groceries. The scar of the wound that had in fact been deep enough to make her drive her Jeep into a ditch off the frontage road. And Karl had used his beat on her, in the way he'd promised himself and Bernadette and the rest of the world he'd never use again, whether or not anyone else gave a shit.

A sob burst from between her lips as she dragged a trembling finger across that scar. Fuck, she hadn't cried in so long. Now just wasn't the time. Now was the worst fucking time possible.

She knew it, and she whispered it to her trembling reflection in that mirror, and it didn't make a fucking difference.

37

WITH WIDE EYES, Leo Tieffler stared at the screen of her
open laptop. The room was thick with the smell of sawdust
and plaster, the metallic tang of open steel and the underlying whisper of work boots and dust and sweat, even though
the renovations had barely started. Over all of it was that
fucking orange-scented, multi-purpose cleaner she hated but
would keep in their regular supply order because John had
told her once that he liked it.

"What's that?" The woman beside her—Shawna, or
maybe it was Shantal—settled an arm around Leo's shoulders and played with the hair at the nape of her neck that had
just started to grow back since she'd shaved it.

"Fuck if I know." Leo slid one hand up Shawna-Shan-
tal's thigh and moved her finger around the mouse pad with
the other. Then she turned toward the woman with a smirk
and wiggled her eyebrows. "Looks like someone's sending
out homemade videos."

The woman let out a high-pitched giggle and took another long pull from her beer bottle, scooting in closer.

Leo ignored the fingers running up the shaved back of her head—why did they always have to play with it?—and opened the new email from an address she didn't recognize. But the subject line had been more than eye-catching: *'You know you want to stop running...'*

The message itself was only a few lines sprawling across empty white space.

'This is what happens when you stop being someone else's bitch. They're not our "family" anymore. They can't do what we can do. That can change.

Out of all the fucking poison they pumped into us, only one made us what we are now. Have you figured it out yet?'

The video attached to the email had a title just as fucking confusing—'Tijuana, Mexico 2031'. Just as confusing, and now Leo was even more curious.

Shantal-Shawna tipped her beer bottle toward the laptop and snorted. "That doesn't even make sense."

"Watch it with that thing, huh?" Leo tipped the bottle back up and gestured toward her laptop. "You spill that all over my computer, I'm gonna have to start charging you for all those drinks."

"You don't even have a liquor license yet." The woman puffed out a laugh and stuck out her lower lip in a pout that wouldn't have been nearly as endearing if she wasn't nearly as drunk.

"Cute." Leo squeezed the woman's thigh, and whatever

the fuck her name was giggled, leaning in to press her lips against Leo's neck just below her ear. "Okay, hold on—just stop for a sec. Hey." Laughing, she grabbed the woman's face and gave her a quick kiss just to stop all the groping. "I'm serious. I wanna see what this is."

"Fine." Starts-with-an-S thumped back against the newly installed booth and wiggled her head. "But if it's longer than like three minutes, I'm leaving."

Leo snorted. "Okay."

She clicked on the video, which pulled up a shot of some run-down street, apparently in Tijuana. Everything was a dusty brown, broken, dry, like the whole damn town had just given up. And a few yards away, a bunch of dudes stood outside a faded, washed-out building in front of a line of motorcycles. The audio crackled with a gust of wind and dirt against whatever was used to record the damn thing, and the frame wobbled just a little. Then a woman stepped into the shot, her face framed by a glistening curtain of straight black hair. Dark, almond-shaped eyes widened at the camera, those thin lips pressing together in a line of amusement bordering on insanity. Leo's stomach dropped lower than it had a right to be.

"This is what we were made to do," Kaylee said, staring straight at the camera. "Don't try to fight it."

"Fuck." Leo slammed her finger down on the space bar to pause the video, then minimized the internet browser and turned her head toward whatever the fuck her name was. Leo's eyes, somehow, wouldn't leave that computer screen. "You need to leave."

"What?" The woman laughed again and tried nuzzling

into Leo, her beer breath spilling all over them both. "Come on, baby. You said we'd go back to your place after you closed up."

"I said get out. I'm not fuckin' around."

"But we *could…*" Slipping a hand between Leo's thighs, the woman bit her lower lip and blinked slowly with the kind of sluggish ignorance only the young and wasted seemed to master completely.

Leo pushed her away and pointed at the front door of the place she planned to call Tracey's when it was finished. "Get the fuck out already."

The woman's mouth popped open, then she scoffed and leaned away from Leo, glaring at her. When Leo just kept staring at her computer, Shantal-Shawna-Shitface slammed her beer bottle onto the table and slid clumsily backward out of the booth. Then she stood and slapped the tabletop like she thought she was fucking scary. "You're a real cunt, you know that?"

"Yeah, you too."

With a grunt of disgust, the totally pissed—in more ways than one—chick whirled around and nearly crashed sideways into the wall on her way to the front door. "Oh. Yeah. And this fucking bar's gonna be a piece of shit too!"

Leo turned her head toward the front door but couldn't take her eyes off the screen and that face filling the frame. "I know."

Growling, the bitch who thought she'd be too good for this dive bar yanked on the door, again and again, until she finally realized it was the push-out kind and stumbled out into the darkness at almost midnight.

Leaning over the chipped, faded bar they'd just sanded down that day, John snorted. "Why do you even keep her around?"

"I don't. She just keeps coming back."

He laughed and tossed the wrench onto the bar, giving up for the night on the plumbing repairs. "Maybe not anymore."

"Hey, come take a look at this, will ya?"

"Sure, boss."

Normally, she rolled her eyes at that. The huge, muscular guy wasn't here as a real employee, whenever the hell she'd finally end up needing employees. But if his nursing skills in a past life—before they'd been thrust together under circumstances only Fate in its infinitely fucked-up wisdom could conjure—were half as good as he said his bartending was, whatever hospital he'd been snatched away from down in Colorado must have really missed the guy. Until they forgot about him altogether. It had been long enough for that now. No, Leo didn't *keep* John around, either. They'd made a deal without any words at all. John stayed, because he was all she had these days—John and this monster of a bar renovation and that crumpled, faded photograph of the redheaded woman laughing in the sunlight.

And she shared with the guy what she had. Because she could. Because she couldn't *not* share it with him. Leo had gotten over not wanting to admit how alike they really were, especially after Vanguard.

John lumbered around the long bar and stopped on the other side of the table. Leo thumped the back of the wooden booth beside her and nodded at her laptop. The huge guy squeezed himself into the booth with a grunt. "This another one of those fucked-up news clips?" he asked. "Things are gettin' weird out there, man."

A dry, bitter laugh caught in the back of her throat. "Not a news clip. Definitely fucked up."

He stuck his legs out under the table and finally looked up at the laptop screen. "Holy shit. Is that Kaylee?"

"Yup." Leo ran a hand through the longest parts of her hair—much longer than the shaved-but-growing-again hair at the back of her head. It all flopped back down against her forehead and around her face, and she shook a little of it out of her eyes. "She's saying some real crazy shit."

"Well play it."

Biting her bottom lip, Leo pressed the space bar again and let the homemade video roll on.

Kaylee's frozen face moved again. Her dark-brown eyes were wide, glistening with a sickening eagerness that hadn't been there seven months ago—except for when she or Leo or both of them were naked. And there sure as shit hadn't been anyone around back then to catch that fucking look on camera.

Goose bumps prickled across Leo's shoulders.

The chick in the frame—the same girl and a different girl at the same time—flashed a wide, completely insane grin at the camera. It only lasted a second before disappearing again into that cold, emotionless expression of absolutely nothing. Leo knew better.

Then Kaylee turned around and took a few steps across the dusty road in Tijuana toward the dudes standing around with their bikes. They all looked up at her. A few of them glanced quickly at whatever she'd used to record this shit.

One of them shouted something in quick, angry Spanish and headed toward Kaylee. He nodded toward the camera, pointing, and Kaylee's low voice rose from her mouth, barely louder than a whisper. The words were carried away by the wind still buffeting the camera and all that dust across the street.

The biker screamed and clutched at his head, staggering away from the tiny half-Chinese girl in a black tank top and jeans, her shoulders darkened now to the same golden dusty-brown of the road. Then he dropped into the dirt, doubled-over on his knees, and kept screaming until he couldn't do anything anymore.

Two other bikers raced toward Kaylee, shouting in Spanish, trying to snap their friend back to consciousness. The first one with a black bandana around his head threw his hands up to his throat, choking and shaking his head, his eyes wide with terror while the rest of his sun-darkened face turned a darker shade of purple. The second lurched forward across the dirt like he'd been shot in the back, his arms flying behind him as he cried out. Kaylee took one sideways step when he fell at her feet, dust and dirt spraying up from beneath him. He convulsed one more time before a gush of blood and spit sprayed from his mouth. The next second, he was too dead to care that his face had dropped right into the puddle of it.

The roar of motorcycle engines rumbled through the laptop's speakers even louder than the crackle of the wind. Boots shoved against kickstands. Legs swung over seats.

Exhaust exploded from chrome pipes, and the panicked bikers shot Kaylee terrified glances over their shoulders as the whole crew churned up dust and gravel beneath thick rubber tires.

Kaylee turned after them but stayed in the frame. The low, growling tone of her voice rose above the roar of fading engines. "…who favor fire. But if it had to perish twice, I think I know enough—"

Screams erupted from grown men's mouths, too far away from the camera to differentiate one from the other. But close enough to hear every fucking last one of them. Engines revved, rubber skidded across dirt, whole beasts of metal and leather crashed against each other and against bodies, over bodies, across dirt and dust. None of it was in the frame. Only Kaylee, her profile small and unwavering, her chin lifted slightly as she spun her beat into the wind.

And then it was over.

Kaylee turned slowly and walked with a calm, unaffected confidence toward the camera. A few motorcycles still rumbled in the background. The frame jolted when the girl removed the device from whatever she'd used as a stand, then it panned to the right to capture what she'd done.

A dozen bikes and bodies—one giant mass of black and silver and brown—were strewn across the dirt road, piled up haphazardly in an attempted and failed escape. Dust whirled up in thin plumes from where the still-turning engines pumped exhaust into the road.

Those dark eyes centered in the frame again, joined by the slightly flattened nose and lips set in a straight line of feeling absolutely fucking nothing. Voices rose somewhere down the street, shouts of surprise and confusion, but they fell silent again. Kaylee's eyes burned into the camera, and she sighed. "The world is changing. Don't let yourself get caught up in the storm, fucker."

Then the frame shivered again, rustling and clicking harshly before the recording stopped on an angled shot of clear blue sky.

Leo's next breath leaked out of her in a shuddering hiss. "Jesus fuck…"

"What's she doing in Tijuana?"

She leaned away from him and shot him a condescending frown. "Fucking murder spree, John. What the fuck else does it look like?"

Her hand slammed down on the pack of cigarettes beside her laptop, and she pulled one out and lit it right there, because she could, because this was her goddamn bar, because if she didn't focus on a task as simple and necessary as flicking her thumb across that lighter, she'd end up pulling out her hair.

The first drag puffed up into the air, swirling beneath the low yellow lights over the bar. She dropped her forearms on the table on either side of her laptop and stared at her email. First Poe with this chick, and now Kaylee had moved on to Robert Frost. "What is she *thinking*?"

"Who do you think she was talking to?"

Leo cocked her head and closed her eyes. "Probably the person she fucking sent it to, man."

A long silence floated up between them, mixing with the thin stream of gray smoke from the cherry tip of her cigarette.

John cleared his throat. "What happened between you two?"

Another sharp laugh burst from her mouth. "Not enough to make me understand this shit. If Kaylee ever sat down to write a love letter, I'm pretty sure this is it."

"Damn."

Taking another drag, Leo closed the laptop. What the hell was she supposed to do with something like this? What fucking poison was that fucked-up chick talking about?

Her cell phone buzzed behind her laptop on the table. She and John both frowned at it, then he leaned forward to pick it up and handed it to her. Leo didn't recognize the number. Just before 12:30 in the morning wasn't exactly the most popular time for phone calls, but that didn't mean it didn't happen from time to time. Fuck it.

Leo accepted the call and brought the phone to her ear. "Hello?"

"Leo?"

"Yeah, who's this?"

"Holy shit."

John looked up at her, watching her eyes widen in surprise. Not the surprise of watching that little homemade movie from a woman he barely knew. Something almost like happiness in those brown eyes. She nodded at him and slid from the other side of the booth beside the end of the bar, her knuckles rapping twice against the wooden wall like they always did when she stood from what she now called *her* table.

"Everyone okay? Yeah. I'm fine out here. Yeah, he's still with me." Leo walked across the room and turned to shoot John a smirk. "I don't think he's going anywhere. I know. I know, man. Yeah, it's fucking crazy. Sure, just tell me what you… Woah. For real? Yeah. The place isn't even officially open yet. We deserve a fucking vacation anyway. Just text it to me. Probably a few days. All right, thanks. Hey, man. It's fucking good to hear from you. Yeah, you too."

John stared at the closed laptop, waiting until he was needed, and then he'd do whatever she asked him to do. He owed her that much. If it wasn't for Leo, he'd still be strapped to that bed, screaming himself hoarse where everyone in that fucking building could hear. And no one ever came. No one but Leo.

Plus, he'd really grown used to being around someone who was pretty much allergic to bullshit of any variety.

She ended the call and shoved the phone into her back pocket. Another drag, another exhale. He'd brought up the second-hand-smoke thing only once, and then he'd given up. Her place, her rules.

"Shit…" Leo's little chuckle this time was full of surprise and a halting, unsure nostalgia. "John."

"Yeah."

"Find us a couple Greyhound tickets, huh? First bus outta here. Put it on the business card."

"Right now?"

She laughed again. "Yeah, man. Right now. Fuck, I'm

not getting any sleep tonight. I'm gonna make some coffee. You want any?"

John shrugged. "If it's there, sure."

"All right." Shaking her head, she snuffed out the cigarette in the top ashtray stacked on all the others on the bar. "Shit. A whole conversation. Like he never even stopped."

"Hey, where we goin'?"

"Oh." Leo turned back toward him with a crooked smile and shrugged. "Somewhere I've never fucking been before. Just get us the first bus headed relatively south, yeah? We'll figure it out."

"Okay…" He opened the laptop and pulled up the Greyhound website. They'd figure it out, sure. Whatever it was. They always did.

38

BERNADETTE STUCK THE last of the dishes in the dish-washer and turned to smile at Mirela. The woman sat at the kitchen table, nursing the three-day-old baby with a sleepy-eyed look of exhaustion and pure bliss. That was how it was in the beginning, wasn't it?

"You settle on a name for her yet?"

Mirela shrugged as much as she could with the bundle in her arms. "Brad really likes Skylar. I think I just wanna make it Skye. With an E, you know?"

"That sounds pretty perfect to me." Bernadette finished drying her hands on the dishtowel and hung it neatly back up over the handle on the oven door. It was the least they could do, to keep things as neat as possible while David and Marianne had been more than kind enough to put them up even for this long. But they were running out of time. Something was bound to catch up with them sooner or later, and the fire that had already been burning in Charleston when they got there wasn't contained to just that city. It wasn't contained just to South Carolina, either, or the South. Everywhere they went after this, there would be more and more people shooting them wary glances, prying, ready to turn on their heels and turn on strangers because of what they thought they knew. Because of who the world thought Sleepwater and people with the beat really were. It was all bullshit, but bullshit was like a can of gasoline for that kind of fire, wasn't it?

Mirela let out a tired little laugh. "You know, Peyton's convinced her name is Natasha."

"That boy's had nothin' but brilliant ideas since we got here." Bernadette headed toward the table, pausing for a moment as she pulled out another chair just to look down at the baby's tiny, precious head against her mother's breast.

"I know. I'm already taking notes from David and Marianne. They look like they've really gotten this whole thing down."

Bernadette tried to contain her laugh. "Thing is, nobody ever really has it down, honey. You just do what you gotta do for that baby and hope you don't fuck it up too much."

Mirela wasn't ignorant to the message behind the older woman's words. Pressing her lips together, she looked up at Bernadette and gave her a knowing nod. "I know."

The baby's head popped up, and the child blinked sleepily at her mother, that tiny mouth open in milk-drunk satisfaction.

"All right, now." Bernadette reached for the baby, nodding, waving that warm little bundle toward her. "I heard you telling Brad you needed a shower."

"Oh, that's okay. I'll go get him to—"

"Don't play around, honey." Bernadette laughed. "Give me that baby and go take a nice long shower. Hell, take a bubble bath. Stay in there for an hour. We'll be fine."

With a little chuckle, Mirela lifted the baby into Bernadette's arms and tucked the soft blanket below her daughter's chin. "Thank you."

"That's what family's for." Family she hadn't had herself. Family she'd been much better at supporting and protecting than her own flesh and blood. And that didn't seem to matter much now, anyway.

"Oh. Here." Mirela draped the burp cloth over Bernadette's shoulder.

"We got this." She lifted the baby up over her shoulder and took in the agonizingly sweet scent of the little girl's head as it bobbed over the cloth. Then she turned and walked back through the kitchen toward the living room. "Brad. Go help your wife. She needs some time, and I'm giving it to her."

"Yeah." Brad jumped up off the couch, pausing briefly to lay a kiss on his daughter's head before meeting Bernadette's gaze. "Thank you."

"Uh-huh. Go on." She smiled after him, then stepped into the living room and glanced at the TV letting out a low hum of newscaster's voices. "What's this, now?"

On the floor in the corner beside the empty fireplace, the twins sat propped in different positions, both of them reading a book taken right off what Marianne had called her library shelf. Don nodded toward the TV without taking his eyes off the page. "More fake news."

"Huh."

Randall was leaning over his long legs, forearms propped on his thighs with his hands clasped in front of his knees. More than anyone else, he seemed the most interested in what the man on screen with oiled hair and the woman wearing too much makeup had to say. "Shooting in Texas. They're making this asshole out to be some kinda fucking hero. Like he was justified in it. Four people in a living room."

Bernadette closed her eyes and patted the baby's back, swaying from side to side. "Something we should be worried about?"

The man bobbed his head, his brow creased in pain and concern and something close to defeat. But not yet. They couldn't let that happen yet. "Yeah, we should be worried."

Sitting at the other end of the couch, Cameron sank farther into the cushions and didn't say a word.

"All right. Y'all need to turn that shit off. Marianne and Olivia should be back in an hour, and I promised them we'd have this floor looking spotless by the time they stepped through the door. Come on." That was the closest she could get to talking about her daughter without really talking about her. Olivia was here with them just long enough to make sure Mirela and the baby had what they needed before this Sleepwater group moved on. She'd made that perfectly clear, more than once. For now, that was enough. It had to be, because Bernadette didn't have it in her to try making something more of it. Not with what they were all facing now. Even Olivia.

With a sigh, Randall readjusted his glasses and pushed himself up onto long, lanky legs. Cameron groaned but stood anyway too. "What about you?"

"Cameron, do you see this baby in my arms?"

He wrinkled his nose. "Yeah."

"I did all the dishes and cleaned that kitchen spotless. Now I'm on baby duty, and y'all need to make yourselves useful. Especially before we get back on the road."

Rolling his eyes, Cameron snatched up the trash and dirty dishes from the coffee table. Randall shut off the TV and started gathering up the pillows and blankets scattered all over the living room. The twins put their books down and slowly climbed to their feet.

"Anybody wanna head to the store?" Bernadette smirked at them. "Peyton told me this morning he wanted to make pizza."

"No one wants to make pizza," Cameron muttered.

"Well *he* does. Can't deny a four-year-old when his mama told him we could do it, so—"

A loud, firm knock came at the front door, and everyone froze. A few glances were tossed around, eyes wide with the unknown and that ever-present fear that whoever knocked on the other side of that door would be in uniform. With a gun. With or without identifying badges or an official nod from the higher-ups to come get the job done. The knock came again.

"Fuck…" Cameron ran a hand through his floppy hair.

"All right, now. Just… hold tight. I'll go look." Bernadette thought she'd be walking forever before she reached the front door, but then she was there, leaning sideways into it to press her eye to the peephole looking out onto the porch. Her breath caught in her throat.

"Shit." The dishes clattered back to the table, and Cameron raced toward the hallway. "I'll get the bags—"

"Don't you move." The command was just sharp enough to make him obey. Cameron skidded to a stop, and the whole room held its breath. This couldn't be real. It had to be some kind of trick, some new way to lure them in, make them feel safe. Or maybe she'd finally started her journey down the road of senility, because Bernadette couldn't really have seen what she'd seen through that tiny circle in the door.

Not daring to breathe, she opened the front door and let it swing wide open.

The woman on the other side gave her a lopsided smirk, blinking at the baby in Bernadette's arms. "That's new."

"My God…"

"Well, not really. But thanks."

The man standing with her on the front porch chuckled. "Can we come in?"

Bernadette couldn't find her voice, couldn't believe this was real. She stepped back, nodding like a fucking idiot.

"Holy shit." Cameron stepped down the entryway toward the front door as it closed behind their new arrivals. He squinted at the woman with much shorter hair than any of them remembered and poked Leo's shoulder, like he wanted to make sure just like Bernadette that she was really standing there. "What the fuck are you doing here?"

"Good to see you too, asshole."

Randall burst out laughing and walked out of the living

room with a grin each one of them had almost forgotten how to wear. "Both of you. Huh. You gotta be kidding me." He looked Leo and John up and down, cocking his head in that way that made him look so much like some kind of long-legged bird. "You guys look good. You doin' good?"

Leo ruffled a hand through the longer hair on the top of her head and shrugged. "Better than you guys, from what I hear."

"What did you hear?" Bernadette's heart fluttered in her chest, and she just kept patting the baby's back even though the child had already burped and was most likely falling asleep over her shoulder.

"That you might be in a little trouble."

"Ha." Randall stuck his hands on his hips and just stared at the two people they'd all thought had gotten out of this mess. For good reason. "Unreal, man."

"Yeah, I know." Leo's smile faded a little when she met Bernadette's gaze. "There's something I need to show you guys. 'Cause, uh…" She glanced up at John, who just shrugged his massive shoulders, hands thrust into his pockets. "Well, you deserve to see it. And I might know a little more about what's happening… everywhere. Another chapter got in touch with me too."

"Yeah, I was about to make a few calls." Bernadette nodded slowly, taking in the color in Leo's cheeks, the haircut, the new quiet, unassuming confidence that had replaced the slouch and the wide-eyed, overwhelming cynicism at some point over the last seven months. "Well don't just stand there. Come on inside and tell us all about it."

Cameron folded his arms as Leo and John headed into

the living room. "We thought you were the fucking cops."

Leo snorted. "Sorry to disappoint."

She stopped just inside the living room when she saw the twins and gave them both a quick nod. "What's up?"

Don's mouth had dropped open. "Dude…"

"You too, man."

Bernadette finally managed to stop her brain from unraveling as she headed toward the couch with the baby. This living room—this house—suddenly didn't seem to have enough room for the size of that tiny, skinny girl, let alone the former nurse built like a linebacker. "How'd you find us?"

Leo's half smile made her look so much older, somehow. So much wiser than the rest of them, even Bernadette. "I got a call."

Randall stepped past her into the living room and turned around to ask, "From who?"

The girl bit her lip and narrowed her eyes, like she wasn't sure if she should say anything at all. And that couldn't have been the worst thing she had to tell them that she thought they deserved to know, could it?

Across the living room, Tony cleared his throat, his hands shoved deep into his pockets as he stared at the floor. "I did."

Beside him, Don's mouth fell open again. Everyone else in the room stared at his brother. Tony just nudged his twin with an elbow and leaned away, but he slowly looked up and met the gazes all aimed at him from around the room.

Cameron snorted, and now he was grinning too. "No shit."

"The whole world's changin', isn't it?" Bernadette smiled at the twins.

Leo grimaced and tipped her head toward her shoulder, like she was trying to brush off an ache or something crawling across her narrow back. "Yeah… that's what we need to talk about."

Thank you, Dear Reader, for grabbing this book. If you enjoyed it, please consider leaving a review on Amazon and/or Goodreads. It is *the best* way to thank any author!

Looking for More?

Visit KathrinHutsonFiction.com for news and updates on more LGBTQ+ Speculative Fiction, Dark Fantasy, and Dystopian Sci-Fi. You can also sign up for Kathrin's newsletter, where you get some exclusive dark surprises not seen anywhere else.

Do you like Dark Fantasy?
Check out Kathrin Hutson's other series:

The Unclaimed Trilogy (NA Dark Fantasy)
Sanctuary of Dehlyn
Secret of Dehlyn
Sacrament of Dehlyn

Gyenona's Children Duology
(Grimdark Fantasy)
"The Jungle Meets Kill Bill... with dragons!"
Daughter of the Drackan
Mother of the Drackan

About the Author

International Bestselling Author Kathrin Hutson has been writing Dark Fantasy, Sci-Fi, and LGBTQ Speculative Fiction since 2000. With her wildly messed-up heroes, excruciating circumstances, impossible decisions, and Happily Never Afters, she's a firm believer in piling on the intense action, showing a little character skin, and never skimping on violent means to bloody ends.

In addition to writing her own dark and enchanting fiction, Kathrin spends the other half of her time as a fiction ghostwriter of almost every genre, as Fiction Co-Editor for Burlington's *Mud Season Review*, and as Director of TopShelf Interviews for *TopShelf Magazine*. She is a member of both the Science Fiction and Fantasy Writers of America and the Horror Writers Association. Kathrin lives in Vermont with her husband, their young daughter, and their two dogs, Sadie and Brucewillis.

For updates on new releases, exclusive deals, and dark surprises you won't find anywhere else, sign up to Kathrin's newsletter at kathrinhutsonfiction.com/subscribe.

author@kathrinhutsonfiction.com
kathrinhutsonfiction.com
Facebook.com/kathrinhutsonfiction
Twitter: @ExquisitelyDark
Instagram: @KathrinHutsonFiction

Thank you so much for picking up this book and diving in for the crazy ride. If you enjoyed it, please consider leaving an honest review wherever you purchased this book and/or on any of your favorite review sites. This is the best way to thank any author, and more than that, it's the best way to show other people who love good books as much as we do that this, right here, is another good book to be read.

CPSIA information can be obtained
at www.ICGtesting.com
Printed in the USA
LVHW022207150920
666084LV00004B/780